Acclaim
Skip Macalester

"If Holden Caulfield were reincarnated today in the body of a queer African-American adolescent, he might be Skip Macalester, the narrator of J. E. Robinson's new novel. Robinson understands teen angst and ennui, but he also understands teen idealism, teen energy, teen friendship, teen family relationships, and teen wit. The novel is also sensuous to a degree that I've not seen in a long while. *Skip Macalester* reminds us of the intensity of adolescent senses, including the feel, taste, and smell of teen spirit. Robinson resists stereotypes, including stereotypes of blackness. In a pop culture saturated with ghetto minstrelsy, UPN-cloned you-go-girl finger-snapping sistahs, and gangsta poseurs, *Skip Macalester* teaches us about the African-American professional class, what W. E. B. DuBois a century ago called the 'talented tenth,' whose lawyers, physicians, executives, and politicians trace their roots to free people of color in the nineteenth century. In today's political climate where race and sexuality are tense social fault lines, this novel is most welcome."

—Dr. Thomas Lawrence Long,
Professor of English and Chancellor's
Commonwealth Professor, Thomas Nelson
Community College; Editor of the *Harrington
Gay Men's Literary Quarterly*

NOTES FOR PROFESSIONAL LIBRARIANS
AND LIBRARY USERS

This is an original book title published by Southern Tier Editions, Harrington Park Press®, an imprint of The Haworth Press, Inc. Unless otherwise noted in specific chapters with attribution, materials in this book have not been previously published elsewhere in any format or language.

CONSERVATION AND PRESERVATION NOTES

All books published by The Haworth Press, Inc. and its imprints are printed on certified pH neutral, acid-free book grade paper. This paper meets the minimum requirements of American National Standard for Information Sciences-Permanence of Paper for Printed Material, ANSI Z39.48-1984.

Skip Macalester

HARRINGTON PARK PRESS®
Southern Tier Editions™
Gay Men's Fiction

Skip Macalester

J. E. Robinson

Southern Tier Editions™
Harrington Park Press®
An Imprint of The Haworth Press, Inc.
New York • London • Oxford

For more information on this book or to order, visit
http://www.haworthpress.com/store/product.asp?sku=5589

or call 1-800-HAWORTH (800-429-6784) in the United States and Canada
or (607) 722-5857 outside the United States and Canada

or contact orders@HaworthPress.com

Published by

Southern Tier Editions™, Harrington Park Press®, an imprint of The Haworth Press, Inc., 10
Alice Street, Binghamton, NY 13904-1580.

PUBLISHER'S NOTE
The development, preparation, and publication of this work has been undertaken with great care.
However, the Publisher, employees, editors, and agents of The Haworth Press are not responsible
for any errors contained herein or for consequences that may ensue from use of materials or information contained in this work. The Haworth Press is committed to the dissemination of ideas and
information according to the highest standards of intellectual freedom and the free exchange of
ideas. Statements made and opinions expressed in this publication do not necessarily reflect the
views of the Publisher, Directors, management, or staff of The Haworth Press, Inc., or an en-
dorsement by them.

This is a work of fiction. Names, characters, places, and incidents either are the products of the
author's imagination or are used fictitiously, and any resemblance to actual persons, living or
dead, business establishments, events, or locales is entirely coincidental.

Cover design by Lora Wiggins.

Library of Congress Cataloging-in-Publication Data

Robinson, J. E. (John Eric), 1965-
 Skip Macalester / J. E. Robinson.
   p. cm.
 ISBN-13: 978-1-56023-576-7 (pbk. : alk. paper)
 ISBN-10: 1-56023-576-4 (pbk. : alk. paper)
 1. African American teenage boys—Fiction. 2. African American families—Fiction. 3. Upper
class families—Fiction. I. Title.

PS3618.O3267S57 2006
813'.6—dc22

                                                                              2005018757

For my friend,
who read me first
and understood

It is not your memories which haunt you.
It is not what you have written down.
It is what you have forgotten, what you must forget.
What you must go on forgetting all your life.

James Fenton
"A German Requiem"

I and the public know
What all schoolchildren learn,
Those to whom evil is done
Do evil in return.

W. H. Auden
"September 1, 1939"

Chapter One

I

"Let's see," he began in a soft Southerner's lilt, "you look like a Trey Ellis reader."

He was near me as we attended to business in the boys' room between classes the first Thursday in September of my junior year, a tall man, slender enough and with enough of a haircut to have been called a human mop. I remember his smile, on lips exquisitely blood red and a face as pale as a pearl. He had rimless glasses not unlike my father's, the Judge. Nowhere was there a sign of facial hair.

Positioned a urinal away from me, his hands looked artsy, almost delicate. I could clearly see his knuckles fluctuate beneath his skin. I glanced away when he looked my way and his head turned a blur of Irish-setter brown. When he spoke, I looked at him carefully. Being still summer in St. Louis, he still had on jeans and loafers. I had not seen the guy before, but no matter: our school, Milton High School, was big. I assumed he was a senior.

"Excuse me?" I asked.

"I said you look like a Trey Ellis reader. Either that or Darryl Pinckney."

I assumed they were authors. I knew I had seen Darryl Pinckney in the Judge's library. Ever the chauvinist, I preferred Charles Johnson. "Are they on the order of Ralph Ellison?" I asked.

He did a cute semifrown with his mouth. "No one is on the order of Ralph Ellison." Finished, he shook and flushed. "Really, you should read more Mick Fitzgerald. He is just right for a young man like you."

He winked and left the boys' room. Watching him, I called him a fruit.

Soon, I saw him standing at the door to Doctor Levin's English classroom. Our eyes met and he smiled. From the opposite direction,

Drew Ford appeared and caught me just short of the door. He pulled me into an alcove.

I had known Drew since eighth grade, and since then he has been my best friend, tennis partner, and protector. I loved his gray eyes, particularly when they turned full of expression, like that day.

"Now you did it," Drew said breathlessly. "It's all over the school about yesterday."

"What about yesterday?"

Drew almost fainted. "About you and your cousin. Didn't you hear it in history?"

I had to be honest. I didn't. The only thing untoward there was Kay Reece looking at me, turning away, and laughing, which was par for the course from him, and had been ever since eighth grade. No one mentioned a thing about me roughhousing with my younger cousin, Alan Morgan. I barely shook my head.

"Jesus Christ, Macalester! I told you something like this would happen! I told you you gotta be careful around the pricks that go here!"

"What did they say?"

"They said you touched your cousin," Drew said. "And it wasn't a good touch, either; it was a bad touch."

Stepping away as the starting bell rang, I shrugged. "I guess that's it, then."

"You mean you aren't going to do anything about it?"

"There's not a whole hell of a lot I can do," I said.

I went to Dr. Levin's class, with Drew not far behind. The senior I met a few hours before closed the classroom door behind us and watched us go to our seats.

In time, I would become comfortable in Dr. Levin's room, but less than two weeks into the year I still found it rather intimidating. She had bookcases lining two of the four walls, with overflow books stacked on the bookcases' top shelves. The three walls of chalkboards, wiped clean, boasted pictures of Emily Dickinson, Arthur Rimbaud, Gertrude Stein, Herman Melville, Lorraine Hansberry, and James Baldwin, among other writers. Opposite the flag was an autographed photograph of Audre Lorde. On a table near her desk, Dr. Levin had a congressional-era picture of the Judge as a much younger man, signed "To Genie, As Always, Best, Alfred." In the picture he seemed to have been smiling more enthusiastically than I would know him to be later.

Whenever we entered her classroom, Dr. Levin would be seated on the stool at her lectern, reading Psalms, because, she always said, the King James Version was fantastic poetry. Later, I was to discover her love of Psalms occasionally got her in trouble, for reasons that had to do with their religious connotations. Later still, when I would know her as a friend in my college years, should would confide in me, "I don't give a shit what those assholes say. I'm reading my Psalms." The sentiment's incongruity floored me.

The day I noticed that guy in the boys' room, Dr. Levin read Psalms. She had her salt-and-pepper hair pinned back by a stylish indigo scarf the Judge would later admit he had given her following a visit to a West Bank town not far from the settlement where she worked the summer after high school. I remember Dr. Levin wearing a sleeveless aqua top that day; when she lifted her arms, one could see she didn't believe in shaving. Completing her outfit was a light-colored pleated skirt. She wore no hose.

That day, Drew and I took our seats in the vast circle Dr. Levin liked putting her students in. Dr. Levin waited until all were quiet, then she raised her hand and showed the full, rich beard beneath her arm.

"Listen to this," she said. "Psalm 137."

She read it, and it spoke to me. "'By the rivers of Babylon, there we sat down, yea, we wept, when we remembered Zion . . . For there they that carried us away captive required of us a song; and they that wasted us required of us mirth, saying, Sing us one of the Songs of Zion. How shall we sing the Lord's song in a strange land?'"

Closing Psalms, Dr. Levin closed her eyes and pressed the volume to her heart. She said something in Hebrew and smiled, as she always did after reading Psalms. Though hardly the only kid in class, the words seemed special to me. It was then that I realized I sat just a few seats from Kathy Lawrence, the blonde of my heart, who, days before, had been such a figment of my imagination. Drew told me she liked me. I told myself I liked her back. Such was the beginning of junior year.

"For this quarter," Dr. Levin began, "we shall be joined by a student teacher from the university. Mr. Armstrong."

The guy from the boys' room stood. He tried looking friendly. I think he also tried looking at me.

Drew nudged my arm. "Fruit," he whispered.

I smiled a bit. I was a fox casting off the chase.

"I'm very glad to be with you for a time," Mr. Armstrong said in his lilt. "As this is my first time working with high school students, I know this will be a learning experience for both of us, for me as well as for you."

"Told you," Drew sneered.

"Where you from?" I asked Mr. Armstrong.

"Skip, I know you know you are to raise your hand," Dr. Levin said.

Okay, so I had to jump through that hoop. Smirking, I raised my hand. Then I was recognized. "Where are you from?"

"Mississippi," Mr. Armstrong said. "I was reared just outside of Jackson, the state capital." He smiled and adjusted his glasses. "Now, please don't hold none of that stuff against me."

"Which?" Drew asked. "You coming from Mississippi or you coming from Jackson, or something else?"

Mr. Armstrong smiled again. His eyes twitched behind his glasses. "I only go back there for weddings and funerals." He waited for someone to chuckle, but no one did. "As for the something else bit, it's been my experience that kids use their imagination in that department." His eyes twitched again, almost shutting this time. Again, he waited for someone to chuckle. No one did. "But like I was about to say before, I'm really very glad to be here. I really look forward to working with you."

A couple kids nodded, as if to say "that's nice." Mr. Armstrong fumbled back into his seat, careful to catch no one's eye. He seemed awkward, like the caught little boy made to sit at the teacher's desk because no other desk would do. And I couldn't help but smile at the irony: I had shared the toilet with a Mississippi peckerwood and nothing happened! Wait until I told Grandma.

We had been studying the beginnings of American literature. For that day, Dr. Levin moved the class to a discussion of Jonathan Edwards and puritanical poetry. I kept my eye on Mr. Armstrong. His hair flipped over his eyes shyly as, chin in palm, he followed Dr. Levin reading "Sinners in the Hands of an Angry God" in the textbook. Then, when she finished, he closed the book softly and looked up. He had long lashes.

"I hope you remember that," Dr. Levin said, "in the privacy of your own rooms."

Drew nudged me and smiled. "Remember that, Arthur." He winked.

I turned to the opposite direction, toward Kathy, who was dutifully taking notes. She had a floral handwriting, I could see, full of curls and Os. In the midst of my looking, she glanced up. I quickly looked busy.

"For our first book," Dr. Levin began, shifting her weight on the stool, "we shall see how Puritanism was depicted in a non-Puritan time. We shall read not a book, as in a novel, but a play. Arthur Miller's *The Crucible.*"

She held an almost thinnish, white book in the air. It showed two young women in 1600s era cap and frocks, all in black and white cover photography. After a few minutes of hoisting, she brought it down.

"Will we get parts?" one of the girls asked.

"We could," Dr. Levin said. "It's been successful both doing it with assigned parts and in not doing it that way. Frankly, I prefer giving out parts, and, in the past, this class has even staged the play. But first, everyone must read it."

"That's the best way to enjoy it," I heard Mr. Armstrong mutter. I guess I was the only one paying attention to him, because I was the only one to smile.

Dr. Levin went to a stack of like books on one of the bookcases and counted the spines. "*Shi*—" she hissed. "I'm short!"

We looked at each other. Dr. Levin, we thought, was a tall woman. She looked at the class and counted each of us.

"I don't know how this could have happened," she said, "but I have miscounted. I don't have enough books for this class, and I'll need about twenty-five more for the seventh hour class. Could a couple of you go to the English library and get about thirty books of *The Crucible?*"

A question like that was an invite for volunteers. I almost raised my hand, but Drew pinched my shoulder and said, "Don't you dare." When no one volunteered, Dr. Levin dropped her hands.

"Guys," she moaned.

"I'll go," Mr. Armstrong said, "if Arthur and a couple of guys go with me."

Everyone snickered. "Arthur" meant me, and it was a name I scarcely used past the first day. Most of the class had already forgotten that was my first name. Most except Drew. Obviously, Mr. Armstrong's ears were good enough to overhear him calling me that. Much too good. I stood.

"Don't," Drew whispered.

"I'm the only Arthur."

"Brown nose."

Mr. Armstrong stood and clapped his hands. "Who else wants to go?"

"I think we'll need about five," Dr. Levin said. "And I don't want to be sexist. Young men as well as young women may go."

As it turned out, none of the young women offered. Frank Kotter, a Whitmaner whose baggy Bermuda shorts showed off fantastic soccer legs, and Joel Whitney, a quiet little guy with the bug eyes of a sick baby bird, were volunteered by Dr. Levin. Drew chose to go, to keep an eye on me, he claimed.

The English library was on the fourth floor of the Main building, situated across from the student parking lot called "the Pit." The Main is an impressive, ornate building from the Jazz Age, with an edifice Jay Gatsby would have died for. Built on the side of a continuous hill, the Main is framed by the school auditorium and the boys' gym, which were attached to the Main by narrow corridors like Lincoln's arms and to each other by diagonal sidewalks across a sculpted courtyard. The auditorium and boys' gym hit a person in the nose harder than Mike Tyson. Beneath them, the Pit was always packed with kids on break (it was lunch for some at that hour). There, some Whitmaners played pitball, whatever that was.

It was a beautiful day, practically hot, as early Septembers are still
in St. Louis. Being on the Illinois side of the river, less than two miles
as the crow flies from the Mississippi, it was also extremely humid.
The school had a rule against guys taking off their shirts and going
bare chested, but some of the Whitmaners ignored the rule and
tanned their chests and stomachs, lying on car hoods and tops. It was
a righteous scene.

"You stare too much," Drew whispered. "You stare too much and
people notice. It's disgusting."

Then, Frank Kotter flashed his eyes. "Let's make this last," he
shouted, and he raced down the hillock for the Pit, skidding on grass
into a parked car and bouncing into the path of someone trying to exit
the parking lot. Luckily, the driver hit the brakes, and Frank hitched
up his Bermuda shorts and banged on the car's hood. "God! I *love*
these women!"

The driver, a brunette in a ponytail and black baseball cap, smiled
somewhat and probably said something, but I couldn't hear her. Joel
said the brunette lived in his subdivision in Whitman Township.

"I think we should make this as painless as possible," Mr. Armstrong said. "Dr. Levin's expecting us back."

Hitching up his shorts again, Frank sneered. "Ah, Mr. Armstrong,
it's your first day. Be the man."

Drew had something to mumble about that.

"We're all good guys," Joel said to Mr. Armstrong. "We'll be
good."

Mr. Armstrong did that blinking again, furiously. For some reason,
he looked at me. "I don't know. What do you think, Artie?"

"*Shit!* The man's name is Skip!"

It was Drew. His explosion made some of the guys sunning themselves look in our direction. Frank snickered a little. Joel didn't know
what to do. Neither did Mr. Armstrong, who could barely smile and
blink again. Drew looked like he could have shaken the life out of the
guy.

"Skip?" Mr. Armstrong said.

"Yeah?"

"What do you think?"

I looked at Frank. I looked at Drew. I looked at Mr. Armstrong. I looked at Joel. He kind of looked out of it. I didn't know quite what to think.

"It seems to me," I began, "that, perhaps, we should get it over with and get back to Dr. Levin with her books."

"That was just my thinking," Mr. Armstrong said.

"I just bet it was," Drew said, in a faux Southern lilt that bordered upon an effeminate lisp. Frank, who would laugh at almost everything, giggled.

We crossed the Pit in the middle of a pitball game in which Frank stepped in as a fielder. A ball had been hit all the way to him, and he dropped back, extended an arm, and caught it by the tip of his fingers. The hitter was out. The guys sunning themselves cheered. Then, Frank hitched his shorts and zipped the ball past the pitcher before hitching his shorts again and jogging to join us at the door to the boys' gym wing.

"That's par for the course," Joel told Mr. Armstrong. "There's always some kid doing something like that around here."

Then came the blinking again, this time with raised eyebrows, as if the news meant he had to reconsider some things about Illinois.

The doors to the Main are made of shatterproof glass and heavy steel. Using what strength the little guy had, Joel forced open the door. There was the dull echo of guys doing roll call in the gym one flight above. We climbed the stairs and heard the roll call echo louder and more insistent until it became just a mass of sound. Drew, who was a little faster than the rest of us (he always took stairs two steps at a time), got to the gym door first and waited for us to come. He looked into the gym and waved at someone.

"That's enough staring, Ford," bellowed one of the PE teachers, Mr. Moore, a Neanderthal. Even now, I can see the whistle worn like a choke chain around his neck, his lower leg jutting at an angle from his knee. Mr. Moore blew his whistle. "Okay, you pricks! Concentrate on me."

We moved quickly. Mr. Armstrong, head down, trudged past the door. Joel didn't dare look up. As I passed, there was nothing to see; the guys were gathered together beneath a far basketball hoop. And

Frank? Frank hitched his shorts and trotted down the hall. Either he was in sore need of a larger behind or a stronger belt.

We got to the fourth floor. Mr. Bruggeman, the English teacher given responsibility over the English library that hour, looked at us from behind his desk through half-moon glasses. He looked like a sketched owl. Because even Mr. Armstrong seemed a kid, Mr. Bruggeman was none too pleased. He sighed heavily, so heavily in fact that his unruly, salty, mad-professor hair flitted.

"Let me guess," Mr. Bruggeman said. "Dr. Levin just remembered the rest of her books."

We said nothing, and Mr. Bruggeman rested his chin and jowls in the oversized fist of his hand and stared us down. I suppose that, being students, we waited for Mr. Armstrong to say something, but he was quaking with the rest of us. Then, without fanfare, Mr. Bruggeman stood. And stood. He stood well over six feet tall.

"Come along, then, gentlemen," he said. He led us to the door at the far end of a classroom and jiggled a set of keys trying to find the right one. I could see it was a long, rectangular key, made of brass so vivid it could have been gold, were gold keys still being made. As he unlocked the door, Frank spoke up.

"That's Dr. Levin's student teacher," Frank said.

"Uh-huh," Mr. Bruggeman said. "Tell me something else."

"I'm from Mississippi, sir," Mr. Armstrong said.

Mr. Bruggeman opened the door. He straightened his back and stared directly at Mr. Armstrong, who, like the rest of us, knew enough to look down.

"Is that a fact?" Mr. Bruggeman asked tartly. "Welcome to America."

Intimidated just a little, Mr. Armstrong handled the transaction of books nonetheless. "Thirty *Crucibles*," they agreed, and Mr. Bruggeman went through the stacks like a bat until he came to the right title. The room was classroom size, with a slanting ceiling and seemingly with as much shelf space as a small supermarket. Walking it was like walking a mausoleum.

"*The Crucible*," Mr. Bruggeman said, pointing to the books stacked on their sides on a top shelf. "Right here."

Drew and Frank got Mr. Bruggeman a stepladder and they steadied it enough for him to climb aboard. He needed only to mount the
third step to reach the shelf, and, once there, he counted the books
until he got to thirty.

"There are five of you," Mr. Bruggeman observed. "Quick, Whitney, what's thirty divided by five?"

Joel's eyes turned big and blank. Pop quizzes always scared him.
Since I was next to him, he looked at me for help.

"Six," I whispered.

"Six," Joel said.

"Wonderful. And you say you're taking Algebra II-Trig this year?"
Mr. Bruggeman shook his head and took six copies of *The Crucible* into
his hands. "Let's see if you are any quicker with this. Catch."

With that, Mr. Bruggeman dropped six books into Joel's hands.
Joel had to act fast to catch them, stepping forward and bracing himself. Most of the books were caught, though the last two ended on the
floor.

"Good catch, Whitney," Mr. Bruggeman said. "Good to see jerking around with the computer improved your eye-hand coordina-
tion."

Joel tried to smile and he moved to the back of the line. Mr. Bruggeman dropped ministack after ministack into our hands. When it came
my turn, I held my hands out like a wide receiver, and almost closed
my eyes.

"Oh, come on, Macalester," Mr. Bruggeman bellowed.

I opened my eyes and Mr. Bruggeman dropped a set of six books
into my arms. They burned. Mr. Bruggeman smiled what must have
been his most devilish smile.

"Good to see that, too, hasn't been bred out of you, Macalester,"
Mr. Bruggeman said.

I smiled as well, for whatever he meant by it.

Once each of us had his allocation of books, we left Mr. Bruggeman, who was kind enough to watch us struggle to open the classroom door. The hall monitors, newly out, were used to seeing books
leave the fourth floor. They turned their heads.

"In my old high school down south," Mr. Armstrong said as we left the third floor, "if you didn't have a pass, your hide was toast. It would happen just like that."

Drew, who was walking ahead of Mr. Armstrong and me, tossed a look over his shoulder as dispassionately as tossing a bit of thumbnail. Then he shook his head. "Bet you loved that."

By the time we got back to the boys' gym, the Big Ben–looking hall clock said (if it were right) that class was almost over. Frank pointed this out and wondered aloud whether it would make better sense to head uptown rather than to go back to English.

"She's expecting these books," Mr. Armstrong said.

"Ah, Mr. Armstrong," Frank teased again. "Be the man."

Joel looked bird-eyed at Mr. Armstrong as he toyed with the idea of shucking the books somewhere in the hall and skipping the rest of the hour, or rather what was left of it, which we knew Frank would have loved to do. For a minute, I thought seriously about making it a longer day, and leaving the books somewhere in the Pit. The worst thing that could have been said was that I had been irresponsible.

Then, of all things, my cousin Marshall Langston came across the courtyard and reentered the Main at the boys' gym. It was a picture of my cousin I knew very well. He was confidence, like the Judge, only much younger. Hands in his pockets, he sucked a dead black-ink pen like a cigarette holder, and the shirt he wore, a red polo, was wrinkled, as usual. Beyond that, he was every bit a Lockean New Negro, mercurial, contemplative, the visual personification of those Byronic adagios he plays on his cello, whimsically styled, with a dash of Mr. Mistoffolees within his streak of Old Deuteronomy that made most white guys—Whitmaners and otherwise—hate him so. Someone had given him aviator sunglasses, which did not quite look his part, but, from the way he sucked on the pen, he certainly didn't care.

"*Ah! Froehliche Tage sind noch einmal hier, Schwester,*" Marshall sang.

I laughed. I knew enough German to know he was singing Franklin Roosevelt's campaign song. "Huh?"

"If you weren't asleep during that part of social studies in eighth grade," Marshall said, "you might've caught it, cousin dear."

The blinking started again. "You two're cousins?"

"No shit, Sherlock," Drew mumbled. Frank heard him and started to chuckle again. Joel heard him as well, and didn't know what to make of it. And Mr. Armstrong? The poor guy looked so utterly surprised.

The books started to seem somewhat heavier for us, even if they were paperbacks. A couple of us shifted them in our arms. There was a slight, tense moment. Then, Marshall had to speak.

"You doing your good deed for the day, cousin dear?"

"Always," I said.

"We're doing this for Dr. Levin," Mr. Armstrong said. "She needs these books for her classes."

Marshall smiled broadly, jutting up the pen. "Then, you'll be in her good graces for a while, unless you do something wild, like go to a baseball game."

In a flash, Frank looked as though he were struck by lightning. "*Cardinals!*" he yelled loud enough for the teachers in the classrooms nearby to look out and say we really didn't belong in the building. "My feeling exactly," was Frank's reply.

"You're thinking what I'm thinking," Drew said.

"You better believe it. And they're in town for an afternoon doubleheader."

"Are you guys thinking about making a baseball game?" Mr. Armstrong asked.

"Actually," Marshall said, "they're thinking about having fun."

"Who's in?"

Frank needn't ask. We all thought it was a splendid idea, Mr. Armstrong aside. Of course, that meant skipping the rest of the day. We had the pressing problem of Dr. Levin's *Crucibles*, which Frank unloaded almost entirely upon Mr. Armstrong, even before we crossed the Pit. He took them to Dr. Levin's class. Then, we remembered we left our things there, and Joel had the wondrous idea to send Marshall to retrieve them, because Marshall's father was an assistant principal at the high school and, besides, Marshall could be a wondrous liar.

We waited in the Pit. Drew looked at me a couple times while we waited and said, "You've never tried this much trouble," which was true. A few times Drew volunteered, "Tell 'em it's my idea," which made sense, since blaming him was like blaming Frank. Frank grinned a little, and watched the pitball game end.

In a few minutes, Marshall emerged from the building with our things, which went into the trunk of Drew's car. By then the bell had rung and a massive flow of kids poured from the buildings around us.

"Any problems?" Joel asked.

Through the sunglasses, Marshall looked indignant. "For me?"

"Sorry."

"What did you tell her?" Drew asked.

"I told her 'Dad' had you," Marshall said. He looked us over. "But I didn't say which dad."

Frank thought that was excellent, to say the least. He clapped enthusiastically, and hopped into Drew's car. "Fantastic! We're off!"

"What about tickets?" Joel asked.

It would have to be Joel Whitney to throw cool water on an otherwise foolproof skipping plan. Frank, however, whisked the question aside with the wave of his hand. "No need to fear," he said. "Have money? Will ticket. Get me to a phone."

Then, it became a matter of finding a phone far enough from school not to be discovered, and removed enough from the principal's office not to be monitored. That was a chore. We drove through uptown looking for a phone that was in service and that was not occupied. No luck. Then, when we passed the high school for a fourth time, Marshall said "I know," and he had Drew drive to my house.

Great idea, Marsh. Why didn't you order him to *your* house?

Marshall and I lived within blocks of each other, in Jefferson Heights, on the other side of Jefferson Park, next to the high school. My house was Tudor style, with terraces, built by the Judge just before he left Congress, a few years before my birth. It has a wonderful view of the park's arboretum. Sometimes we see deer in our front yard.

Drew had been to my house many times. He knew the way. But, like me, he questioned the wisdom of going to my house. Marshall seemed to pat him on the head.

"The Judge's house," Marshall began. "No one would have the balls to ever dream of checking a federal judge's phone."

At least Frank thought that made sense. Drew was not quite sure, but still he brought the car up my drive. All eyes looked toward me as the car doors were opened and we piled out. Then, perceptive Joel spotted the Volvo coming down the lane. He pointed it out to me.

"Oh, shit," I said under my breath.

"There, there, cousin dear," Marshall said. "All you got to do is lie."

Now, Marshall knew us better than that. He knew that Volvo was my mother, home for lunch from her law firm, Macalester, Wharton, Stone, and Parker. He knew she, a perceptive counselor, could sniff out a lie as readily as Paul Drake, Perry Mason's private investigator. As Mom parked the Volvo on the lane, I thought about each lie I could have possibly used to make her leave us alone, but every one fell flat. She opened the car door and stepped out, and there she was, in her midfifties, lawyerly in a cream and lime summer skirt suit, carrying a lawyer's satchel. I felt cold. At that age, at almost sixteen, whenever I was confronted by her, I always felt cold.

"Where's the party, Mr. Skip?" she asked.

"We were hoping it would be in St. Louis," I said. Shocked, Joel nudged me.

"St. Louis?" she said.

"We were going to catch the ball game."

Mom chuckled and unlocked the front door. "And I suppose you were going to catch the game here?"

Even Marshall said nothing. We all looked at our feet.

"We'd like to use the phone, Mrs. Macalester," Drew said, "if that's all right."

"I don't mind you using the phone," she said, "but in the middle of the day?"

"We're on lunch, Mom."

Mom gave me a look. It was not just the type of look an adolescent hates coming from his mother, the type that said she knew all too well what we were trying to do, but it was her look, her coldest look, the kind of look she gave the Judge when she found him talking intimately on the phone. I felt like I needed to hide, fast. Nevertheless, she jiggled her keys and pushed open the front door, then signaled for us to enter. Marshall entered first, of course, being family, followed by Joel and Frank, who remembered to wipe their feet.

"We'll be just a minute, ma'am," Drew said to her, crossing the threshold. Mom did a little nod and smile.

I followed Drew. "Thanks, Mom."

Before I got my second foot in, Mom had ahold of my arm, tight, and she held me fast. She pulled me toward her ear.

"This better be for lunch," she whispered. "Because otherwise you'll be in your worst trouble."

All the guys, except Marshall, stood in the front hall awaiting some direction allowing them to enter the living room and sit. Joel, who had never been to my house before, craned his neck to watch the masks of the Dan climb the stairs into the second floor. And he didn't hold the banister to do it; instead, he leaned forward, awkwardly, until Drew tapped him on the shoulder.

"Don't," Drew said.

Joel nodded and stopped staring. He peeked into the living room, at its antiques and objets d'art, like he was in a house museum. His bird eyes got bigger and bigger. I suppose he had never been in a house in Jefferson Heights before.

Marshall was not with us. I had no idea where he had slipped off to until a toilet flushed and he reappeared with the phone. When he saw Joel looking scared, he swatted his flat behind. Joel jumped.

"This ain't Mars, guy," Marshall said.

Mom was gone, leaving her satchel on the stairs. I imagined she headed for her study in the attic, where I think she had left a brief. That left Marshall to hand Frank the phone. Frank dialed a few numbers, then listened for a tone.

"What's the number here?" Frank asked. "I'm dialing a page."

Marshall told him, and Frank repeated it as he dialed. When Frank hung up, we all went into the living room, sitting on the antique chairs the Judge was so proud of. Five, no, ten minutes passed before the phone rang.

"Answer it," Marshall commanded.

Frank handed the phone to me. "If it's Wallace, give it back to me," he said.

I answered the phone. Mom had already picked up the extension, but once I said "I got it" it was just me and the caller. In the background at the other end of the line I heard a din, like locusts feeding on a field.

"Hello?"

"I got a page," a kid said. "This is Wallace."

I handed the phone to Frank, who draped a leg over a love seat arm and lounged that way until Marshall removed his leg. That did bruise Frank's ego a little, but he caught himself and began talking.

"I want a deal," Frank said. "Cardinal tickets. Five. You can do better than that. Better. Come on, Wally, old buddy, old pal, I'm your boon coon. Is that your best boon coon rate? Gimme a break. Shit, what are you selling, a kidney? Bleep that, I don't need 'em that bad. Good night!"

He hung up. Did he know he, a Whitmaner, skin tanned and hair amber, had used a slur in a black family's house in the middle of a black neighborhood? Even Joel, nice, white-bread, thought it was not quite the thing to do, as he got awfully tense. Drew slugged Frank in the shoulder.

"Take it from a mick," Drew said. "In here, kill the coon shit, kraut."

Frank realized what he had done. He smiled an apology to Marshall and me. He stood and hitched his shorts, then he stroked his chest. "I'm thirsty," he said, looking around. "Where's the liquor cabinet?"

"We're Methodist," Marshall said.

"So?" Frank asked. "All that means is that you drink a little more Diet Coke with your Seagram's. That's all. Is there something to drink here, Macalester?"

Mom must have been eavesdropping. She came into the living room and went straight for the Judge's liquor cabinet. There, she took a highball tumbler and poured a deep, stiff drink from the crystal decanter of Grandma Macalester's bourbon. She offered it to Frank, who drank it, drank a little too much of it. It went down the wrong way and left Frank coughing.

"That's good stuff, Mrs. Macalester," he managed in a hoarse voice.

Mom offered it to everyone else, but Marshall, who knew Mom's version of aversion therapy firsthand, shook everyone off. No one took her up on her offer. Frank never finished the drink. He had done a little too much.

Mom returned upstairs. The phone rang once and no one answered. The phone rang a second time and Frank put his hand on it. He answered it on the third ring. He had a grin to beat all grins, like he had someone by the short hairs.

"I'm sorry, Mrs. Macalester," he said, "it's Frank Kotter. I think this is for me. Yes, ma'am. Bye, Mrs. Macalester." His smile got bigger, and he showed teeth. "Wallace? I don't think I need them. No. How good are the seats? You're kidding. Excellent! And price? A little lower. Yes, lower. Lower still. Is that your best? Okay, then. I'll see you, regular place. Gimme fifteen minutes." Frank hung up and looked around the room. He cleared his throat. We were at the edge of our seats. "We need two hundred."

Joel's eyes got bigger than ever before, if that were possible. "Dollars! For baseball tickets?"

"Five of them," Frank said. "Good seats."

"But, that's forty dollars each!"

"Hey! You in, or you wanna be cheap, panty-snipe?" Frank sunk his hands into his pockets and hitched up his shorts in one sweeping motion. Since he wasn't going to grow a bigger ass, I was about to give him one of my belts. "Five good seats at a Cardinal game are—what—a couple hundred dollars? And we're not getting them for market, either. Gimme a break!"

I was about to say something when I heard Mom coming downstairs. She had reclaimed the brief, which she carried in her hand. Signaling for Frank to calm down and dummy up, I went to the stairs.

"We'll be out in a minute," I told her.

"Just remember to flush the toilet and lower the seat before you leave," she said. She stuck her head into the living room and looked at Frank. She made sure Frank knew she was looking at him. "And do count the silver. You know even boon coons have sticky fingers."

Perfect! She was listening. She was mad as hell. She didn't kiss me before she left. She never kisses when she is mad, no matter how much we want it. Instead, she left. I watched her drive away.

"I'm not being cheap or anything," Joel said. "I'm just saying forty dollars each is an awful lot of money for baseball tickets. Even for the Cardinals. That's just what I think." He turned to Marshall. "What you think?"

"Forty is a lot," Marshall said. "But these are good tickets?"

Recovering a bit, Frank raised a finger. "The best. If not, may I eat—"

"Careful," Drew warned, stopping him. "You've put enough in your mouth."

We decided to get them. Each of us took turns in the bathroom and with the refrigerator before heading to an ATM. Then, once we all had our cash, Frank asked Drew to drive to Whitman Township.

Whitman Township was just outside of the city, a place carved up by subdivisions of tract housing, some respectable ranches, others tri-levels on cul-de-sacs, most tin-walled two bedrooms that would become unglued after forty years. Don't get me wrong: most of my friends, and most of the people in my track at school, were Whitmaners, but most Whitmaners were trash that almost never thought of themselves as trash, no matter what they did.

Drew was a Whitmaner. Were there more Whitmaners like him, I would like them better.

Near the middle school in Whitman Township, Drew pulled the car into a doughnut shop's parking lot and turned off the engine. "Now what?"

"Give Macalester the money, guys," Frank said, "and wait here."

I assumed I was selected because I sat directly behind Frank. Maybe I was trustworthy because money meant so little to me. Whatever the reason, everyone gave me his money and Frank and I went in.

The doughnut shop was practically empty, except for a man and a woman, both in white, tentlike hats, working, and a thin, angular, straw-haired boy sitting on a stool at the far end of the L-shaped counter. From his smacking sounds I could tell he was eating a doughnut, that, and lapping milk.

Frank and I approached from the back. "You sit on that side," he whispered. "I'll sit on this. And remember: look; don't touch."

Okay, so that was something I really needed to hear.

Coming from behind, I felt I knew that backside. As I said, he was thin, his off-white shirt hanging from his slender shoulders, ballooning over the top of the stool. His beige shorts were almost invisible. But it was the feet, in sandals, that seemed most familiar. I studied his heel as we approached, and imagined holding them. I saw he had a something sticking out of his back pocket.

Frank and I sat. The boy seemed not to notice us. He ate his doughnut and drank his milk. "Well," he said finally, "if it isn't Skip Macalester."

I was struck. *Do I know you? Did I know you? Have you heard about me?* I looked at the boy and tried thinking of something to say.

"I'm Kathy Lawrence's little brother Wallace. You came to my house Saturday looking for her. Remember?"

I did remember. Last I saw him he had let Drew and me into their basement family room, where two boys in towels and damp swimming trunks let a guy, slightly older than us, draw on a sketch pad with charcoal. *Did you know that guy was doing their feet, Wallace?* Nothing is a greater aphrodisiac for me than bare feet.

"Macalester!" Frank exclaimed. "You devil!"

The man working at the place approached and pointed at the clock, then he went to the cash register.

"Ain't got time to talk," Wallace said. "Got the money?"

"Got the tickets?" Frank asked.

"Got the money?"

Frank pointed to me and Wallace turned his head. That was my signal. I went through my pockets and produced the two hundred dollars, all in twenties. I started to count them, but Wallace stopped me and grabbed the cash.

"Ah," Wallace said. "That's okay. I know where to find your dick."

Wallace finished the doughnut. He swung toward me and stood. "See ya around." Then, he went to the cash register, paid his bill, and left. Whatever was in his pocket, an envelope, I think, was gone.

Frank got up as well and headed for the door. He had an envelope in his hand, and he tapped it. "To St. Louis."

II

"How was your yesterday?"

That question, asked by the Judge Friday morning as he ate his morning apple and sipped his morning glass of iced tea, hung out in midair like his evening pipe smoke. What did he mean by that? Only he knew.

It was about seven-thirty. After showering, I had opened the bathroom door to find the Judge before me, dressed and eating and sipping. I considered confessing leaving Dr. Levin's class early and going to a teller machine, taking forty dollars from my account, and buying a scalped Cardinals baseball ticket. Easily, I could have confessed taking the Inter-Urban train from our downtown to downtown St. Louis, where the five of us (Joel Whitney included) sat behind home plate and watched the Cardinals beat (again) the New York Mets, whom everyone booed.

There were a couple things I would have never confessed to him. I would have found it difficult to admitting a lit ganja blunt I held for a few seconds before Drew snatched it out of my hand. Where that went, I wouldn't have known. Most likely he had flushed it down the Busch Stadium toilet, where he said it belonged. I would scarcely discuss Frank Kotter's postgame escapade on the Inter-Urban, when he was racked by a girl for fondling her. Luckily, she got off long before we did, before we could offer money for her not to tell.

None of those things would I have dared mention to my father, though the thought did strike me. I looked at him, eating the apple. My hair dripped onto my bare shoulder.

"Fine," I said meekly.

He bit the apple. "Anything special happen?"

"No."

"Okay." The Judge started downstairs. "By the way, get dressed. I'm driving you to school."

"But Drew picks me up."

"Not this time."

Mom stood at their bedroom door, still in a dressing robe, watching. She had much to say.

"What did I do?" I asked her.

"Remember to lower the seat and count the silver, boon coon," she said, "next time."

At a quarter to eight, the Judge stood at the foot of the stairs and opened his lungs. "It's time, Skip."

That was my signal. Brushing my hair, I grabbed my book bag and headed downstairs, almost tripping over my untied shoestrings. The Judge took his briefcase and headed for the Saab. I was not that far behind. He wore his broad gray hat with a wine-red band, all matching his gray suit and wine-red tie.

"I wish you'd tell me what this is about," I said. "I mean, you usually don't take me to school."

"I just felt like driving you. You don't mind, do you?" He looked back at me. I shook my head quickly. "It's been so long, I thought I'd stop by and see what the school is like."

"You mean you want to go inside?"

"You don't mind, do you?"

That was a rhetorical question. The Judge set his briefcase in the backseat and I sat in the front, next to him, as I had done so many times before. Without much fanfare beyond these simple acts the Judge lit his pipe and expelled an engulfing cloud of smoke, then started the engine. He eased the Saab out of the driveway.

It is rather awkward being almost sixteen and being driven to high school by your father. As it was not yet seven-fifty, I could find some comfort in that most Whitmaners were not yet out of their subdivisions to see me. Everyone else didn't matter that much.

But I could not hide the fact. The Judge was driving me to school, like a little boy. Leaving Jefferson Heights the long way, I thought about what could have caused him to do this to me, and I happened upon the obvious when the Judge honked at Leah Langston as she went down Jefferson Avenue for work.

"What about Marshall?" I asked.

"What about Marshall?"

"He was in on it."

The Judge puffed. "He was."

"Yeah."

The Judge puffed again. "Was Drew Ford?"

"Well—"

"He was."

I didn't answer. I looked at my book bag.

"He was," the Judge repeated. Taking the pipe from his mouth, he rested his elbow on the door. "Who else?"

"Two other guys. Whitmaners. You don't know them."

"Try me."

I cleared my throat. "Frank Kotter. Joel Whitney."

"So, you, Marshall, Drew Ford, Frank Kotter, and Joel Whitney were in on it? What else did you do?"

"We just went to a Cardinal game," I said. "That's all."

The Judge turned the Saab onto College Avenue. The high school, just a block away, could be seen through the trees. "Sounds like, to me, that's enough."

I sat silent as the Judge brought the car into the parking lot behind the high school's West building, where Dr. Levin had her room. If you have ever been at a high school before your friends, when only teachers and administrators are there, then you know full well the sick feeling I had. The parking lot was absent of people, though it had plenty of cars. I imagined the dozens of guys teasing, "Skippy got driven by his old man! Skippy got driven by his old man!" and Kay Reece, in particular, sticking his tongue out and roughing my head.

Then, I saw Mr. Armstrong drive into the parking lot in a pale blue Volkswagen Beetle. He seemed intent, as though driving commanded all his faculties. I stuffed my kelly green plaid shirt in my pants again and checked my breath. My clothes smelled like a pipe. Mr. Armstrong waved, parking. I waved back. The Judge merely looked at me.

"You buttoned your shirt lopsided," he observed as he put his pipe in the ashtray and opened the Saab door. I looked at myself. He was right.

I didn't want to be too embarrassed. I rebuttoned my shirt before leaving the car. By then, Mr. Armstrong was out as well. He lifted from the Volkswagen a leather briefcase not unlike my father's and mother's, the kind of satchel that said "lawyer" and "lawyer's kid."

"Good morning, sir," Mr. Armstrong called out to the Judge.

The Judge grunted. I checked my zipper.

Mr. Armstrong blinked. Looking downward, he raced us for the door to the West building.

"You teach here?" the Judge asked.

"Yes, sir."

"How old are you?"

Mr. Armstrong blinked. He held the school door open. "Twenty-five, sir."

The Judge shook his head. "Twenty-five-year-old teachers are looking younger and younger these days."

Mr. Armstrong didn't know quite what to make of that sentiment. "Yes, sir," he said. He looked a little dazed as the Judge and I entered the building. Then he caught himself. "May I direct you, sir?"

"I know where we're going," the Judge said. "Thank you."

As I had dreaded since he "offered" to drive me to school, he headed for Dr. Levin's room, which was on the first floor. I was behind him, and Mr. Armstrong, satchel in hand, was behind me.

"Are you looking for someone in particular, sir?" Mr. Armstrong called out.

"Yes," the Judge said.

"Perhaps, sir, I can get them for you."

"No."

"Are you sure, sir?"

The Judge stopped in the middle of the corridor and turned around. "Very."

With that, the Judge resumed walking. Mr. Armstrong shuffled along behind us.

When we got to Dr. Levin's room it was vacant. The Judge turned on the lights and ceiling fans and positioned himself in the cushioned chair behind Dr. Levin's desk. From the bottom of a good-sized stack of books, he plucked W. H. Auden's *Collected Poems* and started leaf-

ing through it. He removed his hat. He seemed not to notice the picture of himself in his congressional years that Dr. Levin kept on the
table near her desk, a picture that had vexed me ever since I first saw
it, on the first day of school, about a week before.

"Young man," the Judge said without looking up, "is there some
coffee around here?"

For a minute, Mr. Armstrong looked at me. "He's talking to you,"
I whispered.

"Coffee?"

"Yes."

Mr. Armstrong set his briefcase on a student's desk, still set with
other in a circle, and blinked. "I don't know. I just started here."

"Then find out."

Mr. Armstrong shuffled. "Yes, sir."

"I like my coffee fresh, light, and sweet."

Nodding, Mr. Armstrong hurried out the room. The Judge continued reading. I, like a jerk, stood near the lectern with my hands in my
pockets. I thought about reading a *Crucible* that rested on the lectern;
I would have grabbed it, too, had Dr. Levin not come through the
door.

"Don't ever skip my fucking class again, mister," she said.

I couldn't believe my English teacher would say such a thing to me.
I looked at the Judge, who read poetry. He seemed not to have heard
her.

"Genie," the Judge said, "how can you teach this Auden? It doesn't
have 'September 1, 1939.'"

"Did you hear what she said?" I asked.

"Yeah."

"And?"

"Don't ever skip her class again," the Judge said, cleaning up the
phrase. He held the book up. "I just can't see trying to teach Auden
without 'September 1, 1939.'"

"You gave me that book," she said. She rested her red and white
canvas tote bag on her desk. "Remember?"

"I wouldn't have given you it if I had known it didn't have 'September 1, 1939.'"

Dr. Levin didn't respond. She shook her head. "Where'd you go?"

"Just to a baseball game," I said, in a low voice.

"Cardinals?" she asked. I nodded. "Did they win?"

"Yes."

"I hope that was worth it," she said. "Whose idea was it?"

"Do you even teach this Auden?"

"Alfred!"

"What?"

Dr. Levin wouldn't say. She shook her head. "Whose idea was it to go to a baseball game?"

"Does it even matter?" the Judge asked. He closed the Auden and plucked from the stack Robert Lowell's *Selected Poems* and flipped to "For the Union Dead." Holding the book before him, he read, *"Relinquunt Omnia Servare Rem Publicam."* He licked his lips. "Professor Snowden would have my hide, even today, if he knew I forgot how to translate *relinquunt*. Do you know how to translate *relinquunt?*" he asked me.

I shook my head. Even then, Latin was Greek to me.

The Judge patted his lips. "If you didn't skip, old man, perhaps you would know *relinquunt*." With that, he read the poem's first stanza.

Mr. Armstrong came in with the Judge's coffee. He spilled a little on the floor, and smiled and blinked at the Judge's pissed look. The Judge paused and sipped coffee. Mr. Armstrong awaited his verdict.

"Very good," the Judge said, and Mr. Armstrong was relieved. "'Two months after marching through Boston,'" the Judge recited, sipping, "'half the regiment was dead; at the dedication, William James could almost hear the bronze Negroes breathe.'"

Mr. Armstrong grinned and nodded. "I saw the movie."

"Do you know this waterfly?" the Judge asked Dr. Levin. "Oh, yes! 'All surrendered to preserve the Republic!'"

Mr. Armstrong looked at me. His mouth was wide open, like a fool. He had no idea what to make of the Judge.

"Cicero, I think," I whispered.

Closing his mouth, Mr. Armstrong nodded. He looked at me, then at the Judge. Without fanfare, the Judge closed the Lowell and sipped his coffee. "You would excuse us, of course, waterfly?" The Judge sipped coffee, smiled, and nodded. "You won't mind, will you?"

Mr. Armstrong excused himself with his satchel as the Judge leaned back and crossed his legs.

"Was he responsible?" Dr. Levin asked after Mr. Armstrong left.

"No," I said.

"You wouldn't be covering up for him, too?"

"Genie," the Judge said. "What does he have to do?"

That was a nice, open question for my father to have asked. He asked it as easily as a sip of his light, sweet, fresh coffee. He creased his hat's crown and waited for Dr. Levin's answer.

"I will say I'm sorry," I offered. "And I'll never do that again."

"Knowing your father, he probably made you shit fear," Dr. Levin said. Then, she shook her head. "I'll have to give it some thought."

The Judge grabbed his hat and stood. "That's all I need to hear." Putting the hat on, he left, pinching my cheek in the process. He said he had an OSHA case to decide. After he left, Mr. Armstrong fumbled in, apologetic for waiting in the corridor.

Dr. Levin went to her desk, and restacked the Auden and Lowell. "Of all my students, I would never have believed it would be you."

"I'm sorry," I said again, for what it was worth.

"If you ever try playing your father and me for fools again—"

"It won't happen again," I said. "I promise."

"Make damn sure." Dr. Levin, shaking, started going through the things in her tote bag, unpacking the books and themes she had as homework that previous night. As she unpacked, I wondered whether I had missed anything the day before. I thought it best not to ask her, as she unpacked rather furiously. "Since you're here, I might as well assign a *Crucible* to read."

Dr. Levin directed Mr. Armstrong to hand her one of the *Crucibles* on the bookcase, which he did. She removed a card from the pouch in the back of the book. She handed me the card and had me write my name.

When known by a nickname, you can write any of a combination of signatures. Already in a mess, I chose to keep it as simple as possible. *A. M. "Skip" Macalester.* I returned the card. She looked at it briefly.

"Just like Alfred," she said. She filed it by number in a rubber banded stack on her desk. She handed over my *Crucible*. "Start reading."

"How far do I read?"

"Read until you stop. Or until the World Series."

She busied herself with a gradebook and a stack of papers. That was my dismissal. Hitching my book bag to my shoulder, I took *The Crucible* and slinked out of the room. Not far down the hall, I felt someone tug my arm. I thought it was Drew; it felt like Drew; having stood him up it should have been Drew. I turned around, expecting Drew. Instead, it was Mr. Armstrong. He fumbled with his words, wringing his hands.

"I'm really, very sorry," he said. "She asked me where'd you gone off to, and then your cousin showed up, and, by then—well—by then, I couldn't lie anymore. I didn't want to screw up the chance I have to teach here before I started. I hope you'll understand."

"That's okay," I managed to say. I was, after all, a little dumb-struck by this display. We looked at each other, speechless, for a minute. Then he smiled. His teeth were a perfect row of pearls, like a choker.

"I hope you won't think worse of me for that."

"No, I don't. You have a job to do."

"Yeah, and yesterday, it was snitch." Mr. Armstrong did a silent laugh, then he brought his hand to his mouth, as if hiding something. His eyes twinkled. "I'm sorry. My dad's always telling me not to laugh like some old lady."

"Yours too?" I lied.

"Oh, he's just a bear about it. He's a life insurance agent in Philadelphia, Mississippi, where they found those three civil rights workers? Not that you would know anything about it; it was before your time—"

"It was before my father's time."

He smiled. "Exactly. But that's how most people remember Philadelphia, even if it did happen, like, years ago. Not that I'm saying we should forget about it, but—well, you know."

A bell rang. A group of students came inside and headed for class. Dr. Levin left her room and came directly to me. Mr. Armstrong looked unnerved again.

"Young man," she said to me, "you need to be heading to class."

"Yes, ma'am," I said.

"Go."

Dr. Levin seemed disquieted that day. And why? What did I do? All we did was go to a baseball game.

In my second hour class, history, Frank Kotter confided to our classmates that we skipped the previous day for the Cardinals game, and they looked at me in bewilderment.

"Never thought you'd have the balls, Macalester," Kay Reece said. "Did you see any young boys?"

"Young boy this," I said, grabbing my crotch.

"You can't young boy that," Kay laughed. "There ain't nothing there to young boy."

I was so mad that I wished I could bite him. But I had heard that pork from middle white pigs could be rancid, if the mug were too sour. And Kay had the sourest mug.

Not dignifying him was the easiest way to get through history. Frank, his wavy blond hair stroked and shiny, suggested I ignore that part of Kay, because Kay, he said, could really be a good guy. I laughed. "Fat chance."

"No, really," Frank said. "He can be just about the best."

I looked at our history teacher, Mr. Scott, whittling some girl's pencil. "Kay's always been a jerk to me," I said. "I heard it's because I'm Marshall's cousin."

"Why would he give a fig leaf about that?"

I shrugged. Kay and I had a history. I took from Frank my history assignment on the Treaty of Paris, 1783, which he was copying.

"I'm not saying it's impossible for Kay to be like that," Frank said. "I've known him since second grade, and I know he can be such a jerk—I know that firsthand—but, if you look past that, you can really see he is a neat guy."

As earnest as Frank was I had not the heart to say I hated "neat," for that sounded so much like a tailored suit or a vacuumed room. At the sound of that word, I felt like picking lint from Frank's hair.

"I'm not saying he can't be neat," I said. "I'm saying that he can be a jerk."

"Oh, yeah, I agree. Anybody can."

Frank turned his attention to a Supremes song Mr. Scott had on the CD player. He mimed the words senselessly until they seemed a shadow of themselves. I turned to a write up on the treaty and on Benjamin Franklin's machinations. Then, I chose to change the subject.

"Dr. Levin is onto us," I said.

Frank stopped mouthing. "What?"

"I said, Dr. Levin's onto us."

"Oh, shit."

"This morning, before school, she had a meeting with me and my father, and she found out about everything."

"Did you tell? Macalester, if you told, so help me—"

"I didn't," I said. "She knew all about it before I said anything."

Frank started drumming his pencil. Drew always said Frank thought by drumming pencils. "It must've been that student teacher." He meant Mr. Armstrong.

"It wasn't him," I lied.

"You sure?"

"Yeah."

"How you know?"

I didn't answer. I shrugged.

"I'd bet anything it was him," Frank said. "I mean, who else would it be? Marshall?"

"I know Marshall," I said. "He wouldn't tell. He's too good a liar."

Yes, I knew my cousin. He was a politico in training, and he could lie with the best of them.

"Then it must've been that Mr. Armstrong guy," Frank said, resolute.

I said nothing to disabuse him of that perception. The girl who had her pencil whittled had returned to her seat by then; I think she had turned her attention to Benjamin Franklin as well.

"We got to think up something to say," Frank said.

"Too late," I said.

"Macalester, it is never too late to say something to a teacher. Yo, Scott!" he yelled to Mr. Scott, who just glared at him, "it ain't never too late to say something to a teacher, right, is it?"

"For everybody but you, Kotter," Mr. Scott said. "For everybody but you."

The foretelling rang in my ears until class ended. Frank and I gathered our books and crossed the Pit for Dr. Levin's classroom. Drew caught up with us. I thought Dr. Levin would be awaiting us like the mythic, vengeful harpy, but she was not there when we got to her classroom. Nor was Mr. Armstrong, to Drew's satisfaction.

"They must have fired him," Drew said, "the undercooked weenie."

"You don't fool me, Ford," Frank said, "you'd still want to eat that undercooked weenie."

"I'd puke him back up."

Drew sat beside me, saying nothing about me coming to school with the Judge. The class was completely full when Dr. Levin and Mr. Armstrong entered. I half expected her to have preached to him about high school juniors still acting like sophomores and skipping school, but, from the way they looked, they seemed not to have been the preacher and the preached. Instead, they had the comforted look teachers with a plan get, as though, in the meantime, they had plotted more things out than a student could imagine.

We new juniors sat in our circle and anticipated the worst.

"Did you read?" a girl near me whispered. "I'd bet anything it is a test."

"They can't test us yet. We just got the book," someone replied.

"Yes, they can," the girl whispered confidently. "They're teachers."

Dr. Levin awaited silence to read Psalms. Which Psalm, I cannot remember. Something about cedars. When she finished, she closed the book and said something in Hebrew, I think, as her eyes were closed. "Beautiful," she said.

We waited.

She turned her gaze upon us.

Everyone looked for cover.

"As you know," she said, "yesterday, I sent some guys to the English library to pick up some *Crucibles*."

We gulped.

"I would like to see those guys after class," she said.

"But what about the class after this?" Joel asked.

She stared him down. She ruminated about what to say. Her cud: "It won't be long."

"The dip," Frank mumbled.

"What was that, Frank?" Dr. Levin asked.

Frank thumbed through his notebook. "Nothing."

I could hear Mr. Armstrong chuckle.

I should have thought the worst had transpired when the Judge brought me to school, but never, I think, did it get me dreading whatever could have been on Dr. Levin's mind. Obviously, she and Mr. Armstrong had something wicked planned.

For the period, we took notes on Arthur Miller in our journals. Sometimes, I read over the stuff of that year and I am struck by my expansive writing and by the way I intuitively leapt to conclusions. "She's looking at me!!" is one entry from that September; I don't know whether I was referring to Kathy Lawrence or to Dr. Levin. As I could hear Marshall say, perhaps both.

Oddly, Mr. Armstrong remained quiet, almost forgotten. And Kathy? Dutifully, she kept notes. Her blonde hair was pinned at the bangs. She didn't notice that I noticed her.

When the period was over, the bell rang and most of the class moved on. Most, that is, except Joel, Drew, Frank, and me. We stayed in our seats and anticipated the worst. And we really didn't feel so good when Dr. Levin left word for the seniors of the next class not to enter for World lit. Mr. Armstrong had left for the moment (something in the building office, I think, was the excuse). Dr. Levin closed the door. She moved into the middle of the circle.

"How was the baseball game, Joel?" she asked.

"Fine." Joel examined his nails, then filed them with his teeth. "Cardinals won."

"Very good," she said. She folded her arms. "During my senior year, in 1982, they won the World Series. That was when day games were still played. Some of us on the yearbook staff watched the game in Milwaukee between classes."

"Then you were like regular guys," Frank said, grinning.

Dr. Levin eliminated his grin with a glare. "You didn't hear me correctly, Kotter. I said 'between classes.' We never skipped for a baseball game. Did we, Skip?"

"I dunno," I mumbled.

"You should. Ask your father. He remembers."

I looked at my nails. They looked like they could have used a biting. For some reason, Drew cleared his throat.

"You got something to say, Drew?"

He cleared his throat again. "No, ma'am."

"Good," she said. "Because, I do. It's been years since a student skipped any part of my class. That has been a long time. Do you know why it has been years since someone skipped part of my class?"

We shook our heads.

"I'll tell you. And I will tell you about the last students to skip. The last students to skip tried to escape reading Sappho. Before the end of the year, they had to explain the feminist perspective in Toni Morrison's *Paradise*. That was years ago, and, from that time, that kept my students from skipping any part of my class. Until now."

Joel raised his hand. His eyes were bigger than normal. Looking at him, Dr. Levin allowed him to speak. For a quick moment, though, the words were caught in his throat. He mouthed his words, but nothing came out. She was patient with him. She signaled for him to catch himself and to slow down. When he did, the words finally came.

"Is that what we're gonna do?" Joel asked.

"No," she said.

We started breathing more easily, fanning ourselves and patting our brows, until Mr. Armstrong came in and said, "Miss Newman will arrange for the measurements."

We looked at him like he was from some place really strange, like Mississippi. Then, we looked at Dr. Levin, who smiled a little.

"What you will do as penitence for skipping part of my class will be appropriate." She paused to let the next class bell ring and she refused to recognize Joel, who was most likely seeking a pass. "We are doing a play. You will have to act. Be at the theater by eleven o'clock tomorrow morning. You may go."

We left her room with a quiet shuffle. Dr. Levin's class of seniors took our place and, as we closed the door, we could hear her reading more Psalms. Joel rushed to chemistry. Frank went to pitball. Drew and I went to lunch. We were to take his car and eat off campus.

"For a minute there," Drew said, starting the engine, "I thought she was going to do something drastic, like tell my old man. He'd kill my ass if he knew I skipped. If he found out, I would have to genuflect and kiss ass and all kinds of crazy shit. What's the worst the Judge and your mom would make you do?"

"Apologize."

Drew pulled into the flow of the Pit traffic. "Really? That don't sound that bad."

"In my family, apologizing is the worst. Remember?"

He braked for a girl in a red Fiat, then he looked at me. "I forgot." Once the Fiat was on its way, he proceeded to the Pit entrance. We waited our turn to go, then he led the car into the traffic for Uptown.

After lunch came Latin, and after Latin, physics. I spent so much time gesticulating apologies that I almost didn't see that it was two thirty and time to rid myself of some steam in PE. I borrowed Drew's gym clothes. As usual, Mr. Moore put my wallet into a manila envelope in the locker room office and stowed it away. But first, he had some fun at my expense.

"Heavenly Father, Mary, Mother of God, and Joseph, what in the hell do you got in this wallet, Macalester? Fort Knox?"

"Just some cash," I said.

Mr. Moore scratched his crotch. "More like Fort Knox. Did you use it for a baseball game?"

"I wouldn't."

"Yeah, I bet the last time you went to a baseball game Ryne Sandberg was playing." Mr. Moore chuckled. "Hell, Macalester, I bet you don't even know who Ryne Sandberg is, poor kid. I bet none of you know anything about Ryne Sandberg. Hey, Dowling!" He yelled at Jared Dowling, the token white forward on last year's freshman basketball team. "You know Ryne Sandberg?"

Jared's reddish acne-pitted face turned blank and lifeless, as though a gun were held to his head. "What year is he in, Coach?"

Mr. Moore laughed. "Kids. Gimme a break."

I took Drew's shorts and found my place at locker sixty-six, my favorite place, just for its repetition. Standing not far from me was Gary Phillips, also a sophomore. Through his underwear, I could see he sported something of an erection. I smiled. The devil, Marshall would say, was already in me.

"Hey, Phillips," I said, "how's the handball game?"

Gary's little boy looks were startled. He plopped on the bench and slid on his gym shorts, without speaking. I had barely unbuttoned my shirt. I turned to him and slammed his locker. He jumped.

"Hey, Phillips."

"What?" he asked, stressed.

"What language are you taking this year?"

"He's in my French class," Jared Dowling said from the row of lockers behind us.

"French," I said. "Figures."

Gary looked hard at me and put his feet into his gym shoes. "Your name's Macalester, right?"

I rolled my eyes. He really was a sophomore.

Mr. Moore blew his shrill whistle. "*Arthur,* stop molesting the kid!"

Everyone laughed. I thought of a couple things to say, but I had been in enough trouble that day. Gary hurried on his shoes and he scampered up the back stairs to roll call.

"Mac strikes out again," some Whitmaner said. Who it was, I couldn't tell, for he was gone before I found him.

I dressed in Drew's clothes and then stood on the line in the boys' gym upstairs for roll call. Then, Mr. Moore went through the line and called our names. After that, we were all to go out for soccer, or to the girls' gym in the West building for softball, but, before we broke, Mr. Moore saw Ken Langston, a cousin and Marshall's father, standing at the door. Ken pointed at me.

"Well, well, Macalester," Mr. Moore said. He put his blue ink pen into his blue polo shirt. "It's your lucky day: the assistant principal wants to see you."

"Oooos" and "Ummms" by the guys. That was all I needed. I trudged to Ken. He occupied the empty hall almost as thoroughly as he claimed two pews with his jacket, his scarf, his Bible, his paper, his bulletin, and his glasses. As he waited for me, he jingled something in his pocket that sounded like change or keys, but, more likely, it was the large paper clips he liked hoarding. Whatever they were, I didn't feel like confronting them. He waited for me as passively as waiting for a noisy room to silence before making an introduction, with a look commanding and expecting total attention. Before, I had not noticed that his mustache, full and feathery, was longer to the left of his nose than it was to the right (or was it the other way around?). His short hair was gray around the ears. Something struck me, even then, that his ears were uneven, and, when he cleared his throat and looked shrewdly down his nose, it was like being confronted by the Judge again.

"It was just a baseball game," I blurted out.

Ken seemed startled. "Hey, Skip," he finally said.

"Hey."

"What's this about a baseball game?"

I couldn't believe that, in my haste, I had shown so much leg, like a harlot promised a Roosevelt dime by a puckish seventh grader. Quick, think! "Nothing."

For a moment, Ken seemed unconvinced that I had really said nothing, then he stroked the short end of his mustache. He leaned against the same door Marshall entered the day before, and, for a minute there, I thought Ken, too, would speak German, for he taught it earlier in his career. "I was wondering: have you seen Brad?"

My other cousin, Brad Morgan, Kay Reece's friend and almost as much of a jerk, was someone I usually saw only on holidays.

"Brad and I don't exactly run in the same circles, Ken."

"A simple 'yea' or 'nay' would do."

I sighed audibly. It was obnoxious, even to me. "No, I haven't seen Brad. Why?"

"It's between me and Brad, Skip."

I wanted to ask why he was asking me, but little would have restrained him from spanking my tail right there in the hall, if I did. Besides, Mom and the Judge had given him permission to discipline my smart-ass antics years before, and, on a couple occasions when I was younger, he had used the permit. So, I went another track. "Did you try him at home? Maybe that group he hangs out with took him home."

"If he were home, I wouldn't be asking about him."

That slap was just like the Judge's. I reacted as if it had been the Judge: I sighed audibly. Before I could say anything, Ken waved his hand.

"Go and play soccer," he said.

Shaking my head, I headed back into the boys' gym. "He's probably with old Kay Reece," I mumbled just loud enough for someone to hear. I was hoping Ken was listening, but, knowing him, he had crossed the courtyard to get a breath of fresh air before returning to the Main.

And so, my school day, which had begun with such a bang, whimpered out with me playing defense on the soccer field against Jared Dowling and some Whitmaners. In the course of a few hours, I went from evading the Judge and Dr. Levin to playing footsie with sophomores.

When Drew came to the locker room looking for his gym clothes, I could almost kick myself for my decline. Somehow, he made it past Mr. Moore and the other teachers to end up leaning against the lockers as I undressed.

"Hey," he said.

"Hey."

"Going to shower?"

"Why?"

"Why?! So you won't stink," he laughed.

I pulled off the T-shirt and sniffed the underarms. They reeked like fresh oysters in a gym shoe. I couldn't tell if the smell was Drew's or mine. "I'm going home, anyway."

"You don't want to stink going home. You'll stink up the whole house. Your mom won't like that." Drew took the T-shirt, sniffed it, and stuffed it into his gym bag.

Sitting on the bench, I pulled the athletic socks off my feet. They are light, my feet. Almost the color of hard maple. Drew stuffed the socks into the gym bag as well. "Mom won't mind," I said.

"Like hell, she won't. You know PE builds up your sweat."

I borrowed a towel from Drew's gym bag and sponged off what sweat was on my chest and put on my plaid shirt. I handed back the towel. "I don't sweat as much as you."

Drew laughed. "I sweat like a monkey going to vote." He cleared his throat. "I mean, if monkeys could vote."

I removed the gym shorts, which were damp along the thighs. I had heard what that expression originally meant. Drew, I think, had no idea.

Drew took the gym shorts, too. And there I was, sitting bare-assed in my shirt and the regulation jockstrap the school compelled every guy to wear. Drew watched my feet. "Monkeys can't vote," I said.

"Yeah."

I wasn't about to give him the jockstrap. As we always did when we traded gym clothes that year, I took the jockstrap home and washed it with my handkerchiefs and underwear, which my parents insisted I do on my own.

My underwear and pants went on. I zipped up and put my shoes on. My socks went into my pants pockets. The bell rang, ending the day, and I wondered how Drew was able to escape class (government, I think) before class was officially over. Then, without me asking as much, he showed off a pink pass from Ken that said he was excused. I got my things and we left the locker room.

"I've got to turn this in," Drew said, "then, I'll take you home."

"Did he ask you about yesterday?"

"He just thought I skipped. That's all."

"He asked me about Brad," I said.

"Brad? Brad Morgan?" Drew looked blank, as though he couldn't think of anyone else I would call "Brad," without a last name.

We headed for Drew's last classroom. I was right: it was government. His teacher (and mine), Mr. MacPhail, stood ramrod like an old Marine by his door as the hall cleared of students. He took Drew's pass, inspected it momentarily, and nodded.

"I guess this means you are legal for one more day, Ford," Mr. MacPhil said. He looked up. Behind his thick glasses, his dark brown eyes shot through like cannonballs. According to his service pictures taken during the Gulf War that he posted on his bulletin board in remembrance of veterans, he had been a dashing man.

"I promise to take my swats tomorrow," Drew said, shifting his gym bag from hand to hand.

"Then, you best eat up," Mr. MacPhail said. "Because, there really isn't that much to hit. Right, Macalester?"

"No comment," I said.

"Spoken like a true son of a politician," Mr. MacPhail said. "You probably learned that in the womb."

In my family, I could easily have told him, such phrases are passed in the genes. But I left that alone. Instead, I nodded and smiled like an idiot.

The hall had become empty. Idly looking down the hall, I saw Brad Morgan lurking near the exit. He signaled for me to come to him.

At times, it was hard to distinguish Brad from the other kids from Whitman Township. Although he was a relative, like Marshall, through Grandma Macalester's side, he scarcely looked the part. He looked more like his mother, a mix of Polish and British, skin pale and unsuntanable, hair muskrat brown, nose sleek, eyes gray, with lips that—if you looked hard enough—only hinted at some far off ghost of negritude. In a crowd, I had to look twice to see him. Brad leaned against the door.

"You know, Ken is looking for you," I said.

"What did you tell him?"

"What could I tell him? You're friends with that jerk. Remember?"

Drew approached. Brad nodded a "hey" at him. "Tell nobody nothing," Brad said. "I gotta go."

With that, Brad dove out the door and disappeared. Drew touched my shoulder and signaled for us to leave.

Chapter Two

WAITING ON EURYDICE

For so long, things were simple.

In high school, dating was done by Martians. Everyone save I dated. There were those who went out; they had quickies in the back of Fords, or night-longs in someone's room, aborted, occasionally gave birth, sometimes married, but I cowered in the dark and knew myself. A second's satisfaction, rested in guilt, and someone knocked on the door to ask what I was doing. Most of the time, it was my mother, come to see how I was before going off to some meeting with quaint old ladies in discreet dresses and wigs who would ask, "Your baby, Rose, now, he's still available, ain't he?" I told her I was thinking—I was, really, about Romeo for the thirty-fifth time of the day, wondering how in the world someone fourteen and in leotards could possibly get a thirteen-year-old without either set of parents knowing about it.

I wish I had his luck. My parents knew my every move, my every thought even before I did and they had a bevy of friends to help in the surveillance. If I dared thought about looking at a girl sideways through a rearview mirror, they would find out. My father was the best at that sort of thing, his rich black eyes peering through his pipe smoke giving me that sort of "Who you trying to fool? I know what you're thinking" look. This was especially frightening back in first and second grade because he would always leave court in time to pick me up just as I zipped up and came down from Chris Wilson chasing me after school. I almost wet every time I heard his Saab's engine because he saw, I know, and of course I didn't explain: a strawberry-haired ten-year-old trying to touch me and then chasing me up a pear tree is something I hardly think he would ever believe could possibly be done to me. Besides, I couldn't explain, what with the way his eyes warmed up when Chris came and spoke and said, "see you tomorrow, Skip," and he would ask if Chris was sweet on me, as though she were my girl, and invariably it became an issue at dinner, sounding suspiciously like marriage, and, if my older brother Ted was home, he would egg it on, and was I scared. Then, as older, I took refuge in my father. I would lean against his body on the sofa in his den, luxuriating in that slick and queer smell of potpourri that comes from used pipe tobacco grounds burnt by a cigar tip and staring blankly at the green, amber, and red equalizer lights dance to an orchestral, every now and then watching his omnipresent pipe puff clouds topped by rings of smoke that floated upward, fibers twisting and rotating, giving the smoke flight into disintegration, sometimes sucking his cigar until tar peed from the butt, I the pensive, moody, seeking child, always hoping he had no idea what I was thinking, though his look made that hope vain. His hand would lift, the smoke would part, the *fin de siècle* of Brahms complete with hoop skirts waltzing would bid the lights dance, and I leaned against his body like so many children, finding sanctuary, my head bobbing at the will of his lungs, and I would try to imagine my father with my mother on the floor, waltzing, of course, as they had done at my sister Adele's wedding reception in the park across the street, but I saw my mom up in her attic workroom transplanting philodendron cuttings and the Judge down in his chambers shrouded by stratus clouds of smoke and thick drifts of pulp, commanding his clerks to use their heads for something more than just passing kidney stones, and I was left to stare at bodices, careful to stare not too hard. When I did, the masks of the Dan frowned, told my parents, their looks saying that was something I ought not do, and I awoke to the airy breath of my afghan descending upon me in the Captain Black–scented pitch of my room.

I suppose I was fourteen, maybe fifteen, before I saw girls as something other than Amazons and I was told they thought of me as something other than fresh meat. It was slowly turning eleven thirty, and Drew Ford and I laid out on my bed, wrung out from a morning of playing tennis in the continental humidity of July. The room smelled of the quiet rancor of boys sweating, and Drew had it especially bad: before I could get him a towel he had taken off his shirt and used it to wipe the sweat from his face, then hung it to dry down his front. His chest was a water-pale pinkish white, the umbra of his tits standing pink like the tip of a tiger lily's tongue, his upper arms and thighs sunburn red from having used the wrong suntan lotion with the wrong sunscreen, and the light silky hairs of his forearms and lower legs were sweat brown, as dark as his bangs, and there was a large suspended oval pressing against the flap of his fly that I couldn't help noticing. My father's red Abyssinian, Bert, joined us temporarily, sniffed our bodies, and left, her sleek body floating like Torvill and Dean on Bosnian ice. After playing Queen, my stereo was still on and, not knowing so, we were serenaded by a Haydn string quartet that made us languish in the air-conditioning even more. Like Drew, I had a Coors he had carried as a six-pack all the way from his house in Whitman Township—as we played, it stayed with his bicycle in a backpack, making it warm, and for that reason I nursed it. We were alone, my parents at work in their offices downtown and not expected home for lunch, though I listened for any sound saying they were coming, hearing nothing more than the Kidds' husky, Henson, chasing a swift hutch of rabbits Brian Kidd and the lawnmower had spooked out next door. We laid, we drank, he talked about burns, rashes, and pimples, and I listened. After adjusting himself and groaning that he hoped he wasn't coming down with jock itch, he said he heard there was a girl in one of his classes that sort of liked me.

"Who?"

"Kathy Lawrence. She's blonde 'n' big—you know—" He cupped his breasts with his hands. "A real nice body. Not a bad face, either." He found my yearbook and showed me her; from her picture, she looked as he said. When school started in September, he showed me her in person on our way back to the boys' locker room after an activity in the girls' gym; in flesh, she was everything the picture promised, only more so. He wanted to call her attention to us, but I shook him off, letting her concentrate upon chemical formulae rather than see us in our shorts and those irritating jockstraps. Instead, she came to me in the dark and stayed with me a couple nights. I looked for her at school and saw her occasionally in the parking lot with the other Whitmaners and watched her talk and smile easily. I heard Whitmaners snicker. For a semester, I chose things in the girls' gym just so I could walk by the chemistry room and see her up close and, for a semester, Drew went as well and offered to introduce us and, for a semester, I refused; and then the semester ended and driver's ed came in and moved a fourth of us sophomores to a PE hour in which for me there was no Kathy Lawrence en route to the girls' gym. Drew thought it a shame.

The start of our junior year meant meeting Kathy Lawrence, and Drew Ford finally getting his wish. All summer, he tried to get me to think enough about her to see her face-to-face, and he took me out to Whitman Township after tennis to show me where she lived, and he even got her phone number—more than once. He called her wherever we were, handed me the phone, and I always hung up when someone answered. Then, he asked, "Don't you wanna meet her?" Our junior year, he was elated a chance of scheduling had dropped us into the same Dr. Levin American lit class. He came rushing out just before I walked in and, grabbing me, exclaimed, "She's here! She's here!" I looked—in a room half full with hes, the only she was Dr. Levin, hardly something for Drew to get spastic about.

"Who? Dr. Levin?"

"No, no! Kathy Lawrence!"

By then, that name had a way of making me sick and it was doing it again. I couldn't help but stare when she entered, and she stared in kind—"love," I think it was. She was soft in her selection of yellows and whites and the scoops of her chest made me oblivious to almost everything else—away and at a distance, she seemed not quite real, then near she was, and I turned preoccupied with her; to all, I was daydreaming. That sick-to-the-stomach feeling of gas just being gas and heading nowhere came over me and it became worse as I glanced periodically at the slowly nonmoving time pieces of class reaching for the hour of lunch . . . tension made us grin, and she had good teeth. When lunch came and Dr. Levin's class was over, I started my way to her to introduce myself, but she beat me to it.

"Skip Macalester—"

"Kathy Lawrence—"

"Hi."

"Hi."

Casually, we walked to the next hour—I had lunch, she trigonometry with Gerald Banks, whose niece he thought would go well with me. I was gone before Mr. Banks could see me. That was all we saw of each other that day, and it was over a year in the making. Drew called that night to see how we fared without him. "We did well," I said, and he was happy. Come that Saturday, he said, we were to go to her house.

Saturday morning, I was up earlier than usual. Of course, my parents were surprised. They were having breakfast on the terrace in the backyard. The Judge sat back from the table, knees casually crossed, hands leafing through the *Courier* before contemplating the obituaries, two *jodh*-shaped streaks juxtaposed on the face of his black onyx ring shining in the sun, glasses sitting flipped-up on his balding head, fresh cigar smoke dissipating close to the gray left in his hair. Mom was just as intense, removed from the table with some briefs she was mending for the firm, pausing time and time again to pick death from some maidenhair that belonged in the solarium. They looked the Methodist pair at Conference, and it was a shame to break it up. But break it up I did. They looked up as I came through the French doors, their readings and other considerations giving weigh to me, and it was part of that parental intuitive to look me over. Unlike other September Saturdays, I was really dressed. I had khakis like theirs and a red rugby shirt striped oatmeal and blue (both of which our maid pressed for me). I wore no socks; neither Mom nor the Judge liked that. I wore cologne.

I ate a piece of bacon before sitting on the edge of a planter of mixed roses. I read part of the paper and listened to Mom and the Judge go back and forth over a case being granted cert by the Supreme Court last term. Then, they looked at me. Why, they seemed to ask, why, on an early September Saturday morning, why was I up, dressed like that, scented like that, eating like that. Were Drew and I going to play tennis as usual, or could it be I would be off to see a girl?

Drew was my salvation. When he came, the Judge's cigar was down to a stub and he flung it past the roses and waved the smoke away. He always did that for guests. Drew was used to it. As he came around from the front, he was grinning (he always grinned around Mom and the Judge, even though I told him to stop it). They smiled back, and offered him breakfast. When Drew sat down across from me, he looked like he was about to laugh. He was in no place to laugh: he had been cleaned, neatened, and oiled. He smelled better than usual, and had even brushed his hair. He wore his usual shirt and shorts, but he also wore loafers. As usual, he wore no socks. He winked. I looked at the table. Mom fixed him a plate, then disappeared (I think the phone rang). After she was gone, I watched the Judge watch Drew eat. Then, Drew looked at me.

"What's wrong?" Drew asked.

"Nothing," I said. I cleared my throat, and drank a glass of orange juice real slow. I cleared my throat again. "We're going out to see a girl."

"Oh," the Judge said. "Who?"

Casablanca fans and high, arched windows with miniblinds, as they are at the firm's offices in the St. Croix building downtown, sun-and shade-lit, smoked Republican in oyster white paint and walnut parquet flooring—that was the Judge's world. Would Kathy fit? She lived in a tri-level, on a cul-de-sac, in a subdivision, in the middle of nowhere in Whitman Township. The Judge kept three-by-five dossiers locked in the cherry buchershrank in his den—there was nothing there under "Lawrence." Sooner or later, he would ask someone what they knew about her family, but I knew they wouldn't know. I knew she wouldn't fit.

I said nothing. The Judge creased his napkin and set it in his plate. Then, he examined his glasses, cleaned them, and placed them on his knee. Mom finally came out. She began watering the flowers, which could have waited for the yardman, if you ask me. While she did so, she loitered around the terrace. Drew was quietly, blissfully eating. Then he smiled again. Something was feeling my leg.

"Anything the matter?" the Judge asked.

"No," I said. I pretended to drop part of the paper, and, when I picked it up, I looked under the table. Bert was under the table.

"So," Mom asked finally, "what's on the agenda today?"

"Nothing," I said.

"They're going to see a girl," the Judge said.

"Oh," she said. I shrank. "Who?" she asked.

I shook my head. "You don't know her. Just a girl."

It was just eleven when Drew and I left. The clocktower at Main Street Presbyterian Church began tolling from the other side of Milton High School and Antioch Baptist Church to the northwest of us on White Street answered. There were also lawnmowers. On any other Saturday morning, my parents and our neighbors the Howells would be out and, being the same age, they would be reminiscing. I used to hear them talk about their high school years, the time before "prep" became "yup," the years before the world crashed into hell and proved too improbable to fix, and, since September is nearly a month before the start of the Second Season, normally they tied it all in with baseball, the bits and pieces of the Cardinals that won the World Series, and, as always, they remembered the names: Lonnie Smith, Tom Herr, Keith Hernandez, George Hendrick, Darrell Porter, David Green and Gene Tenace and Dane Iorg, Willie McGee, Ken Oberkfell, Ozzie Smith, Andujar and Forsch and Kaat and Sutter. After all these years, the Judge still couldn't forgive Whitey Herzog for trading Ted Simmons. The Judge would shift his weight, cross his legs, and wax philosophical with Mr. Howell over half-drunk bottles of Beck's that cancer is still cancer, the Space Program is still talking about sending a man to Mars within the decade, shopping is still done at the grocery store, chickens still lay eggs and food is still solid, *The Day After* is the closest anyone has come to nuclear war, a ride from Vienna to Moscow is still hampered by border guards, guns, and barbed wire, and walking in the Geneva woods is still the best way for the benignly bellicose superpowers to come to their senses and try acting like everyone else, no behemoth had been born in Bethlehem and hundreds of thousands—like hundreds of thousands a millennium before—left Armageddon on January 2, 2001 after seeing nothing more than a change of four seasons, their alma mater Milton High School still has yet to win a Homecoming game, the earth still revolves around the sun, birth is hard, as is life, and death before ninety is still surer than taxes—the greatest technological changes they witnessed were the death of Ma Bell and the introduction of a counterfeit

Coke that tasted like Pepsi, hardly events heralding a Brave New World. They are all just around sixty, and, for the Judge and Mr. Howell in particular, the lack of change meant little. The Judge's finger goes around the bottle mouth once, then back, and, should they be talking that morning, he would move the conversation back to baseball, since that was Cleveland's year, and, like everyone else, he was rooting for the Indians, because of Satchel Paige. Then, the Judge and Mr. Howell would laugh and the Beck's would be gone.

We left at eleven, while the bells tolled. Sonia Kidd came out with Henson as Drew pulled his car from under the poplar across the street into our drive, backed up, and turned around. Drew asked if I wanted to speak to her. I said no.

Drew had to see Marshall, who lived a block away. Marshall had something from physics class that Drew needed. We found him on the Langston patio. Like me, he wore a rugby, but his was wrinkled and oversized and worn in his own, disheveled, who-cares way. Marshall was reading, irritated, increasingly so, or at least a bit annoyed. He was drinking lemonade and listening to *The Flying Dutchman* on the radio. His younger brother Pik was doing the grass; every now and then, Marshall would watch Pik cut, blowing a whistle and snapping *"Peter!"* each time Pik missed a spot, which annoyed Pik to no end (it was Pik's fault: he worshiped Marshall like no younger brother should). Drew and I seemed almost unnoticed as we sat next to Marshall at the patio table. "What'cha reading?" I asked.

Drew notwithstanding, Marshall showed us. It was a Dartmouth recruiting bulletin, green, slick-glossed, plenty-colored in every photograph. "It's Mrs. Stuart's idea," he said quickly, referring to the white-haired resident liberal of the high school counseling department. "She says they're looking for 'qualified minorities.'"

"And what did you say to that?" Drew asked.

"To *that?* I asked her how big an effort are they putting into looking for qualified whites—you know *her*. She didn't go for that." His Lockean New Negro got up and mumbled "qualified minorities" and rolled his eyes, tossing the bulletin onto the patio table. "What a hypocrite."

"She probably meant nothing by it," Drew said quickly. "Maybe, maybe it was that she just didn't know."

"Maybe," Marshall said, "but she should've. Really, it didn't surprise me all that much. She likes Norman Mailer, after all. Who knows? After reading Allen Ginsberg, she probably even comes through here at dawn thinking she'll find an angry fix." He paused and drank lemonade. Marshall always drinks lemonade when he gets hot. "You're here for that physics stuff?" he asked Drew. Drew nodded.

We went inside. Inside was quiet, except for a radio in the kitchen. Everyone was out doing something somewhere. Marshall was refilling the lawnmower because his parents thought Pik was still too young to do it himself. Before going upstairs, Marshall made a fresh pitcher of lemonade.

"So," Marshall asked. "You two going to see that Lawrence girl?"

"What 'Lawrence girl?'" I asked.

"'What *Law*rence girl,' *please!*" Marshall rolled his eyes, a disgusting habit. "The whole school knows about her, cousin dear. Next time, before trying to deny it, take a bottle of castor oil, go to the bathroom and see what comes out, because, cousin dear, you are a shitty liar."

That said, Marshall ran upstairs to his room. Drew and I stayed downstairs in the living room. Marshall's father Ken came in a little later.

"Looks like you boys aren't tempted to battle Marshall's room today," Ken said, flashing a broad smile.

"No, sir," Drew said, very crisply, like he couldn't forget Ken was an assistant principal at the high school.

Ken excused himself to the kitchen and drank lemonade. The Langstons have this thing about lemonade. Marshall came down while Ken was in there. When I say "came down," I mean slid down on the banister. He tumbled into the living room and landed with a thump so hard it shook the grandfather clock in the hall. Marshall stood. He smiled. He had changed from the rugby into a candy-striped Oxford shirt and a Howard University sweatshirt ("prep," they used to call it—so utterly "prep"). Ken came from the kitchen with his hands on his hips.

"And *what* is supposed to be the meaning of *this*?" Ken demanded.

Marshall looked at his clothes. "I spent all morning looking at Dartmouth green," he said simply. "This afternoon, I wanna be seen in Howard blue."

Ken started laughing and Marshall took Drew and me outside. To his credit, Pik had a third of the yard cut, and he was dumping the bag of clippings into a compost pile.

"I made some lemonade," Marshall announced. "And Dad's here. So, if you wanna drink some, better hurry, else Dad'll get it all."

Pik nodded. Then, suddenly, Marshall picked up a football that laid on the ground, whistled, and signaled for Pik to go out for a pass, and, with an ease belying his size, Marshall threw the ball, sending it on a high, tight, spiraling arc through the air that would have eventually met Pik in a reception, but a wind hijacked it, rendering its spiral and flight eccentric. Pik, however, followed the ball. He faded back parallel to its track and, as its flight quickly corroded, he dove, caught the ball, and landed in a thicket of peonies near the middle of the yard.

"If only Milton could have him," Marshall said. "*Yo!* If only Milton could have you!"

"*Naw*—they'd still lose." Pik wiped his hands on his shorts and stretched his hands along the laces. He gripped the ball and threw it back. The ball bounced past us.

"What's he trying to do," Marshall mumbled, "be funny? *Yo!* You trying to be funny?"

Pik didn't answer. He only smiled and went in for lemonade.

We left. Marshall had to run back in to get his physics notebook for Drew because he had left it in his bedroom. After that, leaving was simple. Drew chose the quick way to Whitman Township: through the heart of Jefferson Heights. Everything on my side blended into flowers, shrubs, and trees. Then came the tiger lilies in the yard of Mr. Howell's funeral home. I could hear Grandma Macalester talk about the way Aunt Hilda said Uncle Bug planted them when Grandpa Macalester's Grandpa Wright owned the place. Our church, Bethel

AME, was before the last turn. Old ladies meant for Sundays in stewardess white and deaconess gray had work clothes on, and the ivy up the red-bricked sides waved at me (or so I thought). The church looked as it did at Adele's wedding. Whenever I see the church, I think about Adele's wedding, and the Judge in his swallow-tailed heather gray morning coat, and Adele in a long, flowing white dress and veil, and Mom crying, and I am always chilled by the realization that, of the millions of billions of people to have graced this planet, everyone—my mom and the Judge included—had come about via something as oedipal as sex.

I told Drew I was thirsty. "And I want ice cream," I said. Drew joked that was from watching the Langstons drink all that lemonade. I thought Drew would take me to his house (I knew he had ice cream, and his house was not that far away), but he made a couple quick turns and we ended up on the state highway. In a few minutes, we were at Steak 'n' Shake.

We had malts. It was still early. Inside, the place still smelled of soap water. Beside us, there was a pair of waitresses whose hair had been teased into Medusan tentacles. One of them kept making eyes at Drew; Drew kept twirling on the counter stool. He turned quiet when seven or eight of our classmates came in. My cousin Brad was among them. Like the Langstons, he was a cousin through Grandma Macalester, although he scarcely looked the part. Brad was vaguely European, and a looker. Drew watched him as well. Like the others, Brad gave a meek, muted wave, veered off quickly, and sat at a table near the window.

Brad's younger brother Alan sat near him. Alan (he preferred that to his more ethnic first name Aaron) was of a type Brad was least comfortable around most, and, though a bit more colored, his was the off-white look of polite compromise between his parents. His nose was a parental compromise, neither Negroid, thanks to his mother, nor Jewish, thanks to his father, but a simple, nondescript nose matching comfortably with his skin, surrounded by freckles by the splattered, as though someone in art had taken a mix of purple and yellow and flicked it at him when the teacher wasn't looking. The boy sweats easily, like that day, and in the sweat and its humidity, his sandy curlyish hair took the consistency of a Libyan's, and he had wayfarers that must have been too sweaty to wear. Give him a few years: Alan will prove a looker, too. He also waved.

I returned to my vanilla malt, and Drew wiped his mouth with the back of his hand. Everything was quiet for a while until something happened at Brad's table and Alan almost walked out. I was able to get him to sit with us. I ordered a root beer float for him. When the float came, Alan stared at the grooves in the glass. He said nothing. He drooped so badly he seemed to collapse between his thighs. He had his straw in his mouth, but he sucked like the suck was forced upon him. He shuddered—or did he shiver? The air was running cold in there. He fidgeted and his shorts rode up past the tanline on his thighs. He looked pathetic. I tried rubbing his back.

"Hey, what's *with* you," he demanded, pushing my hand away. "You *know* I don't go for *that* kinda *stuff*!"

"What happened?" Drew asked.

"Nothing," I said quickly. Then I turned to Alan. "The Judge did that when you were a baby. You used to like it then."

"Yeah, but—that's fine. That's fine for him to've done it back then. But *that* was when I was a *baby*. I'm not a baby anymore, you know."

Drew mumbled an apology for me. Alan shrugged. Afterward, Alan was very quiet. He finished his float, licked his mouth, pushed the glass away, and waited for us to finish. For a while, he looked my way.

"So," Alan finally said, "You guys going any place? Or're you guys just out?"

"Both," I said.

"Skip's going out to see a girl," Drew said. "Judge Macalester just sent me along to make sure he behaves. You?"

"Him?" I asked. "He's just out to get some sun."

"Actually, Brad had to take me out to get something for my bike— just some grease, that's all. Then we ran into *those* guys." Whatever happened at Brad's table was still sore for Alan; he preferred pecking through glass to talking about it. A burst of laughter roared from Brad's table and Kay Reece said "You dick—you *dick*" and pulled ice cubes from his shorts. Alan continued tapping. "I got the grease."

Drew offered to drive Alan home. The Morgans lived in a part of Whitman Township that was not exactly on our way, in a subdivision of trees, marigolds, large yards, and custom-built houses with cobblestone driveways shooting into courts in the back, and in a house owned by the hotel their father Dennis managed. Alan sat back and became lucidly gregarious listening to Drew's music. He rested his head on Drew's gym bag on the seat and began to ramble: So, who was this girl? Was she cute? Did she have any sisters? Brad was "in love," did we know her? He sighed. Was the door unlocked? Brad's the one with the key, no telling when he'd be home. Their little brother Ian had been worrying about his boa, it looked "green," whatever that meant, he might have taken it to the vet. Could he get in through the back? Perhaps he might have to climb through a window. Then, suddenly, Alan sat up and looked outside thoughtfully with his mouth wide open.

"Skip," he said quietly.

"Yeah."

"You like me?"

Smiling, smiling just before laughing, I looked at him. "What?"

"Do you like me?"

"You're a cousin." Third cousin, once removed, yes, but third cousins still count.

"Yeah, I know, but, do you *like* me?"

"How the—what kinda question is that to ask a *cousin?*"

"It's a question for you to answer. Just answer the *god*damn *quest*ion, will you?"

I shrugged. "You're a cousin." Alan fell back onto the seat in frustration. "As hokey as it sounds, being family still means something."

"Being family means nothing, as far as that's concerned. Do you like me? Yes or no, that's all, nothing complicated. Just yes or no."

I shrugged again. "Yeah. Why?"

Alan didn't say. Instead, he leaned forward and asked Drew the same question the same way for the same answer, then plopped back down in the seat. For a stretch, Alan just breathed, staring at the warp-stained vinyl car top. Perhaps he was just thinking, perhaps just thinking about thinking, perhaps just thinking about thinking for the sake of thinking, then a pause, something in the air, thoughts change, the Rolling Stones blaring through Drew's speakers, Alan rages his knuckles with the drums on the back of my seat (most uncomfortable). Then the song ends, Alan stops, silence again.

"I was just wondering," he said suddenly, "'cause, I never know just how you guys think of me, or whether you guys like me or not—you know, sometimes, you guys just treat me like I'm a pain in the ass, or something like that, like I'm just a nuisance 'n' something of a pain and a bore to be around, or something like that—"

His voice trailed off, his body faded, his eyes turned blank. I thought he was asleep, but that was until the music changed. Then, almost immediately, his knuckles began raging again. All became quiet again when the grade changed and we headed down the lane to his house. Alan sat up and looked, not just at each house and at every yard, but at the whole thing, as though all of it (or almost all of it) were new to him. At one point, the sun creased along his chin and turned it as identifiably like my family as Marshall's, or mine, and, freckles notwithstanding, he looked a little more like us. When the sun crinkled and moved away, that look was gone.

The Morgans' house was the last, or second to the last, house. No one was home, and Alan had no key. He ran to the side of the house and climbed the trellis to a bedroom window and we waited in the driveway. For a while, Drew seemed tense, and said nothing.

"You gotta be more careful," Drew finally said. "Promise me just one thing, will ya: that before you *do* or *say* anything, that you just stop a minute 'n' *think*, especially around one of them."

"What's that supposed to mean?"

"Whaddaya mean, 'what's *that* supposed to mean?'" he exploded. "Goddamnit!—you mean I gotta spell it all out for you? You know those guys that were in there! You know where their heads are! You know how they talk! You mean to tell me you got absolutely no clue how that stuff will sound when it gets back to you on Monday? You mean to tell me you just simply don't understand things like that? And, what do you think I'm supposed to say when they ask me what the hell's your problem?"

I shrugged. "I don't know, just call me a faggot," I joked.

"You're a faggot," he yelled. "Now are you happy?"

Things dim here. All I remember is how hurt Drew looked. I think he muttered "Why can't you just understand" as we drove off. He was quiet until after we were on the Post Road across Whitman Township. I remember he made some crack about a kid we passed who was struggling on his bicycle, then he became quiet again when we saw that kid was really a middle-aged woman. I don't think he said another word until after we got to Kathy's house. But, then again, going through her subdivision, I was not paying attention to Drew. I was thinking about her, getting nervous, and for once, I wished I had socks. The car stopped, and Drew mustered something of a quivering smile. He was tense again, or maybe he just never quite relaxed.

"Well, we're here. Ready?"

"As ready as I'll ever be," I said.

"Nervous?"

"Me? Of course not."

"Then, we're in trouble." Then he did something he had never done before. Slowly, almost painfully, he traced the length of my nose, then caught himself. Afterward, he held onto the steering wheel so tight his knuckles turned completely white, and he stared into the speedometer. He was biting his lip. "Skip—sorry. Your lips're dry. They might even be chapped."

"I'll be sure not to kiss her, then."

"No," he said, almost looking at me, but not quite. "No, go ahead. Kiss, if you want. Just be careful when you do."

We left the car (*I* left the car—Drew was a little slow leaving). Amazingly, I felt calm about going to Kathy's door, but, when I got there and was stared at by her peephole, that feeling of gas just being gas and heading nowhere that I had come to know so well came again, and I wanted to get out of there.

"Arthur Melvin Macalester," I heard myself say quietly, "you should leave now, now that you have the chance."

In truth, I had no such chance. Drew was right behind me. Although his eyes were red, he smiled a little and rang the doorbell, then he turned around and snorted. It took a while for someone to open the door. It was a thin, angular boy with straw-colored hair, who took a single, long, skeptical look at us, then let us in.

"You guys here for her?" he asked, taking off his shoes and socks just behind the door. "'Cause, she's not here right now, but that's okay, 'cause she'll be back real soon; or that's when she's *supposed* to be—you know how *girls* are, you never know whether they'll come when they say they're comin'—so, you guys can wait in here for her, if you guys want."

It smelled in there. From the looks of the place, someone forgot to hire a maid. The boy led us through the house to the family room downstairs. It took up the entire basement, complete with a wall of glass overlooking their deck and a small, inground swimming pool. Part of the family room was sunken, and a hearth sat in the middle of it. On the other side of the hearth, two boys in towels and damp swimming trunks lay on a chaise lounge while a guy, slightly older than us, drew on a sketch pad with charcoal. One boy watched me intensely, his hands always moving, always twitching, drumming fugues and tarantellas in a sharp *rattatatat,* a beat, then our eyes met, brushed, blushed, batted down, and then again, again, a little longer this time, a little softer, a little less frightened. The hands stopped, the face flushed, shoulders shrugged for knowing how to shrug, lips puckered as if to speak then fell silent against my almost raised palm, quivering up nervously at the corners into something of a smile and staying there a tense second before easing into something more natural. I smiled back.

"You weren't born for this," Drew whispered into my ear. "So, just *try* to behave—*please.*"

The guy drawing the picture had sharp blue eyes and jet black hair. His skin was naturally pale. He wiped his hands on his jeans periodically. He flipped his head back to get the hair out of his eyes, smiled, and showed us what he was drawing. Did the boys know he was drawing their feet? Nothing is a greater aphrodisiac . . .

I couldn't stay. I left as quickly as I could. Drew was not far behind. Although we must have stayed in front of Kathy's house for only a few minutes it seemed so much longer. I couldn't get out of my mind the boy who was watching me. I think he was twelve, about the same age as Alan and the boy who answered the door. He had hazel eyes and a look that reminds me of Rosy in O'Faolain's "How to Write a Short Story." I still ask myself, while it went on, was I doing it to him, or was he doing it to me.

"Sorry," I finally said in Drew's car. "Thanks for bringing me out here. Maybe we can try again some other time."

"Yeah. Maybe. But don't worry about it."

That was Drew's way of saying forget it. I tried the best I could, but Drew was driving me home, and soon, there was the park, and its esplanade, and its rose garden. In a year, I was to be in the Jefferson Heights Cotillion, and how was I uncomfortable about girls.

Drew pulled into our driveway. Mom's Volvo was gone, but the Judge's Saab was still there. Drew turned off the engine. For a short while we just looked at each other. It was, I think, almost one o'clock.

"I don't think we'd be able to find a court for a couple of hours, if you wanna play tennis today," Drew said, scratching his nose. "So, whaddaya say 'bout just going to a movie later, maybe get some pizza afterward?"

"Okay."

"You find the movie and call me, okay? Around five?"

"Okay."

"Say—" he paused. "You all right?"

"Yeah."

"You sure?"

I said I was. In a way, I found it hard to convince even myself. I watched him drive away. I don't remember much, except for the Judge calling me into his den, and the way he pulled a short strand of brown hair from my shirt and the way it spiraled to the floor. Then, I went to my room to be soothed by Schubert and to sough in dreams.

Chapter Three

Drew and I always played tennis after school. We had a regular date for it. Playing tennis after school was an easy thing to do in our town since there were dozens of courts in the area. On most days, it was a matter of finding the right court, as, on most days, dozens of people had the same date as we. Timing, the essence of everything, was the operative factor.

My needs did not help matters any. Though he traveled with his tennis gear in the car, Drew had to run me back home for me to get dressed, for, in the clothes I had on I was starting to smell like a guy who had on last night's stuff. I loathed that stale, sweaty smell.

When I got home, the maid, Miss Cynthia, was dusting the banister.

"Hey, Cynthia," I said, trotting up the stairs past her.

"Tennis today?"

"Yep."

I closed my bedroom door. Miss Cynthia had laundered my clothes and folded them into my dresser. I was clean for another ten days or so.

Taking out some tennis clothes—a tourist T-shirt from a trip to Michigan and a pair of shorts and socks—I started undressing. I stripped off my shirt and smelled the underarms. Yes, to use Drew's favorite phrase, I stank. I think I smelled worse than I had in a long time. For the heck of it, I removed my shoes. They smelled strong, too. Whenever I removed my shoes I rejoiced at the curve of my foot and found it enticing. I thought of bare feet, barely visible. I unzipped my pants. I figured I had time.

Before I could get anywhere, though, there was a knock at the door. I zipped up my pants.

"What?"

"It's me," Miss Cynthia said. "You want me to get you some orange juice?"

"No, thank you." I unzipped my pants.

"You sure?"

"Yes, thank you."

I started to slip out of my pants. By the time I got to my knees, there was another knock on the door. I sighed.

"What, Cynthia?"

"I was wondering, would you like a snack, like peanut butter and jelly?"

"No, thank you."

"I was gonna make some for myself," she said. "I can make some for you, too."

"Thank you—"

"You want some?"

I sighed again. "No, thank you."

Cynthia was getting to be irritating enough to get me to give up jacking off entirely. I thought it best that I did. Taking off my pants, I balled them up and tossed them into the closet. My shirt went there, too. I was debating about trading in my underwear when a car alarm went off outside. I stuck my head out of the window and saw Drew frantically struggling to turn off his car alarm.

"Drew!" I yelled. I decided to go louder. *"Drew!"*

He was able to turn off the alarm. He looked up and smiled sheepishly. "Sorry. Aren't you dressed yet? Jesus, what are you doing in there?"

I wasn't about to answer that. Instead, I said, "I'll be out in a minute."

"Could you bring some socks down, too? You don't want my feet to get full of blisters, do you?"

The last thing I wanted, though I would hardly admit it, was Drew's elegant feet full of blisters. I opened my sock drawer and, at first, found it somewhat difficult to decide which pair I was willing to give up. Lacking anything better, I chose to surrender the U of I socks, since Drew looked natural in orange and blue. After all, I had to wear the blue and white striped socks. Howard colors. If only the Judge could see me. . . .

Once I had my clothes on, I pulled my tennis shoes from beneath my bed and put them on. My racquet was where I had last put it, between my bed and the nightstand. Drew, I thought, had balls.

I left my bedroom. Miss Cynthia was not there. In her stead there was the distinctive smell of meat sizzling and Bert sat in my doorway, apparently, because the doorway was cool. "Excuse me," I said, stepping over her. I barely missed her. She barely glanced at me. Good thing they were barelies—the Judge would have skinned me if Bert ever screamed.

The sizzling meat came from downstairs. When I got there I looked for Cynthia to tell her where I was going (in case she talked to the Judge or Mom). I found her in the kitchen making a sandwich, which she presented to me.

"Fried baloney," she announced, offering it on a napkin. She had sliced the sandwich in half, diagonally, the way I liked it.

"Thanks," I said. I took it and started eating. She had used wheat bread for toast and coated the fried baloney with a layer of mayonnaise. I got a dab of that on the side of my mouth and licked it off. Taking the other half with the napkin and stuffing it into my pocket, I turned on my heels.

"You going to play tennis?" Miss Cynthia called after me.

"Yes. Later."

Were I not such a brat as a kid, I would have noted the way Cynthia hung her head or the way she smiled, or something about her that would have endowed personhood to her. As it was, I just saw her as "Cynthia," the maid, who came Wednesdays and Fridays by bus because the Judge wanted no dilapidated Chevrolets in front of our house all day. It was the same way my parents saw her, as just someone we hired to do day work, like the Irish Catholic scurry maids not good enough to live on the place. It was how Mom and the Judge trained me, and, trained, I was slow to consider her any more. I can't even begin to describe her. The Judge kept no picture of her, and Mom thought Cynthia was so commonplace.

So, I stuffed the sandwich and twirled my racquet. I headed outside, where Drew couldn't believe his eyes.

"Nourishment," he said, "and before tennis! Arthur, how could you?"

I smiled and pulled the other half of the sandwich from my pocket. "I remembered you."

"I see. Excellent."

Drew took the sandwich and started eating. As he chewed, I showed him the socks. "I thought you'd like these," I said.

"They look nice, but you didn't have anything in Mizzou's colors? Black and gold?"

I shook my head. Like many other people in our area, even those on the Illinois side of the river, Drew considered the University of Missouri his school, and worshipped the black and gold. Anyone giving him anything blue and orange would have committed an act most unforgivable.

Drew took the socks anyway, and finished his sandwich. Opening the car door, he sat in the seat, removed his shoe, and prepared to don the socks. His feet were a fragile study of angles and lines encased in daisy-white flesh. The toenails were a little long, and pinkish-purple. I remember thinking, *You really need to clips those, guy. . . . Can I help?* Brown hair wisps grew at the joints. I wanted to taste them.

I was given less than a minute to enjoy his feet before the socks covered them. Once he had them on, he stood on the grass in his stocking feet and held his hands at his side. "I look like a dork, huh?"

"You look fine, even in blue and orange."

"Just don't tell my uncle you saw me like this."

I agreed not to let on, just in case I ran into his uncle, whoever he may be. We boarded his car, racquets in hand, for the ride to a game. Normally, after school, when the girls' tennis team claimed the Jefferson Park courts, we headed out to the park on the far edge of town, where multiple courts sat as part of a tennis complex.

It was a pleasant ride out. It was not very far, because the town was not that big, even at 42,000 people. Going beneath the railroad viaduct and past the Holiday Inn on the other side of the dental school campus then down the decline beyond the limestone quarry's entrance, we crossed the Wood River and started our way up a hillock. We could see the park just south of us. Vast, the park began life as the nearby state hospital's farm, used for food and therapy. Sometime in the 1970s the state deeded it to the city, which, thanks to the foresight of a general practitioner, conceived it to be Veterans Park, in honor of the men who had served in Vietnam.

Veterans Park had a simple, stockade gate. Its long, main avenue was surrounded by dogwood trees. To one side of us were soccer fields used by every team from pee wees to adults; to the other side was a statue of a World War I doughboy in a courtyard of engraved bricks that served as the town's hall of fame. When I was a young boy, I discovered that one of the bricks was for the Judge, and that another was for Grandma. The Judge's had his full name, Alfred E. Macalester. Grandma's was simply stamped "Madelyn."

Why didn't my mother have a brick as well? Sometimes, that question would come to me and I'd remember that my mother came from the Springfield area, and that this part of the state was foreign to her, at best. Occasionally, I would see the way the townspeople treated her. She was always "Rose, Madelyn's daughter-in-law." Most accepted her as this, but I suppose it galled her for it to be the only way she was accepted.

We passed the dogwood trees. We passed the soccer fields. A colony of baseball diamonds were nothing to us as we slipped through them and made our way to the tennis complex. At the Arnold Palmer–managed golf course, Drew slowed down because he thought he saw someone we knew leave the clubhouse, but, when he saw the person had a mustache, he sped on.

We crossed the creek. Beyond the creek were the tennis courts, clustered around an expansive pavilion that was orange and blue. Our hearts sank at the sound of tennis balls being lobbed, for, with a sound that loud, we were certain all the courts were taken. The parking lot near the courts was lousy with cars, as full as a tick.

"Ah *shit*," Drew said as he brought the car into the parking lot. "It's as many as at Jefferson Park."

I bounced the racquet against my knee. "Maybe somebody will be coming off soon."

"I dunno, Arthur. They're a bunch of old farts and shits. You ever try prying one of these old farts and shits from a tennis court? They'd kill ya."

I strained to look at the tennis players. They didn't seem that old. It couldn't be difficult.

Drew parked the car in a spot almost everyone had overlooked but that someone almost claimed by positioning a minivan over our line. Putting the car into the spot was a trick. Drew had to practically roll up the socks, suck in his toes, stretch open the mouth, and use a shoe horn. In other words, it took a couple of tries to fit the car in, and then we could barely open the doors.

"Goddamn," Drew said, opening the door. "Dangit!"

Somehow, he was able to squeeze himself out. Afterward, he tried slamming the door shut, but he didn't have enough room to get a good swing. My door was easier, and I didn't have to inhale to get out. Disgusted, Drew came around to my side.

"Goddamned shitty old thing," Drew mumbled, reaching into the back to retrieve his racquet and balls. "When I get a job, I'm gonna make damn sure to get me a new car."

I knew Drew hated his car. It was a hand-me-down from his sister. I thought about trying to ease him and get him to think about something else, but he did it instead. He sunk a pair of orange tennis balls into his shorts pockets and took a third and started bouncing it on his racquet. Three, four, five, six times he bounded it into the air and caught it with the racquet, sending it into the air again.

"Betcha I can do this till we get a court," he said. He bounced it a tenth time. His eyes were intent, his mouth somewhat open. His hands stuck out as though he were trying to balance himself. "Here."

In a flash, he popped the ball to me. I had just enough time to get my racquet up. The ball hit the face and bounced away. It would have gotten away from me, too, but I moved quick and got the racquet under it. The ball bounced up like a grape, but I caught it a second time and bounced it up. A third time and a fourth time, and it was like dribbling a basketball, even if I wasn't the basketball type.

Drew snatched the ball after my sixth time bouncing it. "That's enough, show-off," he said. He stuffed the ball into his pocket. "Come on."

We went to the pavilion grandstand, where we watched a pair of soccer moms take a last game. It was obvious they would be getting off soon, because they played with no energy at all. The game was dull. One of the women, a tanned blonde with short hair, kept hanging her head to the side just before serving, lobbing the ball with nothing on it. I found the game behind her, two old men battling points, far more interesting.

"Stop looking at me," the blonde said in our direction after she sent a shot into the net.

I looked around. Aside from myself and Drew, there was no one else in the grandstand. I pointed to myself.

"Yeah," she said. "You. Stop looking at me."

"What's with her?" Drew asked me, as if I knew. "Is it her time of the month? Tell her to fuck herself with her sister's tampon."

Home-training taught me not to be so crude. Were I Marshall, I would not have dignified her. But, being me, I was busy trying to think of something appropriate to say.

"C'mon, Sharon," the other woman said. She settled on her toes and prepared to return a shot. She wiped a wristband against her face and smoothed back her raven-black hair. "He's doing nothing. Play."

"I can't play with him looking at me. He messes up my shot."

"I'm watching the game behind you," I said.

"Yeah, right!"

"Hey, lady," Drew said. "It's a free country. He can watch this crappy game if he likes."

"Please don't swear at me," she said meekly.

"Swearing?" Drew laughed. "If you think 'crappy' is swearing, lady, you don't know swearing, dumb bitch!"

"Drew."

The two women looked at him stunned, as did the two old men in the game nearby. One of them, a white-haired fellow with a sweatband wrapped around his head, left his game and approached the blonde.

"Do you need the police?" he asked her.

"No," she said, touching the man's arm. "I think we'll be all right."

The man looked at her, as if trying to make sure, then he turned to us. "I think you kids should go."

I got up. Drew wasn't budging. He narrowed his eyes. "Up yours."

"*Drew.*"

"Come on, son," the man said. "Not like this."

I started to leave the grandstand. "Drew," I said softly. I jerked my head toward the car. "Let's go."

Drew looked at me. He twirled the racquet in his hands, a sign that he was thinking. He stood. "You're lucky I'm with him," he said to the old man, "'cause I'd kick your ass right here."

Drew started to leave the grandstand with me. We would have made it back to the car, too, and with no fanfare, either, had not the blonde walked alongside us. Who knew what she was trying to do.

"I just want you to know——" she began.

"Ah, go fuck your sister with your mama's tampon, bitch!" Drew spat out.

Shocked, the woman stopped dead in her tracks.

"Go," the old man ordered.

I took Drew by the arm and led him away from the tennis courts. He went reluctantly, mumbling all the way to the car. "How dare they talk to you like that," he said. "I should kick their ass."

"You can't go around wanting to kick everyone's ass just because they talk rude to me."

Drew looked at me, almost in disbelief, as if asking, "Who says I can't?" He bounced his hand against the racquet and looked over his shoulder, back at the courts, then he swung the racket at something in his imagination, a forehand and then a backhand, as though he were trying to coldcock a fly or a gnat. He turned around and took a long look at the games. I looked, too. Both games had resumed.

"Next time," Drew said, "I'll kick their ass! I'll kick their ass!" he shouted over his shoulder. The raven-haired woman waved us off, like we were really bothering her. "Stupid bitch," Drew snorted.

"Come on, Drew," I said, pulling him to the car.

Drew really didn't want to go. He had too much energy to leave it alone. He mumbled things about wanting to trash their cars so bad, he'd get every car, but I told him to forget it, that this type of thing happens occasionally. Even to me.

Squeezing back into the car, we left Veterans Park. Drew bolted out of there so fast it left my head swimming. He drove past the high school and Jefferson Park, where the girls' tennis team was just starting to get warmed up. Soon, he was at the state highway. Before us was a convent, quiet in its cloister of trees.

"We're still playing tennis," Drew said as he made a sharp right turn and went north on the highway.

It was obvious we were going to Ellington College. Its tennis courts were open to the public, and playing on them was about as complicated as playing in a park. He said very little driving there, though, passing a woman-driven truck, he muttered "bitch" just loud enough for me to hear. I said nothing in return.

It is pretty amazing that someone who lived with four women all his life would be so sexist. "You need to do something about your anger toward women," one of the girls in our class said to Drew once, and Drew just looked at her, as though it was over his head.

The college campus with its neoclassical buildings looked practically deserted, so many of the people had gone for the day, though some of the on-campus students still hung around the dormitories. Security met us at the first bungalow. It was a young guy in a T-shirt, with shaving cream still on half his face. He set down his disposable razor for a clipboard and pen. He was about old enough to attend Ellington, were he female. He looked at Drew like it was déjà vu all over again.

"Name?"

"Andrew and Arthur, together again." Drew smiled.

"Clown," the guard laughed. "You know what I mean. You know the drill."

"Andrew Ford and friend."

The guard looked into the car. Our racquets were in the back. "Lemme guess. Tennis?"

"Right-o."

The guard wrote something on the clipboard and handed it and the pen to Drew, who signed his name. Drew signed his name dramatically, like he had a floral quill pen in hand and hordes of admirers awaiting his signature. Then, after signing, he handed the clipboard back to the guard.

"You know the drill," the guard said.

"Yeah, yeah," Drew said. "You got ninety minutes. Go straight to the courts. Stay away from the dorms. ID when asked. Go out the exit. I got ya."

"Fantastic." The guard tore a red visitors decal from the clipboard and handed it to Drew, who hung it from the rearview mirror. "Happy tennis."

"Happy shaving." Drew winked at the guy and drove down the lane. I felt like a wife kept out of her husband's joke.

"Who was that?"

"Just a guard."

"I know it was a guard," I said. "I mean, what was his name?"

"I don't know his name. Kevin, I guess. Maybe Guard." Drew laughed. "Why? What are you? Jealous?"

I didn't answer. It seemed foolish, even to me, to state a reason. Besides, I could have my own reasons.

We got to the tennis courts, toward the rear of the campus, to find we had our choice of courts. No one was there; the courts sat like a succession of puddles after a rain. The chalk lines were stretched tire treads along the perimeters of puddles and, through a computerized chain link fence, they beckoned us to prance around them.

Drew parked the car on the lot above the courts, completely alone. He didn't have to go through all the business of stretching and squeezing to get into a spot. The real issue was trying to get into the computerized gate. We needed a punch code. We stood at the gate ready to punch the code in. "Damn new-fangled thing," he mumbled. "They install all this state-of-the-art junk and—*fuck!*—expect you to use it like a lock and key."

"*Is there a problem?*" a voice asked through a nearby speaker.

"You forgot to give me the damn code."

"*Oh, yeah.*" It occurred to me that the voice belonged to the guard. I wondered if he had finished shaving. "*Try one zero one seven six eight.*"

Drew punched in the numbers and the gate clicked open.

We chose a court in the middle of the area, where there would be a healthy echo of our hits and grunts, and where everyone could see us play.

We ran onto the court. Drew took an orange ball from his pocket and punted it toward me. Stepping forward, I returned it with a two-fisted forehand shot. "Take that," I grunted. Drew caught it with a simple racquet shot that sent the ball directly into the net.

"That didn't count," he said. "I kicked the serve. That point didn't count."

"Okay," I said. I got ready to return serve. "Go."

Drew retrieved the ball and brought it back to the baseline. Tossing the ball into the air, he bent his legs and unleashed an ace. It moved so fast that all I could do was to whiz at it. Drew smiled like the devil.

"That counted," he said.

"Okay, Andrew. Go."

I lobbed the ball back at him. Going over his head, it bounced into the corner. Drew was able to track it down. He lunged for it, missed it at first, then rolled the ball back toward him in such an ungainly manner his ass stuck out (not that I noticed such things at almost sixteen). He prepared to serve.

"Ready?"

I nodded. "Do it."

Tossing the ball into the air, he rocked his heels and sent the ball toward me. This was no ace; rather, it was a simple shot, sent over the net and bouncing in my direction. I needed only to step forward and underhand a return. Drew had to run up a bit. Crossing court, he underhanded the ball back to me. I took it easily, and rocked a shot to the part of the court he had vacated. Drew changed direction and ran for the corner, but he was too late. After bouncing just short of the baseline, the ball bounded out of bounds without even being touched. Drew was breathing heavily. He looked at me. I licked my finger and pointed at him like a pro.

"Gotcha." I reholstered my finger.

Drew retrieved the ball. He bounced it on the ground with his racquet and brought it to the baseline. "Let's try this again. Okay, Arthur?"

Bending to my knees, I twirled my racquet. "Hit me with your best shot."

"Okay."

Drew sent the ball up and smashed another potential ace toward me. I shifted toward my left and backhanded the ball into the forecourt, grunting. He volleyed the ball back to me. I returned the volley, grunting. He returned volley. I returned volley. Back and forth the ball went, turning into just an orange streak. It was a long point, and started to get monotonous until Drew edged toward the service line. He didn't notice that, behind him, a college girl watched. But I did. No matter. My goal was to win the point.

Then, I saw my chance. I edged him toward the alley. When he got close enough to lean against the sideline I chopped the ball into him. It ate him up. His return had nowhere to go.

"*Shit!*" He reeled back his racquet and pitched the ball behind me. "I hate missing that!"

The college girl, a brunette with an obvious tennis tan, applauded. "Great point," she said.

"You again?" Drew said to her, a bit irritated at more than just the lost point. He acted like he knew her too well, as if she had grown up with him, or had grown upon him, but he seemed none too willing to share her existence with me. Were Drew the type, I would have said he had a crush on her and he wanted to keep her all to himself, though he refused to admit it.

"You don't mind, do you?" she asked.

"Of course not. But you jinx me, that's all."

She nodded toward me, smiling. I waved at her timidly. "Who's your friend?" she asked.

"What's it to you?"

"Just asking."

Drew shook his head, and tossed the ball to me to serve. "He's too young for you—"

"You think I'm some sicko?"

"Asking about a little kid like him?" Drew said to her. "Yes."

"Hey," the college girl called out to me. "What's your name?"

"Do you mind?"

I bounced the tennis ball a little. Though Drew's question was directed at her, I really didn't mind. I was kind of flattered. It had been weeks since a college girl had noticed me. "Skip," I said. I smiled a little. Drew glared at me, then at her.

She smiled. "You got nice legs, you know that, Skip?"

I had been told this before. I would be told this later, and often. I just then noticed that she was right: I did have nice legs. But, at almost sixteen, I did not pay much attention to my own legs, although I was a leg fancier. Instead, I was noticing other legs. Drew's, for instance. . . .

"Keep talking," Drew said to her. "He's got a really big old man—bigger than anything you can imagine—and he'd put you in the big house for talking to his kid. And there, you'd end up the sex slave of some dyke named Matilda—"

She laughed. *"Please!"*

"I'm serious," Drew said. "Matilda. Matilda the Honey."

She laughed and prepared to go. She looked like she had heard enough high-school-boy talk to last her through the weekend. "You play pretty good tennis, Skip," she called out. "See ya."

I waved at her as she walked away and looked over the shoulder at me. The fifteen-year-old me was starting to get excited, and embarrassed, eventually, at her nice-looking, well-proportioned body, accented by what even I must admit were perky breasts. In the heat of a St. Louis September she wore shorts and a halter top, with no bra. I could see her breasts jiggle with every step, which seemed to occupy every bit of my imagination. Dear God, how much I wanted to be in my room at that moment, my door closed for privacy, I lying flat on my stomach and . . .

"Will you serve the fucking ball, Don Ho?" Drew demanded. He wanted the game to continue. Scowling, he grabbed his crotch obscenely and prepared to return serve. I bounced the ball again, preparing to serve and wondering in a loud mutter whether his "Don Ho" comment was really a reference to the Hawaiian singer or an attempt to call me a Don Juan (or a *Don Juan*) and just another teenaged male slut. Someday, when I see Drew next, I need to ask him.

I served. It was an interesting game. Drew and I always played interesting games, but we hardly ever kept score. It was a constant back and forth, trying to see who could best whom and they ended, as this day ended, with a smile and a handshake across the net. Drew's hands were larger than mine, warm and moist. When I shook his hand, my hand almost always disappeared, and he would hold onto it long after the shake was over. It was that way on that day. When he did it, I would attempt (in vain, it always seemed) to extract my hand from his, but Drew always took it as a test of strength, a chance for him to let me know that, yes, he was bigger, he was closer to being a man than I, and he could make me stay. When he made that clear to me, he would wink and let me go. And my hand never hurt.

He smiled. "Your hands are still soft. You still putting lotion on them?"

"You wouldn't want me to have rusty hands, do you?"

"Rusty hands? You? *Last one to the car*—" Drew bolted for the gate. I was running right behind him. He swung open the gate and, laughing, slammed it into me. I caught it with my hand and dashed up the steps to the parking lot. Drew reached the car first, hopping onto the hood and folding his arms. I was just seconds behind.

"Let's go to your house."

"Nuh-uh," I protested, doubled over and breathing heavily. "We always go to my house. Let's go to your house."

Drew was reluctant, but I was insistent. I had no idea why he was so self-conscious about letting me see his family. His family was not that trashy. They were just Irish-Catholic. Besides, I felt comfortable at his house.

"Okay," he said, opening the car door. "For you, we'll go to my house. This time."

We left the courts, and left the campus by the exit bungalow, to where the first guard (okay—I'll call him Kevin) had faxed Drew's signature. The second guard, a fat old guy with a mustache, smiled and handed Drew a clipboard to sign.

"Who won?" the second guard asked. He, too, acted like Drew was one of the great regulars on the Ellington tennis courts.

"Oh," Drew began. "In the only match that mattered, I did."

I lightly struck Drew on the shoulder. He looked at me and smiled. "What?"

I smiled. "You won?"

"I did. In the last match. I beat you to the car."

I shook my head; sometimes, Drew had such a male ego. He finished signing his name. The guard took the visitor decal and waved his good-bye. Leaving the campus, we proceeded to Drew's house.

Though he never explained it, aside from offering that there were too many women, Drew rarely took me to his house. He preferred going to mine, which was as quiet as a mausoleum by comparison. The Fords were a seemingly mutt family that occupied a small aluminum ranch in a subdivision in the middle of Whitman Township. Though small, the Fords' home felt warm, a place where even freaks were loved in spite of being freaks and where they could count on a hot bath, a warm bed, and three square meals at least five times a week. And, with that, it mattered little that they seemed common.

I try remembering details about his parents. To me, the son of a judge and an attorney, whose family included a federal judge, two congressional careers, some corporate executives, federal bureaucrats, and physicians of various kinds among more than a handful of educators, Drew's working-class parents seemed unusual. Mr. Ford worked somewhere in St. Louis, doing something with resonance imaging, I think, an idea I got from some very distant grunt Drew used some time in our relationship. Mrs. Ford worked at a printing office not far from the high school; I saw her each time Mom needed a program printed for some club. Mrs. Ford's printing office also did Mom's law firm's bulk printing. Drew almost never visited her; nor, for that matter, did he care for me mentioning that my mother's law firm was one of the printing office's biggest customers. Yet, most days, he took her to work and picked her up after tennis. It was something that day both of us had forgotten.

I looked at the clock recently fastened to the car dashboard. It was already well past four thirty. "Shouldn't you get your mom?"

Drew sighed. He hated being reminded. Just short of the turn to his subdivision, he made a left and ventured onto the state highway. The state highway led to Jefferson Avenue, and, from there, College, and then we turned at the local museum and found ourselves in the back parking lot of Devlin Printing.

Mrs. Ford was waiting for us. Seated on a planter, she was fanning herself with tactboard. In the September weather, her blondish-brown bangs were a mess. To rid herself of them, she had pulled them back and wrapped her hair in a bandanna. She looked surprised to see us. She stood.

"For a minute there, I thought you'd run off to St. Louis again," she said, heading for the car. "It's good that talk with your dad sunk through to you."

Drew said nothing. It seemed being reminded of a "talking to," as his mother tended to call it, was the last thing he wanted me to hear. He reached into the back and stacked his book bag and tennis gear. I got out.

"Hey, where you going?" Drew asked.

"I'm gonna sit in the back," I said.

"Skip Macalester," Mrs. Ford said. "I guess you're not the one to have taught him a thing or two about being irresponsible."

Sheepishly, I smiled. Sometimes, it seemed Mrs. Ford liked Drew hanging around me. She climbed into the front seat and I took the back, though not in that order. She whipped off the bandanna, wiped her face, and seemed to wonder how we could play tennis in September. Her hair whipped in the wind as Drew drove.

"It's the change," she muttered. "Just the change."

"Huh?" Drew asked.

"You know what I said." She turned back to me. "Your mom ever talk about going through the change?"

"The Change" meant menopause. My mother went through it in her late forties. It happened so long ago that I barely remembered it. The Judge sometimes talked about how much more moody Mom became at that time, but Mom never said a word about it. No matter. It was too complicated not to lie to Mrs. Ford about it.

"Yes," I said.

She turned back to Drew. "Slaving all day at a graphics board would aggravate anyone's change."

I saw Drew shrug. Then, Mrs. Ford started talking about her day, how hot and long it seemed, how Charlie Devlin, the print shop owner, was too cheap to turn on the air in September and how she needed another vacation from the place. She moved the conversation to what Drew did that day. I braced myself. *Are you going to mention the play?*

"Nothing," he said.

"Nothing?" she asked. "You mean to tell me you were up at six thirty cleaning and preening yourself, all over 'nothing?' Look at me. Do I look like I was born yesterday?"

I could hear Drew sigh. I imagined him rolling his eyes. He didn't look good rolling his eyes.

Mrs. Ford turned back to me. "Skip, what did he do today?"

"Went to school," I said. "Beyond that, there really was nothing that unusual today."

"No baseball game?"

"I said 'nothing,'" Drew blurted out. "How many times do I got to say 'nothing' before you give it a rest?"

She ran a hand through her hair. "Is it a girl?"

"No," Drew laughed.

"Then what was it?"

At a stoplight, Drew turned back to me. "She won't believe me. She'll believe you."

I shrugged. *Why did you have to drag me into your fight with your mother? Andrew, you know how much I hate that.*

She reached to stroke his hair, but he moved away. "My little boy's got a girlfriend."

"*Mom!*"

"*What?* It is a girl, right? Is she pretty?"

"*No.*"

"You mean, you got an ugly girl?"

"*No.*"

"She's not pretty; she's not ugly. She's a girl, right?"

When the light changed, Drew almost missed his turn. "You *always* do that to me," he said as he drove on.

She sighed a little and stuck her arm out of the window. It flowed freely in the air. She said little more for most of the ride, preferring to feel wind than to talk.

In a little bit came the Fords' subdivision. Its entrance was a long, narrow post road set off by pine trees. I think Grandma said once when we were driving past it that the Fords' subdivision was originally a large nursery, and that the pine trees were part of that nursery, but I could never bring myself to believe it.

The car made a few twists and turns. This subdivision was where Grandma would take the Judge and me to look at lights during the Christmas season, when I was younger and when Mom was in one of her moods, blackened more depressingly by the change. That was before I knew Drew, and, with them, I laughed at their tin-plated hovels with windows in only two of their four walls. Had I known Drew, I would never have laughed so easily.

As a younger adolescent, I used to imagine coming out to Whitman Township late at night (once I got my driver's license, of course, and my own car) to see Drew's bedtime rituals. I was curious whether he washed his face and brushed his teeth before bed, as I did, and whether his parents stopped by his door to say "good night," as Mom and the Judge did, and whether he really slept in just underwear, as he claimed, like some uncivilized heathen too ignorant to worry about pajamas. I imagined that I would peek through his window and stay there until he kicked the sheets off, or got up in the morning, whichever came first.

Whenever I thought about the Fords' house I dreamed such things. And, whenever I did, I would blush over imagined questions from my parents who seemed to know the foolery of such dreams. It would be better to spend a life eternal in a monastic cell, as the first Methodist monk, than to endure a discovery of such dreams.

My face felt like it had been splashed with mudpies when we reached the Fords' house. Why? Did I think they could see right through me? Did I fantasize too readily only to be shocked with reality? Drew parked the car in the driveway, just outside the garage, where one of his sisters had left her bicycle. Mrs. Ford stormed out of the car and went straight for the front door.

"*Hey!*" Mrs. Ford shouted into the open front door. "Get out here right now, little lady, and put this bicycle where it belongs, this very instant!"

The older of Drew's sisters at home, Mavis, came through the front door and headed for the bicycle. Her bare feet, long and narrow, looked like Drew's. Her brother, always self-conscious about his family around me, turned red.

"Can't you put on shoes?" Drew asked her. "We've got company."

Taking her bicycle, Mavis wrinkled her face. "Company? It's just Skip."

"He's still company," Drew said.

Mavis sighed. "Whatever." She walked the bicycle on the grass around the side of the house. The last thing I saw was Mavis flipping her long braid over her back.

"See why?" Drew asked. "Eleven and she's already on the rag."

For a few minutes, Drew stood beside the car with his hands in his pockets, looking toward the cul-de-sac at a kid trying to play basketball with a Nerf ball. For those few minutes, Drew seemed unable to decide whether he wanted to go in or jump in the car. Mrs. Ford came from the house.

"It's a disaster in there," he asked his mother, "huh?"

"It's not that bad," she said.

Mrs. Ford held the door open. Instinctively, I started for it. Drew stayed with the car, looking at the kid.

"Hey," I said. I nodded toward the front door.

Drew seemed to move gradually out of his daze as he dropped the kid and approached the front door. "I bet it stinks in there," he muttered.

Mrs. Ford, who was standing right there, did nothing until he passed her. Then, she swatted his behind. In the living room, just inside the door, the television was on. Mrs. Ford promptly turned it off. Since Drew had mentioned it, I was somewhat conscious of a slight stale odor that was not too noticeable. On such a warm day, they really needed to turn off the ceiling fans and switch on the central air.

I stood in the living room, waiting. Drew signaled me to follow him down the hall to his room. Drew opened the bedroom door.

"What are you doing in my room?" he demanded.

"Mom said—"

"'Mom said,' my ass!"

"*Drew!*"

"She knows better than to be in my room!" he called out to his mother, who was in the kitchen.

"Okay, okay." With that, Drew's youngest sister Fraiser, an eight-year-old tomboy, came out of his room.

"Go into my and Daddy's room, honey," Mrs. Ford directed her. From the kitchen came the sound of running water.

"There," Fraiser said as she went into her parents' room. "Happy?"

"Yes, I'm happy."

"*Drew!* Don't agitate your sister!"

"Well, tell her to stop going into my room when she's put out of the living room!"

"She's only eight!"

"Well," Drew said, "tell her!"

Drew pushed me into his room and closed the door. I sat on the bed; he surveyed his things to make sure Fraiser had not moved around anything in particular. I remembered the fried baloney we had eaten and suppressed a belch.

"Little stinker," Drew said. "It smells like bubble gum in here already." He turned to the door and cracked it open. *"You are to leave my room alone!"*

"I didn't do anything in your room," Fraiser protested.

"I don't go into your room, for anything," Drew said. "You are to keep out of mine!"

"I *wasn't* in your room!"

Drew slammed the door. Then, he fidgeted a little, almost like a tiger in a cage. "I hate it when they do that," he muttered. Then, he opened the window, a narrow, sliding slit of a thing, and started to fan.

"It's not that bad in here," I said.

Drew huffed. "That's what you think."

After fanning a bit, he played some Billy Joel on the computer and plopped down on the bed. He was so close to me I had to struggle to keep from sinking into him. He started snapping his fingers to the beat, and singing, too. It was a comedy show, because Drew, who had a pleasant singing voice, was singing purposefully off key, trying to be funny.

With his singing, I started to relax. I eased myself onto the bed beside him and just lay there, listening to him sing. Again, there was that same warm feeling I had when Drew shook my hand: that I was safe with this guy, that we would be best friends for a long time—forever, if need be. Being so close to another warm body felt good, very good, and I closed my eyes and started to fall into a light sleep, still very much aware of what was going on. Then, when the song changed, his singing stopped, as did the finger snapping. I could only hear, aside from Billy Joel, Drew's breathing, which seemed rapid and shallow.

"Drew," Mavis said, opening the door, "Mom wanted to know if—"

"Jesus, will you knock!"

"Jeez, *ex*cuse me."

Quickly, Mavis closed the door.

"See what I mean?" Breathing heavily, Drew turned off the Billy Joel and started pacing the floor. He seemed to try catching his breath. "They're *always* in your room. They're *always* in your business. They don't give a shit how they bother you. See?"

There was a knock at Drew's door. He opened it and Mrs. Ford stuck her head in. Her hair looked moist, as though the sweat had dampened it, or as if she had splashed water in her face. In the background, I heard bathwater running.

"Sorry to disturb you two," Mrs. Ford said. "I'm gonna take a shower, and then I'll make dinner. Skip, are you eating with us?"

"No," Drew said. "He needs to get home."

"I wasn't asking you; I was asking him."

I looked to Drew, who was shaking his head.

"Thank you, Mrs. Ford," I said in my best voice, "but my father and mother probably are expecting me soon."

Mrs. Ford smiled a little and glanced at Drew. "Okay, play safe. Have fun." She closed the door and went to her shower.

Drew rested with his hands on his hips. "I need to get you out of here."

"Why?"

"'Why?' There's too many people, that's why." He paused. "Too many damn women!"

As much as I may have wanted to stay and fiddle with his Boy Scout memorabilia, which sat talisman-like on the shelves above his bed, Drew refused to hear of it. He practically lifted me from the bed and ushered me to the front door.

"Tell Mom I'm going with Skip," he yelled to Mavis.

"What about dinner?"

"Tell her don't wait up for me."

He pushed me out the door and down the steps. Toward the cul-de-sac, the kid was still attempting basketball with a Nerf ball. Drew plopped down on the Fords' stoop and removed his shoes.

"Before I forget." He started removing the socks. "I need to wash these."

"You don't have to. I'll take 'em like that."

He looked at me. Successfully, he removed a sock. Then he sniffed it and made a face. "Pee*yoo!*"

"I can wash that."

"Don't be ridiculous. I'm not letting you near anything this stinky."

Drew removed the other sock and stuffed both socks into the Fords' mailbox. Then, he stood there, in his bare feet, until he plopped back down on the stoop and put his shoes back on. In a way, he looked funny, with his somewhat hairy ankles borne from the tops of his shoes. Because they were so pregnant with meaning, I chose not to look at them, choosing instead to watch the kid with the Nerf ball. *The kid.* The kid was poetic, trying to get the ball to slide across his arms and back like Curly Neal of the Harlem Globetrotters, but it was futile, making it funny, making me smile a little. Drew stuck his face between the kid and me, and he smiled.

"Let's get you back to the Judge."

"Ah, Drew, let me stay like this."

"With these women? You must think I really hate you."

Taking my arm, he guided me toward the car and deposited my body into the front seat. But, for the duration, I remained with the kid with the Nerf ball, who fascinated me, even as we left the subdivision.

Chapter Four

Mom and the Judge were late coming home. I could imagine them stopping at the college to catch a woodwind quintet, or something. After my business, I flipped through *The Crucible* idly, then busied myself with last night's meat loaf the Judge had prepared and left in the refrigerator. I felt the urge for business again, thinking about Drew's feet. I changed my sheets.

After that, I was bored. I mean, how long can masturbation hold even an almost sixteen-year-old's imagination? A guy can do it only so many times. There was nothing on TV. Radio was in the middle of its "drive time" antics. If I could, if I had a car, I would cruise the neighborhoods, maybe return to Drew's house. But I could do no such thing. I wouldn't even have my own license for another three months.

I called Marshall. It was usually a gamble to call Marshall on Fridays after school, because, usually, he was still at his golf game. But he was home. I thought I could hear him playing an opera in the background.

"Who's that?"

"Gorecki," he said. *"Symphony of Sorrowful Songs."*

"Wanna come over?"

He demurred. "I'm really into the Gorecki."

"You can bring it with you," I said.

"Cousin dear," he began, "the Gorecki is about the Nazis and the Gestapo in occupied Poland. The Gorecki will give you nightmares. You know how Dawn Upshaw sings: she'll haunt your dreams."

Hyperbole, maybe, but I was willing to risk it. "I can handle it, Marsh. Bring it with you. Educate me."

Wrong thing to say to Marshall. His mission was to educate no one. "Buy your own Gorecki and educate yourself. What do you think I am? Some missionary?"

"Please, Marsh?"

He relented. Because he lived just a few blocks away, and was used to cutting through yards, he arrived at our back door in a matter of minutes. I waited for him and opened the door, even though he had his own key to our house. As usual, he carried a book bag, which he set on the kitchen table. Then he began to take yellow pad after yellow pad from the book bag before reaching the CD.

"How was the golf game?" I asked, taking a pair of glasses from the cupboard. "Wine?"

"Rum and Coke," he said.

"Ouch! That bad?"

He shrugged. "Couldn't sink a putt worth a shit. I was great from tee to green, and my chips were on the money, but putting? I needed to stick out my ass like Sam Snead to get it in."

We took the glasses to the Judge's liquor cabinet, where I made the rum and Coke. I can make a great drink, considering Marshall and I had been practicing since we were about fourteen. Marshall liked smoking the Judge's Dominican cigars as he enjoyed a drink, and we smoked on the terrace out back. Whether the Judge knew, I had no idea for a long time. He never mentioned missing cigars.

Whenever Marshall enjoyed his cigar and drink, he turned more intellectual than normal. Dawn Upshaw sang on the CD player, and her voice resonated throughout the backyard. Marshall was quiet then, trying, it seemed, to learn Polish from the text, the same way he first learned German by listening to Wagner and first grasped Italian by listening to Verdi. He had his yellow pads among him on the terrace, and he wrote in them—a story, perhaps, maybe even a novel.

"Just an essay," he said when I asked. "Not 'Letter from Birmingham Jail' or 'On Civil Disobedience,' but kinda sorta close."

Knowing him, whatever the treatise, it would prove incendiary.

"Tomorrow's Rec Night," I observed, referring to the annual event in St. Louis for Howard University alumni, which included both of our fathers. "Going?"

Marshall, still writing, shrugged.

"Well, I am," I said. "It will be my first."

"Good for you. My father hasn't decided about going yet, so I don't know."

Both of us took a sip. I didn't know about Marshall, but my drink was half gone, and, between it and the cigar, the backyard was beginning to tilt. "You can come with us," I said.

"Might have to. I really don't want to miss it. My father will probably end up giving me his ticket so I can go."

I thought it would be great, if he could go. That way, I could have someone to play Ping-Pong with. But I didn't tell him that. I couldn't stand offending him.

Marshall hung around long enough for a second drink, long enough for the Gorecki to finish, then he stuffed the CD and yellow pads back into his book bag and headed home. Rinsing the glasses even as the kitchen seemed to float in midair, I went back to eating meatloaf. Why hadn't anyone called? It was so unlike both of them.

It was after six when the Judge trudged in. He labored beneath a sheath of briefs too plentiful to put in his briefcase, and he had that law-wearied look. I met him in the kitchen. He was making his way in; I was, again, in the refrigerator. Barefoot, I had not bothered to change my clothes after changing my sheets. I had not showered. Drew would say I stunk. The Judge seemed to neither notice nor mind the smell. For the moment, he busied himself with the stack of mail Miss Cynthia had left on the kitchen counter.

"Has your mother called?" the Judge asked.

"No." No one had bothered to call me, not that I mattered. The Judge switched on NPR and listened momentarily before brewing his evening iced tea. Depending upon the day, the Judge preferred an evening's iced tea to a happy hour drink. Between the segments, there was a plucking interlude. The Judge listened to a few plucks, then got from the freezer four ice cubes.

"Kronos Quartet," he said. "*Pieces of Africa*. 'Tilliboyo (Sunset)' by Foday Musa Suso."

By the time he was finished, the interlude was over. There had been a rumor, the correspondent stated, that the Kronos Quartet was breaking up.

"Shame," the Judge said. He headed upstairs. "I thought they would be around forever."

At first, I wondered whether he would wander into my room and see the rearranged stuff that indicated a changed bed. It was more of a fear, like the dread of opening a certified letter at the post office, but that fear lasted as momentarily as cracking the mailbox lid and peeking in. I heard the Judge drop his briefcase upstairs. It sounded as heavy as tympani, a muffled thud. That was the most sound the Judge ever made. Then, he closed the door.

Then, I remembered my allocation of rum with Marshall. I took a glass of water and hastily, quietly poured enough into the rum to make up for what we had drank. As much ice as the Judge put into his drinks, I felt it was unlikely he would notice it to be a little more watery than normal.

I returned to raiding the refrigerator. There was still plenty of meat loaf in there, and it was so good. I was making myself a meat loaf sandwich for the fourth time of the night, with wheat bread and horseradish sauce, when the phone rang. I thought the Judge would get it, but it rang a third time and a fourth time.

"You don't have to get it," I yelled to the Judge upstairs, "because it is your house!"

"Skip, could you get that, please?"

He sounded like he was in the bathroom, so I did him the favor. I answered the phone at about the seventh ring, an unusually long time. I was hoping it was Mom.

"Hello," I said.

"I want your daddy."

It was Grandma Macalester, and only Grandma Macalester could have been so commanding. Besides, she sounded to have been hardly in the mood for interference on my part.

"Just a minute," I said. I went to the foot of the stairs and opened my lungs. "Dad," I yelled. "It's for you."

Over the phone, I heard the extension click and the Judge draw a breath. "I got it," he said calmly.

Whenever the Judge said "I got it," and whenever it was his mother, those were my cues to hang up.

I returned to meat loaf sandwiches. Then, I held it before me and inhaled the curry and Dijon mustard the Judge spices his meat loaf with. My mouth watered. The kitchen was beginning to settle back to Earth, and, with it, my stomach, too.

I had finished the sandwich and was about to drink a Diet Coke when the Judge softly entered the kitchen and stood next to me. Though his tie and jacket were off and his suspenders were down, he looked the same as he did earlier that morning. I should edit that: he seemed more harried that night. He breathed as purposefully as a lion giving birth to cubs, then he stroked the crown of his gray head.

"Mother's coming. Can you bathe?"

"Do I need to?" I sniffed myself and checked my breath. Were the afternoon's activities, the tennis and cigar and drink, weighing upon me?

The Judge declined to answer directly. He left the kitchen. "I'll get a few things," he said through the dining room. "Come on up and get clean."

I brushed the crumbs off my shirt and followed him. "Why?"

"Because."

"Why?"

"Because I said so."

That was not a precise answer. Were I to bathe, and possibly change clothes, even if I did stink, I deserved something better. As he left me at the foot of the stairs and disappeared in his bedroom, I thrust my hands into my pockets and resolved not to go so easily. "That's not good enough," I yelled.

His bedroom door clicked open. He leaned over the railing. A chill went through my back as I realized, perhaps, that was the wrong thing to say. "Then do it because my mother's coming," he said.

Now, that was the only thing that would get the Judge in one of his most commanding moods. Like everyone else, he adored Grandma. A retired principal of Henning Elementary School, she had the distinction of succeeding her late husband on the county board and her elevated son in Congress. To each, she was elected to three terms in her own right, but, whereas Dad's imperiousness commanded others to call him "the Judge" or "Mister Chairman," Grandma's demeanor pooh-poohed anyone calling her anything but Madelyn. Everyone, that is, except her boys. Her boys always called her "Mother." All of them, except the Judge, most days.

I trudged to my room and got fresh socks and underwear; the Judge didn't close his door until he heard me run a shower. I wish I could say I took a real shower. Instead, it was cursory, a wetting of hair and a light, soap-laden scrub of the underarms. As if part of a ritual, I raised my feet to the tub rim and spread soap between the toes. That was the most I did for an evening shower, then I rinsed. Without thought, the spray lingered on me. I turned it off before getting too excited. Grandma was coming.

I remember how fresh evening showers made me feel. It is like carousing through the Park early one spring morning, when dew is real. That evening, the towel felt softer, like fur. I could smell the April-fresh fabric softener our maid put into the wash and that reminded me of frolicking on grass even more.

It was a shame to pass the towel over skin and leave it in a lump on the floor. I put on my fresh socks and underwear without much drama, followed by yet another cursory act, the brushing of the teeth and rinsing of the mouth with minty, cobalt-blue mouthwash. I smiled at myself. For Grandma, I supposed I didn't smell that bad.

I opened the bathroom door to the sight of the Judge setting Mom's matching pewter-colored garment bag and small suitcase at the head of the stairs. He had changed from his workday business suit to less formal red polo shirt and khakis. He had his glasses off, indicating he had just changed. He was in his stocking feet.

"Can you take these down for me?" he asked, heading back to his bedroom.

I was a little self-conscious about standing around in just socks and underwear. "Can't I put a robe on?"

"You look fine." He slipped into his bedroom.

"But what if I catch a cold?"

"If you catch a cold, I'll nurse you."

"Thanks," I muttered.

I wrapped a towel around my waist and lifted the small bag. I couldn't believe how heavy it was.

"What you put in here?"

The Judge left his room. He had on his tennis shoes, like he was ready for his morning golf game, or an evening walk. "Just a few of her things," he said.

"Where's she going?"

He said nothing. Easily, he lifted the small bag and started downstairs. "Bring that."

"Is she going away?" I asked, following him with the garment bag, which was as heavy as rocks; he barely even shrugged. "She's going to be gone long?"

"I don't know."

"You know where she's at?"

He paused. He whipped through the dining room. Obviously, he was heading for the garage. "Yes."

"And? We're going there?"

"Possibly."

I felt my face frown. "'Yes'—'no'—'possibly'—your answers could be more concrete."

He dropped the small bag at the door to the garage. "Nothing's more concrete than one-word answers."

I muttered something. I muttered something about cow chips. That may have been the wrong thing to say. It may have been the wrong time to say anything. The Judge, who was walking through the kitchen just in front of me, came to a dead stop, and I, unexpectant, crashed into his back. My towel dropped to my feet. He looked through me, my father. I had never felt so cold. I was petrified.

"Not this conversation," he said.

Just then, the front door opened. "Hello, hello, hello," Grandma sang from the front door.

"Come on in, Mother," the Judge called out, walking again. Quickly, I fixed the towel around my waist.

Grandma met us in the dining room. Her first act was to embrace my father, which he was slow to reciprocate. "My baby," she moaned. When they let go of each other, she saw me and wrapped me into a bear hug so fierce it undid my towel. "Grandma's conniver," she said, still hugging me. "Grandma's poor little conniver."

The Judge pried me from Grandma. "Let Grandma's poor little conniver get some clothes on, before Grandma's little conniver catches himself a cold."

Letting go of me, Grandma gave him a look, a simple look the likes of which I had never seen. Then she dropped my hand. "Go get dressed," she said. "He and I have some talking to do."

I took the towel and went to my room. There was my green polo shirt and a pair of blue jeans with a ripped back pocket—everything else, freshly washed, was too clean to wear. Bert stared at me from her pillow as I put myself in clothes, then she looked at me as if to ask, "What's the fuss?"

"You're about as clued in as me," I said. I plopped on my bed and put on my tennis shoes. I heard the Judge come up the stairs and go into his bedroom. I figured he was getting his glasses.

We left our rooms together. Perhaps it would not have been so remarkable, ordinarily, but he barely looked at me as we bounded downstairs. Grandma was waiting at the front door.

"Alfred," she said, "go get her things. Let's take my car."

The Judge, it seemed, was unwilling to fight. "Yes, Mother," he said. He headed straight for the suitcase and garment bag at the garage door.

As if part of duty, I went as well. I took the small bag this time, to spite my guts, and it did not seem as heavy as it had previously. I followed the Judge, who had the garment bag, and we took them to the trunk of the open boat, Grandma's graphite Lincoln, outside, Grandma following us all the way. The Judge looked so forlorn.

"Keys, Mother."

Grandma clicked her keys and the trunk opened. In it were Grandma's golf clubs and the remnants of a box of black magazines she was taking to the local women's shelter. The Judge stepped aside and signaled for me to hoist the small bag into the trunk, but I needed help. After all, still a virgin, I was not going to sacrifice potency and guts for just my mother's stuffed suitcase.

"Can you help me, please?" I asked.

The Judge replaced my hand on the handle with his, and he lifted the bag to the edge of the trunk, then tumbled it into the trunk, smashing the box of magazines. On top of it, he spread the garment bag. He closed the trunk.

"It's evening, Mother. You want me to drive?"

"You know where we're going?" she asked.

"I know where we're going," he said.

She gave him the keys and she went to the passenger side and the Judge got behind the wheel. I watched her open the passenger side door, not quite sure whether I wanted to open the back door as well, and slip into a form of something as mute as a Missouri blackfly. Besides, I had no intention of going anywhere until someone told me what the hell was going on. Grandma looked at me.

"Aren't you coming?" she asked.

"Where are we going? Are we going to Mom?"

"Yes, Skip," the Judge said from the other side of the car, "you're going to see Rose."

That was all I needed to hear. I plopped into the backseat, which stretched side to side for me. As the engine started and the open boat sailed into drive, I strained to hear what Grandma and the Judge were talking about, but they talked so low they sounded like bugs. I chose to inject myself into their conversation.

"You wanna know what I did today?" I asked.

The Judge looked at me through the rearview mirror. "What did you do today?"

I looked out the window and saw a newly horned fawn in the park. "I went to school today. That's what I did."

Grandma and the Judge looked at each other and started laughing, as did I. "What?" the Judge asked. "No baseball game?"

I smiled a bit, in spite of myself. "No. No baseball game."

They continued laughing. Perhaps they were thinking about the great incongruity between my past trip to St. Louis (the Judge must have told Grandma, from the way she laughed) and my admission that all I did that day was go to school. All the rest was unimportant. You could say I really wanted to lighten the moment, at least for myself, if not for anyone else, because their low talking had an ominous tone to it. And it did lighten the moment, even for me. I couldn't help but join them in laughing, because it was very funny, once you think about it.

After that, Grandma started talking like normal. "Did I ever tell you about me and Skinny Pickle?" she asked. With that, she launched into the story about a young man she once met in an East St. Louis dive when she was home from college. It was a complicated tale that made both Grandma and the Judge laugh almost uncontrollably. That is not to say I wasn't laughing, too. I remember I was laughing, almost so hard my belly started to ache.

By the time we left Jefferson Heights, I had forgotten that this was a trip to see my mother, who was somewhere my father refused to say, for reasons my father refused to admit. Much of this was because of the way Grandma chattered, about the years before she and Grandpa Macalester got serious about their relationship. Then, she said, she was free to eat at Woolworth lunch counters with the Jones sisters on Fridays and to catch the soon-to-be-famous jazz and blues musicians in after-hours sets down in East St. Louis. She mentioned she admired the Lincoln High School men that city produced, because, she said, almost all of them were dashing.

I lost myself in her talk. I imagined Dave Matthews Band–style saxophone riffs in smoke-scented basements where, she said, the malt liquor and snoots ran free. I imagined my grandfather, Edward Macalester, a man who died when my father was just thirteen and whom I met only in a handful of dreamy pictures and vivid stories Grandma told. She said, among other things, that he frequented the East St. Louis dives. She said she met Grandpa, up from Carbondale, in such a place. She said he always wore a dark suit and a colorful necktie. She said he had his father's hearse; as he gave her a lift back up Route 3, the gurney in the back bumped back and forth as if it were a body.

"It scared the shit out of me," she admitted. "And your daddy laughed so hard."

That was their first date, she explained. At the time, Grandma's family, the Crawfords, lived on the Crawford spread of three houses and as many acres of fruit trees on the north side of town. When Grandpa appeared in the hearse, her Grandma Crawford thought it was someone needing a room. "We don't have a place for anyone,"

Grandma remembered her saying, "try the doctor's house." It was the practice when traveling, Grandma explained, before Holiday Inns, to stay with someone with rooms, because few hotels took us in. The Judge nodded, as though he were around during that time.

"Yes, ma'am," the Judge said.

"Why you 'yes, ma'amming' me? You weren't even a hiccup in my throat at that time. All you ever knew was a stay at the best hotel your dollar can buy. You'd never known, thank God, what it's like to have all the money in your pocket and to ride for hours without even the hope of a spare bed in a mortuary." She turned to me, as if I knew instead. "Does he?"

"No, ma'am," I said, smiling.

The Judge drummed a tune on the steering wheel. "I don't think you have to experience it to know what it means, Mother."

"That's pretty easy for a man who knows everything," Grandma said, "but, for us mere mortals—tell him about us mere mortals, Skip."

"Don't drag me into this," I said.

Grandma huffed. "I forgot your arms're too short to box."

Again, the Judge drummed a tune on the steering wheel. He said nothing as Grandma led the conversation back to Skinny Pickle and Grandpa Macalester's hearse. His silence dominated most of the rest of the ride.

I had not realized we had passed the line between our city and Whitman Township until we were well away from it. I figured, since we were going to see Mom, we were heading to Aunt Carolyn's, who used to be married to the Judge's brother, Uncle Clifford. Though divorced, Aunt Carolyn still kept a good relationship with the family through our women, who communed with her in the National Council of Negro Women.

Thinking about her made me think about Drew, who lived not far from Aunt Carolyn. I imagined he was calling me. Then, I thought about Brad, who also lived in the area, which made me think of Kay Reece. Kay Reece, the white-haired pig of the high school baseball team who had been my nemesis since eighth grade. Kay Reece, the Whitmaner, the banker's son, who loved intimidating me. Kay Reece. That was all I needed.

Then came Aunt Carolyn's house, a one-story contemporary ranch of framed aluminum and brick facing exiled to the edge of a Whitman Township subdivision. Yes, indeed, Mom's Volvo was parked in the driveway, sitting as pretty as it did in our drive. Aunt Carolyn had put holly trees along the street and short, bonsailike shrubs in front of the windows, each in nests of phosphoritic rocks.

Grandma killed the Skinny Pickle talk. She cleared her throat as the Judge parked the open boat behind the Volvo.

"You wanna go in?" she asked the Judge.

"Yep," he said. He opened the door and stepped out.

"You think that's wise?" I asked. I remembered the last time Mom and the Judge were in public together, back that past Sunday, when they argued bitterly after church. Their arguments were always bitter, violent affairs, enough to make a kid run to China and hide. Because of this, I was a coward; I wasn't about to open the door myself.

The Judge, though, would have none of it. He opened the door for me. "Yep," he said again.

Reluctantly, I climbed out and stood at the back of the open boat, waiting for the Judge to open the trunk. But he didn't head for the trunk. He opened the door for Grandma, helped her out, then he started for Aunt Carolyn's front door.

"What about her things?" I called out.

"Get 'em later," he said. He was already halfway up her sidewalk. It seemed to me, if someone didn't open the door for him, he was bound to make one himself.

"If he'd shown half that enthusiasm earlier," Grandma said to me, covering her mouth with her forefingers, "your daddy wouldn't be in this predicament."

As soon as that last syllable left her mouth, she was heading for Aunt Carolyn's front door, too.

No one had to bang the brass knocker to announce our arrival. Aunt Carolyn's Great Dane Horatio woofed our coming loudly. Then, as someone inside opened the front door, Horatio bounced outside, barking, jumping up, and licking the Judge's face. He could do nothing but catch the dog.

"Horatio!" Aunt Carolyn yelled, tugging the dog by the leather collar, "down, girl! Bad girl, bad!"

The dog took the tugging and came down from the Judge's face. She wrapped herself around Aunt Carolyn and started barking.

"Yes, yes," the Judge said to the dog. "I see you, too."

Aunt Carolyn pinched her dark purple kimono over her bypass scar and she led Horatio through the house and out the back sliding door, where the dog stood, looking in. I stood in her front door and surveyed the place. Aunt Carolyn, a tall, piano-key dark woman as elegant as an etude, kept a cluttered house full of knickknacks from trips to the Far East. From Louisiana, she scented her house with all sorts of gumbos and jambalayas, whose recipes tended to make it to our house within the week. She and the Judge regularly passed recipes like conspiracies.

"I'm making turkey stew," Aunt Carolyn said to me as she opened the front door for the Judge and Grandma. When they came in, she kissed them, a friendly gesture, the type that said we were still family, somewhere down deep. Then she turned to me. "I know you're hungry for my turkey stew."

Indeed, I was. I loved her food. Aunt Carolyn's turkey stew was more like a gumbo, thick and rich, served on rice. That was the one recipe the Judge had failed to obtain. Aunt Carolyn refused to write it out for him, very unlike her. Without the recipe, the Judge's stabs at the dish were weak by comparison. The Judge wasn't interested. He was on the scent and he wanted to cut to the chase.

"Where is she?" he asked.

"Right to the point again, Alfred," Aunt Carolyn said in mock sarcasm. "Not even a 'hello, how you doing? Love what you've done to the house' from you at all. I don't even know what I'm thinking."

The Judge sighed. He started to peck her cheek, but he paused, thought about it, and kissed her anyway. "I'm in deep, regardless," he said.

"I wouldn't mind helping myself to some of your turkey stew," Grandma said. "I always get a taste for your particular turkey stew."

Aunt Carolyn signaled for us to follow her into the kitchen, where the smell was intense. When we got there, we saw Mom, fresh from a bath, sitting at the kitchen table wearing a pink kimono of patterned bluebirds. She had a deck of playing cards in her hand and beside her on the table were a pen and legal pad. Though I was behind him, I could see my father smile at her, seated as she was in the glow of the setting sun.

"You are radiant," he said.

"Save it," Mom snapped.

Grandma went to Mom. Reaching out, they clasped hands. "You don't mind if we break bread with you?"

"It's always nice to break bread with you, Madelyn," Mom told Grandma. Mom would have known how much Grandma hated her calling her "Madelyn." But that didn't matter that much. By then, I suppose Mom knew there was no heading back into the family. Mom smiled at Grandma. "You're always such great fun."

I remember Grandma's stiff smile, so underwhelmed, as she sat at the table with Mom. Then, Grandma looked at me. I suppose it was my turn to make nice with my mother.

Mom also looked at me. In a moment, she dropped her outsider look and seemed to remind herself that I was her youngest child, at almost sixteen, still just a boy. She held out her free hand and signaled for me to come to her. I am ashamed to admit I was reluctant to do so. Mom had her distant look on. Mom could be so cold when she looked so distant. But the Judge took my arm and pushed me toward her. Mom stood. Wrapping her arms around me, she hugged me so fiercely it almost pushed the air out of my lungs, then she rocked me like a baby. I didn't feel like a baby. Indeed, I did not feel comforted at all. Rather, I felt on edge, on stage, like I was before someone who was not my mother, the person who birthed me, but just another stranger, whom I did not know completely and who preferred it that way. I had always assumed my hard mother was unmoved by sentimental things, but I was wrong. When she finally let me go, I could see she was crying.

"Get yourself some turkey stew," Mom said. She collapsed back into the kitchen chair, and shuffled the playing cards. She started playing solitaire.

Aunt Carolyn distributed large bowls and spoons and ladled rice and turkey stew. Even the Judge got some, and, once he did, he stood at the kitchen table until Mom barely acknowledged him with a glance.

"May I?" he asked, referring to a chair.

Mom looked up. Grandma and I had taken the two other chairs, leaving one chair, the chair beside Mom, for the Judge. Aunt Carolyn took her bowl at the kitchen counter. Horatio barked and tried nudging the door open. At best, the Judge was on his own.

"Rose," he said.

"Sit there if you want," Mom said. She said it in such a way, so hollow and passive, that it sounded as though she really didn't care whether he sat there or stood on his head in the corner with Horatio's tail in his face.

Carefully, the Judge sat down. Aunt Carolyn offered fresh coffee, which Grandma and the Judge took. The coffee came in clear mugs. The Judge poured fifteen seconds of cream that raged up and boiled through the coffee like volcanic flow. Aunt Carolyn remembered his pack of sweetener, which he shook and thumped and opened and sprinkled into the coffee.

"*Salute,*" he said.

"If you're going to say '*salute,*'" Aunt Carolyn said, "I might as well break out my fine wine."

"I'm driving," he said. "And wine gives me a headache."

"I'll take some wine," Mom said.

The Judge looked at her. "Wine gives you a headache—"

"I've already got a headache," Mom snapped. "And he's five foot six inches, one hundred and fifty, or one hundred and sixty, or one hundred and whatever hell pounds he is, and he is sitting right next to me, so, if I want a glass of wine to get rid of it, I will."

End of subject. We shall not cross that line again, Grandma seemed to say as she blew onto her black coffee. Aunt Carolyn got her stemware and poured Mom a serving of chardonnay. Mom didn't sip it; she gulped it, hands shaking. Then, she set the stemware down and returned to her solitaire game.

"That's one mean drink," the Judge said.

Mom put the ace of spades on the table. Then, slowly, she traced her finger along the rim of her glass. "What are you presiding over, Alfred?" she asked. "An OSHA case? You always have something smart to say when you have an OSHA case."

"You don't have to be caustic, Rose," he said.

"Neither one of you has to be caustic," Grandma said, sipping turkey stew. "So, just quit it. Acting like a pair of spoiled children."

Aunt Carolyn nodded. "Amen."

"Like my Aunt Bertha said," Grandma continued, "you two should just scratch your butt and get glad."

The Judge slinked back into his turkey stew, and Mom retreated into her solitaire game. Seemingly, they agreed not to talk the rest of the meal, which went slowly, even as Grandma tried to enliven it with more on Skinny Pickle. It was a polite attempt, but only Aunt Carolyn nibbled at it.

The meal over, the Judge wiped his mouth with a fresh linen handkerchief before Aunt Carolyn produced a stack of simple paper napkins and set them on the table.

"Just so," she said.

The Judge considered her shyly, wiped his fingers on a napkin, and lobbed it into the garbage can, banking it against the corner of the wall like a good lay-up. He raised two fingers. "Two points," he said.

"Alfred," Aunt Carolyn mocked, "I never thought you were a basketball player."

"Now, now," Grandma admonished her, "none of that."

Basketball, after all, was not an activity of our kind of people. We learn that in the womb.

In time, I finished with my turkey stew. I didn't want to seem the ill-trained guest. I thanked Aunt Carolyn, complimented her for making a delicious batch, and declined her offer of more. Then, I suppressed a belch. Horatio barked and tried climbing up the sliding door. Aunt Carolyn removed my bowl to the sink.

"That's an amen," Aunt Carolyn said about the barking response to my belch. "I guess."

The Judge headed for the front door. "Come along, Skip," he said. "Let's get your mother's things."

We left Grandma with Mom and Aunt Carolyn. The Judge seemed to think they had some talking to do. "Women-talk," I suppose, something my family, a family in love with its boys, allowed the women to do on a regular basis. Outside, the Judge jingled Grandma's keys and unlocked the trunk, then he waited to see which bag I would take. I said nothing.

"Since I can handle the small suitcase," he said finally, "why don't you take the garment bag?"

It sounded like a fair proposition. I had forgotten, though, how heavy the garment bag was. When I lifted it, the bag felt like a headless body had been left in one of the suits. I held it by the hangers, then I tried draping it over my arm. Finally, I slung it over a shoulder. The Judge lifted the small bag out of the trunk and held it with both hands.

"Let's go," he said.

Quickly, we walked back to Aunt Carolyn's house. When the Judge grabbed the door, we could hear the women, dominated by Grandma and Aunt Carolyn, discussing something. The Judge looked at me.

"'Someday,'" he began, quoting Vergil's *Aeneid*, the scene of the Trojans washed upon on North Africa, hopeless, I remember, "'Someday, it shall be pleasing, even to remember this.'"

Carrying the small bag, the Judge went to the kitchen. I let the garment bag slide off my shoulder and tumble in front of Aunt Carolyn's sofa. I couldn't hear what the women were talking about, though their talk finally ended with them laughing. Everyone except Mom. Mom had a peculiar laugh I would have known anywhere. On that occasion, Mom, I could hear, had a forced smile.

"What on earth—" the Judge said.

Grandma shooed him. "Don't worry about it. It was just women talking. Nothing for your virgin ears."

Grandma laughed, as did Aunt Carolyn, who laughs heartily. Mom ended her solitaire game and gathered the cards into a deck, repackaged them, and placed the pack in the middle of the table, near the napkins. Grandma and Aunt Carolyn started another conversation, on what Uncle Clifford and Dad's other, older brother, Uncle Edward, were doing. To Aunt Carolyn, it all must have sounded like she was still in the family. Grandma was about to talk about all of her great-grandchildren when the Judge cleared his throat.

"Where, Carolyn?" he asked.

"The bedroom at the end of the hall," she said. "To the right."

That was enough direction for him. He waddled to the bedrooms (the small bag, I think, was getting to him). The bedroom to the right was lit. Done after a Japanese fashion, the comfortable queen-sized bed had Mom's opened briefcase and her day's suit strewn on it amid the impression of her body, for Mom liked mending briefs in bed. Before heading for the bedroom, I had picked up the garment bag. Its hangers pinched my fingers. I was anxious to get rid of the thing.

"Where?" I asked.

"Just a minute," he said.

He set the small bag on the side of the bed, where it could touch neither Mom's briefs, nor her briefcase, nor her suit. Then, he led me to the closet door and relieved me of the garment bag. I flexed my hand, because, among other things, the hangers had killed my circulation. The Judge hung the bag on the closet door.

"Hallelujah," the Judge said, looking at the garment bag, finally out of our possession. He was as relieved as I. At the time, did I really not understand it was more than just a garment bag that I was getting rid of?

I nodded. "And, amen."

The Judge put his hands in his pockets and looked around the room. With her things on the bed, Mom was starting to put her imprint on the place, as if it was meant to be a very long visit. The Judge shuddered. "I guess this will be——" He didn't finish the sentence. Instead, his body shuddered like an engine struggling to turn over, then he wiped his eyes with his handkerchief. He stuffed the handkerchief back into his pocket as the sound of Grandma and Aunt Carolyn laughing came closer. It was safely stowed by the time Mom, Grandma, and Aunt Carolyn were at the bedroom door. The Judge looked around the room. "I like your tastes, Carolyn," he said.

"Don't you blame me," Aunt Carolyn said. "Blame it on Clifford for taking me to Beijing for our second honeymoon. Before that, I had not a clue."

"You've been divorced from Clifford for five years," Grandma said. "You can't still be blaming him."

"It was a long divorce," Aunt Carolyn said. "I can talk about him in my house if I want to."

Mom ran her fingers through her hair. "Did you do your homework, Skip?"

I assessed the situation. I thought it best to leave my reading out of it. "I got some Latin to do. Some other things."

"Like what?" she asked. "English?"

"Rose," the Judge said simply. It sounded like he was admonishing her, as though she were trying to incite a riot and he called her on it.

Mom looked at the Judge sharply, then she calmed down and looked at me. She smiled. That was the first time she did so since we got there. I'd take it, even though you knew to run whenever Mom smiled at you. "Then you better get home," she said.

"I see you have your homework to do," the Judge said, referring to the briefs. "If you need any books—"

"I'll use the law library at the office," she said. "So don't knock yourself out."

There was an uncomfortable silence as we waited for someone to offer something. No one did. The Judge moved us toward the front door. Grandma and Aunt Carolyn followed his example and headed for the front door. At one point, in the hall, the Judge and Mom were so close a dime's worth of chocolate couldn't have passed between them. For a moment, they looked at each other, as though they were about to touch, but then they looked toward their feet. They said not a word.

In retrospect, I don't remember exactly how we left Aunt Carolyn's house. Maybe, as was her custom, she hugged everyone and we hugged back. I always kissed her after a visit and the taste of salt and makeup would cause a queer sensation on my tongue. For an hour after kissing a woman I can still feel the sensation.

After taking turns with Aunt Carolyn, we must have moved on to
Mom. When she hugged me, I remember she held on so tightly it felt
as though she would burst my sinuses. I let go first, and, once she let
go of me, Mom wiped her eyes. Her kimono was wrinkled from the
hugging, as though it had gone through the wash but not the rinse.
My mother at that moment, for all her faults, was the one thing from
that day that lingered longest. And, I remember, I felt so hollow for
having let go first. How I longed to do it again and to let go last!

"Bye, Mom," I said.

Holding her face, Mom rushed down the hall to the bedrooms. I
think I showed the impulse to go after her, but Aunt Carolyn touched
my forearm. "She'll be okay," she said.

The Judge was a gentleman. He thanked Aunt Carolyn for taking
care of Mom, even though they were really no longer family. Aunt
Carolyn smiled and took a kiss.

We were quiet in the open boat. The Judge listened to a Shostakovich prelude after *The Well-Tempered Clavier* in its entirety before saying how moving the music was. That was a first: the Judge rarely (to
my recollection) called music "moving."

"I'll check on her tomorrow," Grandma volunteered. "If you want."

The Judge thought for a minute. "She likes nice lunches."

"Yes, I remember that," she said.

"Claude's downtown is her favorite place," he said. "She likes their
pies."

We had celebrated one of Mom's birthdays at Claude's, a restaurant in the St. Croix Building. I was thirteen then, and I conspired
with the Judge to bring a wandering violinist to our table to play
something from *La Bohème*. The tip cost ten dollars (I was the bag-
man) and it was so beautiful Mom cried. I remember how disturbed I
was. That was the first time I would see my mother cry.

"Is there something you want me to tell her?" Grandma asked.

"Just the usual."

"That you love her?"

"That, too."

"You have thirty-four years invested—"

"I know."

"I know you know. I'm just saying it."

"Mother—"

"What?"

The Judge shook his head.

"Are you and Mom getting a divorce?" I asked.

I felt the Judge look at me through the rearview mirror. "We're just working some things out," he said.

"That sounds like a divorce."

"It's not," he said.

"Married couples sometimes have their differences," Grandma said. "It happens to everyone."

I folded my arms and watched Whitman Township pass by. "It sounds like a divorce."

"Give us some time, Skip," he said. "I know it's hard, but give us some time."

"You've had thirty-four years," I said. "How much more time do you need?"

Again, he looked at me through the rearview mirror. His glare said he was in no mood to debate me. No matter. I was in no mood for his moods. As usual, Grandma served as the peacemaker.

"Things like this always work themselves out," Grandma said.

Even then, much told me this would not be one of those things. Though I didn't know, someone—I was sure—would be moving out of our home.

I remained silent the rest of the ride home. Once the Judge had piloted the open boat into the driveway, I stormed into the house. The phone was ringing. Thinking it was Mom, I rushed to answer it.

"Hello?"

There was a beat on the other end. "Did you and Armstrong have a good time?"

"Huh?"

"*I said,*" the other end calmed his voice, "did you and Armstrong have a good time? You forgot about my voice, didn't you?"

Then, it hit me. "Drew?"

"That's okay," Drew said. "You don't have to remember me. I'm just your best friend. It's not like I'm your lover."

"Not this conversation, Drew," I sighed.

"Struck a nerve, huh? How does it feel? Not good, huh?"

"Drew—"

"So, where did you and Armstrong go?"

"No place!"

"I bet," he snorted. "I bet you and him couldn't wait to be where you can be alone together."

The Judge came in. He looked as though I were talking to Mom. Quickly, I shook my head, saying it wasn't Mom. The Judge went to his room.

"Stop it," I whispered.

"*Ouch!* That nerve does hurt!"

"Drew—"

He laughed. "Okay. Thought I'd get under your skin a little, so you can see how it feels. So, you were with that fruit, weren't you?"

I plopped down upon the living room sofa. "I was with the Judge and Grandma."

He stopped laughing. "Nothing happened?" he asked, turning serious.

"No."

"Oh. Good. Good, because it'd just suck if something happened to your family. You know?"

I could have told him. I could have told him, but I had nothing to tell. "I know. What is it, Drew?"

"I was wondering," he said. "Have you heard about Brad? He's missing. He's missing and no one knows where he is."

That was all I needed to hear. Yet another bit of family news, about my cousin Brad Morgan, the tough guy. Drew was doing more than just gossip. He was seeking information. I turned the tables on him. "Any ideas?"

"I was going to ask you that, since he is your cousin. I mean, I know you aren't in the same circles. But . . ." his voice trailed off. Then, he cleared it. "I was just wondering."

"Did you try Marshall? I mean, he does know everything."

Drew laughed. "Jealous type. I'll let you say that. No way am I going to get in the middle of a family squabble."

I spun on the sofa, stretching my legs on the cushions, with my shoes on. The Judge picked up the extension in his bedroom. "It's for me," I said.

"I know," the Judge said. "Hello, Drew."

"Hello, sir," Drew said, nervous and solicitous at the same time. "How are you doing tonight?"

"Very well, thank you," the Judge said. "Skip, get your shoes off the sofa."

I slipped my tennis shoes off and rested my feet in the arm of the sofa. For a moment, I looked at my socks and examined the impressions of my toes as Drew made small talk with the Judge. Then, the small talk ended, and the Judge hung up. Drew was drinking something. It sounded like soda.

"I like talking to your parents," Drew finally said. "They're so good to me."

"Yeah." I sighed. "I think they're getting a divorce."

"Huh?"

"I said I think my parents are getting a divorce."

There was a stunned silence on Drew's end of the line. I could hear a door close. "What gives you that impression?"

"Mom's at my Aunt Carolyn's tonight. She didn't come here."

"Oh." I could hear water run, then a flush. I imagined Drew zipping up. There was the squeak of a door opening, then of another door closing. "I'm sure it's nothing. Your parents've been together for a long time, right?"

"Thirty-plus years."

"That's too long to get a divorce," he said. "Don't worry about it. They'll work it out. You'll see."

Without saying much, I nodded. The Judge came downstairs. Crossing the living room, he poured himself a rum and Coke, got himself a cigar, and went into his den. He turned on the radio and the second movement of a Beethoven symphony waltzed from the massive speakers.

"You need for me to get off?" I yelled into the den.

The Judge stepped into the den French door. "You needn't yell. I'm not deaf; at least, not yet. You're all right. Take your time."

"How's he doing?" Drew asked.

"Fine. Who?"

"Judge Macalester."

"He's doing fine."

After that, the conversation lingered, then it died an effortless, natural death. "Don't forget to read your *Crucible*," Drew said, as though I needed reminding. I grunted that I would. Then, I hung up, without saying very much more than, "You gonna pick me up tomorrow morning?"

"Oh, I'll pick you up tomorrow," he said. "Just you make sure not to run off with Armstrong." Laughing, he hung up.

The Beethoven symphony concluded its second movement and jumped into its third. The piece was so familiar that I could have almost placed the orchestra and conductor. Though good, my ear wasn't that distinguished. My curiosity got the better of me. After resting on the sofa, and listening, I wandered into the den to ask the Judge, whose experience made him expert in deciphering pieces.

He was unaffected by the music. Sitting in a straightback chair beneath a halogen lamp, he worked a yellow pad with a pen. On the paper, a study of black lines licked its edges, then ran back toward the middle. Cigar smoke floated in the room like clouds.

"Working on an opinion?" I asked, leaning forward.

"Writing a letter," he said. "To Clifford."

I could see Uncle Clifford, in his Kansas City home, trying to read the Judge's writing, extending his arms and holding the paper to the light to get a fix on the Judge's microscopic writing. "Tell Uncle Clifford 'hey' for me."

The Judge looked up and smiled. "Always do."

"You going to tell him about Mom?"

He rested his pen. "I really haven't decided. I might. I might just let Mother tell him."

I nodded. Bert came in and rubbed against my leg. That made my toes itch. "If you do, tell him Mom's doing fine."

He picked up the pen and wrote a line. "Anything else I should add?"

I thought. "I don't think so."

He continued writing. I stood there, trying to recall my reason for entering his den in the first place. Then, he said, "Don't forget to do your reading for English."

"Did she tell you I got some reading?"

He rested the pen again and looked up. "She didn't have to." He held the yellow pad before him and reviewed his writing. He listened to the music. "Beethoven," he said, "Symphony number four, third movement." He set the pad on his lap and started writing again. Something made him stop. He sipped his drink and mumbled something about putting too much ice in it and about needing to add sugar water to stretch the liquor. Then, my father remembered me. Holding his mouth, he considered me. "Everything will work out, Skip."

I mumbled something. Maybe about guessing so. Then, taking my shoes, I tried to forget that evening and most of the day.

Chapter Five

I awoke Saturday morning with a slightly sour taste in my mouth. I assumed it came from eating turkey stew. On second thought, the bad taste probably had more to do with a bad dream of some sort. It still nags at me.

I remember seeing myself in the mirror and looking a mess. I had tumbled into bed in my underwear and an old T-shirt. I wore the slept-in look poorly. My hair, always short, was nappy. How much I loathed having nappy hair, I cannot begin to tell you. Worst of all was my face. I had slept on it and it looked like I had been slapped silly so hard God's hand had left an imprint.

It was past ten already. I imagined the Judge was somewhere on the fourth fairway, because he had a nine o'clock tee time most Saturdays. He was probably retrieving the ball from out of bounds, because he probably sliced it, and then he'd toss it onto the fairway for his third stroke. Ken Langston and Dennis Morgan were his regular golf partners. They knew to turn a blind eye whenever the Judge played. Who filled out the foursome? I suppose it could be Marshall. He was a good golfer, even as a kid. But that morning, like me, he was commanded by Dr. Levin to appear at the high school by eleven, so he was highly unlikely. Brad also played well, when he was not in heat or trying to prove his "homeboy" credentials by playing basketball with riff-raff in some park. It could have been Calvin Wilson, the Judge's first law partner, who himself retired recently as a county judge, or it could have been Mom's current partner, Vince Wharton, who at times ingratiated himself to the Judge by granting "mulligans," whatever they were. Then, I thought Dr. Kidd, the orthodontist next door, may have been brave enough to join the cousins, because the Judge hated socializing with other lawyers.

I was alone. Hallelujah! I had privacy.

In that context, it just didn't make sense to get up and rush to get dressed on Saturday morning. It made sense to do something only be-

ing alone permitted an almost sixteen-year-old guy to do. I returned
to bed, this time leaving my T-shirt and underwear on the floor.

I was naked in bed. I loved that feeling! Outside, our yardman cut
the front lawn. The sound was enough to make me daydream.

I don't want to tell anyone about my daydreams. At almost sixteen,
my daydreams were complicated stories of seduction, sometimes of
domination. At almost sixteen, I daydreamed about faces I had seen
within the previous day. For whatever reason, my daydream that
morning started and ended with Mr. Armstrong.

In my daydream, I gave him the name Nick, which I soon found
out really was his name. He came into my room and stood before me
in a swagger, like Donatello's *David,* complete with even a feather in
his boot, caressing his calf. He joined me in bed and, like the feather,
his soft, pure hands caressed me until we laid on top of each other,
stomach to stomach, flesh to flesh.

And then, after that, I was ready to get dressed. Since I was alone it
was nothing to walk naked into the bathroom and to shower with the
door open. Showering and washing my face and brushing my hair got
the mess out. After that, I didn't look too bad.

I dressed. Shorts and T-shirt. And, because it was a pretty morning,
I chose to chuck convention. No socks. Prep . . . so utterly prep.

The faint smell of Captain Black in the house confirmed the Judge
was long gone. As usual, he left the radio in his bedroom on, and a soprano sang *"O Mio Babbino Caro"* from *Gianni Schicchi,* with orchestral
accompaniment. Heading downstairs, I considered cloak-draped di-
vas navigating pigeons in Venetian piazze. Puccini always gives me
that thought.

I was hungry. I had a taste for hickory smoked bacon, thanks to the
pipe smoke. When I got downstairs, I heard something moving about
in the kitchen, like a grade school gerbil rattling about in a cage.

"Mom?"

"It's me," a voice said. It was young, male, a little cracked. I knew I
had heard it before. Was it the young man of this morning's daydream?

When I got to the kitchen, I had to kick myself for not realizing
that "me" was Drew. He was at the kitchen table, in Mom's spot,

drinking orange juice, eating toast, and reading the *Courier* business page.

"Good morning, Arthur. Did you have pleasant dreams?"

"Fine." My daydream was something I could never tell him, as it was with all my other daydreams, including those that featured him. I was a bit annoyed at Drew being alone with me in my house, but I tried not to show it. I headed for the refrigerator.

"The Judge said it was all right," Drew said, referring to the toast. "You don't mind?"

I poured myself a glass of orange juice. "His house."

"I figured that. Did you sleep well?"

Were you here when I was traipsing around naked upstairs? What were you doing when Armstrong and I were doing my daydream? Did you peek? "I slept the way I always do," I said.

"On your back?"

I drank, then shook my head. He was getting too many details.

"Stomach?" Drew shivered and smiled. "Ouch!"

Drew started laughing. He was laughing so uncontrollably he was snorting. He did that until I threw a dish towel and got him in the head. Besides, what was so funny about me sleeping on my stomach? Do you always sleep on your back, Andrew, in just your underwear, all the time, there in your room, in the middle of your house full of women? If you think my sleeping habits are funny, think about yours.

Whatever. Time to move on.

I fixed my breakfast, which consisted of a zapped piece of bacon on wheat toast. Drew saw that as an opening for a comment or two. This time, he let his opinion percolate before saying something. By then, I was sitting across from him at the kitchen table. It was still my spot at the table.

"You're gonna get zits like mushrooms," Drew said finally as I ate. "Get something healthy, like oatmeal."

I scrunched up my nose at the thought. In my family, only old people ate oatmeal. Other than that, no one in my family ate oatmeal, because we could afford not to. Must you eat oatmeal to have enough for lunch, Andrew? "Did you get oatmeal?"

"No," he said. "I got toast, but that's beside the point. You're still a kid, Arthur. You need to eat more healthily than a piece of bacon from the microwave."

"Stop trying to sound like my mother." I continued eating. *Even if she's not here, and you are sitting in her spot.*

"Okay," he said. "Be like that. Live in cholesterol city. Die at seventy."

I ate my sandwich. When I was finished, we were ready to go. Drew reminded me to retrieve my *Crucible,* still just inside my room, where I had dropped it the afternoon before. Leaving Drew at the front door, I scurried upstairs past the masks.

"Hey!" Drew called out. "Where's the socks?"

I stopped and looked at my feet. Yes, my ankles were quite bare. "I decided to go without today."

Drew nodded. "Does the Judge know?"

"Whether he knows or doesn't know," I shrugged, "I'm going sockless anyway."

I continued upstairs. I got the book, and returned to Drew. He waited with his arms folded. "Got your key?" he asked.

I checked my pockets. My key was among the things, like change, I stuffed into my pockets after putting my wallet away. But my key was not there. I looked at Drew. Shaking his head, he dangled the house key by the ring's monogrammed "M" fob. I snatched it and put it into my pants pocket.

"Come on," Drew said. He locked and closed the front door and we piled into his car for the ride to school.

There was a standard route Drew took to get to the high school, which, ironically, was the same route the Judge had taken to get me to my early morning meeting with Dr. Levin. We were to go through Jefferson Heights, through uptown, to get to the high school. No sooner did we begin did we stop. Marshall had crossed our path. Drew honked and rolled down the window.

"Hey," Drew shouted, "wanna ride?"

My cousin, independent Marshall, was walking, about to cross the park and go to the high school. The temperature was bound to get up into the eighties again, but Marshall had on his beige Windbreaker, as usual, sleeves rolled up to the elbows. He, too, had a book bag, but he lugged it by its fag end, which barely kept it off the ground and made it seem as though he were ready to brain someone with it. His hair was longer than mine. It looked damp and just somewhat combed. He was busy chewing a thumbnail. He mulled over Drew's offer. "What the hell," he said. He accepted the ride. He sat in the back.

"We might as well go together," Drew said, releasing the brake, "since we're all going to the same place, you know?"

Marshall nodded. It made sense to him. He stared through me.

"Hey," I said.

"Hey yourself," Marshall said.

"Heard about Brad?" I asked.

"Heard about your mom?" he asked.

"What about my mom?"

Marshall rolled down the window and spat out the thumbnail. "Oh, she's doing fine. So claims Carolyn. No more news about Brad."

Drew watched Marshall through the rearview mirror. Drew had a good relationship with Marshall, but, like a lot of Whitmaners, he tended to treat him with a long-handled spoon because he knew how dangerous it was for his kind to get too close. "Where'd he go?"

"Brad?" Marshall sighed. "Who knows."

"He might've gone off to St. Louis," Drew said. "Not that I'm saying he would go off to a baseball game and get lost. It's just that, well, St. Louis is where I'd go, if I disappeared for a day."

There was silence for a few minutes. It was the type of silence that Marshall used for sneering. I looked back at him to see if he were sneering. Staring right through Drew, he had his lip curled, as though there were something rancid in the air, like he was near some trash.

"Hey, don't do that," I said.

"Don't do what?" Marshall asked, blinking.

"That thing that you do."

"What?" Marshall asked.

I tried to approximate that curled lip. The best I could do was to scrunch my nose up. I imagined I even crossed my eyes. Glancing at me, and not getting a full look at what I was doing, Drew laughed. "What?"

"Nothing," I said to Drew. *I don't think you would understand, Drew.* Shaking my head, I mouthed to Marshall that he shouldn't do that again. Marshall just smiled and looked out the car window. My scolding stuck to him like water to a duck's back. So much for subtlety. He knew what he was doing. He knew what he was doing and he knew it would have hurt Drew. Bastard!

We were among the handful of students at the high school that morning. Being a Saturday, the vast majority were members of the football or volleyball teams, or were there for Saturday detention. If the Pit had forty cars parked in it, I'd be surprised. Our instructions were to be at the auditorium by eleven. We were there with a few minutes to spare.

The auditorium—or "theater," as Dr. Levin called it—had its lights on. On the stage a two-tier set from the previous spring's *Man of La Mancha* was still up, having been left for that semester's stagecraft class to deconstruct. To the side of the stage, plaster urns sat with fake philodendron stalks with a sheen of dust on them. Needless to say, they hadn't been watered in a while. Behind the urns the heavy velvet curtains, crimson and drawn back like a girl's hair, stood as silent as tombstones.

Drew and I stood near the stage while Marshall took a seat at the exact, dead center of the auditorium. He draped his elbows on the armrests and waited.

Joel Whitney flew in next. Thinking he was late (which he was), Joel ran down the right aisle, carrying his French horn. He had "sectionals" in the band room that afternoon, a rehearsal requirement for the marching band. He ran past Marshall, then stopped and turned around.

"Where is everybody?" Joel asked.

"We *are* everybody," Marshall pronounced.

Joel sighed and swung the French horn over his shoulder. "Frank, I mean."

Almost on cue, Frank entered, wearing Bermuda shorts again (that was his standard outfit until Columbus Day), and his hands in his pockets. Again, the shorts hung low on his hips. His hair was wet and swept back in sequenced lines, like he didn't have a care in the world. Drew pointed to Frank, and Joel looked his way, then he left the French horn in the aisle, and both he and Frank approached the stage. All we needed was Marshall, but Marshall's posture made it clear he wasn't moving until he had a good reason, and, knowing him, our being there wasn't reason enough.

The four of us stood around, occupied by small talk, until Mr. Armstrong flitted into the auditorium. I say *flitted* because he got on my last nerve running late and making us wait like dildos. Some may say he sashayed or waltzed in, but to me he flitted like a trapped butterfly. Gracelessly, he stepped over Joel's French horn case.

Was this really the guy I daydreamed about within the past hour? He seemed so—so—queer. Why did I have to daydream about such a fag?

"Come on," Mr. Armstrong said to Marshall.

Marshall, carrying his book, approached the stage. He was so underwhelmed by the event, as the totally pissed look on his face made clear. He looked as though he had better things to do with his Saturday, like pitching out of the sand trap at the ninth hole. The rest of us wished he were there, for our sakes. Marshall glared at us. We stood.

"I'm sorry I'm late," Mr. Armstrong said, setting the satchel in a seat near the stage, "but my Tawny called just as I was fixin' to leave and talking to her set me back about fifteen minutes."

He grinned, blinking. We looked at him. Does he really think we'd believe he had a "she," some gal named "Tawny," in his life? What does he think we are? Fools?

"What's the buzz?" Frank asked, folding his arms. "Tell me what's happening."

Mr. Armstrong cleared his throat. He rummaged through his satchel. "It's Dr. Levin's idea. I think she wants each of you to read a part in *The Crucible*."

"The *whole* play?" Joel asked.

"Just a scene or two," Mr. Armstrong said. He produced *The Crucible*. "I think she has it picked out."

"There's not enough of us," Marshall observed.

Blinking, Mr. Armstrong didn't quite know what to say. He shrugged. Leave it to my cousin to throw an apple into the wedding.

"Well?" Drew demanded.

"I'm just the messenger," Mr. Armstrong said finally. "And the message is she'll have something picked out."

"Well," Frank began, "what scene is she gonna give us?"

Mr. Armstrong pushed his glasses against his nose. "She said she was going to bring it."

"Where is she?" Drew demanded.

Mr. Armstrong shrugged again. "I'm just the messenger. No one tells me a thing—I'm just the messenger."

Marshall jumped onto the stage and dangled his legs. Now, he looked like he had Mr. Armstrong right where he wanted him. "She must've told you something."

"Just to meet her here," Mr. Armstrong said, "and that's it."

Marshall, who never wore a watch, looked at his wrist as if he had one, like this delay really had interrupted his golf game. He sighed a little, which said enough.

Before it got extremely ugly, a door opened, and down the aisle came Dr. Levin, dressed in a dramatic, deep blue cape fringed in gold tassels. She wore large, heavy plastic sunglasses that made her look blind. Beneath the sunglasses, a smile sparkled. When she got close enough to say something, she set the red and white canvas tote bag from the day before in a seat in the third row and sat behind it.

"You are all here," she said. "Perfect."

"Why are we here?" Joel asked.

Dr. Levin dropped no beads. "You are here because I told you to be here," she said through a smile. "So, hush up and listen. Gentleman," she continued, folding her hands together, "as you know, you are here for skipping my class to go to a baseball game, necessitating a suitable and appropriate response that will imprint the nonsense of skipping my class. And so," she reached into her bag, "I give you this."

Like the proverbial magician, Dr. Levin produced five booklets, bound with colored cardboard sheets and bright brass fasteners. I saw Joel's eyes bugged out and I heard him gulp.

"This is the play you are to do," Dr. Levin explained.

"The whole thing?" Joel asked.

Dr. Levin's smile broadened. "It is a simple thing, and one I think you will enjoy."

"Is that *The Crucible*?" Frank asked.

Dr. Levin brought the booklets to her chest. "In a way. This is your crucible. After handling it, you will acknowledge the futility of skipping my class."

She stood and handed the first booklet to Drew, who fanned through it and mouthed "Oh, shit." I took my booklet and weighed it in my hands. It felt like a good fifty-minute presentation, at least.

"Who'll get parts?" I asked.

"You all will," she said. She handed a booklet to Marshall, who took it like a used tissue. "There's just enough for each of you."

"Who wrote it?" Marshall asked.

"I did," she said. She gave booklets to Frank and Joel, then tucked her hands beneath her cape. "Did you really think I'd give you something as precious as Shakespeare or Ibsen?"

Before Marshall could spit out anything witty, the door opened again and down the aisle came Miss Newman, the art teacher, whose long, floral, wraparound skirt and pulled-back hair in a combed bun said she had spent a lifetime entering and exiting. Dr. Levin acknowledged her momentarily, then plucked from her tote a thick manila envelope.

"Nick," she said to Mr. Armstrong, handing him the envelope, "you're in charge."

Dr. Levin grabbed her tote bag and started up the aisle for the door. She and Miss Newman barely missed each other.

"But—" Joel began.

"Just follow the yellow brick road," Dr. Levin said. And, with a wave of her hand, she was gone.

"Yeah," Frank said, flipping through his booklet. "This sure ain't Kansas."

From somewhere, Miss Newman picked up a long, broad walking staff that was more than a staff. It was more of a board, which she clomped with every step. Once she got closer, I could see her heavy black eyeliner and a hint of the bluish silver eye shadow she applied carefully above her eyes. When she blinked, she revealed her black Egyptian lids. Her lipstick was the only thing applied with less than deliberate care. The uneven line around her bottom lip seemed to have been put there by an unsteady hand. I had not had much contact with Miss Newman beyond seniors claiming her true occupation was gypsy. She stood before us and cleared her throat.

"I believe," she began in her slight Spanish accent, "she left you in charge, Mr. Armstrong?"

"Yes, ma'am," Mr. Armstrong said. He offered her the manila envelope, but she declined to take it.

"I need a young man who is good with numbers," she said.

We all looked to Joel, our mathematician, who was reluctant.

"You got the 'A' in geometry, Whitney," Marshall said.

"Geometry!" Miss Newman exclaimed. "You must be a genius. It shall be you."

She wrapped an arm around Joel and pulled him up the side stairs to the stage. Joel looked so embarrassed he almost peed on himself, a common response for him. When she got him to the stage, Miss Newman eased Joel to the center of the two-tier set. Then, she let go of his arm.

"Light, please," she said, and a limelight shone from the balcony. "I do costumes for student plays," she explained, "and, at Dr. Levin's request, I shall measure you for costumes. This"—she clomped forward her staff—"shall be the unit of measure. It is marked all the way to five feet. I shall use him, for example. Stand up straight," she commanded Joel, who was slouching. "Mr. Armstrong, assist me, please."

Mr. Armstrong mounted the stage with the envelope in hand. Taking his hand, Miss Newman knelt and brought the staff along Joel's inseam. She steadied it, and made Mr. Armstrong hold the staff against Joel's leg.

"Bet he likes that," Drew whispered, "the fruit."

"Silence," Miss Newman commanded. "Eccentric artist at work." She measured Joel's inseam. "Twenty-nine and three-quarters inches. Write it down."

Mr. Armstrong scribbled the measurement on the manila envelope, letting go of the staff in the process. The staff would have fallen, but Joel captured it by the tip of his fingers. That was the most he did. He didn't go unnoticed.

"Thank you," Miss Newman said to Joel. "Twenty-nine and three-quarters inches. You remember for me?"

Joel nodded.

"Good," she said. "Stand clear."

Joel stepped aside. Miss Newman pointed at Frank and he went up to be measured. She went through him as dispassionately as eating cornflakes. When it came to me, Mr. Armstrong helped steady the staff against my leg, and, in the process, he brushed against my thigh. That was all I needed. I started to get hard. I was afraid I would show. The limelight burned my eyes. I looked for someplace safe.

"Just stand still," Mr. Armstrong said. "It'll all be over in a sec."

I looked at Joel, who stood toward the wings watching me. From the way his eyes grew, I could tell he was watching my groin. He glanced up toward my face. When our eyes met, he quickly glanced away.

"You are just thirty inches, my son," Miss Newman said to me. "Congratulations. Now, stand aside."

Taking my arm, Miss Newman whipped me away, toward Joel, who was still staring, and who still looked away when he noticed I was noticing.

"Joysticker," I muttered as I passed Joel. His eyes simply bugged out, like a little bird.

It was Drew's turn. He leapt onto the stage, declining stairs. He got to his feet and walked into the limelight. Once there, he snatched the staff from Mr. Armstrong. "I can do that myself," he said. Having seen it done before, he steadied the staff against his inseam, resting it against his body. He stood straight. "It's thirty-four," he said.

"I must measure," Miss Newman said.

"I'm telling you," Drew said, chin up and eyes focused on the seats. "It's thirty-four."

Miss Newman looked at him for a quick second and then started to mark his inseam. "Long legs," she said. "Thirty-three and seven-eighths."

"Told you. Thirty-four."

Drew tossed the staff to Mr. Armstrong, who almost didn't catch it. Drew crossed in front of Miss Newman and jumped from the stage to the floor. Marshall was last. We all looked to him.

"My dear, young Mr. Langston," Miss Newman said, holding her hand out. "If you please."

"Skip and I are the same," Marshall said. "Thirty inches."

"C'mon, bro," Frank said from the seats. "If we got to go through this humiliation, you do too."

With his now thoroughly pissed look on his face, Marshall went to the spot on the stage. "I got your 'bro,' *bro*," he said to Frank as Miss Newman brought the staff to his body. She measured.

"Young Mr. Langston is thirty and one-eighth," Miss Newman pronounced. "Just a hair—as you say—taller than our young Mr. Macalester."

Marshall and Mr. Armstrong helped Miss Newman to her feet. Wrapping her arm around the staff, she clapped dust off her hands. "Off," she said. The limelight clicked off. She turned to face me and Joel. "Genius, who got 'A' in Geometry. Add: thirty and one-eighth, thirty-three and seven-eighths, thirty exactly, twenty-nine and three-quarters and—how long are you, Kotter?"

Frank smiled and blushed. "That depends upon what state—"

"Ah, yes!" she exclaimed. She must not have heard him. "I remember now: thirty-three and one-quarter. Now, add. How many yards of fabric we need?"

Joel's eyes got even bigger. He wondered what had he done in Gerald Banks' class to deserve this reckoning. "I need to get my calculator."

"No calculator," she said. "You good with numbers, got 'A' in Geometry. Use head."

"His head is his calculator," Frank mumbled.

"Not using head? I will tell you, then. Four yards and a little over twenty-three inches," Miss Newman said. "You wonder how I know? I will tell you how I know. I used my head. In Havana, we had no calculators. We had to use head," she said, jabbing Joel in the skull, "so, we learned to use head! I knew, because I used my head!"

Gratefully, the bell rang, a signal for the kids in Saturday detention. That was Miss Newman's signal as well. Taking her staff, she left the auditorium, muttering Spanish all the way to the door. Afterward, Frank mocked her, *"We had to use head, so we learned to use head, because I used my head!"* He thumped Joel in the head and laughed. *"Head . . . head . . . head . . . head!"*

"Let's settle down," Mr. Armstrong said. "We still got some work to do."

"Like what?" Drew demanded.

Mr. Armstrong blinked. He opened his manila envelope and took out his copy of Dr. Levin's play. "We still got to decide on parts."

Drew gave him a harsh, cynical look. He slammed his copy of the play against the auditorium floor, which made everyone jumped. He looked like he had something to say, but he just stood there, arms akimbo and head tilted back a little. He patted his mouth.

"Maybe, we can do it in Dr. Levin's room on Monday," Mr. Armstrong suggested. "You know, acting under her guidance."

"That sounds better," Drew finally said.

I picked up Drew's copy and handed it to him. Joel grabbed his French horn and Marshall got his book bag from the seat at dead center of the auditorium. Drew shoved his copy of the play under his arm and Frank rolled his into a cylinder.

"Well," Mr. Armstrong said timidly, "I guess I'll see you in class Monday."

Drew burned him a vicious look. "Count on it."

Mr. Armstrong blinked again. Quietly, head down like a slapped puppy, he went up the aisle and left.

After that, I did not think about opening that play, or about Mr. Armstrong, that much. To me, it was just another assignment, meant for me to give a double-take once, then lose somewhere only I could find while cleaning my room. For me, Drew's behavior was the concern. He had been acting like a little bitch lately. What time of the month are you in, friend?

We had nothing to do that day; Drew and I decided to roam. After all, what was the worst thing they could do to us? Send us to the principal for Saturday detention? We were not that far from Mr. Scott's room, where we knew he had his set of Saturday detainees doing American history as punishment. The thing was that Drew and I did not want to be *seen* going to his room willingly. We had to sneak by. And, sure enough, Mr. Scott waited with a smile. I tried sneaking past him, but he caught me by the neck.

"Macalester," Mr. Scott said, pulling me out of the doorway. "So good of you to grace us with your presence. Say, how many home runs did Brooks and Frank Robinson have, combined?"

I cringed. Mr. Scott had ahold of my neck so tightly I felt the blood being clamped from my head. "I dunno. I hate baseball."

"'I dunno. I hate baseball.' But I thought you love baseball," he said, tightening his grip. "I thought you love baseball so much you'd skip school for it. At least, that's what I heard."

I saw Frank, giggling, try to get past us. He barely got into the door when Mr. Scott grabbed ahold of him by the neck. Frank winced.

"Isn't that right, Kotter?" Mr. Scott asked.

"*Oooh!* Isn't what right, Mr. Scott, sir?"

"Isn't that right that Macalester here loves baseball so much he'd skip school for it?"

"I don't know about that, Mr. Scott, sir!"

"You don't?"

"No, sir!"

"But I heard you and he love baseball so much you'd skip school for it."

Frank winced again. "Where'd you hear that from, Mr. Scott, sir?"

"Where'd I hear that from?"

"Yes, sir!"

"Why, a little bird told me."

Mr. Scott let us go and dropped us into his room. Drew was not that far behind. We went to our seats and tried getting our necks circulating enough blood to ease the pain of having been clamped. My neck throbbed through Mr. Scott's presentation on the Articles of Confederation. His Saturday detainees glazed over. As was the case during the week, we were forbidden from dozing off during one of Mr. Scott's presentations—to do so was as treacherous as flying the Confederate flag on Independence Day.

"What're you in for?" whispered one of the detainees, a sophomore with bad acne burns, who sat in front of Drew and me.

"Why," Mr. Scott responded (the guy had bat ears), "they're in here because they rooted for the Mets on Thursday."

I sank low in my seat as the detainees, freshmen and sophomores all, catcalled their disapproval. Frank got the worst of it, because he was a baseball player. I watched him from across the room. Busily, he prattled through a collection of rolled notebooks and folded loose-leaf papers while massaging his neck, which must have hurt like hell. A pair of girls, flirty girls, not too bad looking, teased him. He teased them back, and asked them to rub his neck, which one girl did, giggling. Mr. Scott looked at them wide mouthed.

"Kotter!"

"What?"

"Can you save your necking for during the week?" Mr. Scott bellowed.

The detainees hooted. Embarrassed, the girl shrank behind Frank. She laughed a little, and turned red. Frank, however, didn't miss a beat. He batted his eyes.

"Ah, Mr. Scott," Frank said with a pronounced lisp, flipping his hand like a tortilla, "you know I neck with only the boys!"

Again, the detainees hooted. Some of the guys flicked spit wads in Frank's direction. Even I did. Mr. Scott raised his hands and tried to regain control, but bedlam had broken out, and there was little for Mr. Scott to do but blow spit wads himself. That was enough of a bizarre thing to make some of the detainees throw back at him, and some of the rest of us stare in amazement. Soon, bedlam subsided. Mr. Scott, who was using the shell of an ink pen to blow, sealed the pen and smiled.

"Now you know how silly you clowns looked," Mr. Scott said. "Like a slew of little kids."

For that, Frank tore off a scrap of paper, wadded it, and chucked it at the man.

Drew did not laugh or hoot, or throw spit wads, for that matter, something he did almost every other day. Instead, I could feel his hot breath on my neck, and occasionally his hands as well, warm and comforting, and trying to massage. He stopped when Mr. Scott's eyes seemed to go our way, only to resume when the man turned around or looked at someone else. Once, in a lull, I put my hand on the back of my neck (my neck still ached), and there was Drew's hand. I felt his short, crewed nails and the light calluses on his fingertips. It seemed I could feel his pulse, his heart beating rapidly. One of his fingers reached up and touched the back of my neck, where the hair was, and seemed to play with it as though it tickled him. I smiled.

"Drew—"

"*Don't touch me!*" Drew blurted out, yanking his hands from my neck.

The detainees oooed.

"Keep your hands to yourselves, kids," Mr. Scott warned, and then he continued with the Articles of Confederation. No matter. He would have to repeat all of it in the future.

Frank, Drew, and I stayed until lunch. By that time, the spit wads had been swept up and discarded by the responsible ones and my neck had stopped throbbing. I was watching some sophomores—those who only had a half day of detention—go up the hill behind the high school, heading toward uptown, and I wondered why I couldn't be a sophomore anymore. I saw a Volvo in the faculty parking and thought about my mother and I wondered how she was doing. I was still in that state when Drew began a breathless tirade.

"Well?" Drew asked. "Did you read it? Did you read what that fruit gave us?"

Frank blinked. "Which fruit?"

"That fruit Armstrong," Drew said. "He's, like, the only fruit on campus. Did you read it?"

I shook my head. Really, I had no idea what he was talking about. Besides, whatever Drew's problem with Armstrong, he really should give it a rest. Then, I remembered the play. I remembered hearing Drew leaf through pages in Mr. Scott's room.

"You, of all people, should really read more," Drew said to me. "I dunno how you can keep from reading it."

We entered the West building, for no better reason than it was where Dr. Levin's room was, and we were hoping for the offhanded chance that she was still there. Drew gave the subject no rest. He pursued the conversation. He kept saying "it . . . it." Frank stopped just short of Dr. Levin's room. "What's wrong with it?" he asked.

"'What's wrong with it!'" Drew exclaimed. "You tell me. Take a look."

In the middle of the corridor, Frank did just that. He took out the play, rolled into a cylinder, and flipped through it. "So?"

"'So?' Is that all you got to say? 'So?' Take a look at the parts."

Frank turned to the front. I tried looking, too, but Frank was too tall for me. "I'm looking," Frank said.

"And?"

"And—"

Drew huffed. He smiled hello to Dr. Levin, who was still in the building, getting work done in her room. Then, those gray eyes flashed. Drew gritted his teeth. "There are no parts for guys."

"So?"

Drew almost exploded. "You wanna do the play in drag?"

"What're you worried about?" Frank laughed. "You got good legs."

Frank put away the play and we headed into Dr. Levin's room. Dr. Levin smiled at us as we came in. "Got measured?" she asked. We nodded and sat in our seats. On the chalkboard before us were her plans for Arthur Miller. Monologues, readings, reports. Our work on *The Crucible* was to stretch ten days. At the end of her plans was a starred note. PERFORMANCE IN THEATER, it said.

"Is that us?" I asked.

Dr. Levin swiveled in her chair to take a look at the board. In doing so, she gave me a full view of my father's congressional picture. "Yes," she said. "That is you."

She said it so matter-of-fact that it seemed she had said so countless times. She said it the way an experienced teacher would. I think I had heard someone say that, by my junior year, she had been teaching about thirty-six years. I had also heard someone say teaching is an art. If so, Dr. Levin had that art down cold.

I was so transfixed upon Dr. Levin that I did not notice my father, the Judge, standing in the door. Drew saw him first. He stood for my father, which tipped Dr. Levin off. She looked to the doorway. I followed her eyes. Behold, the Judge was there, fresh from his golf game.

"Lunch, Genie?" he asked her.

"Excuse us, gentlemen," Dr. Levin said.

The performance was something for another day. We stood as though a dismissal bell had rung. Before we left, though, Drew stood in the doorway, next to the Judge, arms crossed for some reason until the Judge's glare made him uncross them. Dr. Levin was still at her desk.

"Dr. Levin," Drew said. "There's something we got to talk to you about."

Dr. Levin folded her hands behind her head. "Make it quick. I can't keep Judge Macalester waiting."

"Oh, it's just about selecting parts," I said, quickly. Drew glared at me.

"It's more basic than that," Drew said. "Tell her, Frank."

Frank looked dumbstruck. Then, Drew gave him a look, eyes very intense, like shooting daggers. "Oh, that," Frank concluded. "It's about the play."

"What about the play?" she asked.

Frank sat into a seat and unrolled the play in his hands. "I personally think it's a very good play."

"Thank you. What about the play?"

Frank looked at Drew. Drew gave him that look again. "It's just that—well," Frank paused, "about the parts—"

"What about the parts?"

Frank sighed. "Well, it wouldn't have been written for a bunch of girls, would it?"

Drew threw up his hands. Dr. Levin didn't seem to notice. The Judge did. His look said he liked that not one single bit. "That drama really wasn't necessary, Mr. Ford," he said. Drew mumbled an apology.

"The play was written for five young men who skipped my class. Anything else?" Dr. Levin looked to Drew, as did Frank. Drew was scratching his head.

"All the play's parts're for girls," Drew said. "We can't go on stage playing girls—"

"Why not?" she asked.

"Why not?" Drew repeated. He furrowed his brow. "It's just that people'll think we're weird, playing girls. That's all."

"What's weird about it?" she asked. "Most crossdressers are hetero-sexual. Is that what's bothering you?"

"*No.*"

"Then, what?"

We all looked at Drew, who looked at his feet. After that, the sub-ject died. Dr. Levin opened the play and assigned the three of us parts. I was given the role of Laura, "a good girl," according to her character description.

"It's meaty," Dr. Levin explained. "The type of something you can sink your teeth into."

I tried not to smile too much. Thanks to braces years before, I was somewhat self-conscious about my teeth.

After that, we left quickly. The Judge closed the classroom door behind us. That perplexed me a bit—I mean, what was between him and my English teacher? I tried not thinking about it. On our way to his car, I looked at Drew. I could see he was a little irritated. From the way he looked, I dared not ask him.

"I ain't playing no girl," Drew blurted out when we got to the Pit. "You can do what you want. For me, I ain't gonna play no girl."

"What's the worst thing that can happen?"

"The worst thing? The worst thing is that one of those major pricks can pick at you and pick at you until you are a girl." Drew threw open his car door and slammed his play into the backseat. "And I'm not gonna take it, and, by Reagan's nose, I don't think you should take it, either. And it's because of that fruit Armstrong." He jabbed his car top with his finger. "And, what I'm gonna do is tell that fruit Armstrong just where he can stick his goddamn shitty play."

"It's not Armstrong's play. It's Dr. Levin's."

"It's that fruit's play," Drew reiterated, jabbing his finger into the car top. "That pass-the-buck act might work in Podunk, Mississippi, but like hell will it work in Illinois."

Drew climbed into the car, as did I. Before driving off, he sat be-hind the wheel, breathing heavily. I was almost too off balanced to say anything, all things considered. We sat there for what must have been five minutes.

"What're you going to do?" I finally asked.

"I'll find something."

"No, I mean, are you going somewhere to eat or are we just gonna sit here and rage, or what?"

Drew looked at me for a moment. Then he started laughing. "What, Arthur? Hungry?"

"Yeah, I'm hungry. After this morning, I'm interested in finding something to eat."

Drew continued laughing. "Okay. For you, we'll find something to eat."

He started the car and led it out of the Pit. For the moment, at least, Mr. Armstrong and Dr. Levin's play were relegated to the backs of our minds, where they would stay until we dredged them up again and the old conversation would kick us in our faces.

Chapter Six

After lunch Drew and I played tennis. When I returned home, the Judge wasn't there. It was after three o'clock; did lunch with Dr. Levin take so long? I was hungry again. The Judge's meat loaf was long gone. In the refrigerator, I found spinach lasagna, which Cynthia made earlier that week, on Wednesday. I had eaten that alone, Mom and the Judge busy with whatever well into Wednesday night. Bert twisted around my ankles.

"Well," I said to her, "it's you and me again. Alone again, naturally."

A chunk of the spinach lasagna went into the microwave. When it was finished, I looked at it on its paper plate. I was sitting in my chair at the kitchen table. What sense did that make? I was alone. Mom was at Aunt Carolyn's, and who knew where the Judge was? I could afford to sit anywhere. I tried the Judge's chair. It had a good view of the doors and windows, its back tucked into a window and into a tall rose of Sharon bush outside, which sprouted soft purple flowers. The Judge's chair was scary. I was afraid a lightning bolt would strike me down for putting my butt there. I moved to Mom's chair, which was close to the refrigerator. That way, I could get refills with no problem. I could see why Drew chose it over the Judge's chair that morning. No lightning bolt.

Mom's chair was meager consolation. I looked at Bert, sitting as she did in the Judge's chair (she was very brave), and I wondered what did I do to deserve eating alone so frequently. My mother had abandoned me; so had my dad. Drew, where are you when I need you most? I could barely eat. In the middle of my meal, I could hear the house settle around me. I felt entombed.

After my first serving, I turned on Queen. "Bohemian Rhapsody" echoed from the living room CD player. I felt such rage at finding myself alone that afternoon that I would have even considered eating with the Ford sisters a considerable improvement. Why did everyone

have to forsake me? I couldn't even trick myself, to find company in
my images of Kathy Lawrence and Mr. Armstrong, to tell myself it
wasn't necessarily bad to be alone on a Saturday afternoon. At that
moment, everyone I could claim seemed so removed from me. Thinking about it, and hearing that song, which I liked but occasionally
found more depressing than usual, got to me. I took off the CD, and
hurled it into the living room wall. I cried.

"Skip?"

I wiped my nose with the back of my hand. "Dad?"

At the dining room doorway, Marshall appeared, wearing a St.
Louis Cardinals baseball cap. Yes, he looked like he had just arrived
from sinking the ninth hole. *Cousin, dear,* as he so often called me, *even
you are the best sight I had ever seen all afternoon.* I wanted to kiss him. He
looked too perplexed to be kissed. "Have you been crying?" he asked.

"Me? No." I smiled a little and hoped he missed the Queen crashing
against the wall. "I was just having spinach lasagna. You want some?"

"Finish eating, then we shall go."

"Go where?"

Marshall didn't answer. He picked up the sand wedge he had next
to the dining room doorway and examined the head, smeared with
fresh grass stains, then gripped it over his shoulder like a baseball bat.
He headed for the back door.

"Go where?"

"To Cousin Madelyn's," he finally said.

"To Grandma's?" I asked. "Why? Is something wrong?"

"Nope."

"Then, why?"

"You'll see." With that, Marshall went out the back door.

I finished the spinach lasagna. It took just three servings to do that.
I picked up the Queen and put it back into its case. I went out the
back door. In the backyard, Marshall was chipping yellow golf balls
against the house. It sounded like soft raindrops.

"Full?" Marshall asked.

I nodded and wiped the corners of my mouth with my thumbs.
Crossing the yard, Marshall picked up the golf balls and put them
into his pockets.

"Let's walk," he said.

You should have seen Marshall. The club went from baseball bat to chipper to walking stick in a matter of seconds. Twirling it, he led the way as though it were his grandmother's house we were headed for. In a way, my grandmother was his grandmother. Marshall, like all the Langstons, looked up Grandma Macalester for the best sage advice possible, even when his own grandmother was in the room. That spoke as to how well the rest of the family viewed my grandmother: a wise grayhead, almost a mother hen (a comparison I was to learn she loathed).

It was a glorious September afternoon. It was still a bit warm, but the sky was as crisp a pale blue as it sometimes is around Easter. I saw squirrels leap through trees. Soon, they were to make nests for the winter hibernation. I remember thinking about Frost poems, and about being a swinger of birches. It was as if all of the stuff in those recent days had evaporated, and, miraculously, I was back to being a kid. But then, the problem of the moment brought me back to adolescence. I had to know what the buzz was about.

"What's going on at Grandma's?" I asked.

"You'll see." Marshall leaned to his right side, brought the club's grip back, and whacked the hell out of some grass, as though he were playing polo. "Meeting."

"What kinda meeting?"

"You'll see." Again, walking, he steadied the grip, brought it back, and took a couple passes at a rock, which refused to be hit. "Crawford meeting."

"Damn."

"It's not that kind of meeting." He slid the clubhead to the ground and made a one-handed croquet shot at the grass growing in the cracks of a driveway. "At least, not yet."

A Crawford meeting—a meeting among the Macalesters, Langstons, *and* Morgans—was the type of meeting that was most grave. When we have a Crawford meeting, the whole family comes together to discuss issues so serious that they have repercussions for the entire family. What was the topic of discussion that day? Who knew. Could it be about the situation with Mom and the Judge? Indeed, that would be serious enough for the Crawfords to meet. Did the Judge call our cousins together to talk things over? Could Grandma have preempted him and gathered us? I didn't know. I knew merely that Marshall had been sent to fetch me, as my presence was required. If it were required so desperately, desperately enough for the family to endure Marshall's puffed-up reactions, why was I being kept so far into the dark?

The subject vexed me. Marshall and I walked the three blocks to Grandma Macalester's house in a degree of august silence. Throughout the walk, I could not imagine what could have compelled the Crawford family together, nor what could have sent Marshall after me, nor what could have required my presence. It must have been big.

Then, when we got to the block with Grandma's bungalow, I almost froze. It was a big Crawford meeting. Cars, including the Judge's Saab, were parked on both sides of the street, and, although it was still light, we could see the living room lamp through the windows. Her three-foot-tall black lawn jockey, set at the head of her brick walk, waited for me. I stopped at the gate.

"She's your grandmother," Marshall said. With the sand wedge, he held open the gate and signaled for me to enter.

My curiosity got the better of my reluctance. I followed Marshall up the brick walk and waited beside the lawn jockey while Marshall rang the bell. Cousin Mariah, Grandma's niece, came to the door, her shoulder length, naturally straight, gray-streaked hair still pulled back into a comb. She was cafe au lait complexioned, like Grandma, but with freckles, which she set off with indigo lipstick. By profession, Cousin Mariah was a marketing executive. The Judge said that meant she sold things. Cousin Mariah, could you sell me on being comfortable? That would be a trick. For the time being, she just sold me on coming inside. She held the door open.

"Just in time," she said. "We were just beginning to talk about you two."

"We would have been here sooner," Marshall said, "but Skip had to finish eating."

"What did he have?"

I knew I recognized that voice. It was as irritating to me as the scent of curry that permeated the house. Stepping onto the enclosed front porch, I followed Cousin Mariah. And, there was my sister Adele, arrived from Washington, sitting in an American colonial stuffed straightback chair beside the lamp. In the lamplight, she looked exactly like Cousin Mariah, only younger, a little darker, and lacking gray hair. She sat cross-legged, her black pumps off her feet, which were dressed in sheer nylons. Her knees jutted up through the slit of her light gray business-suit skirt. Her white blouse was open at the neck. Most likely, she had flown in from Washington after some meeting at the National Endowment for the Humanities, where she worked. She seemed to call me "kid," her favorite nickname for me.

"When'd you get in?" I asked Adele, laughing.

"Is that Skip?" the Judge called through the kitchen. "Tell him to get on in here. I need his taste buds."

I left the living room and its Crawford women, and barely missed stepping on Marshall's grandmother, Cousin Ruth Langston, who was stretched out in a chair by the piano. A television was on in one of the bedrooms; the door to the other bedroom was closed.

I went into the kitchen. In it, the Judge was at the stove, wearing an apron. He still had on his golfing outfit. Ken Langston entered the back door from the deck outside.

"Get a fork," the Judge commanded. "I need you to try this."

I did as I was told. I got a fork from Grandma's hoosier cabinet and inched toward the stove. Marshall pushed past us and went onto the deck. I imagined he wanted to do more chipping. The Judge took a saucer from the cupboard and ladled a sample of what he was cooking onto it and he handed it to me. It was piping hot, a jaundiced piece of chopped chicken breast and a few pieces of chopped onion.

"Kid," Adele yelled, "now, don't let him give you all that curry."

"Too late," the Judge said. He opened a package of white rice and measured two cups. "Eat."

I was about to eat it when Grandma and Dennis Morgan came out of one of the bedrooms. "I'd just tell her, 'this is what I'm going to do,'" Grandma said to him. She followed her nose right to the pot the Judge was cooking. She inhaled. "If you cooked like that thirty-six years ago," she said, "she might've put up with you. You wouldn't be in this world of trouble."

The Judge pulled out another saucer and ladled out another sample. "Get a fork."

"Don't do it, Aunt Madelyn," Cousin Mariah yelled from the dining room, laughing.

Grandma looked at the dish skeptically. She looked at me. "You, first."

My job in the family was always to be the Judge's taster, even at Crawford meetings. I blew onto the chicken breast. Then, I took a bite. The Judge made terrific curry chicken, but, because his roommate in law school had been on medication for manic-depressive disorder, he knew all about cooking without salt, and, sometimes, those talents failed him. That was the first thing he wanted me to tell him. But his food was usually too hot to taste for salt. "I— *ow!*"

"What did he say?" Ken asked.

"He said 'it's hot,'" Grandma said.

"I know it's hot," the Judge said. "What does it need?"

I chewed a little, once I got used to the heat. Then I swallowed. "Needs salt." There. That was my usual diagnosis.

"I could have told you that, Alfred," Grandma said, "but you don't think I know what I'm talking about, when it comes to cooking."

"Eat, Madelyn," the Judge said.

"Don't you call me 'Madelyn,'" she said. "You call me 'Madelyn' again, and I'll swell your lips past your eyes."

"Eat."

Grandma took out a fork. "I'm not doing this because of you. I'm doing it because I'm hungry." She blew onto the chicken breast and carefully took a bite. It was also a bit hot for her. She fanned her mouth and drank water. Then, she nodded. "Just a teaspoon of salt."

The Judge whipped out the salt and, over the sink, poured a second's worth into his hand, which he splashed into the pot. "Anything else?"

"If you add that," Grandma said, "that'll be enough."

With understatement, the Judge turned to Ken. "Hit the dinner bell. Send in the troops."

Ken opened the back door and whistled. Then he cleared his throat. "Better come on in, because, otherwise, Skip and Cousin Madelyn will get all of this for themselves."

A line formed behind Grandma and me. Ken passed out the paper plates and plastic flatware and the Judge dished out the curry chicken and white rice. After getting the food we went to the deck, sitting on the steps and on Grandma's black wrought iron patio furniture. Cousin Ruth opened the table's umbrella and Dennis positioned it just right, then the Judge joined us with his own serving of food. I looked at my helping, high in protein. It smiled at me. It didn't matter that I had enjoyed spinach lasagna less than an hour before. It was my father's cooking. I was hungry again.

"Where's Alan?" Cousin Mariah asked. "Aunt Madelyn, I don't think Alan got anything."

I had not known Alan Morgan was at Grandma's. Apparently, it had also skipped everyone else's mind. Dennis started to stand up and go back inside, but the Judge said "just a minute" and turned toward me.

"Would you mind?" the Judge asked.

I knew what that meant. I had to put aside my plate and fork and fetch Alan. I sighed a little and made a show of a frown as I placed my plate on the table. It was my best put-upon show. "Don't even think about it," I said to Adele. She swatted my butt anyway.

I wish I could say my thoughts were simply to feed Alan, for he must have been hungry, but my mind was busy considering other things. The house was silent, save the sounds of the television in the bedroom, and of a boy laughing. I followed the sounds. When I got there, I considered the sight. Alan was stretched out on the bed, eyes glued to the television. Those shapely legs, wonderfully tanned, teased me. Olive drab shorts were pushed up to reveal his full thighs. His feet were exposed by flip-flop sandals, and he rubbed them together like matchsticks. His white T-shirt boasted the name of the YMCA camp. Obviously, he had been swimming.

I had seen him swimming before. His thirteen-year-old body moved through the water like a tadpole. Then, he would bring his upper body above the water, the water dripping from his hair onto his face. He would smile. Alan, you have the cutest smile, a smile with dimples, a smile I know that made the seventh-grade girls melt before you. And, wait until they see your legs. Those beautiful legs, shapely legs, the Crawford legs that, more than anything, mark the men in our family. In the water you are no longer thirteen, Alan. Rather, you are a young man. Easily close to my age. Easily fifteen or maybe sixteen. Almost sixteen, easily, like me.

"Hey," I said.

"Hey," he said through a laugh.

I looked at the television. "Three Stooges?"

"Yeah." They did some slapstick and Alan laughed again. "They're the best."

I watched the black-and-white picture. Though funny, their antics made no sense. Maybe it was just me and I was simply past the Three Stooges stage. The Crawford meeting was a little too near for me. I could see the Judge through the window; could he also see me? Through the wall, I could hear Grandma and Cousin Ruth talking. Can you hear things in this room, too, Madelyn? "The Judge made something to eat," I said.

"What?"

"Curry chicken. Ever have it? It's really good."

Alan laughed at something on television. I doubted he heard me. He was concentrating so very much upon the Stooges. I had to be recognized. I cleared my throat.

"Alan—"

"What?" he asked, laughing.

"Would you like some curry chicken?"

Alan finally looked at me. I shivered. He had beautiful eyes. "Is it good?" He asked. He looked back at the television, and laughed again.

"It's the best."

"I'm watching this. Can you get me some?"

The fact was I would have gotten anything for Alan. As it was, I got him curry chicken and rice. As I got out his paper plate and prepared to ladle his dish, Marshall came in. He took a look at me, paper plate and ladle of curry chicken and rice in hand, and frowned a little.

"He's only thirteen," he said.

"Huh?"

"You heard me. He's only thirteen. Just remember that."

Okay, Marsh, what was that supposed to mean? He wouldn't say. He wouldn't let on, like he could read me like a transparent book, like he could read me and he didn't like what he had read. With just a look, Marshall returned outside.

On the bed of rice, I dished out a couple spoonfuls of chicken, trying to keep a nice, balanced, presentable plate going. It took some adjustment to get it right. Once it was, I got plastic flatware and a paper napkin and carefully took them into the bedroom. Why did I do that? Wouldn't you have done something similar, too?

Alan had changed positions. He was now seated on the floor, his knees up and his forearms crossed between them. Through the leg of his shorts, his tanline was exposed. All that laughing at the Stooges had put a perpetual smile on his face, and his eyes twinkled.

I must be careful here. I don't want to be misunderstood. I remember wrestling with Alan, as we had done so many times, but Alan was not going for it. "Nuh-uh," he said. "Nuh-uh." He was not going to let me beat him, and, for good measure, he scratched me. Twice.

After the second time, we moved to opposite ends of the bed, where we waited, catching our breath, as if a referee would come and start us over again. On the deck, the family laughed heartily. My heart beat rapidly as I heard the family move, because I was scared to death they would come into the bedroom, see an exercised Alan and the scratched me, and conclude we were in there doing not just a boys' thing, but something ugly, debased, and sinful.

It was about ten minutes before Marshall, sent in to check on me, opened the bedroom door. My heart stopped as the door creaked open. Alan had tried eating. As though nothing had happened, he chewed with his mouth barely open. I had moved from the floor to the bed. I tried standing as the door opened, but Marshall moved almost too quickly; the best I could do was to obscure the scratches on my face. Marshall had that censorious look going. He signaled for me to join him in the hall. When I did, he closed the door and smacked me across the face. It hurt. Then, Marshall raised a finger.

"That," he whispered, "is because it would kill your parents to do it."

My assault was something I bore by myself, as Marshall excused himself into the bedroom. I went outside, like nothing had happened.

It may have been hard to believe, but the curry chicken was still hot. No one had moved it from its place on the table. Though Alan had scratched my face and Marshall had slapped me, no one seemed to have noticed the red streaks across my cheek or my reddened, watery eyes. I ducked my head when I saw Dennis, who was a tall man whose chestnut eyes eerily looked right through me. I picked up my plate and started eating as though nothing had happened.

"Good to see your interlude inside did not ruin your appetite," the Judge said, lighting his pipe.

"Don't you start that smoking here," Grandma said. "And, don't you call me 'Madelyn.' You call me 'Madelyn,' and I'll knock that pipe and tobacco clear back to old Virginny."

The Judge took the pipe out of his mouth and set it on the deck rail.

Adele turned to me. "We were just talking about you, kid. Ken said you and Brad don't travel in the same circles."

I looked at Ken. He sat near the bedroom window, where Venetian blinds and a large cactus kept the interested from peeking. The light was on in the bedroom. I wondered how long Alan would hold out before Marshall bolted outside for me. Ken looked back at me. I picked at my food.

"What the hell happened to your face?" Cousin Mariah asked.

"Wrestling," I shrugged. "About Brad, just because we're cousins doesn't mean we hang out together. It's not like me and Marshall."

"You got no idea where he could've gone?" Cousin Mariah asked.

I looked at Cousin Mariah. Grandma had always said she looked like the women in her mother's family, all those Crawford women who came north from Missouri. All of them, Grandma said, had a fullness about the lips that seemed incongruous with the rest of their passable features. Looking at her, I was reminded I was looking at least five generations into our past. She, and our ancestors, seemed to accuse me. I shrugged.

"Well," Dennis said, turning to Grandma, "who else can we ask? Marshall doesn't know. Skip doesn't know. Brad's friends, they don't know. I don't know, Cousin Madelyn. I wish I did, but I just don't."

Dennis put his face in his hands. Grandma and Cousin Ruth tried comforting him, but he seemed in such despair. And, in Dennis's state, he would have made short work of me.

The Judge sniffed his pipe, then set it back on the rail. "I hate to change subjects, but—"

"Ah, yes, Alfred," Cousin Ruth said, "your situation."

Dennis rubbed his eyes, then looked up. "We need to resolve it."

"Skip is out here," the Judge said, "and we can e-mail Ted to get his take on things, but I need guidance."

"You don't need guidance, Alfred," Cousin Mariah blurted out, "you need a good swift kick—"

Cousin Ruth gasped. "Mariah!"

"Well, it's true. If not for Aunt Madelyn talking to Rose, Carolyn and I would have done it so fast—"

"Not in front of the boy," the Judge said.

"'Not in front of the boy,' my foot!" Cousin Mariah set her plate on the table and huffed. "Running back to her, after all these years!"

The Judge had little to say. He reached a hand to Adele, who took it, held it for a little while, then let go. "Well?" was all he could muster.

"The question is," Grandma began, "do you still love her?"

"Which one?" the Judge asked.

"'Which one?'" Cousin Mariah moaned. "Dear God! Gimme a damn break!"

"Which one do you love, Alfred?" Grandma asked.

The Judge thought amid dead silence. During the silence, I saw the bedroom light go off. Marshall must be coming.

"I love Rose," the Judge said softly. "She's the mother of my children."

Adele started to sob, comforted by Cousin Mariah, who rushed to her. I was too numb to do much of anything but stare at Adele and the Judge. Grandma tried stroking my leg, but her touch was foreign to me and I jerked away. Did I hear the Judge's pronouncement clearly? Clearly, with that sentence, the Judge had ended his marriage to my mother.

We waited for Grandma and Cousin Ruth to draw breath and say something, but Cousin Ruth was taken aback by how things had transpired. The door opened and Marshall and Alan came out. Still a little boy, Alan went to Dennis and tried sitting in his lap. It was an unusual sight, a big boy like Alan climbing into Dennis's lap. I watched him for a minute, but, when our eyes met momentarily, both of us looked away.

"I can't think of anything to say, Madelyn," Cousin Ruth said. "Everything leaves me."

Grandma thought for a moment. "Much is in Rose's favor," she said. "Besides being the mother of your children, her marrying you made your career. You would never have gotten what you had if you stayed with Eugenia. Not then. Not in this country. Rose had earned her place in this family. However, Eugenia will be given every opportunity to re-earn hers."

"Amen," Ken said softly.

"I wanna go home, Daddy," Alan said in a low voice, resting his head against Dennis's shoulder. He looked toward me a hot second, eyes vacant, then flashed away. "I'm tired."

For what it was worth, I felt the need to comfort him the way Grandma and Cousin Ruth comforted Dennis, but Marshall, who was watching me like a hawk, made that impossible. He shook his head, and seemed to say that I had done more than enough.

I picked at my food. Between the guilt of what I had tried to do to Alan and a sense of guilt about my potential role in the end of my parents' marriage, I was too numb to feel like eating. My fork went over the plate idly, like a hand leafing through a book.

"You don't have to finish that," the Judge said.

I set the plate on the table and scratched my nose. The smell of Alan was so identifiable and intense I had to scrub my hands.

Chapter Seven

I needed to forget that smell, as well as other things. I was alone, again. No one would understand why I did what I did, why I tried what I tried, nor how I felt afterward. Besides, I was afforded no opportunity to let the experience of my actions settle upon me; at least, not for that night, for it was the annual Howard University Alumni Rec Night in St. Louis. It so happened that, after years of being relegated to a minder and left to slumber with Drew on the phone with The Three Stooges and Chevy Chase in the background, it was my first chance to join the Judge and Grandma Macalester at the games.

I looked forward to it like a kid looking forward to a jaunt to the orthodontist. I had forgotten this event, which Grandma in particular anticipated every September. Having not attended a Rec Night before, I had no idea what to expect, except for one vague notion that it was to be spent with men and women not unlike my father, who believed earnestly that God was a Howard alumnus with a Phi Beta Kappa key. That was enough to make me look at the event with foreboding. But, what exacerbated my dread was the understanding that I would engage in such triviality, entertained in a convivial atmosphere, so soon after my father had ended his marriage to my mother and so soon after I had attempted to force myself onto my cousin. Would anyone notice that Judge Macalester's son looked so down and so guilty? I thought they would. I assumed someone would. I figured a person would end up leading me into custody, be it a ward of the state or a guest of the sheriff.

Adele wasn't coming. She preferred to spend the night at Aunt Carolyn's talking to Mom, or maybe having sorority talk with Cousin Mariah, a like-minded sister in Delta Sigma Theta. Given my preference, I would have wanted to have Drew on an overnight. I tried broaching the subject as the Judge drove me home.

"You know, it's Rec Night, Dad."

"Yes."

"You still want me to come?"

The Judge took the pipe out of his mouth. I could see him scrape his tongue with his teeth. Apparently, there was a bite in the bowl. "Don't you want to go?"

"I know you bought tickets for me and Mom—"

"You don't have to go, Skip," he said. "If you'd prefer, you could always stay home. Invite Drew over to spend the night and eat a pizza. Wouldn't you want that over going to Rec Night with your grandmother and me?"

I hated that question. Whenever he mentioned Drew coming over, it always sounded to me like he had assumed something, like there was something between Drew and me, like we were a pair of fags.

"I want to go to Rec Night," I said quickly. "Really, it would be good to see some of the guys you went to Howard with."

I tried sounding convincing. He must have believed me. He relit his pipe. He said nothing more on the subject.

I had about an hour before we would leave. I began to prepare shortly after getting home. I showered again, then brushed my hair. In just briefs, I spent the better part of fifteen minutes trying to decide what to wear when I thought I heard Mom yelling that Marshall was on the phone. It was my imagination playing tricks on me. It wasn't Mom. Rather, it was the Judge. But, rest assured: it was Marshall on the phone for me. Not having a phone of my own I took the call in my parents' room. The Judge was in their bathroom, dressing.

"Almost sixteen years," he droned, "almost sixteen years, and you still act like some newborn baby. Put your robe on!"

Almost sixteen years, I thought, and I am still treated like a newborn baby. Were I as crass as some Whitmaners said they were, I would have stuck my hand down my briefs and said something disrespectful, but, I did little more than smile stupidly and pick up the phone.

My fear was Marshall had heard something from Alan, but it was just a fear, unrealized. All he had were a couple of questions.

"Two things," he said. "You're going to the Rec Night tonight, Right?"

"I have my whole existence revved for that," I said, trying to be sarcastic but not sarcastic enough for the Judge to hear me. "What's the other thing?"

"That was just the premise," Marshall said. "My real question is, can I go with you?"

"What about Ken?" I asked. "Is he going?"

"Skip," the Judge said, "if he needs a ride, we can give him a ride."

I ignored the Judge, as far as I could ignore him. Since Marshall's father Ken was also a Howard alumnus I felt it was a reasonable question to ask. I mean, what else was worth asking?

"No," Marshall said. "He's not. Ask the Judge if I can get a ride."

I had to scratch myself because my balls itched. It was hell to do anything with the Judge nearby.

"Skip," the Judge said firmly, "does he need a ride? Tell him we'll give him a ride."

"What was that?" Marshall asked.

"That was just the Judge," I said. I switched the phone to my other ear. "Listen, if you need a ride—"

"It won't be a problem?"

"*Skip,*" the Judge said from the master bathroom, a little louder so he could be heard by the dead.

"Just a minute!" I yelled. "Marshall, no. It won't be a problem. We'll pick you up!"

"Around seven-thirty," said the Judge.

"Around seven-thirty?" Marshall asked.

"Yeah," I said. "Around seven-thirty!"

"Well," Marshall said. "That handles point one. Now for point two: what are you wearing?"

"Dress to play tennis," the Judge said.

"Dad said I could play tennis," Marshall said, "but you know how lousy I play. Besides, golf's my game. I could dress for cards."

"Wear what you wore today," I said.

"That'll be good," the Judge said.

"I can't wear that tonight!"

"Why not?" I asked. Marshall, dressed prep in a Howard University polo shirt, looked the part.

"He can wear something similar," the Judge said.

"Wear something similar, then," I said.

"That would be fine," the Judge said.

Hanging up the phone finally, I returned to my room. Little could underwhelm me more than a trip to see Howard University alums with Marshall, who would fit right in. I had seen him when our parents took us to the Charter Day dinners each March like outings with the old Jack and Jill. Marshall laughed at the right old Dean Snowden jokes and blended into the alumni like he was born to it (which he was). And, though Mom and the Judge may have thought he was going to keep me company, it was really the other way around. I was meant to service him.

I dressed. Following the Judge's suggestion in spite of myself, I dressed for tennis. Just because it was Howard, I wanted to wear a Morehouse College T-shirt Aunt Carolyn brought back from an Alpha Kappa Alpha boule in Atlanta, but the Judge pooh-poohed it, saying that was in as much bad taste as showing up at an NAACP convention in a Mississippi Rebels uniform, Confederate flag blazing, so I nixed it. My father was more than willing to compromise: I could wear something Illini.

So there I was in my orange and blue striped polo shirt and matching athletic socks, sitting in my tennis shorts waiting for the Judge to finish dressing. Strike that. I was waiting for something else, as if Mom had to finish. I sat in the kitchen, bouncing the tennis racquet against my knee like it was a ball.

At 7:15, the Judge stood at the bottom of the stairs and opened his lungs. "It's time, Rose," he bellowed. Then, looking lost momentarily, he headed for the garage. "Come on, Skip." At 7:16, the Judge eased the Saab into the driveway and almost hit Marshall. The Judge stuck his head out of the window.

"I said we would pick you up at seven-thirty, Marshall. Didn't Skip tell you?"

Marshall, who was again dressed prep in his Howard University sweatshirt, sort of shook his head, and climbed into the backseat. At sixteen years old, he had a way of getting anxious.

Our first stop was Grandma Macalester's.

The Judge sent me to fetch her. Though she was a treasure and her house was a simple two-bedroom bungalow, the place was rather imposing. To go there twice in a few hours seemed much. I mean, I love my grandmother, but you just can't lie to her and get away with it.

"Why don't you get her?" I whined to Dad.

"Because you are on her side of the street," he said.

As much as I might protest it, his logic was impeccable. Conversation over, reluctantly, I opened the door. I went through the gate and walked up to the house. Before I could ring the bell, the door opened.

"Hello, hello, hello," Grandma sung. She grabbed my cheeks and brought them to her face for a kiss, which was followed by a strong hug. When she let me go, I looked her over. Though eighty-five, she carried herself like a woman my mother's age. She had two piercings in each ear, and had tasteful, ageless earrings. She refused to let herself go gray. Nevertheless, she allowed her stylist to smoke her hair, giving her the impression of a constant, angelic halo. People who knew her said she looked the same about the face for almost eight decades; Grandma always replied either that she had found the fountain of youth or that she was the oldest looking child in Creation. Her cafe au lait complexion was accented by Fashion Fair. She wore a "Howard Mom" pin on her rust brown, kente-fringed pantsuit, not a bad outfit, but one keeping with her Congressional reputation as the black Millicent Fenwick.

As I looked her over, her smile turned into a gasp. She blinked.

"We're going in that?!" she asked. "Did your Daddy lose his mind?"

She approached the Saab and opened the rear door. Marshall smiled and waved.

"Alfred," Grandma said, "you can't get all of us riding to St. Louis in this! We'll be squooshed like sardines!"

"It can fit four people," he said.

"Sure, and it can fit five," she said. "So can a Mustang, but that's not saying much. Let's ride in my car."

That meant the open boat. The Judge loathed driving the open boat. He groaned, "Oh, Mother," and backed the Saab up to let the Lincoln out.

I forgot to tell you before how much I liked riding in Grandma's Lincoln. It was so elegant. We climbed into her Lincoln in our usual pecking order: The Judge drove, Grandma (who liked being chauffeured as much as chauffeuring) rode shotgun. In the backseat Marshall got in behind the Judge, while I got behind Grandma, bouncing my tennis racquet on my knee.

We were meant to go to St. Louis that way. But, before we went to St. Louis, the Judge drove through town a little. "A little detour," was how he put it. Grandma rolled her eyes. "You say," she said. "I'll believe it when we cross the bridge."

In Middletown, on an exquisite hill that the Catholic high school's ski team used for practice in January, the Judge parked in front of a small red brick house with three windows in the front. I had heard—from Marshall, of course—that such a house was a German worker's house. It had steep, cut stone steps to the front door, and was dressed in hollyhocks, hyacinths, and canyons, the scent of which must have been heaven in spring.

"Don't start nothing," Grandma said to the Judge.

"I'm not going to start a thing, Madelyn, not while you're here," he said.

"Don't you call me 'Madelyn,'" she shot back. "You call me 'Madelyn' again, I'll start something you won't be able to finish."

The Judge smiled a little, and went to the front door. Wondering what was going on, I looked to Marshall. "You mean, you don't know?" he asked.

The Judge acted like he didn't even need a warrant. He unlocked the door and walked in, like he had done it dozens of times, like he would do it dozens more. Grandma sighed audibly. She turned back to Marshall and me.

"Alfred's acting like he's your age again," she said to us.

"Is she coming with us?" Marshall asked.

"She, who?" I asked him.

Inside the house, someone moved among the discrete Venetian blinds. The person, this she, looked at us, then let the blinds be. Shortly afterward, the Judge returned outside.

"She's got more sense than you," Grandma said to the Judge as he got behind the wheel.

"She, who, Madelyn?"

"Don't 'she, who, Madelyn' me," Grandma shot back. "She knows better than you not to run around with that band still on your finger. Genie got more sense about what's proper than you'd ever let on. And, you call me 'Madelyn' again—"

"You'd cut it off," he said.

"That's right!" Grandma caught herself, for the Judge's *it* could have been more than a finger. She wagged her finger at him. "Don't get fresh with me!"

This "Genie" intrigued me. Was this "Genie" the same as Dr. Levin? Was this her house? I wondered.

Now we were ready, the Judge declared. We crossed the river for St. Louis. We lived north of St. Louis, where the Mississippi runs east and west. Opposite us were flat St. Charles County and full North St. Louis County. To be honest, we don't spend much time in North County, which Grandma could not forgive for growing by leaps and bounds after 1960, when it became even more of a refuge for the Germans and Irish fleeing blackening North St. Louis. It was before my time (hell, before the Judge's time, if there could be such a thing), and I never thought about it much beyond it being a place from which some Whitmaners moved years before. To me, it was more of a conveyance than a symbol, and it made sense to go there to shop for things we otherwise had to go downtown to get, or to go through it to get to the Central West End of St. Louis, to West County, or to the airport. It was hardly a destination.

When the Judge said the Rec Night was to be in North St. Louis County this time, my heart sank. North County was like a desert. The snob in me simply could not bring myself to think about going there, no matter who was with me. It was just beyond my comprehension. It was like being sent to exile, toward a place no one would dare go.

We were lost for a good part of our trip, adding insult to injury. Grandma kept asking whether he knew he was lost. Of course, being omniscient as well as omnipotent, the Judge denied it, denied being lost and needing some guidance. Besides, the directions he was working on, from a woman he called Tamara, were enough for him, he claimed. As he drove, and as Grandma asked more insistently if we were lost, the angrier the Judge became at the directions. He became increasingly short-tempered, and snapped at even Marshall, his favorite cousin, whom he loved like a son, when he dared ask a question. This continued for a good while, both down the Interstate and then down a frontage road, which took us back in the opposite direction. It became obvious to me that we were lost, but I was no fool. Unwilling to be cast down the mountain for broaching such a subject, I kept my mouth shut. Then, the Judge stopped for directions at a gas station. While he was gone, I thought about Adele for a minute. She had weaseled out of this expedition. Maybe Adele traded it for some "quality time" with Mom and Aunt Carolyn. If she did, I would have traded places with her, gratefully.

"Don't get a big head, Madelyn," the Judge said, bringing the car into the gas station's parking lot.

"Don't you call me 'Madelyn,'" Grandma said, leaning toward him. "You call me 'Madelyn' again, I'll knock you back into the Seventy-fourth Congress."

As was his arrogance, though, the Judge smiled at the thought and parked the open boat. I bounced my racquet on my knee and tried to disappear. I stared at a guy who waited outside the gas station on his bicycle, reading a book.

He was about my age, maybe a little younger, maybe just turned fifteen. He had pure, peachfuzz legs that shifted form every few minutes to get comfortable. His mother, also on a bicycle, removed his helmet and stroked his hair and flapped mosquitoes away, but still he read. He wore George Bush–style aviator glasses and he needed a haircut. Seated as far from him as I was, I could tell he had gray eyes that looked right through me when he looked up. Yes, he was breathtaking, and how I wanted him, too.

Twisting my knees against each other, I tried to deny the simplest interest in him. Still, I couldn't help but fantasize. Later, after arriving home, I would resolve to remember the fantasies and to enjoy them alone in my room. At almost sixteen, I had an idea I knew I wanted us to do *it*.

Marshall nodded at the guy. "In a way, he kind of reminds you of Alan," he said. "Right?"

Marshall looked right through me, unsmiling. He meant that question to sting. Grandma didn't hear him, because she was anticipating the Judge's return, trying, I think, to prepare the next quip she would use were he to call her "Madelyn" again. Little did I know, her quips came naturally. I tried concentrating on that idea, but Marshall continued looking at me. His lack of smile grew into a disgusted frown.

Then, the Judge returned. "It's just a little bit back that way," the Judge said.

"See?" Grandma asked. "You should have stayed on the Interstate, like I told you, and turned like I said."

"I told you not to get a big head, Madelyn."

"Don't you call me 'Madelyn,'" she shot back quickly. "You call me 'Madelyn' again, and I'll backhand you so fast, you'd think I'd play backgammon."

The Judge smiled. I cowered in my seat. Hopefully, he didn't notice I was staring.

We started driving again. The sun was starting to set when we saw a man in blue and white standing among blue and white party balloons amid a sign saying TURN HERE. The Judge turned, a left this time, and at the back of a long industrial drive was a firm concrete building with cars parked before it.

"This is the place," the Judge said.

As it turned out, it was a good thing I did not have my Morehouse T-shirt, which the Judge wanted to burn, for the place was more bedecked with blue and white than *The Hilltop* at Homecoming. Blue and white dripped from the cars in the parking lot, and they were smeared over the entrance to the place like so much lamb's blood. I couldn't crane my neck enough to see the interior, but, knowing these people, it too was blue and white.

The Judge saw my apprehension. Through the rearview mirror, he smiled.

"Don't you wish you wore something a little more appropriate?" Marshall asked me.

"We're from Illinois," I said. "What's more appropriate than the Fighting Illini?"

"A Howard bison," the Judge said as he parked the open boat.

A pair of middle-aged chocolate-flavored women in matching navy blue tops and white tennis skirts was our welcoming committee. They held the door open for Grandma as she climbed out of the open boat and stretched for the sake of stretching.

"Which one of you is the Howard person?" asked one of the women.

"Him," Grandma said, pointing to the Judge.

The women smiled. "Welcome," they said.

The Judge put his hand to his head, as if he were tipping a cap. "I would just like to know what genius gave us those marvelous directions."

"That must be Tamara or Neil," one of the women said. She had a wrist full of clanky bracelets that shifted noisily as she removed her sunglasses to clean them on her top. "Was it a man or a woman?"

"It was a girl," the Judge said.

"Alfred," Grandma said, "don't be so sexist."

"All right," Dad said. "It was a woman."

"That was Tamara," the other woman said. Her voice sounded sultry, a natural female bass. Bessie Smith–sounding, the blues singer whose recordings Uncle Clifford so often played. "She's inside, just inside the door."

The Judge closed the car door. "Fantastic. Let's go meet her."

He strode across the lot with a purpose that said he was out for blood, following Grandma, whose mind was set on making friends, again. Marshall and I took the rear.

I was somewhat self-conscious about wearing University of Illinois colors to a Howard University event, but I took a page from Grandma's book, written in Blackburn College's script, which she bore with an alumna's pride. Blackburn, she often pointed out, was good enough for her; it fed her sons. There was no shame in being proud of that. So, I walked like her, forgetting that I wore Illini colors.

Grandma reached the door to the place first. With a deep breath, she flung it open. The Judge waltzed through as though the Fates had opened it just for him. Marshall squeezed by, naturally. It was shut by my turn. For a second, I stood there and wondered if I really wanted to go inside. Marshall turned around and opened the door.

"It ain't automatic, cousin dear," he said, holding the door open. "Either you slip in after others have opened it, or you have to open it yourself. Either way, you can't just stand there."

Prophetic words, I thought. I grabbed the door and let myself in.

God! Did I feel out of place in my University of Illinois colors! However I felt, I walked right in. Near the entrance, a thin young woman in Delta Sigma Theta red adjusted the miniature elephant on her collar and waited for the Judge to quit inspecting the premises and register. Grandma, talking, engaged her. The young woman smiled a little bit and handed Marshall a white Bic pen that wrote blue ink. As he bent over to register, I moved over.

The young woman smiled. She had white, cadaverous teeth. "Welcome. Are you in the right place?"

"I should say so," I said.

"Are you sure? This is Howard University Alumni Association's Rec Night—a fund-raiser."

"Oh, he's in the right place," Marshall said. "He's only dressed like that because he thinks it is really April first."

She smiled. In those teeth, she looked like she should have been in a corner, suspended from a short chain. Marshall handed me the pen and motioned for me to sign my name. Setting the tennis racquet between my knees, I bent over. A man brushed against my backside accidentally. It was a queer feeling. When I looked, I saw that he had walked on. He, too, was a tennis player.

The Judge stepped forward. He glared at the young woman. Taking the pen from me, he lifted the registration clipboard into his hands and, in his meticulous script, wrote "A. E. Macalester, BA, Classics, Howard University, 1987; JD, Yale Law School, 1990. U.S. District Judge." He clicked the Bic against the clipboard and handed both to the young woman. She looked over the registration form.

"Thank you," she said, smiling. "And how are you today, Mr. Macalester?"

"It's Judge Macalester," he countered, "and we would like to meet the genius who gave us directions. I think her name was Tamara."

The young woman's smile faded. She knew she could easily meet her Maker. "I'm Tamara."

The Judge looked down his nose one hot second and then extended his hand. "Thank you. Those were marvelous directions."

The poor girl did not know whether to shake his hand or faint. Stunned, she smiled a bit and left the Judge out there for a few moments until Marshall leaned forward and said, "If I were you, I'd shake his hand." Then, she got out of her daze and smiled a little more broadly, again with those deadly teeth, and shook the Judge's hand.

"You see," the Judge said, "that didn't hurt."

Before she could answer, the Judge turned his back to her and headed for the men's room across the hall. I didn't notice the young woman's reaction, for she adjusted the elephant on her collar and quickly busied herself with the registration forms, as if she were trying to get her mind off some insult. It all happened too fast to pity her.

Grandma and Marshall occupied a table between the handball and tennis courts, not far from the open bar. Tennis and handball echoed from both sides. Grandma took out a fresh deck of cards and broke the seal. Opening the pack, she found the jokers and threw them out, then started to shuffle. "Ever play bidwhist?" she asked Marshall. Marshall shook his head. "When we first met, Edward and I used to play bidwhist all the time. That was one thing Edward could do: play cards. That, and chase women."

Marshall nodded. Like I, he was used to hearing about my grandfather Edward Macalester chasing women. Grandma Macalester claimed chasing women was the most enduring trait Edward Macalester passed to his descendants. That, and beautiful, well-formed legs.

The Judge emerged from the men's room shaking his hands dry and he went straight for the open bar. "You want anything, Madelyn?"

"Yeah," she shouted, "if you can't get me a man, come back with a whiskey sour. And don't call me 'Madelyn!'"

I sat at another table and bounced the racquet against my palm, trying to match pace with the handball games. There were at least two acres of tennis courts beneath the stretch-fabric dome, and all but the last court were taken. Some playing were pretty good, while others bounced like pikers. I had my eye on a mixed doubles game, where a middle-aged pair in matching blue and gold sweatbands played a point like it was before the King at Wimbledon. When the point was finally over, the other pair applauded and crossed court to shake their hands. By then, the Judge was back with Grandma's whiskey sour and Grandma was initiating Marshall into the rudiments of bidwhist. A couple of men, who looked like doctors, came out of the handball court winded and, seeing the Judge, shook his hand.

The Judge made the introductions. Indeed, they were doctors; their practice, in Creve Coeur, in western St. Louis County, was limited to optometry. They wore gold and purple wristbands, and one of the doctors had a brand on his bicep. Marshall leaned forward and whispered, slumming, as it were, "Them's Ques," meaning, they were members of Omega Psi Phi. Sweating, they exchanged the goggles they were wearing for eyeglasses and wiped their peppery mustaches with the backs of their hands. They asked about Mom. The Judge missed not a beat, but lied beautifully. "She stayed home with our daughter, who is visiting," the Judge said. They believed him. The doctors were glad to meet me and Marshall. When the one with the brand took my hand he squeezed it so hard I grimaced, much to Marshall's delight. I guess Marshall thought that was my comeuppance. The doctors didn't have to be introduced to Grandma. They could never forget Grandma.

"You're going to play some cards, Mrs. Macalester?" one of the doctors asked.

"I'm going to introduce this boy to some good times," she said, pointing to Marshall. Marshall smiled and took a deal from Grandma into his hand. "And, please, call me Madelyn."

The branded doctor smiled and turned to a chocolate-skinned woman in a peach top, who sat cross-armed a couple of tables away, staring at a tennis game. "They're gonna play cards, honey," he said.

"What kinda cards?" she asked.

"Bidwhist," Grandma said. "And I'm gonna clean up! Are you in?"

The woman, who was fair-sized and also had an elephant pin, moved so quickly she was there before Grandma could move the dummy. As the Judge surrendered his seat at the table and as she took his place, I smelled her. She had the scent of cocoa butter after a spring rain. The Judge talked with the doctors affably. In the middle of the conversation, he looked down at me.

"Why don't you find a nice tennis game?" he asked me.

I was beginning to get a little self-conscious about being alone. Not only was the Judge occupied, but Grandma was consumed by her bidwhist hand, watching Marshall play aggressively. The chocolate-skinned woman carefully drew a deuce from her hand, and Grandma and Marshall stared at her like she was crazy.

"I don't know anyone to play with," I said.

"You can do better than that." The Judge pointed at a seated man drinking Gatorade at the bar. "Go ask him to play with you."

Asking strange men in a strange place to play with me was not my forte, but neither was being alone. He seemed such a forbidding man, the gent with the Gatorade. He was tall and muscular, built like the proverbial football player, and his head was shaven. As he drank, Gatorade soaked his mustache and, occasionally, he dried it with a towel draped over his shoulder. He considered the world through dark sunglasses. He was watching the front door; whenever someone entered, he waved. Looking at him, I realized he had been part of the pair that had played that middle-aged couple so well.

"I can't ask him to play," I whispered to the Judge. "He's good."

"Well, you're good, too," he said.

With that, and without much more prompting or any protests from me, the Judge strode over to the man, who straightened his slouched sitting and wiped Gatorade from his face. I went, too. The man removed his sunglasses and revealed light, walnut-brown eyes that sent shivers through me. The Judge stood against him, hands on his hips.

"Would you mind playing with my son?" the Judge asked.

The man's lips trembled a little. I looked down at the tightly wrapped grip of his racquet, leaning as it was against the bar. When I glanced up, I noticed him reading me as if I were a portfolio magazine on a shelf, or an unmarked deck of cards.

"I'm good," I blurted out.

"I bet you are," the man said in a satin, ebony voice, a deep baritone.

"He plays almost every day," the Judge said. "I'm willing to wager he'll give you a pretty good game. He might even win."

"You can't beat me if I don't know your name," the man said.

"His name is Skip," the Judge said.

A thin smile traced over the man's thick, somewhat discolored lips. He put on his sunglasses. "My name is Jimmy."

Jimmy was tall. When he stood he towered over the Judge, who seemed a little miffed that he would be so big in his presence. Taking the court, his great hands squeezed the tennis balls between his fingers like seedless grapes. He flung the towel against the wall behind him. At first biding his time, he rocked behind the service line. He was a big cat ready to pounce. He looked at me through those dark sunglasses and smiled.

"Let me see what you got," he said.

He volleyed a tennis ball to me so forcefully it could have been a serve. Unsure whether to return it or to catch it, I simply stuck my racquet out and let the ball bounce against it, then die before me. I looked at Jimmy, who smiled a little.

"That was my quasi serve," Jimmy yelled across the net.

"That's okay," I said. "That was my pseudoreturn."

Quickly, I retrieved the ball. I dribbled it with the racquet as I took it behind the service line. I glanced toward the table where Grandma was playing bidwhist with Marshall and the lady and saw the Judge, his back toward someone eating buffalo wings and Swedish meatballs while engaging in a conversation. Rest assured, he was watching me. Jimmy pulled up his shorts at the thighs and hunkered down, ready for a return. He seemed to have instantly grown a foot and at least a hundred extra pounds.

"You sure you don't want to serve?" I asked.

"You got the ball," he said.

Taking a deep breath, I hurled the ball into the air above me, then unleashed my racquet. I went through the ball so effortlessly I thought I must have missed it completely, but, to my surprise, I sent it bounding into the far court. Jimmy hurled a rocket back toward me. I thought it would eat me alive, but it was just a matter of a couple of steps, of bringing the racquet head back, and of meeting the ball with a competent, two-fisted volley.

The Judge was right. I was good enough to play Jimmy well. Though he would win the set, it was a series of spirited points, including a couple of points I would win. More than a few times I got Jimmy diving for the floor hoping to make a shot like Boris Becker; and, when his shot failed to back me off, I lobbed a volley back to the far corner of the service line, which he, helpless, could only watch. Each time, I smiled.

The truth was Jimmy was more masterful with the finesse game. Point after point, he coaxed me to the net and teased me with little shots, which I returned, and the ease of that play lulled me into forgetting there was an entire court to cover, which he would remind me with a smash. That happened with such regularity I kicked myself. It was on such a play the set was finally lost.

The set over, Jimmy grabbed the towel and leapt across the net and waved the towel. *"No mas,"* he said. *"No mas."* He extended his hand, which enveloped mine like an oversized burlap sack. "If you were legal, I'd buy you a drink. But you're not legal, right?"

"No," I said automatically in a low voice, not quite sure what he meant by the term *legal*.

"Thought as much. If you were legal, and if your daddy weren't here, I'd give you a ride home. You'd like that, right?"

Still dumb, though wising up, I shrugged. Jimmy took that as coy enthusiasm and scribbled his name and phone number on the back of some cellular phone salesman's business card.

"When you get legal," he said, handing the card to me, "or when you wanna think legal—" he smiled broadly. "I think you know the rest."

As we walked toward the bar, I thought how hamfisted he was. I wanted to ditch the business card in some used plate and wash my hands, but I somehow didn't. Who knows? Perhaps I thought it best to hang onto it, to look at it in the privacy of my room, and to imagine vain things.

The Judge was smiling when we returned to the bar. He saluted us with a raised Bud Light. "I saw you play," he said. "You played like Arthur Ashe."

"I lost," I said.

He shrugged. "You win some, you don't. It was a good set."

When I was younger, I had to learn to take my father's praise when it came, because his praise was rare. Most of the time, he snorted his approval, to which I would snort a retort, and between our snorting we would reach a compromise agreeing to something of significance. In the Judge's world, Arthur Ashe was high praise; when he reiterated his approval by insisting it was a good set, I smiled to myself, satisfied, and I looked at Jimmy, who nodded in agreement.

Jimmy poured two disposable cups of Gatorade from a large yellow cooler on the edge of the bar and handed one to me. The one he kept he drank with gusto and he smiled and gave a huge "Aaahhh!" With the towel, he wiped the excess Gatorade from his mustache. He seemed to have wanted conversation, but the best he did was open his mouth a little. Nothing came out. His eyes flitted a bit, then he smiled.

"Who won the card game?" I asked the Judge.

He shrugged. "Mother and Marshall played together. I think they won a couple hands."

"Do you play cards, too?" Jimmy asked me, stepping toward me and lowering his voice so the Judge seemed an interloper. He smiled again. Later, I would know that smile and that body language as flirtatious, the type of thing employed by a hunter upon the hunted, but, as such a realization would come only after I had turned twenty and be employed after I had turned twenty-five, I was ignorant. I didn't even smile.

"No," I said.

"Then," Jimmy said, "I guess you don't even play backgammon."

"He's too young to play backgammon," the Judge said. He seemed to look down his nose at the thought, and, nervous, Jimmy drank Gatorade.

Because Jimmy stopped talking, I gravitated toward the bidwhist game, where Grandma and Marshall had several books to the chocolate woman's couple. Another woman the color of fresh sun tea was her partner. Not knowing the game, still I knew Grandma and Marshall were winning.

"Playing for any money?" I asked.

"If we did," Grandma began, "your daddy would be paying for this boy's college education—"

"And I would make sure it was expensive," Marshall said with a smile.

Jimmy returned with a plate of food. If for nothing else, this Jimmy was a persistent fellow. With not even a nod the Judge went to the food. That was Jimmy's in. He leaned forward and his voice dropped to a whisper.

"Call me," he said. "It doesn't matter what time."

Chapter Eight

I awoke the next morning, a Sunday, with a slight headache from the Gatorade and a most fantastic feeling that I had been carted away to someplace magical. Past recalling something vague about playing spades with Grandma before Rec Night was declared over, I couldn't remember what I did after leaving Jimmy, aside from eating. I didn't even recall returning to the open boat, which I must have done, since, at almost sixteen, I was too big to be carried.

Amazingly, I was without my pajamas. I was splayed on the bed still wearing my Illini polo shirt and socks, but without my shoes and shorts, as though someone had barely dumped my almost undressed body on the bed, and shut off the lights. I had in my nose the sour stench of slobber, which must have come from sleeping with my face in the pillow that night.

The phone rang. That and the odor shook me from sleep most rudely. I stared at my clock. It was already eight thirty; Sunday school was at nine. Like a bolt, I popped up, but I was weighed down by an enraged erection, a "piss boner," as my cousin Brad called it, and, as any adolescent boy knows, I had to contend with that first before getting on with my life. I tucked it in my underwear and hid it in my robe, and I hurried to the bathroom hoping the Judge was up and about.

I took a leak. As any guy knows, it was a chore directing the stream into the bowl. Before long, I was finished and I could hear the Judge calling for me from the foot of the stairs.

"Just a minute," I said.

Rather than take the time to enjoy myself, I tucked myself, washed my hands, and rushed to the stairs. The Judge, in his robe, was already having a pipe. I did my best to obscure the hard-on with my hands in my robe pockets.

"Are you going back to bed," he asked, "or are you up?"

"I'm up," I said.

The Judge puffed his pipe. "It's too late for Sunday school, but I am going to church, since it is a first Sunday. Do you want to come?"

I blinked. Church, an optional activity? In our family, Sunday school and church were compulsory, and attending church for communion was a no-brainer.

Our church had been our church since World War I, in a denomination that had been our family's since we came to this country a little after the Revolution, even when we absented ourselves from it in disagreements with our bishops, when we would miss it sorely. We were African Methodists, part of one of the oldest institutions in the black community, and second only to the United Methodists in its size in the Methodist family.

An average portrait of us would show the African Methodists to be a most highbacked clan, founders of the first and best newspapers, insurance companies, and universities before our first members fissured off into the Congregationalists and Episcopalians. When I was a young boy, active in our Young People's Division, I considered the John Greggs and the R. R. Wrights—our famed bishops—with such intense awe that it seemed they, long dead, could still see right through me.

The Judge pooh-poohed my fear. He would tap at his great-great-grandfather in the picture taken so many years ago in front of a revered stone chapel and remind me that a distant cousin had been a presiding elder, and had performed Grandma Macalester's wedding and arrived to give words at Grandpa Macalester's funeral. That cousin later stood for bishop and, losing, was transferred to South Africa as an honorary white for his trouble, just in time to witness Mandela's release from prison. The cousin retired in Florida and died a most unspectacular death.

I never met that relative, nor others who were deaconesses, trustees, lay readers, and General Conference delegates. I knew only Grandma's cousin Charles, the minister who married Mom and the Judge, who once—before he died a few years ago—preached at our church that God made Adam and Eve, not Adam and Steve. During the sermon, the Judge nudged my shoulder and whispered, "That is Charles's favorite sermon. He has been practicing it almost forty years."

I was twelve. I spent that Sunday obsessed with a boy I saw at school, whose face was as pure as Michelangelo's David. After that, I made a point of not daydreaming on Sundays for a year.

"Anything special?" I asked.

"Just communion," the Judge said, "and the new preacher should be there."

"What's his name?"

"Hollingsworth, or Collinsworth, or something like that," he said, puffing. "Somebody 'sworth. Paul [the presiding elder, the Judge's friend] told me his name, but I can't really remember."

"I guess with all those precedents in your head, you got to delete something."

The Judge puffed a long, mean trail of smoke. "Are you going?"

I shrugged. "Might as well. I didn't know I had options."

"There are always options, kid. You know where breakfast is."

With that, in a puff of pipe smoke that wafted past my head, and dissipated in the window behind me, he left the stairs.

As had been the case Saturday morning, the Judge was on the terrace, sitting in his robe at the head of the table. He had the Sunday *Post-Dispatch,* fresh from St. Louis, which reminded me of a picture of him as a two-year-old, taken by Grandma, holding the Sunday comics upside down, with Grandpa reading the news in the background. A wonderful picture.

My nose was right. There was a plate of bacon sitting on the table, and, as was in my imagination, he had made fresh French toast. Because it was Sunday and Sundays are for leisurely breakfasts in our family, the Judge had taken the time to section honeydew melon, coming out of season, and leave it in a bowl.

I looked at the Judge. He seemed confident with his pipe, robe, and newspaper, not alone, as though Mom was gone to some bar association conference. It seemed as though he knew she would return, become seated facing him, as she had done after every trip in my childhood. I failed to believe such things. My earliest memory as a three-year-old, taken from when my sister Adele was in high school, was of Mom going on a long trip and not returning for a long time, possibly a week. When I was older, I asked Adele what that was all about. "Mom just needed some time away," she said. Was this one such occasion? I wondered. I hoped that was all it was. But something in me said "no."

I ate in relative silence, though the Judge did mention again this reverend, Something 'sworth. As he quoted the presiding elder, Something 'sworth sounded like an enigma. I wanted to see Something 'sworth for myself. After breakfast, I yielded to curiosity and eschewed going back to bed. I dressed for church. We Methodists have a custom when dressing for church: we wear our best clothes, the kind of clothes one wears to a funeral. In my case, it was my khakis, a white pinstriped oxford shirt, burgundy tie, and blue blazer—my "spring/fall outfit," Marshall called it. He loved my penny loafers.

I waited downstairs. Then, at ten fifteen, the Judge stood at the foot of the stairs and removed his pipe from his mouth. Someone rang the doorbell. Peeking out, I saw Mom, fixing a clasp to her earring. She wore one of my favorite suits, a cream-colored jacket and skirt and matching shoes with a lime green top. She seemed to glow. Beneath her arm was a clutch bag. I opened the door.

"Mom!" I said, surprised that she would be there before me, at our house again, on a Sunday. I wanted to hug her, but you never hugged Mom in that suit.

"Rose," the Judge said. "You're beautiful."

"Going to church?" she asked. "Want a ride?"

I looked toward the driveway. Standing beside the car, dressed in a lively, light skirt suit, was Adele. Apparently, it would be like old times.

We rode in Mom's car, with her driving. Like the open boat, Mom's Volvo was graphite color, kept clean by whatever youth group's car wash she happened upon. She liked keeping her car immaculate, almost to the point of wiping behind me with a rag when I rode in her car as a little kid. And, with Mom's car, as with Grandma's, there was an order to our sitting. I sat in the front with her, with the Judge sitting in the back with Adele. He liked doing that whenever she drove. It gave him the idea of being chauffeured.

Church was a couple of blocks away, on Jefferson Avenue. Mom eased the Volvo out of the driveway and almost hit the Kidds' husky, Henson, which scampered from the park to their house next door.

"How did he get out?" Mom asked.

Undeterred, Mom continued to reverse. Getting to the street, she maneuvered the car into the right direction and eased it onto the road. Past that, it was nothing to get the car to Jefferson Avenue, a fast shot.

Though he was behind me, I could sense the Judge shifting his weight and easing toward me. I looked back to meet him, if only halfway. I decided to speak first.

"Yes?" I asked.

"Nothing," he said. The Judge turned to Adele. "I hear the kid has Eugenia Levin for English, too."

Why did my father have to mention Dr. Levin? Mom seemed to ask the same question. Immediately, Mom hit the brake, almost sending me into the windshield, had it not been for my seat belt. With a fire in her eyes I had rarely seen except when she was angry at me, she whirled toward the Judge.

"Did she call you again?"

"I called her," he said. "It's been years, Rose."

A little steam gushed from her head as she looked at him. She seemed unconcerned that cars behind us were beginning to honk, or that we were stuck in the middle of an intersection. For her, it was more important, it seemed, to take off the Judge's head.

"It hasn't been years enough," she said. She looked at me. "I have told you once, and I'll tell you again: I want my son out of that woman's classroom."

"Why?" I asked, whining.

"Rose," the Judge said, "let's not pull the kid into it. The year's just started; he has friends in that class. Pulling him out at this stage would just draw attention to it."

"Besides, Dr. Levin is one of the best teachers at the school," I said. "You can at least tell me why."

Mom gave me a parting glance, as if to say, "stay out of this, mister," and then she glared at the Judge through the rearview mirror. "We'll discuss this later, Alfred. We aren't finished with this."

She shifted to the gas and the honking stopped as we moved on. Though I would try to pry the information from my father, the most he would say was that Mom had "some issues" about Dr. Levin that, eventually, I would come to know and understand. For the time being, he said, those issues were best left to him and Mom, with my duty being to do the best I could in class, so that the two women need not meet.

Adele decided to change the subject. "Dad," she said, "I'm going to have a baby."

"You're *what?*" I asked, turning around. Where did that come from? How did that happen?

"Spencer and I are going to have a baby."

Mom was still mad. The Judge gave Adele a kiss and congratulated her on making him a grandfather, with another child, Adele's first, joining my brother Ted's little boy Caleb, who had been born in Sri Lanka three years before. For myself, I couldn't get out of my mind the idea of my brother-in-law Spencer, "Sleeping Beauty," the creased shirt, the architect in angles, the wus, forcing my sister to bear his child. It made me want to puke.

When we got to church, Mom parked the Volvo at her usual spot beneath the linden tree on the street. She grabbed her clutch bag and crossed the bricked street before the Judge and I barely got out of the car.

"Kid," Adele said after the Judge left the car, "do all of us a big favor. Anything about Eugenia Levin, tell me. Keep it from Mom. Dad's judgment, when it comes to Dr. Levin, is just pretty bad."

I nodded and we crossed the street.

I should tell you something about a Methodist service whenever a new preacher has been assigned. It is packed, usually, and usually by folks unseen at service on any other occasion. Never mind that the new preacher (this fellow, Something 'sworth) was to be here for a few weeks until the pastor the church wanted, Reverend Hale, finished defending his doctorate and made himself available. That was among the conditions made thirty years ago, when the three African Methodist churches in town finally converged and formed Bethel AME Church, a simple name, the only one Grandma Macalester said most in the three churches could agree on. Hence, we were saved from becoming a church in the wilderness. The bishop at the time, a light-headed, sick man, agreed to grant the congregation the power to call its own pastor in exchange for the Conference naming a preacher when the pulpit went empty.

So, it happened on that day, when Something 'sworth was to fill the pulpit for the first time, Marshall and the rest of the Langstons were there, as were the Morgans, all except Brad, who rarely showed for church services anyway. I stared at Alan. From where he was standing across the vestibule, Alan waved at me, cautiously. Once I waved back, he carefully came up to say hello. Naturally, the Judge spoke first.

"Good to see you this Sunday, Alan," the Judge said, extending a hand, which the kid shook, very carefully. "Good to see the Morgans out in strength."

"Everybody except Brad," Alan said.

"Any news?" he asked.

"I dunno. I guess Mom and Dad still expect he'll come home soon."

Someone opened the sanctuary door and the organ prelude filled the vestibule. "Nearer, My God, to Thee." The Morgans slipped into the sanctuary, and Alan, dressed in his stylish pinstriped charcoal suit with a blood red necktie he somehow got by without tying completely, pulled us in with the rest of his family. He turned to me. Though he smiled, his eyes were plain, like stone.

"Thanks for the ride last Saturday," Alan said, not looking directly at me.

"Don't mention it," I said.

We followed Alan into the sanctuary and took our seats with Mom and Grandma in the fifth pew on the left, which everyone knew to have been the Macalesters' from the day Trinity was consecrated. I watched Alan as the Morgans wandered from pew to pew looking for a place. When they crossed our path for a second time, Ian Morgan, a cute little boy, smiled and shrugged.

"Dennis's kids are darling," the Judge said to Grandma, "don't you think so, Madelyn?"

Grandma nodded. "They are. And don't call me 'Madelyn.'"

The Morgans found a spot in the front just in time for the choir's processional up the aisle. The choir was mixed, wearing rich green, red, and black robes. Behind the choir was the lay reader, Judge Calvin Wilson, the Judge's old law partner from his days before Congress, and the supply preacher, Reverend Something 'sworth, who wore a traditional black robe with the customary AME anvil and cross on the stole. Something 'sworth was an unremarkable, mustached, bespectacled man about the complexion of a chocolate chip cookie. His close chopped hair sported a modern haircut.

"*Shi—!*" Grandma whispered when Something 'sworth passed our pew. "It's that old pest from Conference!"

"Not in church, Madelyn," the Judge said, and Grandma shot him one of her "now, I'm warning you" looks.

As he approached the pulpit, I remember looking at Something 'sworth and thinking he seemed such a small man. No bigger than me, he mounted the steps to the pulpit hunched over, like he was hiding something. Then, when he turned around and faced the congregation for the opening, our eyes met briefly before he glanced away.

Judge Wilson led us through the service. It was a very traditional, very Methodist service. The music consisted of anthems and hymns— none of that bluesy, pseudo nightclub stuff so many called "gospel music." That stuff had been banned a long time ago, and, though we allowed "Precious Lord, Take My Hand" and "Peace in the Valley" as nods to Thomas Dorsey, the stuff we played and sang emphasized the admonition that we good Christians are to be silent and know He is the Lord. Knowing Bethel was a black church and comprehending little beyond that, some white visitors came to our church expecting to hear good music and left more than a little disappointed that our music was as good as what they had in their own churches. They were always amazed, it seemed, that while we made a joyful noise, we did not make Him deaf.

Regular music played, and the liturgy went its regular way. Then, when it came time for the sermon, Judge Wilson introduced Something 'sworth.

"And now, dear church," Judge Wilson began, "as you know, Reverend Hale is doing his doctorate in Chicago. For the time being, the bishop, in his wisdom, after consulting with you, dear church, and after much prayer—"

"He was a lot briefer when his mama was alive," the Judge whispered to Grandma.

"If you had his mama," Grandma said, "you would be briefer too. She was a battle ax."

I had heard about Judge Wilson's mother. Grandma said she kept him in diapers until he was fifty.

"—after much prayer and thought," continued Judge Wilson, "the bishop has supplied to us a temporary pastor. Reverend Michael Shuddlesworth—"

"That's it!" the Judge said.

"—from Indiana Conference, who will render us with a message."

I knew there was bound to be some rumblings about him coming from Indiana Conference, as one of the complaints the three churches had was about the bishops using the Illinois Conference as Indiana's pissing ground. Nonetheless, Reverend Shuddlesworth smiled at the congregation, revealing a gold-tipped front tooth.

"Good morning, church," the Reverend said.

"Good morning," some of us said.

The Reverend removed his glasses and checked them for spots. "If I may borrow—" he said "borrah," really, "—the words of our glorious and dear—" okay, he said "dearah," "—opening, 'I was glad when they said unto me, let us go into the house of the Lord.' And I am glad—" (Okay, both times he said "gladah") "—to be with you today. Can I get a witness?"

We stared at him. Was he really a Methodist, or just a refugee from the Pentecostal tradition? Reverend Shuddlesworth seemed not to know the answer. He patted his mouth and put back on his glasses. "For the Lord had moved my heart to be in your company today, and to rejoice with you in His goodness today."

"In other words," the Judge whispered to Grandma, "the bishop made him."

Grandma chuckled. The couple sitting in front of us, a pair of visitors, there for their idea of our music, probably, glanced at her and almost laughed. I think my eyes sparkled just a bit, as though I had been laughing too.

"And the dear Lord has made us a glorious day," Reverend Shuddlesworth continued. "Such a glorious new day. And He has touched my heart to partake with you the goodness of our Lord and Savior Jesus Christ—"

"In other words," the Judge began, whispering. "While I'm here—"

"—a message—"

"I must talk," the Judge continued.

"—of the Good Lord's mercy and goodness."

"To earn my fee," the Judge continued. The couple sitting in front of us chuckled and shook their heads, as did Grandma.

"He should just say, 'Hello. I'm here. I'm going to talk,'" Grandma whispered.

The Judge shook his head. "Too simple. The goal of these preachers is to always make things as complicated as possible."

"*Shhh!*" Mom said. She leaned into my ear and dropped her voice to a whisper. "Tell your father he is setting a bad example."

For a moment, I looked at her. She seemed serious about it, to say the least. Besides, she seemed to say, we have visitors. With a simple, insistent look, she urged me to relay the message, but by then Reverend Shuddlesworth's introduction had ended and the Judge had settled in to hear the message.

I was right. Reverend Shuddlesworth pronounced almost everything with a discernible "ah" at the end of it. He talked about evangelism. What exactly he had to say about it, I don't know, for he lost me partway through the thing. He caught my attention and pulled me in when he removed his glasses again and checked them for spots. The church organist, an observant older woman, took that to mean he was almost finished, so she sat at the organ and began a hymn. Reverend Shuddlesworth cut his eyes at her until she stopped. Then, chuckling, he put his glasses back on.

"Church," bellowed the Reverend, "I know you are used to someone winding down at about here. But, Church, Reverend Shuddlesworth is not winding down. Oh, no! I'm here to tell you Reverend Shuddlesworth is just winding up."

I looked at the sanctuary clock. According to my reckoning we had been in church for over an hour and Reverend Shuddlesworth had been talking for almost twenty minutes. How was I to know checking his glasses was just at the halfway mark? While he spoke, I considered geometric equations. Staring at the man, I blurred my eyes until his face appeared as a glob of cookie dough. More geometry. Then, after a few minutes, I squinted again. Then I found myself thirsty. And I had to go. I climbed over Mom and incurred her sharp stare.

"Excuse me," I said.

She continued staring at me.

I slipped down the side aisle to the back pew, which the ushers guarded with stacks of bulletins, envelopes, and collection plates. One of them, Mrs. Easton, sat at the end of the pew and gave me a long, hard look. She was what the Judge said Aunt Sister called a "stout" woman. Coal black, with her hair a close-cropped natural, she was the shape of a Sherman tank, and she seemed to dare me to bring my body anywhere near hers. Nevertheless, I approached. I stood at her like a suppliant at an altar.

"You're not thirsty," she whispered, her jagged lower teeth barely visible above her lip. "And you don't need to pee. Does your mama know all you doing is stretching your legs?"

I nodded. I looked up and saw Marshall pass his usher on the other side of the church and pardon himself into the vestibule. As he did, he wagged his finger at me. Mrs. Easton was not about to let me by on her own accord, so I started to prance. I really did need to use the bathroom.

She relented. She shifted her massive weight and pivoted her body, holding her white usher's uniform so the hem still reached her knee. "Go before you have yourself an accident," she said. I squeezed my body past hers (believe me, it was a chore) and slipped out the door.

My first thought was to find Marshall. It had almost been a dozen hours since I spoke to him last, and, to be frank, that was one of the longest stretches (aside from vacations) we ever went without talking.

While we were growing up, Marshall was like me: short in relation to six footers but tall for five footers, and he had a layer of baby fat that made him look a little heavier than his one hundred and forty-five pounds. Marshall moved at a contemplative pace, except when he wanted to get someplace. Then, he would run over his own mama.

Where Marshall went, I did not know. He had moved too quickly for me to find him. Standing in the vestibule, I heard a restroom door (with a creak) open and the side door (with the birds) close. I went to the side door. Beyond it, Marshall stood on concrete, watching the cars go by.

"Hey," I said.

"Hey, yourself," Marshall said. He turned to me and offered a roll of Life Savers. "Mint?"

"Do I need it?"

"After today's sermon, cousin dear, everyone will need it."

We took Life Savers and started sucking on them. Some bootleg U2 fan drove by in a truck and shouted something about Negro boys going to church. Marshall flipped him off.

"How many card games did you win last night?" I asked.

"Ask Cousin Madelyn. She kept track."

Nodding, I sucked on the mint.

"Adele's pregnant," I said.

"Boy or girl?"

"Don't know," I said. "I think it's too soon."

"Pray for a girl," Marshall said. "We got too many boys in our family for you to know what to do with yourself."

That was bewildering. "What's that supposed to mean?"

Marshall wouldn't say. He simply let that rest on me for a while. Hands in his pockets, he looked at me. Then, his eyes returned to the street. "You should take your leak, cousin dear, before someone comes out looking for you."

I examined my front, thinking I was showing, and I went back inside without saying anything very intelligible. I passed Pik in the vestibule and he looked at me as if he were searching, and, knowing it was for Marshall, I pointed toward the side door. Pik nodded and smiled a thank-you.

The ushers opened the sanctuary doors and the hymn of invitation, "Just As I Am, Without One Plea," filled the vestibule. At the head of the church, Reverend Shuddlesworth came down from the pulpit and extended his hands. He looked at me briefly, then looked away.

"If you do not have a church home," the Reverend said, "or want to know the Father better, come forth now. The doors of the church are open."

No one came.

Judge Wilson descended from the pulpit and whispered something to Reverend Shuddlesworth, who adjusted his glasses. The Reverend turned around and faced the mounds beneath white linen on the sacramental table, then he nodded.

"I beg your pardon," the Reverend said. "Holy Communion. Let the words of my mouth and the meditation of my heart be acceptable in Thy sight, O Lord, my Strength and my Redeemer."

Marshall had come into the vestibule. He leaned into my ear. "That was your chance, cousin dear," he said. "That was your chance."

I smiled and Pik smiled. Marshall winked and proceeded into the sanctuary, followed by Pik, as the church stood to take communion. Mrs. Easton held open the door for me and I entered. With the ushers up and prepared to conduct the congregation to communion through the center aisle, it was nothing this time to navigate the back pew and up the side aisle. Mom came out and let me in. As I passed, she pinched my arm, a sign of displeasure.

"Ouch," I mouthed.

"*Shhh!*" someone said.

Rubbing where she pinched, I took my seat between Mom and the Judge. The Judge held open the hymnal to the litany for communion and, like the rest of the congregation, I recited the words in hopes of purifying, if only a little, my sinful thoughts of the previous week. We sang "Let Us Break Bread Together" so peacefully I thought I was daydreaming again.

Then came time for the church, pew by pew, to proceed up to the Reverend and our rather matronly stewardesses and take communion. It is almost as tedious as altar call, which almost always found me praying for absolution and quick sermons. One by one, the ushers signaled for the pews to go forward and take the host, which tasted like copier paper, and drink the wine, which, being Methodist, was really grape juice.

I waited for our turn, reminding myself I was parched from having been so good at church for so long. I remember doing a little dance because my bladder was beginning to scream. Grandma noticed. She looked at me for a little bit and put a hand on the Judge's wrist.

"You need to take that boy to a doctor," Grandma said.

The couple in front of us considered me briefly. I smiled at them.

When it was our turn, Mrs. Easton signaled for us to go. While we were in line, I saw Marshall in the congregation. Again, he wagged his finger at me. I waited for my turn at the host and wine. Once it came, I stood at Reverend Shuddlesworth and tried keeping my mind as empty as possible. The Reverend seemed frozen, until one of the stewardesses, Mrs. Bozeman, said his name. He said words to me that had been said dozens of times before. They were rote and flat. He then placed the host in my hands, and I ate it, and he placed the grape juice in its thimble there, too, and I drank it. I gave Mrs. Bozeman the thimble and returned down the side aisle to my seat, feeling strangely examined.

The end of the service finally came. Preceded by the choir, Judge Wilson and Reverend Shuddlesworth came down to the sanctuary door. The Reverend raised his hands and together we said the benediction.

"'We give Thee but Thine own, Whate'er the gift may be; All that we have is Thine alone, A trust, O Lord from thee.' 'The Lord watch between me and thee, when we are absent one from another.'"

Without sitting again, the congregation retrieved its things and shuffled to the vestibule. I almost knocked down old ladies trying to get to the restroom. When I got there, I had my choice of urinals for a brief second. Then, Alan wormed his way in. He froze when he saw me, then, head down, pushed on to the urinal and started to leak.

"What a talker," Alan said finally. "I thought he would never finish."

I looked at Alan. He stood a good step from the urinal and shot the piss into the porcelain. I looked away.

"He did talk up a storm," I said.

"Man, did he ever." He was so cool it felt like January.

Reminding myself about being in church was unsuccessful, as the blood was beginning to flow. I tried to blunt it by thinking about my mother, or Grandma, or Mrs. Easton, but that helped only momentarily. Then, Alan finished, zipped, and flushed.

"Done," he said. "See ya."

Almost as fast as his entry, Alan exited. Next thing I knew, I was in a toilet stall.

"You aren't being satyrical in there, are you?"

It was the Judge. Engulfed in my thoughts, I did not hear him enter the restroom. He stood on the other side of the stall door.

"No, Dad," I said.

I could sense him leaning into the door, then he backed off. "Be sure to wash your hands," he said.

Quietly, he left. Unable to return to my fantasy, I waited a few minutes and then flushed to sound legitimate. I found the Judge waiting by the water fountain. I smiled and rubbed my hands on my shirt.

"I washed my hands," I said.

He considered me. For a second, he seemed to see right through me. I stopped rubbing my hands and I waited. Then, he looked away.

"How would you rate Reverend Shuddlesworth?" he asked.

"I'd give him a C+," I said.

He smiled. "Really? I'd give a snap and a half twist. I cannot afford to be that generous." Folding his arms, he fixed his gaze upon the women's restroom. "Now all we have to do is wait for your mother, and mine."

He waited a few minutes, then he opened the women's restroom door a crack and closed it, saying nothing. Mom, Grandma, and Adele came out talking.

"The best I could give," Grandma said to Mom, "is keep on walking and keep your big mouth shut." The women went straight for the Judge, and, when they reached him, Grandma leaned forward. "I know that was you," she said to him. "Just pull that again."

"Let's not threaten," he said.

"I'm promising," Grandma retorted.

The Judge nodded and said it was time for the Macalesters to meet the temporary preacher. A line to shake his hand had formed in the vestibule and, gradually, it went down to where Reverend Shuddlesworth and Judge Wilson were shaking hands. When we came to them, Judge Wilson's gray eyes sparkled and his pink, lined face drew a broad smile.

"And here are the Macalesters," Judge Wilson said. "Two lawyers, two congressmen, a federal judge, a principal, a bureaucrat, and Skip!"

Reverend Shuddlesworth grew a shy smile. He took Grandma's hand, which, of course, was first. "You must be the judge," he said to her.

"No," she said, chuckling. "I may be judgmental, but I am no judge. I'm the principal and one of the Representatives. My son Alfred is the judge. Before that, he served in Congress almost fourteen years. Rose to become chairman of the Rules Committee."

Reverend Shuddlesworth took the Judge's hand. "Democrat?"

"Republican," we all said, and the Reverend begged our pardon.

"The Macalesters have been among the pillars in this church and its predecessors for years, real builders," Judge Wilson said.

"We go back in this county, in one form or another, to the 1840s," the Judge said.

Grandma, having none of that, waved her hands. "Never mind that stick in the mud," she said to the Reverend. "I am plain old Madelyn. Welcome to Bethel."

Not wanting to monopolize the Reverend's attention, Grandma stepped away and let him finish shaking the Judge's hand. Then, he looked like he wanted to stop, but the Judge was just getting warmed up.

"I'm friends with Paul Bland, the presiding elder," the Judge said.

The Reverend nodded. "I hope you will give the Presiding Elder a good report on me," Reverend Shuddlesworth finally said.

"Don't worry," the Judge replied.

Mom said hello. Judge Wilson introduced her as one of the best lawyers in the county. She said he was just saying that because he retired from the bench. That was probably true.

Then came my turn. Reverend Shuddlesworth, who had been a one-hand shaker, extended both hands and flashed a broad, gold-toothed smile. "This must be the Skip," he said. "Is your name Alfred, too?"

I shook my head.

"His real name is Arthur," Judge Wilson said, "but I think no one calls him that."

"No one living, at least," Mom said.

There was a wait of a few minutes. I had difficulty getting my hand from him. My hand didn't warm in his, but turned cold and hard. I had to say something to get my hand back. "I really enjoyed today's sermon," I said finally.

His smile quivered. "Now, how could you know I done a good sermon if you left in the middle of it?"

What was I to say to a man who had an eye on me? I smiled. "What was I to do? Have an accident?"

His smile faded a little. He looked at Judge Wilson, who tilted his head in a dimly Reaganesque manner. Mom grasped my arm so firmly she almost cut off the circulation. I almost said something else.

"He's only fifteen," Adele said.

"Ah," the Reverend said, "to be fifteen again!"

"It's one helluva age," the Judge said. Then he looked at me. "Wouldn't you say?"

Mom having hold of my arm notwithstanding, I smiled, and the adults eased me away from the Reverend and Judge Wilson.

"Will you let go of my arm?" I whispered to Mom when we got to the street. I tried wrenching myself away, but her grasp was tight. I looked at her. She walked resolutely, as though she were just a mother enjoying a walk with her son. "Did I say something?"

"Just inappropriate," she whispered back.

Grandma and the Judge were ahead of us. They talked about dinner and they agreed, with Mom, to eat at the Moonlight, for they had a taste for Moonlight fried chicken.

"But don't tell nobody," Grandma said. "We do have a reputation."

"Oh, I ain't gonna tell nobody, Madelyn," the Judge said.

"Don't you call me 'Madelyn.'"

Turning briskly, she boarded the open boat and started the engine. She waited for us to get into Mom's Volvo. We returned to our usual positions, and I looked back at Reverend Shuddlesworth, who glanced at me a hot second before we drove off.

Chapter Nine

In spite of my best efforts, dinner at Moonlight on the far edge of town moved at a leisurely pace. Grandma, the Judge, and Mom all saw people they knew from the moment we entered, as Moonlight had been a favored haunt for decades, in part because it was one of the first places to serve blacks on a nondiscriminatory basis. Its reputation was furthered by serving as a workshop for patients from the nearby state hospital, who could have been anything from alcoholic or depressed to psychotic or retarded. One frequented such a place because it had done right by people, and the frequenting was a way of saying "thank you," if ever so briefly. The owner, Mr. Castelli, was grateful for the loyalty. He came out to greet us, because, Grandma said, the Judge mentioned him and his restaurant on national television at the Republican convention some years before.

Mr. Castelli was a yeasty man. He had a white beard that helped him play Santa Claus at the Catholic Children's Home. After speaking to us, he whistled and said, "best table for Madelyn and her family," and the Moonlight staff quickly busied itself like elves in a woodworking shop. They produced Grandma's favorite table, a round one in the middle of the main dining room, and a pair of middle-aged waitresses in matching pageboy haircuts stood ready with water, coffee, and lemonade, and took our orders.

At first, I chose fried chicken, legs and thighs; my mouth watered so much I wolfed down planks of fresh Italian bread. What could I say? Moonlight served great chicken, and I was so very hungry. Then, my appetite changed. Kay Reece arrived. He would have had a field day seeing me eat fried chicken, like the stuff he had seen in *Birth of a Nation* was really true. To make matters worse (if they could ever be worse than eating around Kay), he was seated at a table near us. Now he could see my whole family eating fried chicken! Like we were pickaninnies from a plantation! I excused myself. I wanted the waitress so I could change my order.

Kay was a member of what Marshall called "the pointy-head jingo set." A Whitmaner and standout first baseman, Kay had the pug face of a newborn middle white pig, with platinum blond hair and skin wisping from his head to boot. As a sophomore, I had been told Kay hated my guts, for no better reason than being Marshall's cousin. (Brad told me . . . so, what about Brad? He's Marshall's cousin too.) When I mentioned it to Marshall over a cigar and a drink, he said Kay hated being called "pink eye" (I think his eyes were brown, maybe blue), and he hated anyone who could tan better than he. Marshall spat out a fingernail. "Don't sweat the prick, cousin dear," he said. "Kay's just white trash like the rest of them." I had two classes that year with Kay, history and English. I thought it would be a rough year.

I found the waitress lifting a tip from a bussed table in the lounge. At first, she looked at me as though she were trying to place me, or like I was there to lift the tip from her. Then, when I said my last name, her mind clicked and she stood at attention.

"What can I do for you, Mister Macalester?" she asked.

"I'd like to change my order."

"You had the fried chicken, all dark, right?" she asked in a loud voice. I tried shushing her, because Kay was not far away. "What did you decide, sir? Go with breasts or livers instead?"

"I decided to go with something else," I said softly. "Something Italian."

That struck her for a minute, then she shrugged. Because I couldn't think of anything off the bat, she sat me down at the bar with a menu, and the bartender set before me a glass of iced milk. Moonlight was just as well-known for its Italian dishes as it was for its fried chicken. Mostaccioli? Lasagna? Linguine with crab and lobster sauce? Linguine with a garlic and white wine sauce? Fettucine alfredo? Manicotti? Cannelloni? My mouth watered like mad. I drank milk, chewed ice. If it weren't for the elders paying for it, I would have chosen a little of everything. The cannelloni kept my eye. Even the Judge made cannelloni. Moonlight's cooks made good cannelloni. I decided on cannelloni. The waitress put the order on the back of a credit card receipt.

I had saved the dignity of my race and class from the ridicule of scum. I had done my duty. I headed back to my table. Kay passed me, heading for the men's room. He looked at me from the men's room door and smirked.

"Jerk off," I muttered, and I practically ran after him.

I entered the men's room. Kay stood at a urinal, head tilted back and eyes closed. Dressed for church, his tan suit hung from his frame as if it were still on a suit rack, and, for the first time, I noticed he had no ass. I had dreamt of him, for one year, in seventh grade, longed to be with him alone in a men's room, and there he was, finally; but instead my thoughts were *this guy ain't got no behind!* I couldn't help but smile at the sight of the great Kay Reece in a toilet. Then again, he knew I was there.

It was a similar place, with a similar smell of soap, back in seventh grade, that I found Kay, years before, alone and doing something in a toilet stall. The rest of the boys were outside doing calisthenics. The PE teacher, Mr. Dorsey, sent me back to get Kay.

For a moment, Kay looked at me, disgusted that I would find him exposed, playing with himself. Then, he eased and put his hand on my shoulder. "Sit," he commanded, closing the door. Once I sat on the toilet he put his hand at my jaw and made me open my mouth. Perhaps "made" is the wrong verb. I was a very willing participant.

He was finished directly; he pulled up his shorts. "Tell anyone, you faggot, and I'll kick your ass." I was almost repulsed by him, for, at thirteen, Kay was not the cleanest kid. But every Wednesday for a month I volunteered to look for him, when he was the last kid in seventh grade to come out for PE. It climaxed with me leaning against a wall, legs together, as Kay leaned against me. Mr. Dorsey interrupted him, and he sent me on my way. The only other remarkable thing that happened that day was Kay and Drew fighting during a softball game.

"*Fuck!*" he moaned in the Moonlight men's room. "That feels so *fucking* good!" He glanced at me and sneered. "I always thought you were the kind of faggot to sneak up on a guy taking a piss."

"Be sure to wash that jizz off your hands," I said.

"Ah, Macalester, I was hoping you would tongue me dry again." He held out his hand, coaxing me to come to him.

He was disgusting. I wouldn't go to him, even if we were thirteen again. But, something in me, my curiosity, I suppose, led me to lean forward to get a better look at his penis. Kay batted me away, dismissive.

Before Kay could say much of anything, his father, a big man with a senator's white mane of hair, came in and clamped ahold of the back of Kay's neck. Kay turned beet red. "Finish," his father ordered. "Finish! Now, shake and zip!"

Grudgingly, Kay did as he was told, and the man guided his son to the sink, where he washed and dried his hands.

"Will you let me go?" Kay asked.

"I'll let you go when you behave yourself, little buster," his father said. Then man guided Kay out of the restroom. I left as well. Considering Kay's old man in action, I shouldn't complain about the Judge.

I returned to my table. The elders looked like I had deserted them. "I really had to go," I said, and, for some reason, that got Grandma and the Judge laughing so hard they just about fell over.

"I didn't think it was that funny," Mom said, acting very serious, which got Grandma and the Judge laughing even harder. Even Adele looked at me and laughed.

"What?" I asked. I rubbed my spoon with a napkin.

The laughter died down enough for the food to be served. At first, the elders thought my cannelloni was a mistake, but I assured them it most certainly was not. I ate quickly, making sure Kay caught me eating Italian, and not fried chicken.

We had dinner. The conversation was mostly Adele telling Grandma about life in Washington, DC. "I'm here until Tuesday," she said. "Then I'm flying back." The work at the National Endowment for the Humanities required her to be back by Wednesday. Mom cringed whenever Adele mentioned NEH. She had always felt her daughter should have been a lawyer. Since Ted was a diplomat, and I was yet to be anything, Mom thought she should have at least one child was a lawyer.

Dinner was over. We had no dessert. We called for the check. The waitress brought it immediately and waited for someone to approve the bill before leaving us alone to figure out who was paying for what. The elders each paid for their own, and my meal and Adele's were divided between Mom and the Judge. Each of the elders left three dollars for the tip, which got Grandma to talking about how the Judge and Mr. Howell, and a few of their friends, had lunch at Jo Jo's one afternoon during his freshman year of college, and left as a tip pennies and nickels in an ashtray. The Judge smiled.

"That's like you and Dad leaving that restaurant in Chicago without tipping and the girl running out after you. Now that was bad," the Judge said.

"That was your daddy," Grandma said. "The waitress asked, 'don't you believe in tipping?' and he said, 'obviously not, I didn't leave you any.'" She laughed heartily. Our waitress, who was eavesdropping, looked at her in horror. "That was your granddaddy," Grandma said to me. "He was quick like that."

I looked for Kay. Kay and his family were gone. So much for thinking about him.

In Mom's Volvo I looked at the clock. It was almost two; a good part of a good day had already been used up. Mom chose the most measured way back home, stopping for a minute at a supermarket because she said Aunt Carolyn needed toilet paper.

"Will you go in for me?" she asked, digging into her handbag for her wallet.

"Do I have to?" I whined.

"In a few years, Mr. Skip, you'll want times like these after eating like that," she said. She found her wallet and handed me a few dollars. I huffed.

"Do what your mother asked, kid," the Judge said.

"And don't get that cheap stuff your father likes to get," Mom said. "I'm giving you four dollars. You can get four good rolls for around three seventy. Get it."

I tried sighing audibly, but both Mom and the Judge ignored it as so much protestation. I took Mom's hemp-fabric grocery bag from the backseat and entered the supermarket, going straight for the toilet paper. I must have been inside all of five minutes. I rushed back, change and toilet paper in the bag. When I got back to the car, Mom and the Judge were sitting in an awkward, strained silence that told me they must have exchanged words. Adele, looking miserable, as she almost always did when she was stuck with our parents, twisted in the backseat. I tried humor.

"Who's dead?" I asked.

Mom glared at me. "Not funny, Mister."

With that, she shifted the Volvo into drive and drove away.

For as pretty a day as it was, it was a cool drive home. Mom said nothing beyond her initial response to me and the Judge watched the cars go by, like he had nothing better to do than twiddle his thumbs. They remained icy until we got to our street. Drew was parked in front of our house, waiting. My heart sank.

"*Please,*" I prayed.

"'Please' what?" the Judge asked.

I looked back at him. "You know."

The Judge waved and smiled at Drew as we passed. "I'll call whomever I like, Rose," he said.

Mom was the first to rage inside. She pulled the Volvo into the driveway, grabbed her handbag and the grocery bag and left for the front door. She engaged small talk about the weather with Drew and stormed inside. In her fit, I knew she locked the door. I looked at the Judge, who was just then leaving the car.

"I said 'please,'" I said.

The Judge shrugged and entered the house through the garage. He did an ever-so-light nod at Drew. Drew came over, wondering what was wrong. At least, he seemed that way. When he saw that I noticed, he lightened up and smiled. I left the Volvo and started for the front door. Adele stayed in the car.

"How was church?" he asked.

"Church was church."

"New preacher?"

"A temp," I said. "Our pastor is in Chicago, finishing his doctorate."

Drew nodded. I used my key, which I kept pinned in my pocket. I opened the door and stuck an ear inside to see if there was any yelling. It was past the arguing stage. All I heard were a couple of doors slamming. I closed the door and turned to Drew.

"You went out to eat?" Drew asked.

"Moonlight," I said, putting my hands in my pockets. "Saw Kay Reece there."

"Bummer. Did that dickhead say anything?"

"No," I said. I could hear another door slam inside. I stepped down from the stoop and belched. "I'm hungry, though."

"I can see how seeing that dickhead would delay your appetite," Drew said. "What do you say to some ice cream? You can even get some on that wondrous suit of yours."

I told him I would love some. We got it from the Dairy Queen uptown, then Drew took me to a ridge in Jefferson Park so lush and green it couldn't possibly be in town. I had a root beer float, Drew a chocolate milk shake, and we drank next to the pines, and, to use Drew's words, "watched the queers looking for men drive by."

It was a pleasant stay. After drinking, Drew put the cups aside and we took turns resting our heads on each other's stomach as the clouds went by. Drew was in his usual shorts and T-shirt. As I lay on him, his belly heaved with the persistence of a cuckoo clock.

"Sorry," he said when he made a gastric sound. "I guess it's the ice cream."

"I should say so."

I did not have to look at Drew. I had seen his sly, crooked smile often enough to know he was doing it then, and I knew he was enjoying my head on his stomach. I was enjoying it too, as I was getting hard. I tried to conceal myself. My hands brushed against his thigh as I pivoted to my side. Drew might have noticed me, for he lifted his head and smiled.

"You'll get grass stains all over your Little Lord Fauntleroy suit, Arthur," he said. "And grass stains don't rinse out."

"I'll just dry clean them," I said. "They ain't permanent press, after all."

He dropped his head. "You know better than to say 'ain't.' What are you? Slumming?"

He rested his hands behind his head and returned to the clouds. So did I. Soon, I turned soft again, though, in the meantime, I could feel Drew's stomach muscles tighten again as his attention shifted from the clouds to my pants. Then, he looked at his watch.

"We've been jerking around long enough," he said. "It's time to get you back home."

He sat up, as did I, and he took me home. He parked the car in its usual spot on the street. The Judge's car was home. I figured Mom and the Judge had gotten tired.

"Hey," I said, "how about me shucking these duds and us playing some tennis?"

He said, "Great." Drew agreed to wait for me while I ran inside to change and fetch my racquet. I would have let him in, but the Judge was in there, and who knew what state of bickering he had been left in. I used my key to enter the front door. I found myself in a house with little sound. I wondered if they had done each other in.

"Hello?"

Mom and Adele were gone. The Judge was watching the Washington Redskins play the Oakland Raiders on TV. I couldn't find my racquet.

Loosening my tie, I ran upstairs to my room. I stumbled out of my shoes, stepped out of my socks, and dropped my pants before flipping my tie off and removing my blazer. Then, I unbuttoned my shirt all the way to the navel and remembered Drew was waiting outside. I peeked out, and saw him leaning against his car. I opened the screen and leaned out of the window.

"You wanna come inside?" I yelled at him.

"No, that's all right," he said. "I'm okay."

"I'll be a minute."

"Just make sure you got some clothes on, Arthur, will ya?"

I closed the screen, and shucked the shirt. Bert, who had slipped into my room, tripped me and screamed because I stepped on her tail. "Sorry, Bertie," I said. She ran downstairs, thinking football games were safer.

I wore what I always wore for tennis: T-shirt, tennis shorts, and socks. I laced my tennis shoes. Where was my racquet? When I opened my closet, where it usually was, I didn't see it. Lifting the screen, I stuck my head out of the window again.

"I'll be there in a minute," I yelled at Drew. "I have to find my racquet."

"If you gotta," Drew replied, "you can use one of mine."

That was an odd thing. Drew knew I had a plethora of racquets. But the one that was really mine, gripped for me to use that year, was missing. I could play with one of my old racquets, bearing a previous year's grip, but I needed the one for that year. Then, the phone rang. I got it in the kitchen. "Hello?"

"You got to be Skip," said a deep, ebony, satin voice.

"Who is this?" I asked.

"Please tell me it's Skip," the voice said.

"It might be," I said. "I'm really busy. Tell me who you are first?"

The voice chuckled. "This is Jimmy. From last night."

I could not believe hamfisted Jimmy had tracked me down. I wondered, did I give him my phone number? I thought I should ask, in a roundabout way. "How did you get this number?" Okay, so that was more direct than roundabout.

"So, it is Skip. How you doing, Skip?"

"Fine."

"It got so busy last night, you left without saying good-bye."

"How did you get this number?" I asked again.

Jimmy paused. "I can get at almost everything I want, once I put my mind to it. As you will find out, eventually. But, more to my reason for calling: you left something last night, and I picked it up."

"What?"

"Guess. It's something I think you desperately need."

"I hate guessing games," I said, using a line I heard in one of Grandma's videos. Besides, I dreaded thinking I could have done anything with Jimmy, like lose my shorts.

Jimmy laughed. "My, you can really be the tough guy, can't you? Who taught you that line, Gene Wilder? Never mind. Let me just say I got your tennis racquet. It is a fine instrument, and since you play almost every day, I thought you might need it real soon. So, son, let me get it to you."

"You want my address, or something?"

"Do I want your address, or something?" he asked. He laughed a little. "No, no, Skip. Even I am not so forward as to attain your address. I figure, since you aren't legal yet, the best thing to do is meet someplace neutral, out in the open. Since you aren't legal."

It sounded like a fair proposition. We agreed to meet at a shopping center, in North St. Louis County, in about a half hour. I hung up wondering what I had done to deserve such attention, though, I really should have been grateful that he found my racquet. I ran out to Drew, when was sitting on the front step.

"Take me to Jamestown," I said, referring to the shopping center.

Shielding his eyes from the sun with his hand, he looked at me. "You want me to take you across the river?"

"Some guy's gonna give me my racquet."

Drew asked no details and I didn't offer any. He squinted at me. He looked like he found something to say.

"Well?" I asked

"Well, let's go get your racquet," he said, getting up.

He brushed off his seat and we trudged to his car, which was still warm in spite of the near-fall day and in spite of the windows being down.

His front seats lay low. The combination of the seat and the engine made me feel as if I were riding a rocket, or something equally cylindrical. Be it the seat, the car, or Drew's driving, I had yet to feel comfortable enough with him behind the wheel to fall asleep, my comfort barometer. Hell, I had yet to fall asleep to anyone's driving. I could never confide this to Drew. I liked him too much.

Drew smiled and the engine ignited easily. "Well, Arthur. Here we go. We are going to get your racquet."

The sound turned to Billy Bragg, then to The Clash, as Drew went across town to the bridge across the Mississippi. Though I might like their politics better, I sometimes told myself, growing up, that I preferred Marshall's Wagner.

"You like this?" Drew asked about a Clash CD. "I can make a tape of it, if you like it enough."

I nodded, charmed by the proposition, and I wondered how my rather ossified parents would take to me bringing something punk into the house. Knowing them, they would probably pass it off as just a phase and go about their business, as though nothing had happened. Then Drew thought better of it.

"Perhaps, since you're into rock, you should get something simple, like the Beatles." He smiled a little. "That way, we can get your parents up to speed, too. Then they can take the really hard stuff."

It was my turn to smile, like I really could see Mom and the Judge singing to the White Album.

Once we had crossed town it was just a couple of easy turns to reach the bridge. Though over thirty years old, the bridge was still known as the new Clark Bridge. The old Clark Bridge, which spanned into Second Street at Langdon Avenue, was a high, narrow, former toll bridge from the Jazz Age; its tollbooth, Grandma said, sat in the middle of the legendary state line, where no one had the option not to pay.

The tollbooth was gone by the Judge's time, though the funniest story he had ever told was about him and the old bridge, which he drove across during his second stab at Practice Driving (he had flunked his first pass), when the Practice Driving teacher, Mr. Macias, a good friend of the family, had a girl drive across the narrow old Clark Bridge and the narrower old Lewis Bridge across the Missouri, and had the Judge drive back. The Judge was saying the Lord's Prayer, he said, and Mr. Macias, a good Catholic, said the Rosary. Mr. Macias, the Judge swore, turned white in the process.

A drive across the Clark Bridge, "new" as it may have been, always resulted in thoughts about the old bridge. According to the Judge, once the bridge was installed and its construction ran as an episode on *NOVA,* property values in town went up, and we were flooded with Missourians.

Driving across the bridge and the Mississippi, we passed a line of Missourians anxious to go up the River Road. We said nothing about them, but let the Clash rant punkish at them, as they were using Illinois, like a whore, for their playground.

I would never admit it to my parents (nor to Drew's, come to think of it), but that was the first time Drew had driven me across the river. During the next year, when we were older, Drew would escort me to St. Louis clubs and Cardinal baseball games, but, until that moment, he had never coaxed me beyond the county line. And Missouri seemed a most forbidding territory alone at that age, a place where kids at school claimed the guys were older or more strange, as though stunted development made them odd.

I had never known Missourians to be unusual. Rather, I thought Illinoisans pedestrian by comparison. The fascinating ones, it seemed, hailed from across the river.

Crossing St. Charles County and the Missouri River, and getting to the Jamestown area of North St. Louis County, Drew headed for the mall. The shopping center was a sprawling, acreage-sucking shopping center anchored by five massive department stores, an ever expanding multiplex, and a whole lot of shops. The Judge enjoyed going there. He visited the place's Tinder Box to get his cigars and pipe necessities.

"You know what this guy looks like?" Drew asked.

"He's big and bald," I said.

"That's helpful." Drew took a spin around a turn and entered at the far parking lot. "What kinda car does this big-and-bald guy drive?"

"I dunno."

"Well, where around here are we supposed to meet this big and bald guy?"

"By Famous-Barr, I think," I said, referring to one of the department stores.

Drew nodded and whipped around another department store, Dillard's, heading to Famous-Barr. "Which entrance?"

"I dunno."

"Let's see: you are to meet this big and bald guy in Jamestown, and you think it is at Famous-Barr, but you don't know what entrance, and you don't know what car he drives," Drew summed up. "Is all that right?"

"As far as I know."

"Then, we got a problem."

Drew completed a turn around Dillard's and we saw the acres of parking stalls that was the Famous-Barr parking lot. Next to the building was a sleek white automobile that favored a new rocket car. I told Drew to try that car. He made a curt pass at it, and, seeing nothing through its dark, tinted windows, spun around and doubled back. Then he turned and faced the car, engine running.

The rocket-car door opened slowly and out stepped Jimmy wearing an off-white, summery suit and his dark sunglasses. He looked even bigger than he was on the tennis court and he moved piously, like a mortician. He reached into the rocket car and produced my racquet, which I would have recognized anywhere. Closing his car door, Jimmy leaned against the vehicle and folded his arms. With an index finger, he beckoned me.

"Maybe I should just drive up to him and get the racquet," Drew said.

"No," I said. "I can get it."

"It might not be safe."

I smiled, opened the car door, and stepped out. I crossed the thirty feet or so between the two cars as rapidly as you can imagine, for the sole thought in my head was retrieving my racquet, which I wanted, like, now.

Jimmy seemed otherwise occupied. Through his sunglasses, he watched cars driving around the parking lot. He seemed not to have noticed too much until I was practically on top of him, and, when he did, he barely cracked a smile.

"Who's that?" Jimmy asked, nodding at Drew's car.

"Just a friend."

Jimmy pulled his sunglasses down the bridge of his nose a hot second with a long, manicured finger, then pushed them back in place. "Snow queen," he said. He handed me my racquet. "Have fun."

"Thanks."

Taking the racquet, I trotted back to Drew's car. I imagined Jimmy waved at Drew, because I saw Drew wave back. After that, I heard the rocket car's door close and the engine rev. Jimmy, I imagined, had enough of kids. He was gone before I entered Drew's car.

For the first few minutes we drove from Jamestown, Drew said practically nothing. Then, after we crossed the Missouri, he decided to speak.

"I don't think you should be with him."

"What?"

"I *said* I don't think you should be seeing that big and bald guy," Drew said.

I had no idea where that came from, so I asked. "Why?"

"Why?" he repeated. "No reason in particular. I just think he's too old and too big for you, that's all. How did he get so bald, anyway? You sure he didn't get like that because of some type of disease?"

I laughed. "You'd like me getting a disease."

"I'm serious, Arthur. Besides, he's—what? Thirty-five."

I had no idea. Jimmy's age was never a topic of interest for me.

"I'll never know," he said, shaking his head. "What you see in this turkey, I'll never know."

I had never thought of Jimmy as a "turkey," but as an older guy with whom I played some tennis. What he meant, what that encounter meant for Drew to have read, was nothing to me at the time. Jimmy failed to register anything more for me. It was impossible to impress any of that onto Drew. Driving the car, fingers and jaw tight, he seemed impregnable as the elders, so I refused to try. I sat in my seat and watched the flat St. Charles County lowlands spill into the dammed up basin, and, once we got to the river, I watched the barges navigate the Mississippi, and I wondered to myself what it would be like to escape and float idly downstream like Huckleberry Finn and Jim.

Chapter Ten

When I got home from tennis with Drew, I was alone. Again. It was a state I was getting very used to, in spite of myself. Mom was long gone; Adele must have left with her. Where was the Judge? Though his essence, spilled through pipe smoke, pervaded every room, I wondered where he went, and what he was doing. Did he return to that German worker's house with the hollyhocks in front? Had he gone off to play golf with Ken? Who knew? Who could know? All I knew was that I missed him, and I wanted him in his house at that moment, sitting in his living room, listening to his Schubert or Shostakovich string quartet, and drinking his tea with his pipe going strong, as if he were the Homeric gatherer of clouds.

But the Judge was gone. I was alone. Nothing to be done. I simply stood in my room, uncertain. Dr. Levin's play tried calling me to it, but I did not heed the call. Instead, I listened to the house settle. A creaking floorboard. Maybe a pipe croak. The phone rang in my parents' room. I stood there and watched it ring. It rang at least five times. I was certain it was someone unpromising, someone who would impose himself upon me, as if it were to be an ordeal. I was paralyzed. Then, a new view came again. I took the caller to be my mother. Call it "intuition." Call it something worse. Whatever it was, the "intuition" passed through me like a sugary confection and left me shaken. Something might have been wrong with my mother. Perhaps she needed my help. Perhaps it was just my mind going strong. No matter. I would never know just standing there. The phone rang an eighth time. I thought it best to answer the thing. So, I did.

"Hello?"

"Have mercy. Is this Skip?"

"Yes."

"Skip," the voice said. "I was really thinking about you. I was thinking and steadily praying. I guess you don't know who this might be."

The voice sounded ghetto, like it had had too many chitterlings in too much grease. It wasn't the voice of our kind of people. Obviously, it wasn't the Judge or Marshall. It was a man's voice, so it certainly wasn't Mom or Grandma or Adele. I was sure none of us knew anyone like this guy. And he was playing with me. Okay, I'll play with you, too. "Rumpelstilskin," I said.

The voice laughed. It was an ignorant, belly laugh, like something Norman Lear would have used. "This is the Reverend Michael Shuddlesworth. How ya doin', Skip?"

"Fine." I really tried to sound bored. After all, why was this guy calling me? Didn't he have communion to bring to the sick and shut-in, or something? Why can't I go ahead and read my play?

"Glad to hear it," he laughed. "I guess you don't remember me."

How could I forget him? My skin still crawled from him holding my hand. "You're the minister subbing for Reverend Hale."

Again, he laughed. He laughed like a spook, and a simple one, at that. "Guess you'd remember me after that message I gave. It was pretty good, if I do say so my own self."

I sighed. I didn't remember much about his sermon, except I needed to pee. That was par for the course. I wanted to cut to the chase. Besides, I had homework to do. "How may I help you, Reverend?"

He laughed a little, that ignorant laugh again, then he stopped and cleared his throat. "Like I was fixing to say, is your daddy home? The presiding elder gave me a letter, and he wanted me to hand deliver it to him, personally."

"Well, I wish I could help you, Reverend, but my father is not here."

"Is your mama?"

"No."

He laughed once more. That laugh had become, how should I say? more sinister than simple, like he had something up his sleeve that he now felt ready to reveal. Later, remembering that laugh, I would feel my skin become cold and moist, my throat turn dry, and my body shake. I would loathe that laugh, that new laugh, as an even greater betrayal than his simple one.

"Well, Skip, that means you are all by your lonesome. I think we can still do some business, don't you? I can leave the presiding elder's letter with you, and you can make sure to give it to your daddy. I can come down and drop it off, and be out of your hair in no time."

That seemed reasonable. How was I to know any different? He was a clergyman, someone I felt could be trusted, simply by his position. I saw nothing wrong with giving him our address. As I hung up the phone, I had the premonition that his visit would be the real ordeal. I remembered what Grandma had said that day about Reverend Shuddlesworth being a pest at Conference. What did she mean? No matter. My thoughts turned instead to getting him out of the house before the Judge arrived. Hell, I wanted to get myself out before the Judge arrived.

I stood at the front door and watched the street. The sun was setting; a fawn and its mother frolicked in the park. In a way, I expected Reverend Shuddlesworth to come in a respectable Buick, but a motorcycle's obnoxious yawp announced his arrival. He wore a fire-engine-red short-sleeve shirt and a black Southwestern-style string tie. He had on skintight black leather pants and what seemed to have been snakeskin cowboy boots. A gold chain looped under his collar and over the tie. In his hand was a white envelope. He wore black gloves.

Was this really an ordained minister? Really, he looked more like your average street fool. I had no time for street fools. I felt like the thing I should do was lock up the family silver and secure the Depression glass. Grab the family jewels and hide them deep in my pockets!

He swaggered to the door the way a gunslinger swaggers into a saloon in the movies. When he got closer, I could see the large, rhinestone buckle of his belt. He reached to ring the doorbell, and I opened the door.

Reverend Shuddlesworth laughed. It was back to that simple laugh. And he laughed so loud it echoed outside. His laughing was getting on my nerves. I mean, what would the neighbors think?

"Skip," he said, enchanted. "Have mercy. Good to see you. How ya doin'?" He extended a hand. I looked at it.

"Is that the letter?"

He offered me the letter. It was held out like bait, then snapped back when I grabbed for it. His gold-tipped front tooth flashed.

"Ain't you gonna show me your house? Since I'm here? You know, play nice for the visiting pastor?"

It makes little sense now, but I let him in to get rid of him. I suppose I was willing to expose the family jewels to this philistine for a short while. Reverend Shuddlesworth stepped it, brushing against me ever-so-lightly. He stood in our foyer like a Vandal in Rome. He reeked of cheap, musky cologne. After getting an eyeful of the antiques and objet d'art in the living room and of the crystal in the dining room, he returned to the foyer and laughed.

"So, you got this big old house all by your lonesome?" he asked. "Have mercy."

"I live here with my parents—with my father—and my sister is in town from Washington."

"DC or Seattle?"

I rolled my eyes. To me, there was one Washington; the other place was Washington State. "Washington, DC."

Reverend Shuddlesworth nodded. "She got legs like you? 'Cause, if she got legs like you, she must be tough enough, indeed."

I wasn't about to dignify that. Everyone liked my legs. That was all good. He still had the letter. I would have grabbed at it, but he kept playing keep-away with it, making a point of changing hands whenever I got close to it. To make matters worse, he seemed unwilling to leave. He stopped smiling and he pointed upstairs, pointing at the masks of the Dan.

"I'd love to see where all these masks lead to. They're from Africa, right?"

"West Africa."

"West Africa," he said. "Doorway of No Return. Land of our ancestors."

I looked at him, a bit like Marshall would have, a little incredulous that we should have ancestry in common. Whichever tribe his ancestors were from had slipped into the slave trade by mere stupidity and had survived the Middle Passage by mere dumb luck. He was standing very close to me. I covered my nose. His cologne was starting to get to me. "Is there something else, Reverend?"

"Your crib up there? I'd love to see the place where you stay."

I tried everything to indicate annoyance. I sighed. I rolled my eyes. I made sure my diction sounded snippy. Nothing worked. So, I did the only thing I could think of. I gave in. I led him upstairs.

You must forget yourself. You are not alone. As much as you may want to be, you are captured by a Vandal, a part of the Germanic horde that has invaded your city to gawk and to disspoil it of its treasures. You, young Romulus Augustulus, have invited him into the city. Now you cannot rid yourself of him. Or, are you really Caesar? Could you be one of the effete sons of Priam, could this be Troy, and could he be some Greek hoplite? You imagine it could. It could all be true. If so, the only Trojan prince you can think of is Ganymede, the boy, the cupbearer. Have you been an eagle, Vandal? Are you prepared to whisk me away to Olympus, to make your wife jealous? Really, you thought it was your father, the Judge, who had the power to translate himself into an eagle.

"Have mercy," he exclaims as you lead him to your room. *The cat looks at the sight frightened, by his stench, probably, then she slips from the windowsill to underneath your bed. You almost hear her disapproving gaze at the man in your room, the Vandal, who, dudded up like a cowboy, studies your CD collection gathered on the bookshelf above your desk.*

"What's this? Johnny hates jazz? Where's the Tupac?"

"The Tu-what?"

"The Tupac. The hip-hop. You know," *he does a little dance, a bob and weave, moving, it seemed, like an eagle in flight.* "Rap."

You had heard about such things, at the Black Rep a few years ago, during a trip with Jack and Jill; the actors breakdanced on the stage. Remember? You didn't understand it, but you applauded. Marshall was the one to sit on his hands. You are most underwhelmed by the thought. "Oh. That."

"You got classical. Rock. Everything except Average White Band and Niggaz with Attitude."

He smiles, and the gold-tipped tooth sparkles. You do like gold like an eagle, dear Vandal. Do you think it imprudent to stay with ivory? Considering it, you think how much better his mouth would look with something less ostentatious.

The game is like tennis. Feel the lay of the court, if you need reminding. He has moved himself to the net, forcing you to come closer with quick, chopping shots. He must have seen you play to know you are naive enough to fall for that.

Now, with him almost looking dead in your eye, he is ready for the winning shot, the smash, the lob, the stroke near the alley, too far from your forehand.

"Where's your people from?" he asks.

"Illinois," you say.

"Whole family? No one from down home?"

"Down home for my family is Crystal City, Missouri," you say. "We haven't been there since we moved from the place after the Civil War."

The Vandal moves into your face. His stench, the road musk, the funk from playing tennis too hard at his age, repels you. "The Good Lord don't like no liars. And He don't like ugly. You know what He do to nigger boys who lie?"

"I'm not a 'nigger boy.'"

Touché. He had tried his winning shot, but it went over the line, out of bounds—not harmless, but still out of bounds.

You stand outside your room, dear Ganymede, the cupbearer, as the Greek hoplite, the eagle, gets one more look.

You are—you were—not the kind of guy who would be in a place like this at this time in your life, but you are, and you cannot say the terrain is entirely unfamiliar. It is true. You know this place all too well, and it is a place you would rather not be.

But, you are here. This is the bed where you sleep. That is the chair where you sit. There is the cat. Where are we?

Your mind turns to the clock. How long has this volley been?

The tennis match is over. Your opponent, who had tried to trick you, leaves the court. He gives you something. A light kiss on the cheek. A tap on the butt, manly, like a grope. A smile. He smells like an eagle. Then, sticking to "Thou shalt not steal" like a broken record, he disappears into the twilight on an obnoxious horse, whose braying resonates like a snoring hog.

I had to shower. How could I explain to you the thoughts that raced through my mind as the water baptized me? I tried to extinguish the heavy feel of being in Reverend Shuddlesworth's presence. I tried expelling his essence which seemed to have permeated me through osmosis. I think I had bitten his hand.

At this moment, you may be interested in what I felt, emotionally. The fact is, the fact is, I felt just the disgust at myself for letting the man into my home. Anything else, I was beginning to learn, ought to be suborned so thoroughly it dare not show his face. Some sores, you must remember, are too easily touched, too readily irritated, too surely bled. Feel nothing.

When I finished, I still had his smell. I scrubbed again. Then, I changed clothes.

I didn't know what happened to the letter.

My mind went blank. Oh, I tried halfhearted things. I prattled through the *TV Guide* and thought about watching cable, but they didn't interest me. I turned my attention to Dr. Levin's play, to *The Crucible* as well, but I couldn't concentrate. I had a rum and Coke. Twice.

Still dressed, wearing a fresh T-shirt, Dockers, and socks, I went to bed. It was around eight, and night had fallen. I listened for Bert doing something, even leaving the litterbox, as a way of reminding myself I was not alone in this world, and I heard just the house settle. Two minutes passed, then six, then ten. It was about eight thirty. I heard the Saab's engine come down the lane and into the driveway, followed by another car. Deep inside, I thought I heard the Judge and Adele enter the house. Then there was the sound of doors opening and closing. The next thing I knew was Adele hoisting her bags to the top stair.

"You could at least help," she called out.

"You talking to me?" the Judge asked from downstairs.

"I'm talking to the gentleman, my little brother," she said to him. Then, she called for me. "Kid! Kid!"

"I'm asleep," I yelled, curling into a ball and bringing the covers over my head.

"If you're asleep," she retorted, "you wouldn't be able to hear me. Kid! Expectant mother! Kid! Come and help me!"

I relented. I got out of bed and went to the stairs, where a garment bag and a smaller suitcase waited. Adele couldn't help but notice I was still dressed.

"Sorry to disturb your beauty sleep," she said sarcastically. She took a good look at me. Perhaps she also smelled liquor on my breath, or maybe the oppressive scent of Reverend Shuddlesworth's cheap cologne. She screwed up her face. "What the hell happened to you?"

I grabbed at the luggage. "Nothing."

The Judge came to the foot of the stairs. He was still in his jacket and tie. In hand was his tumbler. "You need help?"

"No," I said. "I got it."

Prepared that the women in our family stuff garment bags, I took the luggage, heavy, as I had expected, and dragged them to the room that, just ten years before, had been Adele's. I heard Adele remove her black pumps.

"Shame to see Moonlight's cannelloni disagreed with you," she said.

I dropped the luggage on the floor and rubbed my arms. After Reverend Shuddlesworth, I was almost glad to have something other than my nose throbbing. But, I couldn't admit to that. Adele came into the room behind me. I almost jumped. Adele looked at me as if something were very wrong, a very concerned look, then she slowly became normal.

"Grandma said you saw Mom at Aunt Carolyn's."

"Yep."

"How'd she look, then?"

"Fine."

She looked at me for a minute and then reached for my arm. I recoiled. She didn't consummate the touch. "I'm going to see her again tomorrow," she said. "Wanna go?"

"I'll see."

She dropped the light pumps beside the bed. "If you're busy—"

"I said I'll see."

Adele nodded. She unzipped her skirt, removing it and standing in her slip, and then she dropped onto the bed. "Spencer's fine. Thanks for asking."

"I didn't ask."

"No, you didn't." She unfastened the comb in her hair. "You don't look too good. Is everything all right?"

What was I to tell her? "Peachy."

The Judge had come upstairs with his nightcap. He looked inside the bedroom, then proceeded to his room, where he would undress and get ready for bed. It seemed he had had enough of his children for the evening. There, from his room's CD player, came the beginning of a string quartet, deliberate with the cello and viola, meditative with the violins. Adele listened for a few measures, then she did like the Judge.

"Dvorak," she said. "String Quartet number twelve. *American.* Second movement. He's thinking about her."

"Mom?"

"Mom or Eugenia." She dropped her voice to a whisper. "He always puts that on when he's thinking about her."

"You two talking about me?" the Judge yelled from his bedroom.

"We're *always* talking about you," Adele yelled back. Then, she shook her head and smiled. "Men. *Our* men. All of them. Always the same."

Adele got into the music. She closed her eyes and let it wash over her. She looked peaceful, like Mom sometimes did among her plants. I tried being peaceful, too, but Reverend Shuddlesworth's scent still lingered, and it got me out of the mood. Besides, there was still this "Eugenia" woman. Was there another Eugenia, besides my English teacher?

I excused myself and scrubbed my hands so furiously they became softer and red. The smell was horrid. I thought about getting gloves, but gloves in the house in September would have proven too egregious to lie about, and then I would have had to tell. What would I have said? That Reverend Shuddlesworth was in my room? *"What was he doing there?"* they would ask. *"Why did you let him in?"* His kind, I would have been reminded, belonged in the backyard, no further than the garbage cans. They would have compelled me to explain. I would have had to explain too much, and those explanations would have stretched credulity.

The Dvorak was coming to an end when the phone rang. The Judge answered. My heart almost stopped when he said, "Hello, again, Marshall," and they small-talked for a bit before he put down the phone and entered the hall. "It's for you," he said.

"I'll take it downstairs."

I went to the kitchen and picked up the phone. The Judge hung up. For a few seconds I said nothing, just listened to Marshall breathe. In the background was music. It sounded like Verdi. It sounded like a duet between men, maybe between a tenor and a bass. The sound splashed against me, like waves in a tumultuous, green-eyed storm.

"Skip?"

"Yeah?"

"Hey."

"Hey, yourself." I smiled a little. "I think Mom and the Judge're divorcing."

"Yeah. I know. Just look at them today."

"Bummer, huh?"

"Yeah," Marshall said. "Bummer. Skip—"

"I started reading *The Crucible*—Dr. Levin's play. I started reading it. You?"

"I looked at it."

"It's pretty good. Something we can sink our teeth into."

"Yeah, and get them gooey, like mozzarella. Skip, I'm calling about Alan—"

"Huh?"

"Alan. Our cousin."

That was what I thought he had said. "Oh."

Marshall waited for a minute, as if trying to coax me into saying something. I was more fixed upon the evening's tennis match I played with Reverend Shuddlesworth. "He told me what happened yesterday," Marshall finally said. "I didn't tell anyone about it. I don't think I will, for at least a while, and I don't think he would tell again. So, you need to."

I stared at the kitchen walls, done in alternating black and white porcelain tiles, like volleys on the court. I started to cry. I was thinking about Alan and Reverend Shuddlesworth. It was my realization that I had moved that evening from Zeus the Taker, which I had been for Alan, to Ganymede the Taken, as I was for Reverend Shuddlesworth. That was upsetting. I had been no one's victim, not even Kay Reece's. Now I was. *"Thou shalt not steal . . . thou shalt not steal . . ."* I had been stolen. Was there a way of stealing me back?

I cried like a baby.

"I'm sorry," Marshall said softly. "But it is the truth."

"I know," I sobbed.

"You have to."

"I know. What'll I say?"

"Well—" Marshall smacked his lips, a sign that he was drinking lemonade. He must have been enjoying his Verdi, too. "You want to practice with me?"

"I dunno what to say."

"You want to start with what happened this evening? You can trust me."

To use Drew's truism, "trust" is a four-letter word some wench stretched into five. Perhaps, I could trust Marshall, but a confession, even to him, was a confession still. Doubtlessly it would get back to my parents. And, what truism would I trust him with? I buried my face into my hand. My best efforts notwithstanding, his smell was still with me. I sobbed louder.

"Cry," Marshall said softly. "Cry."

"I don't wanna tell anybody."

"I know."

"Ever."

"I know," Marshall said softly. "But you know you can't keep it to yourself forever."

"I know." I lifted my head long enough to wipe my nose on a paper napkin. "I know, but it hurts."

I could hear Marshall blink. It was an awkward second. He had interrogations down pat, he could have been one of Yezhov's men, a pious fellow in a blue hat helping Stalin find enemies of the people. If I were cynical, I would think Marshall was pausing for dramatic effect. It might have been just that his attention was divided, between the Verdi, the lemonade, and me. "You might feel better, if you tell."

"No, I won't."

Marshall's cajoling beside the point, I refused to say anything more. I think I let him know I would carry the embarrassment of that weekend to my grave. That must have been sufficient for him, for then. He gave up and we said our good nights. I hung up the phone.

I used the next half hour to straighten myself enough to venture back into my room, the place of my dishonor. I spent that time in the family room, lying on the sofa, hugging a cushion, in the dark. I had stopped crying. I had long since stopped crying. I suppose I really wanted my mother to hold me, which she almost never did. I would have taken being hugged by my father, which happened much more regularly. Then, I fell into a light sleep.

"Skip," the Judge said softly. "Skip."

"Huh?"

"It's Dad, Skip. Go on to bed."

I opened my eyes. The family room lamp was on, and in its glare was the Judge. He was still in his dress shirt and suit trousers. The odor of his pipe filled the family room like incense. It was the best smell I had smelled all day. I rubbed my eyes and patted my mouth.

"It's almost ten, Skip," he said. "Go to bed."

"Lemme sleep here."

"Here? Isn't it uncomfortable?"

I didn't answer. I just yawned, groaning, and stretched like a cat. Then, I rested my hands under my face and closed my eyes. I almost dozed off again. The Judge shook my arm.

"Skip."

"Please?"

Even with my eyes closed, I could sense him relent. He left, and, a few minutes later, he returned with my pajamas and a pillow and bed linen. I changed in the kitchen while he made the sofa. He was finished and seated in a chair, smoking his pipe, when I returned. His face was still obscured by the lamp glare.

"It's important for me," he began, "for you and your brother and sister to know I will never stop loving your mother, no matter what. Do you understand?"

After everything the past few hours, the last thing I wanted was a heart-to-heart with my father about his marriage. For that day, I felt myself meant to go the path of least resistance. I piled my bare toes on top of one another, "Uh-huh."

For a moment, he considered me. I could see pipe smoke tracing its way above him. He sounded like he was licking his lips. "When you become a father, old man, you will understand."

Adele came down, bearing an envelope that smelled familiar. She handed it to the Judge. "This was in the bathroom," she said.

The Judge opened the envelope and started reading the contents. "From Paul," he said. "The presiding elder. I wonder how it got into the bathroom."

He was looking at me when he thought aloud, as though he expected my response. For a moment, I played dumb. I couldn't tell him. But, he continued looking at me, like a black-coated *Oberführer*. Then, when his stare remained intense, I played like Saul, newly sighted on the road to Damascus.

"Oh, yeah," I said, sitting on the sofa and acting as if everything were coming back to me. "That reverend, Something 'sworth—"

"Shuddlesworth," the Judge said.

"Yeah, him," I said. "He brought it by this evening. I guess I just took it into the bathroom when I had to go, and just forgot about it."

The Judge watched me as I nodded, until I cleared my throat. "Good for us you didn't remember it," he said, "in the bathroom." He refolded the letter and returned it to its envelope. He looked to Adele. "This is a growing boy. He needs his nine hours of sleep."

He stood and left the room. I imagined he went to his den. Adele commented about the concerned look he had on his face. I didn't know; whenever I looked at him, all I could see was light. There was a pregnant moment. Adele looked ready to talk. I had to bring myself to say something.

"How's your flight?" I asked.

"Let's talk about that in the morning. For now, get some sleep. You look tired. And, be sure to brush your teeth in the morning." Turning off the light, she headed out of the family room. "Night, kid."

"At least tell me how long you'll be here," I said.

"For the duration. Night, kid."

Adele left me seated with the night. I sat there and let it relax upon me with a ringing as hollow as Marshall chipping golf balls against the house.

Chapter Eleven

Even in the privacy of the family room, where hardly anyone went unless they were entertaining (the family room was Mom's room, after all), I had trouble sleeping. I kept waking up, on the hour, every hour, whenever I heard something creeping on the floor. I stared at the clock by the television clicking the time. I tried closing my eyes and getting back to sleep, but each time, in a light, suggestible sleep, I dreamt of tennis balls and of racquets, of a match against someone who enticed me to the net, who seduced me with sweet shots, and then who betrayed me with a violent smash. Then, I awoke. I stayed awake until another light, suggestible sleep hit me.

So it went until two o'clock. I sat up and watched the clock. Ten minutes passed, then fifteen. At two twenty I realized that for that night my problem was sleeping in the house. I needed a place to crash. I called Drew.

"Hello?"

"Drew—"

"Huh?"

He still sounded asleep. "C'mon, Drew. It's Skip. Wake up."

"Skip?"

"Yeah. Skip."

He yawned. "Skip, come back to bed. I'll stop hogging the covers."

"Drew, wake up!"

Too late. He hung up the phone. Of all occasions, he had to hang up on me that morning. I knew that, if he were halfway awake, he would have been more than happy to have me sleep over, like what we used to do in eighth grade. He would have introduced me again to his bedtime rituals, to washing his face, to making a sandwich, to talking until sleep came upon us like a shroud, sending us into ignorance, where we would do ignorant things, the things neither of us would be willing to admit we had done when morning came and when we were fully awake.

Back in eighth grade . . . that was when Drew still wore pajamas. I remember him in powder blue pajama bottoms and a T-shirt, bent over the sink, brushing his teeth. He looked at me in my full set of pajamas, blue with white polka dots like my father's; in my black slippers next to his bare feet; and in my robe. "Don't you get hot like that?" he asked. I smiled. I wanted to ask him whether he is enticed to do things so close to naked as he was that night.

But we were not back in eighth grade. Rather, we were in eleventh, in our junior year, and I so longed to get to sleep—with Drew, even, if possible. I sat in the kitchen, unable to decide what to try next. Then, I remembered that cellular phone salesman's business card from Saturday, and Jimmy's number written on it. All right, I was thinking about my dreams, and the card came out of the blue, but my mind worked strangely that night.

The number, I knew, had been in my tennis shorts from Saturday. The card must have been placed in my box in the basement laundry room.

Because it was Cynthia's work space, the laundry room was neat, with its selection of mops, buckets, toiletries, and cleaning supplies put in particular spots like paint-by-numbers violets and pansies. Above the washer and dryer was a shelf with shoeboxes marked "Alfred," "Rose," and "Skip." I reached for the one marked "Skip" and pulled it toward me. It had two black ink pens, one with a chewed cap from when I loaned it to a Whitmaner one afternoon, an orange tennis ball (how did that get into the hamper?), the cigarette-rolled remnant of the scalped baseball ticket, three small brass paper clips, a chocolate-smudged section of waxed paper (where did that come from?), a dollar and forty-seven cents in change, and, beneath it all, the cellular-phone salesman's card.

I took the card. It seemed in the same condition it was in Saturday. The Judge must have pulled it out while preparing the wash. Like a thief, I conveyed it to the kitchen phone and dialed Jimmy's number. The phone rang a couple of times before being answered.

"Hello?"

"Jimmy?"

A yawn and stretch. "Yeah."

"It's Skip Macalester, from the tennis match Saturday? At Rec Night? You brought me my tennis racquet this afternoon?"

"Skip Macalester?"

I gave a sarcastic smile. "Yeah."

He became awake, and scolding. "Do you know what time it is? You need to be in bed, not calling folks."

"Yeah, I know." I looked at the microwave clock. Quickly, the time was approaching two thirty. As late as it was, Jimmy didn't sound asleep. He sounded like it could have been two thirty in the afternoon, for all it mattered to him. I pressed on. "I know I should be in bed, but, the thing is, I can't sleep."

"What's wrong, snow queen? Unpleasant dreams?"

"Sort of. I—I need—I need someplace safe. For the night."

"You mean, you're not safe at home?" he asked, turning serious.

"No, don't get me wrong. I'm safe at home. It's just that, for the night—"

"How old are you, again, Skip?"

Why on Earth did he ask that? "Almost sixteen."

"Then, you're fifteen. And you want someplace to stay? With me?"

"It's just for the night."

"For the night." He thought for a minute; I could tell. "I can pick you up in a half hour or so. Tell me where."

I gave him directions to Boyd's, an all-night diner uptown. All I needed was to dress, gather some things, and get there.

Getting dressed was the easy part: I slipped on the Dockers and T-shirt I had put on after, well, you know. For the risqué heck of it, I opted to go sockless. As late as it was, no one would care that a Macalester, the Judge's son, was going sockless, like I couldn't afford a clean pair. Besides, I wanted to go out prep.

Gathering some things was a little more complicated affair. I had to get a bag, preferably my gym bag, which I hardly used, and stuff a change of clothing, my brush, and toothbrush without waking anyone, namely the Judge. All that meant I had to return to my room. I wasn't sure if I was ready for that.

I felt my way to my room. When I got there, that smell was still there. It was so overwhelming I had to open the windows. Without turning on too many lights, I gathered my things and stuffed them into my gym bag. For reading material, I picked up *The Crucible* and Dr. Levin's play. I popped on my Cardinals baseball cap. After that, it was lights off.

I went to get my toothbrush. There was no need to turn on any lights because my childhood night-light, which Mom kept for sentimental purposes, was on in the bathroom. All I had to do was snatch the toothbrush and stuff it in.

It was that sense, a sense of completion, that made me relax and prepare to leave. According to the clock, it was two forty-five; to my reckoning it would take a little over fifteen minutes to walk to Boyd's. Most likely, I would get there just after Jimmy. Though my faith was a bit shaken, I prayed he would wait.

Taking my tennis racquet, just in case I felt like playing in the morning, I wrote no note. Notes would have been maudlin. I'd rather give a call later. I headed for the front door. Just as I reached for the doorknob, though, a living room lamp clicked on and, sitting in front of the front picture window was the Judge, dressed in khakis and red polo shirt. His black eyes, peering through rimless glasses and beneath a Monarchs baseball cap, startled me.

"I just need a place to stay," I blurted out.

"All right." He turned off the light. The next thing I heard was him jiggling his keys.

Without saying much, the Judge took me to the garage. The engine started. The Saab purred. "Get in," the Judge commanded.

"Where are we going?"

"You tell me." He opened the door. "To where?"

"Boyd's?" It was more of a question than a direction. Didn't I know where I was to meet Jimmy? "In Uptown?"

He nodded. "Boyd's in Uptown, it is."

"But you don't know why I want to go there."

"All I need to know," he said, "is that you want to go there. If you want to go there, I will take you."

He signaled for me to get in. Needless to say, I dropped my butt in the front seat, putting my racquet in the back. I held onto my gym bag. Have you ever driven through a small city in the middle of the night? All who are out are police occupying otherwise vacant parking spots. Driving around, there was an eerie silence, like a CD player gone dead after the *1812 Overture*.

In retrospect, it was strange to have picked Boyd's. It was not that accessible to Missourians, who often got lost trying to happen upon Uptown. Just up the hill from the high school, and within blocks of a middle school, an elementary school, and the dental school, Boyd's had the perpetual feel of a student hangout, complete with framed varsity letters. That feel changed after midnight, when the cops stopped by for coffee. Then, for six hours in the morning, it was for the insomniacs, who tried getting lost amid Hegel and American fries.

When we reached Boyd's, Jimmy had yet to arrive. All we could see through the diner's window were a pair of men, dental students, apparently, wearing caps, talking in a booth. The Judge parked the car.

"We're at Boyd's," he said, opening the door.

"Where are you going?"

"Oh, Skip," he mused, not impolitely, "do you really expect us to wait in the car like common whores?"

He climbed out of the car and stood on the curb. With a look and a hand on the door, he insisted that I come out. I didn't know how it would look, walking into Boyd's with my father, so I kept my head down, and hoped Jimmy was nowhere to see. I took my gym bag and racquet.

"Don't look so defeated," the Judge said as he opened Boyd's door.

I stepped in. When the Judge entered, the man behind the counter, a burly, older fellow boasting a blue captain's hat and fading petunia tattoos on his biceps, hailed him.

"Good morning, Your Honor," the man said, removing his hat and smiling. The man gave the Judge the hi sign. "What brings you to these parts this time of night?"

"Family business," the Judge said. Though his mouth smiled, the rest of him seemed tense, like a string bow ready to spring. "A cup of warm milk," he added, "for me and the old man."

The burly man nodded and started heating milk. We took a booth by the window. Within a few minutes, the man brought two steaming mugs. The Judge flicked a packet of sweetener and poured the contents into his warm milk, then swirled it with a table knife.

"All you need is a spoon of coffee," I said.

He smiled. "Heaven forbid."

I took my warm milk plain, after blowing on it a couple of times. While I drank, I caught snips of the conversation in the booth behind me. One of the voices sounded familiar. I could place it as a school voice, but what kind of school voice? I turned to look, but all I caught were capped heads.

"Skip—Skip," the Judge said softly, catching my attention. He touched my wrist, which sent a shock wave through me. He released my wrist and smiled. I hoped he couldn't tell how uncomfortable him touching me made me. "You know it's rude to eavesdrop."

"But I know that voice," I said, pivoting back toward the other booth. The Judge reached to take my wrist again, almost instinctively, but I snapped it away.

The Judge smiled again. "It's still rude."

Curiosity got the better of my manners. I left our booth and moved to the other one. Both men were hunched over plates of half-eaten biscuits and gravy (*yuck!*) and almost empty glasses of orange juice. Their hands, set up by their mouths for privacy, obscured their faces. From behind one of the hands, the voice I recognized had a definite Southern lilt. It was clear: Mr. Armstrong was in that booth.

I cleared my throat. "Excuse me. Mr. Armstrong?"

The man to my left, whose New Orleans Saints baseball cap was pushed down just above his eyes, did a double take, then blinked, and smiled. "Skip!" He sounded as if we were the only customers in the diner.

The other man, to my right, smiled a little. He looked scruffy with his beard, but he had cool, brown eyes that seemed friendly.

"This is one of the kids from the high school," Mr. Armstrong said to the man. "What on earth are you doing out and about at this time of night? We got school in the morning."

"Out with my father," I said, "drinking warm milk."

Mr. Armstrong raised himself above the booth to see the Judge. The Judge glowered. Mr. Armstrong blinked nervously and smiled a "hello." The Judge cracked not a smile. He continued glowering at the student teacher.

"Hello," the bearded man said, offering a hand, a left hand, of all things. "I'm Daniel." He smiled again, a little broader this time. He wore braces.

I said my "hey," which took Daniel as a strange salutation because, obviously, he was not from around here. I did shake his hand, my right to his left, a queer combination, like holding hands. He had cold, clammy hands. It gave me the creeps. After that, Mr. Armstrong and I looked at each other for a few minutes, uncertain what to say.

"Well, Skip," Mr. Armstrong finally said, clapping his hands, "you read both your plays yet?"

"I have them," I said. Then I remembered more completely that they were in my gym bag. "They're here."

"He takes them wherever he goes, I bet," Mr. Armstrong confided to Daniel, who nodded a little. "Daniel's studying to be a dentist."

Daniel smiled and tapped his teeth. "Orthodontist, Nick."

Mr. Armstrong blinked. "Orthodontist. And he'll be the bestest orthodontist there ever was."

I wanted to say that my orthodontist, Dr. Kidd, our neighbor, was the "bestest" one around (whatever that bastardization meant), but it seemed to make as much sense as Whitmaners dropping names, so I let it go. Again, Mr. Armstrong and I stared at each other, until we dropped our eyes and started looking at each other's hands. As I remember, he had fine, graceful hands.

"Skip," the Judge said softly, "your milk is getting cold."

I pulled my cap against my scalp and smiled. "My father. He says my milk's getting cold."

Mr. Armstrong blinked. "Then you got to go drink it."

As I left, we waved good-bye, like we would really see one another in Dr. Levin's room that morning. The Judge continued glowering even after I had returned to my milk. I drank it with a smile and licked the excess from my lip. It still felt warm.

"Good to see you're doing that this morning," the Judge said.

"Doing what?" I asked.

"Smiling." He drank milk. "When we left the house, you acted like it was too early to smile. Care to talk about it?"

I knew that would have meant talking about why I couldn't sleep in the house, which would have meant talking about why I couldn't sleep in my bedroom, which would have meant talking about what happened earlier that evening. I couldn't talk about that. I had not the words. I shook my head.

Mercifully, it was a few sips before I saw Jimmy's rocket car pull up to Boyd's and park. I watched him stride to the door. He came in. He seemed bigger that morning than he had during the weekend, his white Bermuda shorts seeming to let his legs go on forever before stopping at his untied beige canvas deck shoes. Without giving the place the once-over through his sunglasses, he came right for us and stood at the table until recognized, then, he removed his sunglasses and dropped them into the pocket of his bile green, short-sleeve oxford shirt.

"Excuse me," he said. "Judge Macalester—"

The Judge seemed hardly interested. He seemed more interested in keeping his milk sweet and warm. He stirred the milk a little, then he licked the knife. "Yes."

"I'm Jimmy Williams. We met at Rec Night. Your son and me—I—I played tennis. We talked this afternoon."

"I know who you are," the Judge sniffed. "Are you going to play with my son again tonight?"

"Dad—"

"What?" The Judge turned to Jimmy and placed his knife on the edge of his napkin. "As I said earlier, my son is not yet sixteen. I want you to remember that."

Jimmy nodded. "Yes, sir."

"He doesn't need to get any older than he is already. He's not yet sixteen; let him remain not yet sixteen."

With that order, the Judge pulled three smooth dollar bills from his khakis' pocket and set them beneath his mug. He stood, almost brushing against Jimmy. The Judge took hold of my cap bill and made me look up, then he smiled and flicked my nose like a little kid's, like he used to do when I was much younger. I think he would have said "I love you," were I not so old. Taking out his handkerchief, he left quickly.

His car had moved by the time Jimmy and I left Boyd's. By then, I think, it was approaching three thirty. Jimmy took my gym bag from me, leaving me to carry my tennis racquet, and headed for the trunk.

"Since you're going to be staying with me tonight," he said, "I ought to let you in on a few things."

"Like curfew?" I smiled. I was only half joking.

"Like—" Standing at the trunk, Jimmy clicked open the door. "You'll see."

I looked inside the rocket car. It didn't seem that unusual. The brown leather upholstery smelled as though it had been polished with a special emollient, but that was nothing too extraordinary. The veneer dashboard was a study of digital dials and doodads, like what one comes to expect in rocket cars. In the rear window was a Howard University alumni sticker (figures!) and there was a Howard University Bison, complete with football pads, hanging from the rearview mirror. Between the front bucket seats Jimmy had a standing CD rack; I wondered if he had all rock and roll. Barely visible in the streetlights, a pink blanket stretched over either golf clubs or tennis gear.

Jimmy went to the driver's side. "Get in." He himself climbed in.

I climbed into the rocket car, and kept my tennis racquet on my lap. "What kinda things you got to tell me?"

He put on his sunglasses and started the car. The radio was on the jazz station. Jimmy leaned almost into my lap. A light saxophone played. "Grover Washington Junior," Jimmy said in his most ebony voice. "Best of the best."

Jimmy revved up the car and, like a rocket car, it shot out of the space. Top speed for a rocket car, at that time, was, like, two hundred miles per hour; Jimmy drove it like it was reaching top speed. He cornered without braking, changed lanes without signaling. He drove wickedly, like a tumbling run-on sentence falling on top of itself with benefit of no dash, no comma, no semicolon. When he hit a stop sign, he tapped his brake, checked the intersection, then sped on. When he hit the stoplight at the bottom of Jefferson Avenue he throttled the engine and idled it a bit.

"I just hate these Illinois stops," he yawned.

"Why?"

"Because."

Do you know, dear Jimmy, Illinois police loathe Missouri drivers—except when it came time to issue tickets. Then, they can't get enough of you.

The light changed. He moved the car into gear, sped up, and turned. He jooked the rocket car onto the Clark Bridge. He was moving so fast past the bridge's golden spans I almost laughed. I felt like rolling the window down and letting the rocket-car-driven wind butt against my hand. I laughed out loud.

"What are you laughing about?" Jimmy asked.

"Nothing—this is so cool."

"'So cool?' Slang? I thought you didn't talk slang, not with the family you got."

I smiled. "In my family, we have lessons on slang."

As we reached the Missouri side, I looked back at my hometown. It was a study of lights, pearlish, really, strung together in a sequined choker set on an undulating pad. Somewhere near the clasps was Jefferson Heights, and somewhere in there was Reverend Shuddlesworth, preparing Sunday's sermon, perhaps a parable on lust. The Grover Washington Junior got dreamy, and, with it, I started to close my eyes. I imagined greeting the good Reverend with the choker and helping him fit it to his neck, tighter and tighter until the teeth of the pearls turned red.

Then, I saw the Judge. I could see . . . I could see the Judge ringing Grandma Macalester's door, and Grandma opening it up for him, even though he had a key. I could see her hugging him. "My baby," she'd say. "Mother's poor little, sickly baby. . . ."

Could I see my father crying? I had never seen my father cry before. I couldn't see him cry that night, though his eyes were red, watery, looking ready to pour out. Yes, I could see Grandma dabble his eyes with her hand—it is too late for a handkerchief. . . .

"I need to sleep, Mother," he will say. He couldn't bring himself to call her "Madelyn." He will explain that his house is too big for one person, and his "friend"—this female friend, this woman who had gotten between him and my mother—wouldn't dare go there.

"Mother can offer her baby the sofa." No, she wouldn't put it like that, but it would be close. Perhaps it would be, "Yes, Mother wants you here." Something like that. Something maternal, friendly, comforting. It is late, after all, hardly time for small talk and little pleasantries.

And my father, the Judge, now just Alfred, her son, would enter and tell her about what it was that upset him so. Will he admit to missing Mom? Would he tell her about me? I could see her listening very carefully to him describing my strange behavior, the way I slept in the family room, the way I proposed to bolt from the house in the middle of the night. I could hear him describing demons for her, people like Jimmy, whom he looked upon with an unsettled feeling. *Come on, Dad, don't you know Jimmy is a safe man for me? He is far safer than any minister, sent by the presiding elder or not . . .*

But, I had forgotten—the house would not have had just the Judge. It would have Adele as well. In the middle of the night, morning sick, she would get up and go to the kitchen for something to quell her stomach. Then, perhaps then, she would see I was gone . . . she would call for the Judge, but he wouldn't answer. And then, knowing Adele, she would sit up until someone came home.

I awoke. Nude trees, petrified by the Great Flood of 1993, whipped past us in the dark. They waded in the basin like Baptists, lifting their skirts and feet from the water like the slaves that used to gather there for services. They were as peaceful and as disquieting as a cemetery. After that, my side faded into a levee of darkness.

"You doze off?" Jimmy asked.

"No."

"You can, if you want to."

"I usually don't sleep in a moving car," I said. I lied.

Jimmy nodded. "I'm just saying, don't feel obligated to stay awake on account of me, or anything like that."

That was a nice thought, but I scarcely felt obligated to anyone for anything. Again, I closed my eyes.

I opened them as Jimmy pulled the rocket car into a driveway beside a decor lamp. What looked like lamb's ears were planted beneath

the lamp. Jimmy turned off the radio. Thinking I was asleep, he
shook my arm.

"Hey," he said softly. "Wake up. We're here."

I looked at Jimmy like Dorothy, landed in Oz. Even in black and
white, his was a Technicolor world. Sunglasses on, he opened the car
door. He stepped out and he handed me my gym bag, but soon he
had his head back inside the rocket car, this time in the backseat, and
he grabbed ahold of the pink blanket.

"Hey," he said softly again. "Wake up. We're here."

I half expected the golf clubs or tennis gear to lift up and yawn, but
nothing happened. Jimmy reached for the pink blanket and lifted it
and its contents into his arms. I was coming out of the car by then,
tennis racquet and gym bag in hand. Jimmy smiled and stood beneath the decor lamp.

"Skip," he said softly. "This is Chimera."

He pulled back the pink blanket and revealed a sleeping toddler
the flavor of rich Dutch chocolate.

"Is that your daughter?" I asked.

Jimmy smiled a little and maneuvered me toward the front door.
After attempting to balance the child and unlock the door simulta-
neously, he handed me the skeleton-looking key and pointed to the
large brass lock.

That was my signal to try it. It took a mean turn, but I was able to
unlock the door, and then we went inside.

At first sight, I rather liked Jimmy's house. In the lamplight, it was
a long, brick ranch not unlike some in Jefferson Heights, with flower
beds to either side of the door. In them, someone had planted shrubs
that spread like holly. Inside the door, the living room sat between a
fireplace and a picture window, which seemed to smile at a rolling
lawn that ended at the roadway far below the trees.

Stepping in, I recognized Romare Bearden and Jacob Lawrence
prints on the walls, but there was also a photographic portrait of an elderly couple, taken before a skylike background. There was plenty of
light, with bugs clustered on the windows, but little sound aside from
the pedantic nasaling of a soprano saxophone.

"What's that?" I asked, pointing toward my ear.

"Kenny G."

"Kenny who?"

Jimmy smiled. "Lemme put her back into bed, snow queen, then I'll take care of you."

He left me in the living room, looking at a *Migration* print. Shortly after he had left, that irritating nasaling stopped. A few minutes later, a door closed and Jimmy returned to the living room.

"My cousin's little girl," he explained. "He does shift work, and I keep her here when he works nights."

I pointed at the elderly couple. "Your parents?"

He shook his head. "Auntie and uncle. Auntie Saundra and Uncle Tiff. They raised me. If it wasn't for them, I don't know what would've happened to me. I would've been out on the streets, maybe. And Philadelphia, they got some mean streets." He plopped onto the cream-colored sofa and rubbed his eyes, yawning. "Why am I talking to you about mean streets? For you, mean streets're anyplace that won't give you back your library card." He removed the sunglasses and set them on the coffee table. "One of these days, I should take you to Philly, just so you can get a load of mean streets, *real* mean streets, for your ownself."

Jimmy yawned again.

"Sorry to have gotten you up," I said.

He waved me off. "I was up already. Chimera almost never sleeps the whole night through, and I'm on vacation anyway. Besides, you need a place to stay. What happened? You tried playing Tchaikovsky, and got into it with your old man?"

This time, I waved him off. "Long story."

"'Long story,'" he sniffed. "Now this I gotta hear. But you probably won't tell me till you're legal, right?"

I shook my head and yawned. I had no earthly intention of telling him a thing. Besides, I had not the words to call it.

He rubbed his eyes again. "I guess you'll just have to tell me that when you're good and ready, huh?"

I didn't answer.

Jimmy looked at his watch, a discreet thing on a black band, and then he rocked forward and clapped his hands softly. "I guess it's nighttime for you."

He stood. I followed him down the hallway to the linen closet, next to a bathroom, where he handed me a towel and wash cloth, which he called a "face towel." Then, he took from the closet white sheets and pillowcases. He also took out a green comforter.

He led me to the master bedroom, where a modern, king-size bed sat in middle of the floor clothed in silky, tan sheets like a great buddha. It was large enough for two people. I wondered if we were to share the bed.

"With Chimera here," he began, stripping the sheets, "and the third bedroom being used for my den, I'm just gonna have to put you here for the night."

"Where—where will you sleep?"

He wrapped the top sheet into itself and tossed it past me into the hall. "Well, I'll tell you one thing, girlfriend: I sho ain't gonna spend the night wit'chu," he said, putting his hands on his hips. "Almost sixteen or no almost sixteen. That's the one thing I do know for sure. I'm gonna spend my night on my own sofa, where I know everything's legal. And, don'tchu get no ideas about comin' over 'n' visitin' me, either."

He finished changing the sheets. Fluffing the pillows, he pulled back the green comforter and put his hands on his hips again.

"There," he said. "Everything except a chocolate kiss on your pillow. Now, don't go expecting that, too. That would just be pressing your luck."

"I want to thank you for this. I really didn't expect this."

Again, he waved me off. "Anything for Little Lord Fauntleroy, snow queen. Maybe, if I give you these acts of kindness, you'd learn to give a brother a chance, my little brother." He smiled. I simply stared at him; had he known me any better, he would have known better than to call me "brother." My staring caught him on. He stopped smiling. "Well, as Meat Loaf says, I'll let you sleep on it tonight."

After that, Jimmy left me. I plopped onto the bed and felt the soft, down comforter caress me. I almost slept.

Chapter Twelve

In the morning, Jimmy placed his long, lotioned legs against the planter and stretched. "Gotta get into the habit," he said as he brought his nose down to his knee and held it there. One bounce, two bounces. He lifted his nose and reached for the top of the decor lamp. "C'mon, snow queen. Get with it."

I still felt full of Shuddlesworth. I wanted to sleep. It was not yet seven when Chimera tugged my arm in Jimmy's bedroom. Somehow, sometime, I had shucked my pants and curled onto the bed, pulling the comforter over me. It was a sound sleep; I did not dream. I am certain I did not dream. Still, feeling Chimera got me to thinking she was the Judge, then Jimmy boinked me on the head with my own racquet (I knew it by the bounce), and I opened my eyes.

"Tennis, anyone?" he had asked.

I was still sore from the Shuddlesworth affair. I was not in the mood for trusting anyone. Jimmy convinced me tennis would make me feel better. He had pulled me from his bed. Half asleep, I put on my tennis shorts. I had the sense to brush my teeth.

"Don't bother with your hair," Jimmy said. "Just slip a cap on. You don't need to look pretty, snow queen, to play tennis."

I had followed him out the front door. I thought of Chimera. What about the little girl? "Her daddy's here," Jimmy said, flexing his upper body on the decor lamp. "He'll get her ready for the morning. Besides, I gotta get you some tennis. See if that match Saturday was a fluke."

He continued stretching. I bent over and tied my shoes.

"You'll mind my saying—" he said.

"I'll mind you saying what?"

He shook his head. "Never mind. Stretch!"

"I am." Actually, I *was* touching my toes.

"No," he said. He stopped flexing his upper body and then he sent out his arms, making a T, and he rotated them back so the fingertips touched. "Jump up and down."

I was too sleepy to jump up and down. I would rather return to bed. Still, I bounced on the balls of my feet.

"Do it again!"

I did it again, for what it was worth.

"Now," Jimmy said, windmilling to touch his toes, "face me and touch your toes."

I sighed. I faced him. I touched my toes. I farted a little, accidentally. "Sorry."

"Kids." Jimmy started to jog in place. "Ready?"

"To play?"

"To jog. We will run to the courts, play, then, if we got energy, run back." Jimmy started to jog down the driveway.

"What about my racquet?"

"Bring it!"

I was not about to be left. Tucking my racquet under my arm, I trotted down the driveway, where Jimmy waited.

We did little talking jogging to the tennis courts. Mostly, it was a matter of me struggling to keep up with that long-legged pace Jimmy set. He didn't run so fast that I couldn't keep up, but he ran fast enough that, for me to keep sight of him, I had to really run.

We ran through his subdivision, and through the woods adjacent to it. He took me along a bike path and over a creek bridge. We ducked under a few hardwoods and crossed a field of snapdragons. A couple of rabbits hightailed it into the brush. Some squirrels, harvesting acorns, scampered up an oak tree.

"Can you slow down?" I called out to Jimmy.

"Can't slow down," he called back. "Gotta keep movin'. Like the Moody Blues. You know them, snow queen?"

Yes, I heard of the Moody Blues, but I thought Jimmy was a part of the Earth, Wind and Fire set.

The bike path took us by a middle school, where only the administrators and custodians had arrived. From a propped-open door, I could hear the plodding resonance of woodwinds beginning a piece. I stopped.

"Brahms," I said after the introduction, smiling the way Marshall did when he said "Gunter Grass" in a decisive German accent. I listened a little more. While I listened, I couldn't help but look at myself in the mirrored glass of the door.

I was a sight. My Cardinals cap on my matted head, the bill failing to hide my face. That morning, I was the light flavor of very light maple syrup, smattered with butter. My nose was angular, maybe at sixty degrees, maybe at seventy, certainly too great to be acute and rounded and too shy to be a Grecian right angle. At almost sixteen, I had the beginnings of a mustache, which really would not come, straight and full, for another seven years. My lips were not full, but somewhere between sparse and bountiful. The core of my Adam's apple stuck out a little. I saw myself through dark eyes. I had healthy legs.

That was the image I was used to seeing. I used to see myself, like my father at five, standing in his grandparents' house, wearing a beige Christmas sweater. I thought myself, like my father, an almond-scented kid with smiling eyes. At almost sixteen, though strange men sometimes licked at me, apparently for my freshness, I could reach deep within and know myself as I really was: at almost sixteen, even still, I was Loki, the enchanter, the trickster, the hoarder of secrets and lies.

Jimmy jogged back for me. "Stop studyin' yourself, snow queen. You make the flowers stop blooming."

I started jogging in place. "I was just listening. That's Brahms' Serenade number two."

"Next thing you'll be wanting to tell me is who's playing." Jimmy winked and signaled for me to run along with him.

"It sounds like the Saint Louis Symphony, under Leonard Slatkin," I said, "but don't hold me to it."

Jimmy seemed to chuckle.

I was out of breath and sucking on intestinal fortitude by the time the bike path ended at a vacant parking lot. Jimmy was still running. As I doubled over, he circled the lot and returned to me. He still pumped his legs.

"What's wrong, baby?"

"I had to stop," I gasped.

"Hm! If you waited around for a brother and not gone off with the snowman, maybe you'd build up some endurance."

"Don't give me that," I said to him. "Not today. Okay?"

"Anything you want, baby."

"Okay." I spat. "How much further?"

"Actually, other side of those trees."

I looked toward a cluster of trees on the other side of the parking lot. Vaguely, I could hear the hollow pop of tennis balls.

"Okay," I said. I darted for the trees. Running from Jimmy was like chasing Drew. In other words, it was hopeless, against a more suitably equipped athlete. Jimmy overtook me easily. Apparently, we Macalesters weren't bred to be runners.

Jimmy caught me halfway across the parking lot. Laughing, raising his arms and his racquet, he buzzed to the trees, which opened to reveal four tennis courts, caged by chain-link fencing and tied in a row. I knew there was no hope. I stopped running.

By the time I got to the courts, Jimmy had had his drink of water (I could tell by his wet lips), had caught his breath (he breathed moderately), and was steadily hitting volleys off a corkboard wall. On the other hand, I had almost completely forgotten about my embarrassing moment with Something 'sworth.

"You finally made it," he said between hits.

I headed for the fountain. "Yep."

"If you and that snowman weren't——"

"Yeah," I interrupted. It was more about Drew, which I had heard before. "Yeah, I know."

He hit one volley especially hard. "You know what?"

I shook my head. I really didn't want to hear more about Drew, or anyone else, for that matter. "I'm getting water."

By the time I got back, Jimmy had worked up a second sweat. I had caught my breath. I wiped my mouth with the tail of my shirt. In Drew's words, I stunk. Jimmy headed for a tennis court.

"I wanna see if that match we played——"

"Yeah, yeah," I interrupted. "I know."

I headed for one end of the court while Jimmy took the other. He pulled up his shorts and hunkered down. He smiled. He remembered *he* was the one with the balls. He took out a ball and dribbled it with the racquet, preparing to serve.

As he tossed the ball up and recoiled, I felt like telling him that the "snowman" he liked putting me with was the reason I was any good at tennis in the first place. We played frequently, more frequently than that week, whose events conspired against us. I imagined Drew arriving at my house that morning, expecting to take me to school, with a tennis match to follow somewhere that afternoon. I imagined the Judge would meet him at the door. Perhaps they would share something. Could the Judge let him down easily? Please, Dad, let him down gently.

"Hey! You dreaming of a blizzard, or what?"

I shook my head.

Jimmy looked disgusted.

I went back to the fence behind me and retrieved the ball, which had bounced uncontested past me. I volleyed it back to Jimmy.

"If you're gonna play," Jimmy said, "play. Get your head into the fucking game."

Watching him bounce the ball, I hunkered down and prepared to return serve. As Jimmy sent the ball up, I thought about my first tennis game, against my brother, Ted, who had just graduated from Amherst. Ted lobbed the tennis ball toward me, first serve, and I held onto the racquet with both hands and, somehow, lofted it back. I remember Ted moving toward the ball, bringing the racquet back. I thought he would kill the ball, but he missed it, dramatically.

I smiled. I was five. Verily, I was smitten.

"Ready or not!"

Jimmy sent the ball toward me with a slight grunt. It was a good shot, with almost the right force to skip past me, like the last one. It came right for me, and, to return it, all I needed to do was to step forward and meet it with a simple forehand. The ball went cross-court. Jimmy had to move to reach it. All that jogging helped. He used those big feet and those long legs to dance to the ball. While doing so he brought the racquet head back. When he hit the ball, it had the hollow sound of a burnt peanut shell that splattered its contents in your lap.

It was a rocket, like his rocket car. The ball shot over the net and came into me fast. I had just enough time to put the racquet up and meet the ball. I was able to fashion my defensive stance into a lob that went straight up and sailed to the far corner. Jimmy scooted back, lifted his arms and smashed the ball across the net. It bounced like a football and headed for my waist. It took another defensive stance for me to send the ball across court. Jimmy had eased a bit, then he moved toward the ball, and, with a ground stroke, he sent the ball back toward me.

The ball came fast. It seemed the size of a grapefruit and my racquet head the size of a pin. There was little to do but bring the racquet head back and pray to hit it. It was a forehand shot. Elegant, the stroke sent the ball behind Jimmy and it landed practically on the line.

I scored the point. Jimmy was winded.

"You ain't got no mercy on an old dude, snow queen, do you?"

"No."

After all, I had to get even with him for running me all over the place. Barely breathing heavily, I went behind the line and prepared to return serve.

Jimmy retrieved the ball and dribbled it to serve. With his T-shirt's arm, he wiped the sweat from his face. He was just then catching his breath.

"That was a lucky shot, my little brother," he said. "Lemme see what you can do with this here."

Again, he sent the ball over with a slight grunt. It looked like an ace. It moved so fast it was just about an ace. Having practiced on Drew's aces, I moved fast enough to get my racquet on it. Still, I was not able to put anything on it. The ball ended up in the net. I ended on the court. Jimmy strutted.

"Yeah, yeah," he said. "See who's bad, see who's bad?"

I got up and dusted myself off. I had the makings of a fair-sized scrape on my right knee. "Lucky shot."

"Ain't no luck to it," he said. "Skill."

Wounded knee engaged, I got the ball from the net and volleyed it to Jimmy. I had an idea this match would prove longer than it felt.

Unlike Drew, Jimmy kept score. I found myself in more love points than I liked. For the most part, they were hot shots and difficult shots and shots coming out of the wazoo so fast even Superman couldn't have caught them.

Then, after each shot I couldn't handle, Jimmy smiled and clapped and crowed. He pointed at me each time I got up and he flashed the peace sign. He wasn't even breathing as heavily as I. He was enjoying it more. A lot more.

I remember, in the second set (we played only two), with him leading decisively, Jimmy presented a respite. I was about to serve. He pointed his racquet at me.

"You gotta win this," he said. "For all the snow queens in the world, for all the princesses in this world in love with Prince Charming and his white steed, you gotta win this."

I didn't know quite what he meant, but I took it as a challenge. Ready to serve, I stood at the line and rocked my body. I tossed the ball in the air. "For the snow queens," I grunted, hitting the serve with all my might. The ball shot over the net to Jimmy, who returned it with a forehand. I charged the net and sent a volley just soft enough to make Jimmy run for the ball, to catch it before it bounced twice. Jimmy lobbed the ball into the air. I scooted back, until I was just under it.

"For the snow queens," I mumbled as I returned the ball with what proved a mean overhead smash.

Jimmy was there. Without much fanfare he sent the ball back to me with another lob, this time toward the corner. Moving into position, I waited for the shot to land in bounds, then I rocked a quick backhand that ended up in Jimmy's forecourt, just short of the alley. All Jimmy could do was watch it slip out of bounds.

"For the snow queens!" I yelled.

Jimmy looked at me. "I see Big Daddy's just gonna have to take you out, once and for all."

In the next few points, he did just that. In a little bit, it was I who cried, *"No mas, no mas."* Jimmy won, two sets to none.

I had built up a sweat. That really didn't bother me. What bothered me was that I played so poorly, as if all that playing beforehand meant nothing. Later, I would understand it was not all the playing I did, but all the playing Jimmy did, which was much more, that made the difference.

I started to think Saturday's play was a fluke. I walked like Saturday's play was a fluke. Jimmy saw how I walked. He extended his racquet.

"Nice game," he said, patting my butt.

I snapped a look at him. No one had touched me there since Shuddlesworth tried, and I didn't like Jimmy trying it, either.

"Sorry," he said in a low voice. "You're right."

"Huh?"

He cleared his throat. "You're right. About the way you play, I mean, about you being good."

"I lost."

"You win some; you lose some. After you've been playing for years and years you can beat some kid that's not even sixteen. You can get to running around, like a fool." He smiled. "You win; you lose."

He held the gate open for me and let me pass. As mad as I was about losing, I wasn't set to take second place to him again. We started walking, I going ahead of Jimmy until I realized I had no idea where I was heading. I turned to him and put my hands on my hips.

"You *won*," I said.

Jimmy nodded. He moved ahead of me.

In many ways, it was a shorter walk back to Jimmy's house than was the run. Because it must have been an hour later, the bike path was more alive than before. Joggers and cyclists were traveling that way too, as though they had also opted to play hookey from school.

We passed the middle school. The Brahms was off, the students were in their seats busying themselves with the hour's assignments. One of the kids, a sheet-white fellow, reminded me of Alan. Sitting at his desk, he concentrated his efforts upon a math problem. He squeezed a pencil tight as he repeated a series of equations his teacher had projected onto the screen with an overhead.

Yes, the sheet-white fellow reminded me of Alan. What are you doing today, Alan? Did you, too, fake sick in hopes for a day with the Simpsons and Bugs Bunny? If you are home, I really don't want to wrestle with you again. Let Brad do it. After all, he is your brother. No chance for sickening rumors with him.

"Hon," the teacher said through the window. "Hon!"

I focused upon her. She was gnarled, with salt-and-pepper dreadlocks and magenta lipstick. Her cheeks were as seasoned as fresh peach flesh.

"Hon," she said, "are you all right?"

I nodded. Jimmy was standing beside me.

"Is he with you?" she asked Jimmy.

"Yes, ma'am," he said.

"He needs to be at school," she said. "He shouldn't be around these younger kids."

"Yes, ma'am," Jimmy said. He took me by the arm and got me walking.

I had thought, running, that Jimmy's house was a piece of road away from that middle school, but, walking, it seemed not as far. Back through the snapdragons, back under the hardwoods, back across the creek bridge, and, in a little bit, we were in Jimmy's subdivision, heading for Jimmy's house.

Jimmy's house was just around the bend. And so was the Judge's Saab, parked in Jimmy's driveway.

"*Shi*—*!*" I exclaimed. I ran for the Saab. Passing Jimmy, I heard him call my name, trying to stop me, but I couldn't stop. I wouldn't slow down. "That's my *father*!" I yelled back at him. Jimmy was running after me.

We cut across a couple of neighbors' yards. There were hedges in our way, but I hurdled over them as gracefully as a billy goat. Jimmy, I knew, hurdled them like a gazelle. Then, we ran across Jimmy's yard. We ran right into the Saab. All I had to do was look in and see his pipe, the remnant of a smoke cloud dissipating at the seats.

"It's him," I said. "He's here."

Jimmy was about to say something, but before he could get anything out, I had turned and started marching straight for the house. Jimmy walked alongside me. When we got to the door, he flipped over the welcome mat and picked up a copper-colored key. I knew my father better than that. I opened the front door.

"Okay," I said, coming through the door. "Why're you here?"

You must know my father enough by now to guess what he looked like that morning; I will tell you nonetheless. He was seated in a stuffed chair next to the sofa, hands in his lap, as was his charcoal hat. In his dark suit and tornado-red-sky tie, he was dressed for court. I noticed his wedding ring was missing. He was humming "As Time Goes By." He smiled.

"Well?"

"I'm here for my morning coffee," the Judge said. "You won't mind, would you, Mr. Williams. I like my coffee fresh, sweet, and light."

Jimmy nodded and went into the kitchen. It was as if it was the Judge's house, and Jimmy was one of his retainers.

I rolled my eyes. "No, Dad. Why are you here?"

"I'm here to see how my youngest child is doing. That's all right, isn't it?"

"I'm fine, Dad," I sighed.

He drummed his fingers. I could see they could have stood some lotion. "Answer the question, Mr. Macalester."

I rolled my eyes again. At just fifteen, I was still at the right age for that sophomorism. "Yes. It's all right."

He smiled again. Fresh coffee wafted from the kitchen. Racquet in hand, I plopped onto the sofa and covered my eyes. There I sat, until Jimmy brought the Judge his coffee. The Judge sipped slowly, like the Grand Duke.

"Dad," I said after a few minutes. "Why are you here?"

"I'm here for my morning coffee," he said again. "That's all right as well, isn't it? Mr. Williams is so gracious to be a host, I thought this was the least I could do."

I felt like exclaiming "bullshit!" but that wouldn't have worked with my father. He was the sort of man that wouldn't have hesitated about striking me down for using such a word. Patiently, I let him drink his coffee. Then, jiggling his body, he stood. He left his hat on the coffee table.

"Do you have a toilet in this facility, Mr. Williams?" he asked.

Jimmy nodded and pointed toward the hall, at the end of which was the bathroom. The Judge saluted him and headed for the toilet.

"I got no clue why he's here," I said after he was gone.

Chuckling, Jimmy shrugged. He seemed to know more than he was letting on, but what? Who knew. He wasn't telling me a thing about why my father was there. I could imagine they had talked very early that morning, but would Jimmy really betray my confidence so? Remember "trust"—can I afford to trust you, big, bald guy?

Soon, the toilet flushed and the Judge returned to the living room. As soon as he came back, I resolved to play the interrogator's part. I resolved to ask him about his wedding ring, which I had hardly noticed before. That would have been the safest thing to discuss. Forming the question was the easy part; picking the timing was another matter. The Judge retrieved his hat. I smiled. He smiled. He licked his lips. He snapped his fingers.

"Dad—"

"Skip," he said, snapping his fingers again, "isn't there something you forgot to tell me?"

Why did he have to do that again? It was a grain of sand, and I was the clam. I popped up and fumbled, trying to make the grain into a pearl. The Judge winked. Maybe he winked at me. Maybe he winked at Jimmy.

"There is something you forgot to tell me," he said. "I thought, in addition to getting my coffee, I could get you to tell me this thing you failed to mention, if you wouldn't mind remembering it."

My mind went immediately to Marshall blabbing, then I wondered whether Reverend Shuddlesworth tipped his hand at some moment. I chose to play dumb. "What was that?"

The Judge smiled and stroked his tie. "That you saw Brad Friday? With everything else going on, I guess that just slipped your mind."

My cousin's disappearance, a furlough I wished I had taken, was the furthest from my mind. Did he hear that from Drew? Perhaps so. Anyway, I hit myself in the forehead.

"Yes," the Judge said. "That."

"It just slipped my mind," I said.

"Convenient," the Judge said. "Did he say where he'd go?"

I shrugged. It was a sincere shrug.

"All's fair," he said.

The Judge moved toward the door, putting on his hat in a single stroke. His eyes twinkled, as if he had something more to add. I kept looking at his left hand, trying to build up the courage to ask about his ring.

"By the way," he said just short of the door, "Adele will have lunch with your mother. You are invited to come. Be at her office around eleven thirty. And do be sure to bathe. You smell like a fifteen-year-old."

Jimmy got the door. The Judge gave him a dollar bill for his trouble and tipped his hat. And then, he slipped outside.

"He's right, you know," Jimmy said as we watched the Judge drive away. "You smell like a fifteen-year-old. Actually, you smell like a fifteen-year-old that likes rolling around in snow."

He smiled. I felt like lobbing that smile off his face. That would have made me a horrible guest. As I retreated into the bathroom and stripped to shower, I couldn't help but wonder, did Jimmy tell the Judge where to find me? That was the only thing that made any real sense. As the warm water cooled my body, I whipped myself for not asking what happened to the Judge's wedding ring. Maybe, I hypothesized, he just forgot to put it on, like he just forgot to lotion his hands, in the rush of trying to make it here before court.

Dressing, I practiced the scene with my mother. I could see us sitting in her office, Mom, Adele, and me. It would prove just a tearjerker session, I thought, like a visit to a therapist. I wondered how Mom's visit with Grandma went, as if I needed a picture of how Mom and Grandma interact. They had always been bosom buddies, consummate friends. They must have had a grand time talking about the Judge.

I wondered, would Mom and Adele engage in such talk? There was always such tension between them, at least, there was when Adele was in college. Adele would call and hardly speak to Mom; she would talk to the Judge and me. Then, we would have to relay any message to Mom. Weird how families go.

Jimmy knocked on the bedroom door. "Are you finished?"

"In a minute."

"When you finish, come out. I wanna talk to you."

"Okay," I said, brushing my hair. "Okay."

It was a quick two-step to finish my hair, then I stuffed my things into my gym bag. I checked my breath and gargled with Jimmy's mouth wash. That was like gargling with wood alcohol. "Okay," I said to myself. I was ready for almost anything else anyone could hurl at me. I left the bedroom.

Jimmy was waiting for me in the living room. He sat on the sofa with a cup of coffee in his hands. I still couldn't get over adults and their coffee. "Want some?" Jimmy asked.

"Coffee smells like armpits," I said. I would have told him I really needed my morning rum and Coke, but why confuse the guy? "No thank you."

Jimmy scrunched his nose. His eyes flashed and he smiled, then he signaled for me to sit. Rather than join him on the sofa, I sat in the same chair the Judge had occupied. His coffee cup was still on the table. Piss-worth of coffee was in the bottom of the cup, just enough to wet the spoon. I played with the spoon for a minute before feeling compelled to speak.

"You want me to explain myself?" I finally asked.

"You don't have to unless you want to," Jimmy said.

I felt I had to. I called him in the middle of the night; I stared at a middle school kid; I played inglorious tennis. Then, the Judge popped up in the middle of Jimmy's living room, demanding coffee. Talk about weird. I was no fool. I had no intent to show my hand. Small talk it.

"I guess my dad was just thirsty, huh?"

Jimmy drank. "I guess so. I called him while you slept. Told him where you were."

"How'd you get our number?"

He smiled. "I got my ways. Anyway, as Uncle Tiff says, 'that ain't even the fluff in the boll.'"

I looked at Jimmy, and wondered what was he talking about. I returned to the spoon and cup.

"That is what I wanted to talk to you about," Jimmy added. "I invited him here. I felt that, at the very least, he should see you are okay. That was my doing. Now, the key, that was him doing that. He let himself in."

"Oh," I said, "he would've done that anyway, invited or not." After all, I told myself, I knew my father well.

Jimmy smiled. "Like Uncle Tiff said—" His voice trailed off. He didn't finish the axiom. He finished the coffee, though, and returned it and the Judge's cup to the kitchen. "We got some time," he said as he rinsed the cups. "You wanna do anything special?"

"I figure I might as well get it over with."

Jimmy laughed. "It's just your mother."

"Yeah, I know," I said. "Mom and my sister. Real fun."

Chapter Thirteen

At around eleven fifteen, Jimmy pulled the rocket car to the corner of Market and Third streets and brought it to a dead stop, engine idling. He looked at me through his sunglasses and smiled. It was time for us to say good-bye, for the time being.

"Beautiful morning," he said.

"Yeah," I said. "It is."

He stroked his mustache with his thumb and his smile broadened. "Yeah, it is. Beautiful morning."

I wondered what he meant by that, the way he said it as reflexive as clearing his throat. He kept looking at the CD rack between us. It puzzled me, but I felt I should have been cognizant of other things. We were, after all, in front of the St. Croix Building, the place of my mother's offices, on a hill in the middle of Downtown. Someone, no matter who, would see us. How could I explain being with a grown man from Missouri, a big, bald guy, a guy not quite in my league, when it wasn't even noon? I had to move fast before being found out. I grabbed my gym bag, which was on my lap, and prepared to open the door.

"Skip?"

"Huh?"

"Did you enjoy your respite?"

A little amused, I looked at Jimmy and smiled. "I slept, played tennis, and had breakfast—"

"And your father came by."

I gave him a look as if saying, "Please don't remind me," and Jimmy started laughing, but he stopped when he noticed I wasn't laughing, too. He cleared his throat.

"I enjoyed myself," I said.

Jimmy nodded. "When you get legal—"

"I'll probably drop by for a visit." I shrugged. I was enchanted that he took an interest in me, even though I thought of him as just a friend. Still, I wouldn't promise anything. "Who knows."

Gym bag in hand, I stepped out of the rocket car. It was still a nice day; I felt like finding Drew and hitting for the next few weeks. But to do that, I needed my racquet. Before I closed the door, Jimmy handed it to me.

"American Express," he said. "Don't leave home without it."

Whatever that meant. Bouncing the racquet against my knee, I smiled anyway. It was one of those tense moments when there was too little to say, no matter how pregnant the silence may have been. It was like the short time that Saturday when Jimmy drank his Gatorade and handed over the phone salesman's card. It was meant to end simply, with me saying good-bye, but I held the door and waited for Jimmy to stop smiling and send me on my way.

The postal carrier broke the tension. She walked by, heavy pack on her back, and whistled. I looked at her to see what was going on. "Nice legs," she mouthed. After that, I looked at her like she was crazy. It was something I had yet to get used to, someone looking at me and commenting about my Crawford legs.

"Face it, snow queen," Jimmy said after a laugh. "You turn heads."

With that, he revved the engine and waved. The rocket car's door closed and Jimmy rolled down Third Street hill for the street leading back to Missouri.

With Rosemary Clooney crooning on the sidewalk loudspeaker, connected to the radio station in the basement of the St. Croix, I headed up the steps into the building. The St. Croix, a former two-and-a-half-star hotel before a syndicate purchased it at auction and converted it to an office building, had a marblelike plaster atrium with a *David*—in loincloth—set in the middle of a fountain on the ceramic-tiled and Oriental-rugged floor. Around the atrium were the building's five floors, connected by balconies and an elevator. It reminded me of the Old Post Office building in Washington, where Adele worked.

I crossed the atrium, passing the newspaper stand and Claude's, the restaurant where we were bound to eat, and headed directly for the elevator. Someone had the air on especially hard, and, by the time I had walked across the atrium, I was shivering like a Turk in Greenland. Shirley, the elevator attendant, looked at me through her fashion eyewear and pulled back the elevator door.

"Good morning, Mr. Macalester," she said.

"Morning."

"Here to see your mother?"

"Yep."

"Fourth floor, it shall be."

Shirley closed the elevator door and pressed the right buttons. The elevator started to lurch up like a simple push of a volley. Shirley and I looked at each other as Frank Sinatra sang over the loudspeaker, also connected to the radio station in the basement. Then, Shirley looked away, and scratched her smoky pompadour with a fuchsia-glazed fingernail. I shivered.

"They keep it so cold in here," she said.

"Yep."

I stuck my hands in my pockets and fancied saying something more. It was difficult to maintain silence. My gym bag hanging from my shoulder, the tennis racquet under my arm, I seemed as accessible as a kid on the street, and Shirley popped her gum as though she were practicing things to say. I hoped she wouldn't ask what I was doing away from school at noon, tennis racquet in hand, for I didn't know whether my answer would suit her.

The elevator stopped at the fourth floor. Shirley opened the door and I exited with barely a thank-you. I left no tip. She knew better than to expect either from me.

Macalester, Wharton, Stone, and Parker was my mother's firm. Originally Wilson and Macalester, it had been the Judge's firm before he went to Congress, when he and Judge Wilson were younger men. It started out doing corporation and equal-employment law, then branched out to do regulatory law when Mom joined the firm, then tax law when Vince Wharton came on board, then probate and real estate with Tom Stone's addition, then "legislative law" *(lobbying)* under Russell Parker. By the time I was in high school, the firm handled almost everything but criminal law and ambulance chasing, both of which went to a litigator across the street.

Clients from around the state came to the firm. The firm had some pull in Chicago and Springfield, but the firm's real pull came from the cable and biotech companies Mom and the Judge were able to strong-arm a long time ago into putting the firm on retainer. A long time ago, that was enough for the firm's founding partners (Mom, the Judge, Judge Wilson, and Vince Wharton, that is) to get the St. Croix for pennies on the dollar and to refashion it into an office condominium. Five floors of fairly content occupants—doctors, lawyers, accountants, a couple of stockbrokers, and two dentists—were in the building, along with the radio station in the basement. The fourth floor was the firm's. That, and the property manager the Judge and Judge Wilson still owned.

The firm's receptionist was at the far end of the balcony. Reaching her was like ambling through a gauntlet. From across the way she beckoned me. I made my way to her on pins and needles, passing the individual offices of the firm's grubs, who busied themselves with chewing legalistic minutia.

The firm's receptionist, the oldest, most senior employee, who had been Judge Wilson's secretary back when he was a prosecutor, was Bonnie. Nothing ornate, just Bonnie. She watched me coming through half-sized bifocals, and, as she watched, she filed her nails.

"I have been expecting you, Arthur," she said.

"Hey. Is my mom around?"

She raised a plucked, arched eyebrow like a midnight shift's cup of instant coffee. "But of course."

"Don't suppose I could see her, huh?"

"Now, Arthur," she said, pointing at me with the file, "you know the rule: anyone with the initials A. M. M. can see her any day."

I had forgotten that rule from childhood, from long ago, and the fact that Ted, Adele, and I all have the same initials. Both Mom and the Judge used it, to give us free passes anytime we wanted them. I was about to take such a pass and move toward Mom's office when I heard the elevator open and saw the imposing frame of Aunt Carolyn lumber down the balcony. Aunt Carolyn wore her Nancy Reagan red suit; Uncle Clifford used to say, when wearing that suit, she was loaded for bear.

I waited at Bonnie's desk as Aunt Carolyn made her way toward me. I decided to speak once I saw her bypass scar.

"Hey," I said.

"Hey, yourself," she said. "Is your mama in?"

"I think so."

"She better be. She's looked forward to this so much, she sure better be."

Aunt Carolyn needed no more direction than I to find her way to Mom's office in the southeastern corner of the floor. Mom's secretary, Thelma, was busy transcribing shorthand onto a computer. Efficient, she waved us in with hardly a dropped stroke. Through the door, I could hear Mom talking to someone.

"Knock on the door first," Aunt Carolyn warned.

I was a little hesitant, because there was another voice sounding like Adele. Aunt Carolyn met my hesitation and knocked on the door herself. The voices quieted. The door opened.

I was right. Mom and Adele were conversing. Mom wore her cream and lime green skirt suit while Adele had on her typical blue jeans and peach top. After the door had opened completely, they occupied different sides of the room, balanced by Mom's George Washington University law degree and the picture of Mom as a young girl with Patricia Roberts Harris. At first, Mom didn't acknowledge us. Instead, she focused upon the picture of Aunt Marta, Mom's only sister, who had committed suicide, allegedly over a Morehouse man, while a student at Spelman. For her part, Adele leaned against a conference table full of law books. Her arms were folded and her eyes were downcast. With her pout, she looked a little more like Aunt Marta, after whom Adele had been named, than like Cousin Mariah, whom she most often resembled.

"Ready?" Aunt Carolyn asked them.

"In a minute, please," Mom said.

My mother, I am reminded, hailed from Lincoln, Illinois. She had been baptized in the same AME church that had baptized Langston Hughes. Her family, the Merriweathers, worked for the state and for the county in various capacities. After college, Mom was something in some department until she met the Judge on the campaign trail, and, after voting for him, her first Republican, he whisked her away to Washington. After that, she became a lawyer.

It's ironic that I would recall all that at this time, when confronted by Mom in her own environment, free of all things Macalester, except for her children. I saw pictures of my parents' large wedding, complete with soon-to-be Speaker Newt, whom the Judge couldn't stand. The ceremony was at Howard University, naturally, in Rankin Chapel. The cousin the minister did the wedding. I had heard it said, when he talked about being "thy brother's keeper," soon-to-be Speaker Newt walked out. Funny: the Judge said Newt was lucky to find the place.

I was told (by Grandma Macalester, of all people) that Mom went out of the way to soothe Speaker Newt. Grandma said she smiled in his face. I knew the Judge didn't like that. Speaker Newt was an army brat, you know, and army brats were not our kind of people. I would discover later that such behavior meant she was cast out of the family, not a member, but a retainer, hardly much more than the spitter out of children. And she was a pink-clad AKA to boot, in the middle of a family dominated by red-clad Deltas. I would find out later that ate at her. It made sense. She hated being bossed around by the Macalesters. Instead, when we were in her element, she preferred to boss Macalesters around.

"Let me get my bag," Mom said. She removed it from her desk drawer and applied fresh lipstick (lavender, I think—certainly not red) to her lips. She stepped out of the running shoes she had on and stepped into cream pumps. She cracked her knuckles. "Ready?"

Adele removed herself from the conference table. She was still pouting. "I like what I'm doing, Mom. I don't want to be a lawyer."

"Oh, please!" Mom shot back.

"Now, don't you two get into it again," Aunt Carolyn said. "We've got no time for that."

I shifted my weight, wondering what to say next. My gym bag slipped down my arm.

"You can leave that in here," Mom said. "Alfred told me you slept with friends."

"Yeah," I said, dropping the gym bag and racquet behind her desk.

"Drew?" she asked.

"No."

"Who?"

"Just a friend."

"If you don't want to say who—"

"No, I don't wanna say who," I whined. "If I wanted to say who, I would say who, but I don't want to."

Mom shrugged and looked at Aunt Carolyn. "Obviously, Carolyn, I have some of the most communicative children in the world. Are they really Madelyn's grandkids?"

"You're their mother," Aunt Carolyn said. "In this family, mothers like you are the last to know."

Aunt Carolyn held the door open as Adele and I trudged through it. Mom glided by and told Thelma she would be at Claude's should the president call. She wrapped her arm around mine and we proceeded toward the elevator. Adele engaged Aunt Carolyn in small talk, mostly about her pregnancy and the not-so-subtle wish for a little girl.

"Oh, no," Aunt Carolyn said, "for this family, it will be a boy. The Lord as my Witness, I'll lay you heavy odds any day: it will be a boy!"

"That's one thing this family needs," Mom said. "Another boy."

"Name him 'Alfred,'" Adele said.

"That's one thing we really need," Mom muttered. "Another Alfred."

Adele stomped her foot. "Mama!"

Aunt Carolyn put her arms around Adele. "What I tell you, now? We're going to work hard at being pleasant and stay pleasant, even if we just have to fall all over ourselves and get giddy and piss in our pants, as Madelyn says. Now, you two just remember that."

The elevator came and we boarded it in silence. Mom stood between Adele and me, arms twined around our arms, hands clasped as though she waited for someone to say something. By the third floor, Shirley the elevator attendant spoke and got Mom out of her way.

"Got two of the chicks here," Mom confirmed. "All we need now are the rooster and the mother hen."

"Aren't you the mother hen?" Shirley laughed.

"I'm a hen, but not mother hen. Mother hen's the big bird in this chicken coop."

It was enough to leave Shirley scratching her head in silence. That was just an act. It was obvious Mom was referring to Grandma Macalester, who dominated everyone.

The elevator stopped at the first floor. When the door opened, Mom and Aunt Carolyn let Adele and me exit first, then they followed. Again, there was music—this time, Dean Martin singing "That's Amore" It was too much.

"Who's selected this music?" Adele asked as we crossed the floor. "Rocky and Bullwinkle?"

"Don't knock 'em," Aunt Carolyn warned. "They were a pretty decent cartoon."

I looked at them. I couldn't get the idea of my mother and aunt as kids watching cartoons. Adele kept on walking.

We headed for Claude's. It was, after all, Mom's favorite place, thanks to the desserts. She said little to dissuade Adele and me from leading her and Aunt Carolyn there. The lunch crowd had not made it to Claude's yet, so it wasn't a matter of slipping in and finding a table. Claude's owner, a friendly, middle-aged woman named Ann, greeted us with menus.

"Not eating in, Rose?" she asked. "Family outing?"

"Family business," Mom said, "as usual."

Ann nodded and led us to a table by the window, from where we could see mile-long barges pushed along the Mississippi by mite-size tugboats. On slateboards on the walls, the day's menu was written. Soup and salad, sandwiches and pies. My eyes got big when I saw Ann's famous tollhouse pie still on the board.

"Um, Mom?" I said. I pointed toward the slateboard. "Can I have that?"

"Let me guess," Ann said. "The tollhouse pie?"

I nodded, smiling a little.

"As much as your father loves chocolate chip cookies, no wonder, especially when it's a pie." Ann turned to Adele. "You, too, hon?"

Adele paused. She flirted with a fudge pecan pie, but settled on a tollhouse pie as well. Being eccentric, Mom asked for a banana custard; in almost sixteen years of being in our home, I had never seen anyone eat anything banana but Mom. Aunt Carolyn, conscious of her health, opted for gooseberry pie.

Such was a meal at Claude's. Like Pietown Café, which preceded it and was situated on Second Street, folks always ordered desserts first. By the time our waitress came we had selected the salads, soups, and sandwiches of our meal, as well as the particular variant of sun tea or pink lemonade that was part of the fixture of a lunch at Claude's. Then, after our waitress (Angela?) shuffled away, we braced ourselves for the continued "talk" between Mom and Adele, which was on the agenda.

I sipped water and watched Adele and Aunt Carolyn small talk about being pregnant, which, if you have ever been in a conversation with someone who has given birth, you know, can be an eye-opening experience.

"I've talked to Ted and Gia this week," Adele said, "and they describe it as hell."

"It's hard to describe birth to anyone," Aunt Carolyn said, folding her hands. "It's just something you have to experience. And the funniest thing of all is all the cravings you get. Pickles and ice cream, in the middle of the night." Aunt Carolyn shuddered. Then, she laughed. "Madelyn says that, when Rose was carrying you, Alfred sent an intern all over Maryland looking for—what was it?—Ben and Jerry's butter pecan."

"I didn't have cravings like that when I had you," Mom said to me.

"Yes, you did," Aunt Carolyn said. "When you carried Skip, you wanted vanilla extract on Ritz crackers. Mariah and Madelyn both said you had vanilla extract stashed all over the place. In your briefcase. In your car. You'd even have vanilla extract right by you at the baseball game."

"It was all that vanilla-flavored pipe tobacco Alfred smoked," Mom said.

Aunt Carolyn covered her face with her hands and laughed heartily. "Rose, that was nothing but you wanting some vanilla extract on Ritz crackers. That's all, and nothing more."

Mom smiled a little, then drank sun tea.

The lunch time crowd arrived and the waitress (Angela!) came with our meals. I had a special ham sandwich, piled Dagwood high. I started eating. Adele folded her silverware on the plate.

"Sorry, kid," she said to me. Then, she turned to our mother. "Mom, what's this about you and Dad divorcing? You've been married thirty-four years. Why chuck it now?"

"You should ask your father," Mom said.

"I'm asking you."

"And what did he tell you?"

"What he told me is irrelevant," Adele said.

"My foot! Did he tell you about her?"

"*Her?!* You've known about *her* all these years," Adele snapped back. "*She* was part of a package deal. You mean to say, all of a sudden, after all these years of knowing about her, you got indignant?"

"If you continue this," Aunt Carolyn whispered, "I'm going to get indignant."

Adele leaned forward. She caught herself. "All I know is," she whispered, "you've been using her as an excuse all these—"

"An excuse?" Mom leaned forward, too, and dropped her voice to a whisper. She pointed at Adele with her fork. "You have something like this happen to your marriage, and then you can talk to me about using her as an excuse."

"I'll use it as an excuse," Aunt Carolyn whispered. "Keep on keeping on. I'll use it as an excuse."

That ended the conversation. We ate with a tension that was as tight as a freshly strung tennis racquet. Though Aunt Carolyn tried to move us to act differently, neither Adele nor I could get the idea of our parents divorcing out of our heads. It hurt especially that Mom was not wearing her wedding ring, either, like the Judge, choosing to have on her thirtieth anniversary ring, which she cherished because the Judge had it specially fitted for her. And this "her" everybody kept referring to—that was a complete mystery. Someone, clue me in!

The tollhouse pie was tart.

When lunch was finished, Mom took the bill. As she rolled out a pair of twenties, I felt an emptiness, like it was our last supper.

"I know you know you are Macalesters," Mom said as she waited for the change, "but try to remember you're Merriweathers, too. It might not mean much now, but, over the years, it might mean as much."

I scratched my head. That was so out of the blue, I had no idea what she was talking about. Mom spun her heels and turned right into Adele. Briefly, they smiled at each other, as if knowing something.

"I wouldn't wish any of this on my worst enemy," Mom said. "Let alone my only daughter. Our marriage is, in a way, on hiatus—"

"This is not a network offering, Mom," Adele said.

"Maybe not," Mom retorted, "but it feels like it. Believe you me, it does feel like it, and you are still waiting for the laugh track. It will come like *Frank's Place*'s second season."

Mom tucked her handbag under her arm and left Claude's, leaving Adele and me with Aunt Carolyn. Adele was bewildered, as if this whole thing was an act for the nosy folks' benefit and what she really wanted was to be released from a contract before the agreement expired. I was beginning to feel it was just an act, too.

"Can you *believe* her?" Adele said, shaking her head. "That's *our* mother."

I put my hands in my pockets. "Who's this 'her' you keep referring to?"

Adele looked at me, shocked. Didn't she know I didn't know just yet? Aunt Carolyn clasped her large hands.

"How old are you, Skip?" Aunt Carolyn asked.

"I'll be seventeen next year," I said.

"By late October," Adele replied. She hooked her thumbs into the belt loops of her jeans. "Right now, he's still fifteen."

Aunt Carolyn looked at me. I expected her to shake her head and say I was still much too young to know who this "her," the other woman, was. Aunt Carolyn didn't do that. Instead, she guided me to a love seat in the atrium and sat me down. She sat with me, then folded her hands in her lap. I got the feeling this was very bad news.

"Your father and mother," Aunt Carolyn began, "wanted to keep some things from you until you are ready. Certain things about their past."

"The her is Eugenia Levin," Adele blurted out. "Genie."

I felt nauseated. "My English teacher?"

They nodded.

I still felt nauseated. "The Judge's girlfriend is my English teacher?!"

"That's part of the problem," Aunt Carolyn said.

"I'd say that is the problem, if my English teacher is the Judge's girlfriend," I said.

"There's a problem with your verb," Adele said. She was sounding like Bill Clinton. "It's not *is;* it's *was.*"

"Is, was," I said. "It doesn't matter. Dr. Levin is breaking Mom and the Judge up."

Aunt Carolyn grabbed my hand. For a minute, all I heard was the atrium's fountain. "The fact is, Skip—" Aunt Carolyn paused and bit

her lip. "There's no pleasant way of saying it. At one time, Alfred and
Eugenia Levin were engaged."

I exploded. "They were *what?!*"

They shushed me, then they nodded.

"Before he met Rose," Aunt Carolyn said, "Alfred was engaged to
Eugenia Levin."

"You mean, she could have been my mother?"

Again, they nodded. It couldn't get any worse than this, I thought.
All I could do was think about the Judge and Dr. Levin, enjoying each
other. I shook my head. How could I hold my head up at school in the
morning? And, over the loudspeaker, someone had to be singing
"I Got Rhythm."

"It gets worse, kid," Adele said. Aunt Carolyn nodded. "See, they
would've married, if it weren't for Mom."

"You don't mean—"

I could scarcely finish the phrase. Mom, the Judge, and Dr. Levin—
a love triangle. Who would have thought? I started pacing. Adele
paced with me.

"It's not that bad," she said.

"Oh, yeah? You try explaining it!"

"What's there to explain?" Aunt Carolyn asked. She remained on
the love seat, thanks to her heart. "They're grown."

"They're my parents and my English teacher!"

Aunt Carolyn blinked. "It happened so long ago."

"But it happened!"

Adele and Aunt Carolyn both blinked. They looked at each other.

"Had I known this would be how you would react," Adele said, "I'd
never've said anything."

"It's hard for you to've said nothing, with you going back and forth
talking about 'her,' 'her,' and 'her.'" I put my hands in my pockets
and shivered. "*Shit!* It's cold! You thought I wouldn't've noticed?
What you think I am?"

I saw no way out of the conversation but to walk away. After all, I
was stuck in the middle of this. What happened with Reverend
Shuddlesworth was forgotten, as though it was a lifetime ago. I felt

exhausted. Hell, I just felt old. I continued pacing. My mind raced. Then, I stopped pacing. I shivered.

"Are they getting back together? The Judge and Doctor Levin?"

Aunt Carolyn shrugged. "Only they can answer that."

"*Great.* I'm going to be taught by my stepmother!"

With that, I turned and headed for the elevator. Adele tried to go with me, but I shook her off. I was heading for Mom's office, but what would I do (aside from fetching my things) when I got there? Would I say something? And wasn't my anger better suited for the Judge and Dr. Levin, rather than for my mother? After all, Mom had done the first act.

It was still lunch hour. Bonnie and Thelma were away from their desks, replaced by clock faces that clicked away the minutes. Thelma's clock face had a particularly funny sign: ENTER AT YOUR OWN RISK, it said. It made me think twice.

Mom's office door was open. She was steadily working on a yellow legal pad. Letter writing, or maybe making notes for a brief. I stuck my head in.

"Hey," I said. "Mom?"

Mom looked up for a second, then returned to the pad. "Your things are where you left them."

I came in and went around to her desk. I looked at her. She didn't seem the other woman.

"Did you play today?"

"Yeah," I said. "With Jimmy, a guy I played against at Rec Night. Didn't win, though."

"You Macalester men—"

I grabbed my things. "Huh?"

"Just an observation about you Macalester men," she said, still writing. "Ask a question, they give you the Nicene Creed. Whatever you do, you should make sure you have a lawyer with you."

I didn't know what she meant. I scratched myself. "I'll be sure to call Marshall. He can be my lawyer."

She stopped writing and looked up. "Marshall. He knows how to keep his mouth shut."

"You mean he knew about that?"

"About what?" she asked, then she gave me a look the likes of which I had never seen. It was a look that went right through me, and left me quaking in its wake. It made me look at my feet. She resumed writing. "You should be in school. Alfred knows that."

"Adele's going to drive me," I lied. "She's waiting for me. She'll take me back."

Mom continued writing. "It's good you and your sister are so close."

I nodded and shivered.

In retrospect, I felt I should have said something a son would say, but, in my mother's office, I felt as much a stranger as an assistant counsel, stopped by to get some advice. And, like some assistant counsel, all I could do was shuffle my feet and head out the door, having been dispatched. Though I felt like crying, it was clear I would have gotten less sympathy than a subchapter C corporation called in for taxes.

Adele was waiting for me at Thelma's desk. She stood as I approached and she reached for my gym bag. "Want me to carry that?"

I shook my head. I wanted none of that friendly sibling stuff. "I got it."

Adele wrapped her arm around my shoulder. We walked to the elevator. The elevator opened on cue and Shirley stuck her head out. We were still a couple of yards up the balcony, so we had to hurry, but Shirley held the elevator long enough for us to get there.

"There you are," she said, smiling.

We smiled as well, though, truth told, I think neither of us felt like it. We boarded the elevator, and, when the elevator closed and the polished brass reflected upon us, we saw Brad Morgan leaning against the back. Adele and I were both surprised. We thought the elevator was empty, aside from Shirley, and since Brad's disappearance the last place we expected to find him was inside the St. Croix elevator.

Shirley just pushed her glasses up her nose.

Brad seemed to be thinking. He had his hands in his pockets and he was looking down. He was in desperate need for a bath and fresh clothes. His pink oxford shirt and khaki pants had grass stains and he had straw in his hair that Adele reached to brush out. Sockless, his feet seemed muddy. He looked a little tired. I decided to speak first.

"Brad," I said. "Where have you been?"

"Around," he said. He took a deep breath. "'For once I myself saw with my own eyes the Sibyl at Cumae suspended in a bottle, and when the boys asked her, "Sibyl, what do you want?" *respondebat illa*—'"

He balked at Adele touching him. It didn't make sense: *Respondebat illa* is Latin; Brad took French, with the Whitmaners.

"He's been talking like that ever since he got here," Shirley snorted. "Wish he'd quit. Gives me the creeps."

Brad accepted Adele's offer of a ride, but first he wanted something to eat. When we got to the first floor, Adele led him to Claude's, where she ordered him a ham sandwich to go.

"It ain't kosher," Brad said. "I don't want it. It ain't kosher."

Adele was bewildered. Brad was the kind of guy that would eat anything. "Your family doesn't keep kosher."

"We will now. I don't want ham. Order me something like turkey or chicken."

Adele called the counter girl back, and changed her order to a turkey sandwich, to go. Once it came, Brad devoured it like he hadn't eaten in years. Then, Adele offered again to drive him home.

Brad looked up from his sandwich. "Which one?"

"The one in Whitman Township," Adele said through a bit of a smile. "The place where you live."

"I was kinda hoping you could drive me back across the ocean," Brad said. "But I guess that's impossible."

"Let Dennis send you on the Paris trip." I smiled. "He can do that for your birthday."

I meant that as a joke. The Paris trip was that next summer, for third year French students. Dennis had said he wouldn't pay for it. Brad, who was normally irreverent about his father, didn't smile. He wiped the corners of his mouth with the sandwich's wrapper. He smelled as though he had been wallowing with pigs. Indeed, he needed a bath desperately.

"The car is right outside here," Adele said, leading us to the Third Street entrance.

When we got to the door, Brad was a gentleman. He held it open for Adele. It surprised me so much I wondered what had gotten into him. Adele didn't know what to make of it. I mean, he was like so many other Whitmaners before—so flip and crass—this transformation seemed completely out of character.

"What's up?" I whispered to Brad as we headed to Adele's car. Brad just looked at me and shrugged.

The car Adele had was one of those hybrid things that were the fad of the year. Part electric, it had the capability to traverse great distances on a single twelve-hour charge. In a way, it reminded me of the car she had in Washington, which she used exclusively for trips around the Beltway. Seeing it, Brad became Brad again.

"Oh, man," he said. "Righteous."

He ran toward it and saw his reflection in its gold body. It seemed not to have bothered him he had to cross traffic to do it. Adele and I had to wait for a slow mail truck to pass to join him.

"Did you have to drive this all the way from DC?" he asked Adele.

She shook her head. "Picked it up from the airport."

"Can I drive it?"

Adele looked at Brad skeptically. She didn't know where he had been sleeping.

"C'mon," Brad said. "I got my license."

"It's not your license I'm concerned about," Adele said. "It's your insurance. You know how expensive teenage boys are these days?"

"Dennis keeps telling me," Brad said. "But I'm safe."

Adele chuckled and opened the car door. "I bet you are."

"I am. If I were an ambulance driver, I'd be able to get my patient to the hospital, no sweat, no scratch."

"What do you know about ambulances anyway?" I asked, going to the passenger side.

"Enough to know how to drive one," Brad said. "It ain't as complicated as flying a plane, but it works. Just ask Ernest Hemingway."

I looked at Brad. What had he been inhaling since he went away? *A Farewell to Arms?*

Adele wasn't interested in indulging Brad's fancy. She directed him to get into the backseat, where he stretched out and quickly fell asleep. His odor was so strong I had to roll down the window.

"He stinks."

"Kid! He's a cousin."

"Cousin or not," I said. "That guy smells atrocious!"

Unfortunately, the Morgans's house was a ways away from the St. Croix. We had to go through town to the penultimate light and find our way onto the state highway. As we made that turn, I was reminded of the brickyard that used to be there before World War II. Grandma Macalester's family, the Crawfords, worked there; Grandma Macalester's paternal grandfather, Charles Crawford, who died of appendicitis a hundred years ago, was the brickyard's first black engineer. Among the most notable things about him, the Judge said, was said to have been his railroader's pocket watch, complete with a gold chain, with which he timed his children's lunch deliveries of a fresh, hot meal, his favorite being ham. Now, irony of ironies, his distant nephew, descendant from a niece Charles Crawford reared like a daughter, refused to eat ham!

Brad slept soundly, even when we got to his subdivision. Adele turned down the drive and selected the Morgans's house without much prompting. She parked in the driveway.

"Go up and ring the bell," she said.

That was something I really didn't want to do. I mean, what if Alan answered the door? Adele repeated herself. "Kid," she said. "Go up and ring the bell."

"We don't know if anybody's home," I said.

"We won't know if you don't go up and ring the bell. So, go up."

Sometimes, I wonder if it is just me, or does Adele occasionally have a mother's circular logic? It seemed like she really didn't need a kid to be a mother. Or, maybe she had Grandma's knack for arguing. No matter. I didn't feel like belaboring that point, either. I trudged to the front door.

Walking to the door, I thought about Alan. Was he there? What would I say to him? Would I tell him I was sorry? No, I couldn't tell him what happened, really happened, to me. I rang the bell. A chime echoed through the house.

I waited. It was the longest wait I could have imagined, like watching a pot boil. Then, I heard someone move the brass dead bolt and I saw the knob turn. Then, the large, black front door swung open and

I was face to face with Alan, whose eyes were as large as a deer's in traffic.

"Hey," I said.

Alan was speechless. He seemed to gulp.

"Who is it?" a woman called from inside the house. "Aaron?"

I heard footsteps. Then, with a liverspotted hand, Alan's grandmother Myrna Leventhal opened the door. "Yes?"

"Mrs. Leventhal," I said. "I'm Skip Macalester."

She looked at me for a second, then threw up her hands. "Yes, I know you: you're Madelyn's grandson."

I pointed to the car. "My sister and I found Brad."

With scarcely more than that, Mrs. Leventhal trotted to the car. She was a stout woman, her body banging along on what Grandma Macalester said were artificial hips. Alan, in tennis shoes and shorts and T-shirt, was not far behind. I took up the rear. Adele got out of the car and opened the back door. Brad was dead to the world. When she saw him, Mrs. Leventhal put her hands to her face, looking like *The Scream*. Then, she caught herself and shook Adele's hand.

"Myrna," Mrs. Leventhal said. "You must be Adele. Madelyn talks about you all the time. She's so proud of you."

Adele almost blushed.

"Where'd you find him?" Mrs. Leventhal asked.

"In the St. Croix," Adele said. "We finished lunch, then we went into the elevator and there he was."

"We've been worried sick about him." Mrs. Leventhal shook Brad's arm, trying to wake him, then she backed away, covering her mouth. "Heavenly Father from up above!"

I wondered what could have made her exclaim like Grandma. I inched forward and looked through the open door. Above Brad's left wrist was a series of faded, light blue numbers, like a tattoo. Brad stretched a little. His eyes opened.

"Work," he muttered, "it makes you free."

He fell back to sleep.

"Someone needs to call the police," Mrs. Leventhal said. She turned to Alan and me. "Could you guys get him inside? I need to call the police."

With that, she headed back to the house.

Alan and I looked at each other, unwilling to make the first move. Then, Adele directed me to "grab him." It was like a shock on the balls.

"Huh?"

"Grab Brad," she directed.

Like a good little brother, I did as I was told. I took him by the arm and pulled him out of the car. Once I got him standing on the pavement, Alan did like a little brother, too, and draped Brad's arm over his shoulder.

"He's so heavy," Alan said.

"Yeah," I said. "A ton of bricks."

Between the two of us, we were able to waddle him up the walk to the front door. Mrs. Leventhal held the door open. She looked again at the light blue numbers and shook her head.

"What kind of sicko could do that to a little boy?" she asked.

Alan glanced at me. I felt like disappearing.

Having been at the Morgans's for Brad's birthday parties when we were younger, I knew where his room was. We managed the stairs and went directly to it. I kept him standing while Alan opened the door, then we poured Brad onto the bed. We just looked at him. I glanced at his swimsuit pinup girls on the wall.

"He really stinks," I said.

Alan sort of nodded, then he stepped out of the door.

"Alan?"

"Yeah?" He looked in from the hall, a safe distance.

"About what happened Saturday? I'm sorry."

"Yeah."

He slipped away. Next thing I heard was him trotting downstairs. I felt like something scraped off a shoe with a stick.

By the time I got back downstairs, Mrs. Leventhal was on the phone in the living room. Alan had wrapped his arms around her waist and she was stroking his hair. "Don't worry," she said to him. "Nana won't let anything happen to you."

Alan glanced at me for a second, then he glanced away. I sat with Adele on the sofa, as she sipped bottled water.

"She's reporting it as a hate crime," Adele whispered.

"About Brad?" I asked.

Adele nodded. "What else would you call it?"

"Hate crime" would be a logical thing to call it, though I would have called it simply "a prank." It seemed, though, I would have lost that argument.

When Mrs. Leventhal was satisfied with the conversation, she hung up the phone. "They're sending a deputy sheriff," she announced. "We are not to wash the body."

"But he smells like a horse," Alan said.

"Still, we are not to wash the body."

We stayed there until the deputy came. He interviewed Adele and me, and remarked how I seemed such a bundle of nerves. It seemed odd, but for everything else, that I would be interviewed as an eyewitness or as a spectator and not as a victim or a perpetrator.

It proved a fruitless series of interviews. No one knew what happened to Brad, and Brad was no help. The best he could give was gibberish about domed cities and genocidal wars, about burning crosses and riders cloaked like the Four Horsemen of the Apocalypse. No one knew where Brad was for so long, and no one had the slightest idea what happened to him, either.

I watched Alan like a hawk as the deputy asked him questions. "I dunno," was his answer. He rested his head on the sofa arm. He glanced at me a couple of times, then looked away. It was like a code. He had cute dimples.

When finished, the deputy patted Alan's head. After that, Adele and I felt free to go. Dennis had arrived from the hotel by then. Rachel Morgan, notified by beeper that her son had been found, was due in from St. Louis any minute. It would prove a tearful reunion.

Chapter Fourteen

Leaving the Morgans, Adele dropped me off at the high school just as the bell rang and the seniors were dismissed for the day. It was really something to have been let out of one of those hybrid numbers in front of all those Whitmaners, a real boost to my ego, because the Whitmaners must have wondered whom did we bribe to have smuggled such a thing into the area. They were in their Mexican-made Japanese and Korean cars, drooling. Not that I was the type of kid that gloated, but I couldn't help but smile.

When the seniors are dismissed, around two, traffic along College Avenue is as vicious as it is at eight o'clock in the morning or at three in the afternoon. A pedestrian wanting to cross, as I did that Monday, must wait like a driver and patiently choose his point to move.

So I waited. At first, the traffic moved too fast for me to slip by. Then, after a while, a police car came down the hill and rolled to a stop. A girl in a Toyota took the opportunity to speed out into traffic and down the hill. I watched the police officer. She, a real kick-ass looking thug, looked at me through reflecting wraparound sunglasses. I smiled at her. She was stone-faced, and uglier than the Medusa. Still, I smiled. She refused to smile. She signaled for me to cross the street.

Until I started walking up the hill to the West building, I was undecided about what I would do there. Would I really confront Dr. Levin over my parents? That seemed a little melodramatic for me. Would I try going to Ken and telling him about Brad being home? Really, I felt that ought to be left to Dennis. Besides, I really didn't feel like seeing Ken, which would be just like seeing the Judge again. I needed some time before doing that.

The thought occurred to me to try Drew. Drew . . . I have always been comfortable seeing Drew. Besides, I hadn't seen him in almost an entire day. He was in government, of course, in MacPhail's class, in the Main building. Getting him out of there would prove a trick, because MacPhail lets no one out early.

What thought went through my mind heading to MacPhail's class? Good question. Mainly, I tried conjuring something to get Drew out. Though I thought of several scenarios, each seemed to have had its own pitfall and reason for failure. My mind couldn't settle upon anything too rich. And, besides, MacPhail really just doesn't buy certain things.

The Main building was deserted—no monitors in the hall, I mean. That meant a pretty good slip to the government classroom. Having MacPhail myself, I knew what they were talking about. They were going over the Legislative Branch, Article I of the Constitution. I could see Drew's eyes glaze over as MacPhail explained the New Jersey Plan and the Virginia Plan, comparing the two. The clock must have moved especially slow that hour, so close to dismissal, as the talk about Congress blurred into a single, continuous stream, like the faces panned in a shot at the president's State of the Union Address.

Drew must have looked at his watch. His watch must have provided discouraging news. Around him, a few people would be asleep. MacPhail would toss erasers at them. One of the kids would collect the erasers and return them to the blackboard. When I arrived at the door MacPhail had turned to the third page of his notes.

Drew, may we play together, tennis this afternoon? I have learned the best shots. You would like them, I think.

"Yes, Macalester?" MacPhail asked as I stood at the door. I had been thinking so deeply I had not realized I was really there. MacPhail was at his door, hands on his hips. Hearing my name, Drew had popped out of his seat and he trotted behind him. MacPhail barely noticed. "Your father said you were sick today."

"I was." I cleared my throat. "Still am. Contagious."

MacPhail looked me down with his Marine glare. "I bet you are."

I smiled as MacPhail returned to his lectern. Drew took his place at the door. He smiled. It was his funny smile again.

"Got over the old flu bug, huh, Arthur?" Drew said.

"Ford," MacPhail called out from his lecture notes, "back to your seat."

Drew flashed his smile. He had on his nice, friendly smile. Somehow, that smile was able to get him out of that room, for the next thing

I knew, he was given a pass, to someone (Mrs. Stuart, the counselor?) and we were walking down the hall.

"Now that I've done this," I said.

"Now that you've done it," Drew said, "you can go tell your kids. When you have kids. Say, 'I helped my best friend, Drew Ford, skip MacPhail's government class, the class no one ever skips.'"

Naturally, Drew thought himself lucky to have gotten out of MacPhail's class twice in a week. He draped his arm over my shoulder as we walked and it would have stayed there, too, had I not shrugged it off. Drew was shocked.

"What?"

"Nothing," I said. "People will talk."

"You never gave a care about people talking before, so why start?"

I couldn't say anything, except perhaps that what people would say was true. Besides, the fact was that I was not quite ready to be touched by anyone. I didn't think Drew would understand. So, I said nothing as an explanation. "Never mind."

Drew stopped smiling. We stopped walking. We were at the gym. "What's wrong?"

"Nothing."

"Did something happen?"

"No."

"Because I'll kick anybody's ass if something happened."

"*Nothing* happened."

"You sure? You wouldn't just be shitting me? I'm not just shitting you; I really would. I want you to know that. I'd kick anybody's ass to death if they did something to you."

I didn't get the chance to answer. As I was about to say something significant, Marshall came through the very same door he had come through just a few days before, when we made our way to the Cardinal ball game. As I remember, Marshall's schedule called for him to be in class (where we all should have been); why he wasn't was beyond me.

"What're you doing out?" I asked him.

Marshall held up a laminated hall pass and flicked it. "Heard you found Brad."

"Yeah," I said. "We took him home. To his house."

"How's he doing?"

"He's Brad. Only, this time, he's speaking gibberish."

Marshall smiled. "They can take him to a shrink and iron it out. See Alan, too?"

"No."

"You sure?"

"I need to see Dr. Levin," I said after a few moments.

Marshall sighed. He looked like he knew exactly why I needed to see her. "Come on," he said.

We crossed the Pit. I hoped that Marshall would send my episode with Alan to the "family only" part of his mind. Drew, I knew, had to remain oblivious about that. If he knew anything about that, he would kick my ass to death. What I feared most, though, was the exchange of information—Drew telling Marshall about last Saturday morning, Marshall telling Drew about this past Saturday afternoon— and, between the two of them, adding me up. Were that to happen, how would I explain myself? I wouldn't just be able to call myself a "faggot." I would have to call myself worse.

We were at Dr. Levin's room. The door was closed and locked. Through the door glass, we could see the lights were on.

"Where could she've gone to?" Drew asked.

"Wherever she went," Marshall said, "she mustn't've gone too far."

We chose to wait. We crossed our arms and ankles and leaned against the lockers across from Dr. Levin's room.

"We look like The Three Stooges," Drew mumbled.

"Three Stooges," Marshall said. "That brings on a lot of memories. Doesn't it, cousin dear?"

I shrugged a little and tried seeming inconspicuous. A pack of girls in red PE uniforms ran from the girls' gym down the hall. Some, behind hands, giggled and whispered. They looked like a bunch of sophomores.

"They like your legs," Marshall said.

"You got the same pair, cousin dear," I said.

"I guess they know a good pair when they see it, Arthur," Drew said. "You, too, Marshall, believe it or not."

In a few minutes, we heard whistling from the nearby stairwell, accompanied by a rhythmic toss of keys. I tried placing the melody, but it was something this side of symphonic that I couldn't recollect. Then, out of the stairwell came Mr. Armstrong, whistling the melody and whirling a peck of keys on a long, elastic band. In his free arm was a stack of *New York Review of Books*. He looked at us, blinking, and smiled.

"You made it," he said. "For a while there, I thought you'd given up on us for the day."

I found a way to smile at that. A little at ease, I loosened my legs.

"We're waiting for Dr. Levin," Drew said sharply. "He's got to see her."

Mr. Armstrong stopped at us and blinked. "You want to wait for her here or inside?"

"If we could wait for her inside," Drew snapped, "we would. That's why we're waiting here." He rolled his eyes, as if adding "you dope" to the sentence.

Mr. Armstrong shifted the review copies and the keys. He jiggled the keys when he did that. "You can wait inside. She'll be in directly."

It seemed to take a while for Mr. Armstrong to find the right key to the door, and, once he did, he had to turn it a couple of times before getting it right. Backing up with the knob in hand, he held the door open.

"You're in school," Marshall whispered.

"Huh?"

"You heard me," he whispered. "School. Remember that."

Mr. Armstrong deposited the set of *New York Review of Books* on the table behind Dr. Levin's desk and upset the Judge's photograph. Quickly, he picked it up. "Didn't mean for that," he said.

"What?" Drew demanded.

Mr. Armstrong flexed his hand and brushed it against his shirt. "Nothing." A little nervous, Mr. Armstrong busied himself with a stack of themes, which he moved from Dr. Levin's desk to her table. Again, he upset the Judge's picture.

For a fleeting moment I had a vision of Drew kicking Mr. Armstrong's ass. I wondered what it might be like to sic Drew on Reverend Shuddlesworth. I wondered would he, like a pitbull, turn on me. My great fear, almost as great as Marshall and Drew sharing notes, was for Mr. Armstrong to mention that I had seen him with his friend (or, as I would discover later, "friend," if you know what I mean) and to add that he had seen me with Jimmy. I knew Drew would turn angry at that.

Thankfully, Dr. Levin made it in. She took one look at us and she took a deep breath. "I think I know what this is about. You need to speak to me in private, Skip?"

I nodded.

She looked at the others. "Please excuse us for a few minutes."

It was awkward, Drew and Mr. Armstrong leaving. Mr. Armstrong was reluctant to turn his back to Drew, and Drew didn't want to leave first. They left together, like birds of a feather. Marshall was slower to leave.

"Remember," he whispered. He gave me a look, like a kinsman's squeeze, then he left.

It was just the two of us. What does one say, face-to-face with his potential stepmother? What I wanted to say, I couldn't say at school. Though I understood my mother, I felt a degree of anger at this woman for ending my parents' marriage. I felt enough rage to forget myself and lash out at her. As she dropped into her chair, I wanted her to hurt. I wanted her to cry. I wanted her to bleed. She held a clear black ink pen and raked it with her thumbnails. It sounded like a dulcimer.

"I want you to understand me," she said, taking a breath. "I didn't want this to happen to you or to her, or to your sister and brother, anymore than it happened to me thirty-six years ago. Your father and I had an agreement. We kept to that agreement all these years, and even the time Adele was in my class, we didn't break it. I think that's in our favor."

It was a likely defense, the beginning of a Socratic apology. What lurked behind that apology? I slid into a desk and looked at the floor. I dreaded what was to come next.

She interlaced her fingers. "We thought we would grow apart. It was so long ago. But we were wrong." She cleared her throat. "When they moved back from Washington, your mother told him if we ever—she would—"

I wanted to yell at her to stop. I wanted to cover my ears, but all I could do was to start crying. She pushed a box of tissues under my nose, then she returned to her chair. She sat there and watched me. It is hard to say exactly why I was crying. With so much going on, I really didn't know. It was just everything pushed upon me so hard I was ready to burst.

It was what women call a good Oprah cry. When I was finished, I was numb. She brought a tall, woven wastebasket to me and dropped the damp tissues into it. "Are you going to marry him?" I asked.

She scratched her head. "That's premature. He's not even divorced yet."

"I don't want them to have a divorce," I said finally.

"That's understandable."

There was a knock at the door. Mr. Armstrong stuck his head in. "Can we—?"

"Give us a sec," she said.

"Okay." Mr. Armstrong closed the door.

Dr. Levin turned to me. She looked gentle. "I've said my piece. Is there something you wish to say?"

I struggled. "I love my mother."

"I hope you do. And your father?"

I nodded. I supposed, when it was all said and done, I really loved my father as well; but not at that moment. At that moment, I had my fill of him, for tearing my family apart over this woman. It would change after time. After a few months, a year, I would come to love Dr. Levin as a second mother. I would forgive my father, just as he had forgiven me countless times. But those months seemed like an eternity away. At that moment, I wanted to be left alone in my anger.

A second knock on the door signaled it was time to dry my eyes. Dr. Levin busied herself with the stack of *New York Review of Books,* ripping out articles as I opened the classroom door. Mr. Armstrong rushed in, followed by Drew, who sauntered.

"Where's Marshall?" I asked.

"Went to use the phone," Drew said. "He said he'll be back in a few minutes."

Nodding, I sat with Drew in student desks and watched Dr. Levin for a few minutes. Then, Drew touched my arm and looked me in the eye.

"What's wrong?" he asked.

"Nothing," I said. "With me? Nothing. Why?"

"'Cause you look like you've been crying," he said.

"We talked over a few things," Dr. Levin said.

Drew looked at her skeptically. "Like what?"

"That's between me and him," she said.

Drew didn't seem to buy that as an acceptable answer. He seemed to say to her that, if she had said anything to upset me, he would be more than willing to kick her ass then and there. So much, so much. Easily, were I the truly vengeful kind, I would have sent him upon her. Marshall entered a little later. This time, in addition to the laminated hall pass, he carried a pink slip, also a hall pass, which he carried like a pinch of snuff.

"Where'd you run off to?" I asked.

"Had to make a phone call," he said. "The Judge's made plans for dinner. He wants us to meet him at Midtown Restaurant, around six."

How Marshall communicated with my father was beyond me. With him in court all day, it was like ESP. No matter. Move to the next question. "Who's the 'us'?"

"Us," Marshall said. "You, me, and Drew."

Drew was unsure. "I need to check with my mom."

"Why's he want Drew?" I asked.

Marshall gave me a look, as perplexed as barbed wire. "Really, cousin dear."

We left Dr. Levin shortly after that. She didn't let us go before reminding us we had to prepare the play, *both* plays. She was not willing to let us forget it. "Rehearsals begin tomorrow after school," she said. I wished she hadn't said that. I wished she had let us pass on performing that play in drag. But she wouldn't. Come the next day, I would see my outfit and find it interesting. And, when I play-acted, I took to the role like a fish to water. I enjoyed it tremendously, and, because she helped me perform it so successfully, I started to forgive Dr. Levin for her selfishness and want for the Judge.

Our parents were invited to the performance a few weeks later. The Judge came. Mom didn't. She said she had to do a deposition. Sounded like her.

But, back to early September, the Monday afternoon. That afternoon, leaving Dr. Levin's class in anger still, I walked Drew and Marshall back to the Main building. As we walked, I couldn't get out of my mind such questions as why dinner with the Judge that day, and why Drew should join us. It seemed one of the Judge's mysteries, about which he was too reluctant to clue me in. I tried taking Marshall's implied advice and let it pass me by.

I couldn't. Once Drew was returned to MacPhail's class, I buttonholed Marshall in the stairwell. Before I could ask anything, though, Marshall volunteered information.

"I didn't tell him anything when we talked," Marshall said, "but, knowing him, he's got an idea."

"But why Drew?"

Marshall shrugged. "He knows Drew's your best friend. Perhaps that's got something to do with it."

"Don't expect me to talk in front of Drew."

Marshall blinked. Then, slowly, he regained mastery of the situation. He sighed his sigh, bored and underwhelmed as usual. "Finished, cousin dear? Because I need to get back to class sometime before the day ends."

I had to let him go. He was no use to me otherwise. I wondered what he said to the Judge, and what else the Judge said to him. It occupied me the rest of the period as I sat in the library and leafed through magazines, until the final bell rang.

Drew and I met in the stairwell leading to the library. He smiled. "Let's find a phone."

"What about your cell phone?"

"Mavis grabbed it," he said. "She's probably got purple, smelly bubble gum all over it. I'd have to use disinfectant to get it clean."

He went to the pay phone near the Main office, but there was a line at its alcove, which irritated the hell out of him.

"Damn," he muttered.

"You wanna go to another phone?" I asked.

"Like what? The other pay phones're in the other buildings, but they're bound to have lines, too."

I thought for a second, then I happened upon the obvious.

"C'mon," I said.

We crossed the flow of kids and hurried into the Main office. The secretaries and clerks, clerical looking, busied themselves with paperwork. No one noticed us. I had to clear my throat to be recognized. They all looked at me like we had just come in from the rain.

"Is Mr. Langston in," I asked, "or is he still making rounds?"

It was like I was Eris, the goddess of discord, fresh from an apple orchard. One clerk in hideous blue contacts turned to another clerk with tainted hair. "Have you seen him?" the blue contacted one asked.

"I ain't seen him," the tainted clerk said. "I ain't seen him, and I ain't looking for him, either."

"Why'd you want to see him?" a secretary with tusks for teeth asked.

"Why'd he want to see him?" a clerk with bad skin repeated. He paused to chew cashews. "That's his cousin."

"I know that's his cousin," the tainted clerk said. "Tell me something I didn't know."

"I'll tell you something you didn't know," the blue contacted one muttered, rolling her eyes.

"Just tell him if you've seen him," one clerk, filing folders, said.

"I don't think you should tell him," said another clerk, who looked like a grandmother and was closing a set of student passes in a manila envelope and wrapping the envelope in a tease of string. "What if he doesn't want us to say it?"

"It's not like he's with the damn CIA," the bad-skinned clerk muttered.

"You never know," someone said.

"No, you never do," another person said.

"You had to drag me into this?" Drew whispered. "It's like a fucking freak farm in here."

I tried remaining hopeful. "Is there a phone we can use?"

"What's wrong with that one?" the tusk-toothed secretary, pointing through the office's glass wall at the pay phone, asked. To my surprise, the pay phone was free.

We left the Main office for the relative quiet of the teeming hall. The line, apparently out of frustration, had evaporated. Drew found fifty cents in his pockets and made the call to his mother at work.

"I'm having dinner with Skip," Drew blurted out when his mother picked up. He corrected himself. "Yes," he said. "Hi, Mom, it's me.

School's okay. How's work? Yes. Yes. No, it's not. We're going out. Midtown?" He looked at me. I nodded. "Midtown. Judge Macalester, I guess. No, I don't think so. *No,* I got money. I said no. Okay." He sighed. "I'll be there. Yes. Okay. Thank you."

Drew was red faced when he hung up.

"Well?"

"She wants me to pick up some money," he said.

"But did she say you could go?"

"Of course she said I could go. She said I'm to get some money from her. That's how she said I could go." Looking pissed, Drew folded his arms and leaned against the alcove. No one seemed to want to use the phone after him. Drew waited a few minutes, then muttered, "I hate when she does that to me."

"Does what?" I asked.

He cut his eyes at me, then softened. "Never mind. You'll never understand."

I wanted him to try me, as I, too, had parents who foisted themselves on me at any whim, even if it made me uncomfortable around my friends, but saying that seemed unworthy, like chasing after a boy. With Drew, I knew part of his problem was the general self-consciousness with which he understood that we were not of the same class and that I could buy and sell him a couple times over with the spare change in my pocket, if I wanted. It was an understanding that hovered about us from our relationship's beginning to our relationship's end. He would tease me with it, reminding me that he was working class and that he had to work hard to get the things he wanted in life, whereas I—I think you get the picture. For that reason, I was a bit surprised that he would still agree to dine with the Judge and me, and with Marshall, too, even though he would so obviously be the oddest man out.

At any rate, Drew moved himself away from the alcove. We headed for the front doors, which swung heavily on hinges, pivoting upon single pins. The students expelled, the doors smiled self-satisfied upon the courtyard and the Pit at the bottom of the hill, a long line of hard, concrete steps grimacing between dogwood trees.

We came down the steps. It was like descending Borobudur, in Indonesia. Having visited the Great Buddha's lair, we were free to go our way. The students were still going. At the Pit exit, there was still a line of cars.

"I guess I ain't got no choice but see my mom," Drew sighed.

"Don't sound so bad," I said. "It's not like going to see my mom."

"Says you."

We were at his car by the time Drew realized we had descended empty-handed, with little more than a few notebooks in his bag. The rest of his assignments, it seemed, were in his locker. Throwing the book bag into the backseat, he kicked the car door.

"I can't believe I left all that," he said. He slumped against the car door. "I'm not going back after it either."

"What if there's an assignment?"

"Screw the assignment. I'm just gonna have to take zeroes, that's all. I'm outta there; I ain't going back."

He craned his neck to the line of cars trying to get out the Pit exit, then he looked toward the Main building, where, I remember, one of his lockers was.

"Trouble deciding?" I asked.

He scoffed at the thought. "I've already decided. Not going back there today for nothing."

We climbed into his car, which was warm from the windows being rolled up. The upholstery felt hot to my legs. They felt burnt. "Let's get going," I said. "I'm getting singed."

"Your leg'll survive it."

Drew started the engine and, in a little bit, we were a part of the line heading for the exit. We would have made it sooner, were it not for the girl in the Fiat cutting in front of us.

"Stupid *bi*—" Drew honked the horn. "Move it!"

She looked over her shoulder, smiled, and waved. That made Drew mad enough to honk twice.

"Dumb bitch."

"Drew," I said, "that could be my sister."

"But it's not."

"But it could be. Would you call her a dumb bitch?"

"If she pulled some stunt like that, I would," he said. He maneuvered the car toward the exit. "Hell, if it was my own sister, and she made a dumb-ass move like that, I'd call her a dumb bitch."

At the print shop, Mrs. Ford came from the other side of a large copier, hair tied by her bandanna. She carried a ream of goldenrod paper. She signaled for us to cross the counter and go into a back room with her. We did so, and an old man with bushy eyebrows and a bushy beard, a customer waiting for a printing, looked at us as if he were studying pork steaks in the meat case.

"You picked a fine time to come," Mrs. Ford said, closing the door. "Just as Allen Ginsberg there was getting started, for the fifteenth time this project."

"Sorry," Drew said, "but you said."

"I know what I said," Mrs. Ford said. She unlocked a file cabinet and pulled out her purse. "I'm just saying." She handed Drew ten dollars. Drew almost turned up his nose.

"What's this for?" he asked. "I can't get crap—"

"Don't use that language with me, young man," Mrs. Ford snapped. She fixed her index finger upon him. "You're not so big I can't take you down a peg or two in front of your friend! Just give me an excuse!"

Drew glanced at me and cut his eyes toward her. "Thanks, Mom."

"I'm warning you," she said. "If you don't think I will, just try me."

Thankfully, Drew didn't. Winking at me, he moved me out the room to the front, where Charlie Devlin was still "in discussion" with the old man, who was getting as blue in the face as his suit. Drew barely waved at Charlie Devlin.

"I would've loved to hang around and watch ol' Charlie pop his rug," Drew said when we got outside. "That old cheapskate—that'll serve him right."

I smiled. I would have loved to see Devlin's toupee blast off. Though I knew squat about the man (past his name), to watch an adult lose control like a kid was something I thought refreshing. Even if it was someone not in our league.

We climbed into Drew's car. Drew looked at the clock and turned to me. "It ain't even three thirty," he observed. "We got a couple hours to kill. What you wanna do?"

I shrugged. "I dunno."

"Let's kill some time at your place."

I thought a minute. "What about your mom?"

He frowned. "What about her?"

"Don't you have to pick her up in about an hour?"

"She'll get a ride, I think." He thought a minute, then nodded and started the engine. "She'll get a ride."

Chapter Fifteen

For some reason, I remember that evening's smell. It reminded me of syrup. Asleep on the family room sofa with the radio providing the background of NPR, I dreamt of a crusty Texas Democrat careening down a hill of parked cars in what looked like an old-fashioned Buick. Seeing a shirtless young man walking down the hill, the Texas Democrat stopped and spoke. The young man joined the Texas Democrat in the car. The Texas Democrat inhaled; the young man's smell reminded me of syrup.

In my dream, I didn't follow the car. Instead, I just watched. Maybe I knew what the Texas Democrat wanted from the young man. Maybe I knew what the Texas Democrat would get. Maybe I wanted that, too. It would have been queer to attain it.

I could hear the Buick's radio. "Okay," a newscaster, someone sounding like a kid, said. "Time to get up!"

The radio in the family room, which was broadcasting a congressional sex scandal, went off and the family room's horizontal blinds were pulled back to put the bright day in my face. There was a tap against my bare toe, first once, then three times, then someone stepped on it, hard.

"Ow!"

I woke up immediately, rubbing my foot, just as the Texas Democrat smiled at the shirtless young man. In the family room, Marshall stalked away.

"I said 'time to get up,'" he said.

"You didn't have to put it like that," I said.

He shrugged and disappeared into the kitchen.

Beside me, Drew stretched like a cat. He patted his mouth and rubbed his eyes. Beside me, he had drooled onto the sofa. The saliva's smell reminded me of syrup.

"Morning," he said.

"Afternoon," Marshall said from the kitchen.

"What time is it?" Drew asked.

"Time for you two to get washed up," Marshall said. He returned to the family room and rested his hands on his hips. "The Judge is expecting us for dinner and you two are passed out like a bride and groom in the newlywed suite!"

I rubbed my eyes, then looked at him. "Sorry."

Marshall trudged into the kitchen. "Time to change, cousin dear. The Judge is expecting us."

Drew pulled his dishevelled shirt over his belly, which had a line of hair leading to the navel, then he stretched again. "Uh, Skip."

"Huh?"

He pointed at my shorts, which were unbuttoned and whose zipper was partially undone. I quickly zipped up and buttoned. Did I show anything?

"How'd you get in?" I yelled at Marshall.

"I used the door," he said. "How'd you think I'd get in?"

An alternative thought had not occurred to me. Besides, Marshall had a key, in case I had forgotten. Drew and I put on our shoes. "Sorry I asked," I muttered.

Marshall returned with a towel and washcloth, tossing them into Drew's lap. "No time to be sorry. Time's a-wastin'. Gotta move. Fast."

I think it fair to say Marshall would not have appreciated me dallying too long on the sofa. I shifted my weight and prepared to stand. I was trying my best to delay the inevitable.

"You going to your room?" Drew asked.

"Might as well," I sighed.

To be truthful, I dreaded going back into my room. It was my first time there since Reverend Shuddlesworth's visit, and, when I got there, the room still seemed to have reeked of cheap cologne. I stood at my bedroom door and looked at the interior.

"*Uhgh,*" Drew said, holding his nose. "What did you roll around in?"

I couldn't begin to tell him. Still, towel and washcloth tucked under his arm, Drew entered the bedroom and surveyed the place.

"Let's change your bed," he said.

He pulled off the coverings, comforter and padding included, and tossed them down the laundry chute. Luckily, I had gingham sheets, instead of white, as gingham does not easily stain. When Drew returned, he opened the dresser, towel and washcloth in hand.

"You need to put something nice on," he said.

Drew dressed me. He took out a red polo shirt, a pair of boxers, and a pair of dark socks and he handed them to me. Then, he went to my closet and got out some khakis, which he hung on the bedroom door.

"I'd really prefer jeans," I said.

"It's your dad," Drew said. "You can't wear just blue jeans for dinner with your dad."

It was my father. I could have told Drew I would wear what I liked. It would have been a fruitless argument. Taking my clothes, I headed into the master bathroom, while Drew took the main bathroom. As I let the shower wash over my body, I wondered what had happened to Adele. It seemed strange for her not to show up. Then, when I had finished showering, there was a knock on the bathroom door.

"Just a minute," I called out.

Then, the door opened. It was Marshall, tumbler in hand. Indeed, he would have his afterschool cocktail, even if I could not. I barely had time to cover myself.

"What?!"

Marshall smiled. "Just checking." He closed the door.

Because I do it so rarely, I took my time dressing in my parents'— I mean, the Judge's—room. Once I got my socks and boxers on, there was a knock on the bedroom door.

"Just a minute, Marshall," I called out, a little irritated.

"It ain't Marshall. It's me."

I opened the door for Drew, even though I was half-naked. He came through the door wearing the same clothes he had on previously, but his hair was wet and freshly combed, indicating he, too, had showered.

"I put the towel and washcloth over the tub," he said, "but I can't think what to do with these."

In his hand, he held his socks and underwear, neatly folded, as if fresh.

"I dunno," I said. "You expect me to figure it out?"

Drew blinked. "You don't wanna wash them?"

"You can wash your own drawers, Andrew," I said. He could do my wash; I wasn't about to do his. Marshall came up and into the bedroom, this time, without his tumbler. He frowned at me.

"Cousin dear—"

"I'm moving as fast as I can," I said.

"Move faster," Marshall said, motioning with his hand. "Move faster."

Marshall went back downstairs.

"Who the hell does he think he is?" I asked out loud.

Drew gave me a look, like I really didn't have to ask.

I finished dressing, with Drew on the Judge's bed flipping through cable channels. At 5:45, Marshall stood at the foot of the stairs and opened his lungs. "Skip, Drew. It's time!"

Dutifully, Drew trotted to the stairs. I had to stop at my bedroom to get my tennis shoes.

"Don't wear them," Drew said. "Not with khakis."

I returned to the bedroom closet and fished out my loafers. Drew approved them. Then we tumbled downstairs, just as Marshall prepared to bellow again.

Marshall was the first to Drew's car; he stood there like an Old English sheepdog wanting to pee. Drew got the keys from his pocket and unlocked the door for Marshall, who climbed into the back, then Drew threw his underwear and socks into the trunk.

I sat in my usual spot, up front, as Drew climbed behind the wheel. He started the car, then eased it from in front of the house. Next door, Sonia Kidd came out with her dog, Henson. They were to walk. Drew honked the horn at her. Henson, scampering across the street, barely gave her time enough to wave.

Having fifteen minutes to work with, Drew decided to take us on a little ride. He made a couple of turns and got us to Statehouse Square (which was really a circle—go figure) and we headed down Meridian Avenue, situated at the exact center of town.

I loathed Meridian Avenue. It is so marginal, with people we looked upon as general embarrassments to the race. What hurt us most about Meridian Avenue was that the Whitmaners need only look down that street to see the qualities they say all of us have. When they did so, they ignored Jefferson Heights. They preferred residents of Meridian Avenue, who seemed to believe the myth of our race's inherent inferiority.

Marshall watched Meridian Avenue go by. At every other corner, there was some group gathered and talking. "Why can't they go to some pool hall?" he wondered.

"Huh?" I asked.

"I was just wondering why these people can't go to some pool hall and not hang out on the street, like they are still in Arkansas or Mississippi," Marshall said.

"They can hang out, if they want," Drew said.

Marshall looked at Drew as if he had just arrived from the South. "Up here, it's called 'loitering.'"

"Where'd you learn to be such a stick in the mud?" Drew asked, smiling.

"It's in the genes," Marshall said. At a four-way stop, a snaggle-toothed four-year-old girl suspended hopscotch to wave at Marshall. I could hear Marshall curl his lip; obviously, he was looking at the girl's house, which was so dilapidated it must have had newspaper on its walls as a windbreaker. "A broken down little girl," Marshall said, "in front of a broken down little house."

"Marshall," Drew said. Our turn came and Drew drove on before Marshall could say anything more.

After that, we entered Hunterstown, whose site on top of a hill gave it a pretty good view of the St. Louis skyline some thirty miles downstream. Almost all gentrified, rehabbed brick German workers' houses and townhouses, Hunterstown was such a pleasant place to drive through when I was growing up and it contrasted against the poverty of nearby Meridian Avenue. As a boy, I loved the various colors of the flowering trees in front of the houses, as well as those of each and every gaily decorated home. Almost a third of the houses liked hanging out rainbow flags. Only later would I comprehend their significance, and add everything together.

The Midtown was in Hunterstown, in a building whose first story the Judge claimed had been built after the second story. He claimed it was a fact, and more than simply a trick to get people in to look at the menu. It served that purpose, too.

I looked at the clock. It was almost six. The parking lot was full. I didn't see the Judge's Saab, nor, for that matter, the hybrid deal Adele was driving.

"I guess I'm gonna have to park on the street," Drew said.

Drew found a spot on the street, around the corner from the restaurant, within a healthy walking distance.

"Time for exercise," Drew said. "You can handle exercise, can't you, Arthur?"

"He can walk," Marshall said.

I thought about looking at Marshall, but he had a way of staring me down, even when it was the back of my head that was facing him. No matter. I opened the car door and stepped onto the pavement, followed by Marshall, who stood expectant. Drew started to cross the street.

"C'mon," he said.

Marshall looked at me for a bit, raised his eyebrow like Spock, and started across the street. "Come along, cousin dear."

I gravitated to the other side of the street as well, where the crab apple trees were inviting. After that, it was a simple walk. It was still beautiful, the sun just starting to set. It cast fair-sized shadows before us. Walking in silence, our shadows poured themselves over the half-cracked sidewalks like red wine spilled on the ground. They were spooky, needless to say, and difficult.

Drew was the first to the Midtown. He rushed to the Seventh Street entrance and mounted the steps. Turning around and grasping the door with one motion, he pulled the door open, swept his arm across his body, and bowed.

"Talk about service," I said.

"I'd do anything for you, Arthur," Drew said, not quite serious. "Just remember that."

Once in, the piano playing "Mrs. Robinson" in the lounge made for an interesting smile on Drew's face, and made him raise his eyebrows. For my part, I sensed immediately the rude odor of cheap cologne. I thought changing my bed had freed me from that smell. Then, from the lounge came Reverend Shuddlesworth, Miller High Life in hand and wearing a fairly conservative double-breasted gray suit and cobalt blue necktie.

I gulped.

Reverend Shuddlesworth looked at me warily, as if he didn't know what to do. Then he raised his free hand and gave a three-fingered wave.

"Joining us for dinner, Reverend?" Marshall asked. "You remember my cousin, Skip Macalester?"

Reverend Shuddlesworth smiled a bit and nodded. Drew turned to me. I tried not to look scared.

It was an awkward, silent half second. I didn't know what to say. Neither did Drew, though Drew seemed to turn his nose up at his smell. The awkwardness broke itself when the hostess, a tall, thin woman with long, gray-streaked black hair, interrupted and asked if she could help us. Marshall helped himself.

"We're part of the Macalester party," Marshall said.

The hostess referred to her spiral notebook on the podium at the entrance to the dining room. "Party of six?"

"Six?" Drew asked.

"That's Judge Macalester's party," the hostess said. "Party of six."

"I guess that's us," Marshall said. Stepping aside, he turned to Reverend Shuddlesworth. "After you, Reverend."

Reverend Shuddlesworth stepped forward and the three of us fell in behind him. Menus in hand, the hostess led us to the rear dining room, where three tables were lined together, waiting.

Drew was right behind the Reverend. Making a face and turning around, Drew held his nose, as if something really reeked. He stopped once we got to our seats. Oddly, the four of us stood around waiting for someone to sit first.

Reverend Shuddlesworth set his bottle on the table. "If I knew you would be here," he said to us, "I wouldn't've bought this. Wouldn't want you to think I got a bad reputation because of it."

"Oh," Marshall said quickly, "no one from the Indiana Conference has a bad reputation in Illinois."

I half expected him to chuckle. He flashed that gold tooth and started to smile, almost chuckling, but then his smile faded and he picked up his bottle. A concerned look came over his face, and he looked down at the table. Then, after a few seconds, he looked up, as if embarrassed, and nodded. Marshall, who was standing next to the Reverend, smiled and nodded as well.

Then, the Judge arrived, breezing in, like a zephyr.

"Thirsty, Reverend?" the Judge asked as he positioned himself at the head of the tables. Adele, coming in as well, moved around to the other side of the Reverend. She nodded to Drew.

"Yes, sir," Reverend Shuddlesworth said.

"We would've got something to drink too," Marshall said, "but—"

"But you just got here," the Judge said, winking. "No sense chasing an afterschool float, eh, Marshall?" He waited for Adele to sit, and, once she did, he sat, then nodded for the four of us to be seated. He turned to Drew. "Glad for you to join us," he said.

"Thanks for having me, sir," Drew said.

The Judge turned to Reverend Shuddlesworth. "You've met my son's friend?"

"Can't say I have," the Reverend said. He extended a hand across the table. "The Reverend Michael Shuddlesworth."

For a moment, Drew looked at the hand, then he smirked a bit and shook it. Afterward, Drew sniffed his fingers and turned up his nose.

The Reverend smiled a little. "I'm—"

"Visiting," the Judge completed the sentence. A waitress set a glass of ice water before him. "He was here for this past Sunday's service and he's going back to Indiana, isn't that right?" he asked Reverend Shuddlesworth sharply. All the Reverend could do was nod. Then, the Judge softened. "Drew and Skip have—how do the British put it?— 'a special relationship.'" The Judge smiled.

Drew smiled, sort of.

I couldn't smile. I felt like crawling under a rock. That made us sound like a pair of fags.

Adele cleared her throat.

"Oh, yes," the Judge said, "my daughter Adele."

"Where've you been?" I asked Adele from across the table, trying to deflect attention.

Letting nothing slip, Adele smiled. "Around." She forced a smile. Reverend Shuddlesworth offered a hand, extended across the table, but Adele declined to shake it. He looked like a real fool, too.

No, I would never know where she went or what she did that afternoon. I hypothesized it had something to do with Mom.

By this time, everyone had water. The waitress set a menu in the empty seat beside me. Each of us opened the menu, but when the Reverend opened his, the Judge stared him down.

"Reverend," he said, "you are far too busy to join us for dinner."

We all looked up. I think I knew what he was saying. Reverend Shuddlesworth had no idea.

"I'm sorry?" he said.

"I *said*," the Judge began, "you are far too busy to join us for dinner. At least, that's what you indicated when the invitation was extended this afternoon."

Reverend Shuddlesworth still acted like he had no idea what the Judge was talking about. He seemed hungry, and saliva was coming out of his mouth so he used a handkerchief to wipe it away. He mustered a smile. "Am I being uninvited?" he asked, chuckling. The chuckling and smiling stopped as the Judge stared him down.

The Judge closed his menu. "Can you read, Reverend?"

"Sir?"

"I *asked*, can you read?"

"Of course," Reverend Shuddlesworth said.

The Judge nodded. "Good. Were you able to read when—oh, what was that college you attended?"

"It was a small, Christian school in Indiana," he said. "It was real small. You wouldn't know it by name."

The Judge asked. Reverend Shuddlesworth didn't tell. The Judge chose not to pursue. He smiled and sipped water. "I suppose it was all you could get." From his inner breast pocket, he pulled out an envelope and removed from it a letter. "Since you are able to read, perhaps you would like to read this."

The Judge handed Reverend Shuddlesworth the letter, which he read, hand over his mouth, as if shocked.

"The presiding elder sent me that," the Judge said. "It should come as no surprise to you: You delivered it to my house last night. Didn't he, Skip?"

Why did he have to drag me into it? I barely peeped. Drew looked at me. I had no idea what he was thinking.

Reverend Shuddlesworth shook his head. "I—I don't understand."

"Why, you *said* you can read," the Judge said. "It's there in black and white, and in English, is it not? The presiding elder is coming down here tomorrow to see you at the church. After that, you're going back to Indianapolis."

"But I don't understand that part," the Reverend said. "Why Indianapolis?"

"Because, my dear Reverend," the Judge said, "you are to see the bishop. Something about you and a young man at Conference you were—how should I say?—'friendly' with. When I called him, Paul wouldn't elaborate beyond that."

Then, I thought I understood what Grandma meant when she called Reverend Shuddlesworth "a pest." I would call him a pest, too. But what would I call myself?

Reverend Shuddlesworth folded the letter. He tried to pocket it, but the Judge signaled for him to return it. After that, Reverend Shuddlesworth drank the beer. He barely looked at me. He mumbled something. I think it was, "nothing happened."

"In our family's line of work," Adele said, "silence is gold. It's in the Constitution."

The waitress returned and took our orders. To Drew's relief, the Judge said he was paying. Then, the waitress dropped two baskets of French bread before us and went back to the kitchen. Like an eagle eviscerating its prey, the Judge ate a slice, piece by piece, staring the Reverend down. Half finished, a smile traced over his face. The Reverend finished his beer and prepared to go.

"Before you depart, Reverend," the Judge said, "do you mind if I ask you a question?"

Reverend Shuddlesworth didn't know exactly what to say, so the Judge continued.

"In that college you attended," the Judge said, "did you study classical literature? Homer?"

"I've read it."

"Good. Then you know about the myth of Aulis." The Judge ate a piece of bread. "At Aulis, Agamemnon slaughtered his favorite daughter to appease the goddess Artemis. To him, it was important to get the expedition off to retrieve Helen for his cuckolded brother. In that college you attended, did they teach Aulis's moral?"

Reverend Shuddlesworth shook his head.

Looking down his nose at him, the Judge ate another piece of bread. "Why, the moral, dear Reverend, is that everyone must be willing to sacrifice Iphigenia for favorable winds. And, for this play, you are going to be Iphigenia. The question is, who will be Agamemnon?"

The Judge smiled.

Later, I would rehash the sequence of those days and try to piece together some understanding. Later, it would be crystal to me that while Zeus is immortal, he is also flesh and blood and perpetually in love and at vengeance, and while the other gods are immortal too they creep in his presence. And while I may wish it otherwise, I, like every other person, am subject to Zeus's vicissitudes, including those that change me from the actor to the acted upon. I understood that I could go from Agamemnon to Iphigenia and back again, just for the heck of it.

Reverend Shuddlesworth was excused. Grandma Macalester took his place. She made me forget about the discomfort of seeing Reverend Shuddlesworth for the time being as she tried in vain to get Drew to call her Madelyn. Drew seemed too preoccupied to try that.

For the time being, I forgot about the Reverend. I would think about him again when, come the next afternoon, he would be found near the church, kicked to death. No one knew who did it, but someone who caught a glimpse of the perpetrator driving away said it was a white boy.

Drew didn't pick me up that afternoon. We played no tennis that day.

When I first heard the news of the Reverend's death, I tried to imagine what it was like to kick a man to death. Was it a football kick or a soccer kick? Did he just kick with the toe or did he use the sole and stomp? Did he break bones?

It was a topic come the next Sunday, when the presiding elder himself came in to fill the pulpit. Some thought kicking a pastor, even a temp, to death was an awful thing, one hell of a way to die, but I saw my father's semidistant look as though he had just read the Federal Sentencing Guidelines. One of the members proposed a memorial for Reverend Shuddlesworth; the Judge coaxed them into just sending a card to his family, who hailed from Indiana. Ever the good boy, I tried signing the card. Once I was finished, ever the good son, I handed the pen to the Judge. Barely acknowledging it, he walked away.

"I barely knew him," Mom said to a church member, a lady sweet and dark as licorice. "It just wouldn't feel right signing his card."

Mom opened her handbag and took out two dollars. To her, it seemed better to give cash and move on.

Outside, the Judge lit his pipe and started smoking it under the linden tree, near Mom's Volvo. "You need a new parking space, Rose," he said to Mom.

"Still doing the OSHA case, Alfred?" she asked.

The Judge nodded a little and moved away from the car as Mom got behind the wheel and sent it charging down the street. I watched her. Except on special occasions, I never saw Mom at Bethel again. She became Presbyterian.

Then, I had the funny feeling of being watched. I turned around and saw Brad Morgan, standing behind me. He smelled his usual way, of hair gel.

"Hey, Brad," I said.

Brad nodded. "What happened between you and my little brother?"

"What do you mean?"

Brad looked away for a second, then put on Wayfarers. "It's just that, Marshall said something happened, and, if I wanted to know, I'd have to talk to you. So, I'm talking. What happened between you and my little brother?"

I shrugged and kept my cards close to my chest. "Cousin stuff."

"You know, if it wasn't a Sunday and if this wasn't church, I'd say bs." Brad smiled. "Then, that would get both of us in trouble." He moved closer, so close, in fact, that I could smell his gum. "If I find out anything happened to him, cousin dear, I'd kick you to death. Don't ever forget that."

He patted my cheek and joined his family in the parking lot for the drive home. The Judge called for me to come to the Saab, which I did. I wish I could get out of my mind the image I painted myself that day, bearing a red palm print on my cheek, like a big, scarlet **M**.

THE END

ABOUT THE AUTHOR

J. E. Robinson, MA, is an instructor of history at Lewis and Clark Community College in Godfrey, Illinois, and host and producer of "Eavesdropping" on WBGZ radio in Alton, Illinois. His short stories have appeared in *Rebel Yell* (Haworth), *Men on Men VI*, and *M2M: New Literary Fiction*.

Order a copy of this book with this form or online at:
http://www.haworthpress.com/store/product.asp?sku=5589

SKIP MACALESTER

_____in softbound at $19.95 (ISBN-13: 978-1-56023-576-7; ISBN-10: 1-56023-576-4)

Or order online and use special offer code HEC25 in the shopping cart.

COST OF BOOKS_____	☐ **BILL ME LATER:** (Bill-me option is good on US/Canada/Mexico orders only; not good to jobbers, wholesalers, or subscription agencies.)
	☐ Check here if billing address is different from shipping address and attach purchase order and billing address information.
POSTAGE & HANDLING_____	
(US: $4.00 for first book & $1.50 for each additional book)	
(Outside US: $5.00 for first book & $2.00 for each additional book)	Signature_____
SUBTOTAL_____	☐ **PAYMENT ENCLOSED: $**_____
IN CANADA: ADD 7% GST_____	☐ **PLEASE CHARGE TO MY CREDIT CARD.**
STATE TAX_____	☐ Visa ☐ MasterCard ☐ AmEx ☐ Discover ☐ Diner's Club ☐ Eurocard ☐ JCB
(NJ, NY, OH, MN, CA, IL, IN, PA, & SD residents, add appropriate local sales tax)	Account # _____
FINAL TOTAL_____	Exp. Date_____
(If paying in Canadian funds, convert using the current exchange rate, UNESCO coupons welcome)	Signature_____

Prices in US dollars and subject to change without notice.

NAME_____

INSTITUTION_____

ADDRESS_____

CITY_____

STATE/ZIP_____

COUNTRY_____ COUNTY (NY residents only)_____

TEL_____ FAX_____

E-MAIL_____

May we use your e-mail address for confirmations and other types of information? ☐ Yes ☐ No We appreciate receiving your e-mail address and fax number. Haworth would like to e-mail or fax special discount offers to you, as a preferred customer. **We will never share, rent, or exchange your e-mail address or fax number.** We regard such actions as an invasion of your privacy.

Order From Your Local Bookstore or Directly From
The Haworth Press, Inc.
10 Alice Street, Binghamton, New York 13904-1580 • USA
TELEPHONE: 1-800-HAWORTH (1-800-429-6784) / Outside US/Canada: (607) 722-5857
FAX: 1-800-895-0582 / Outside US/Canada: (607) 771-0012
E-mail to: orders@haworthpress.com

For orders outside US and Canada, you may wish to order through your local
sales representative, distributor, or bookseller.
For information, see http://haworthpress.com/distributors

(Discounts are available for individual orders in US and Canada only, not booksellers/distributors.)
PLEASE PHOTOCOPY THIS FORM FOR YOUR PERSONAL USE.
http://www.HaworthPress.com   BOF06